D

"Rosie Danan's *Do Your Worst* has that rarest of tropes: an enemies-to-lovers pairing that is perfectly, lusciously balanced. . . . It would be simpler for Riley and Clark to stay enemies if it weren't for Danan's signature evocation of horniness—blended here with just a soupçon of pain kink, as a treat. The sexiness is more cutting than her previous two books, with a bright acid pop that brings out the richness."

—*The New York Times Book Review*

"I have two words for you: Sex. Rituals. And five more: Curses. Made. Them. Do. It. Did I know I needed this book? No. Am I over the moon that it has been written? YES! Rosie Danan always gifts us with the spiciest, most hilarious rom-coms, and her latest is an enemies-to-lovers, spooky read that I'll be recommending to everyone I meet! Another perfect, sizzling romance by one of my favorite authors!"

—Ali Hazelwood, #1 *New York Times* bestselling author of *Deep End*

"Rosie Danan has taken expert sexual tension to the Scottish Highlands. Need I say more? As always, this author is an auto-buy."

—Tessa Bailey, #1 *New York Times* bestselling author of

It Happened One Summer

"Danan is on our short list of must-reads for every new and established romance reader. Her heroines are the ones we worship; her heroes are the ones we deserve. Rosie Danan's romances deftly and seductively move the genre forward."

—Christina Lauren, *New York Times* bestselling author of

The True Love Experiment

"Delightfully spooky, sexy as hell, and dappled with Rosie Danan's trademark wit, *Do Your Worst* is quite possibly my favorite romance this year. This book is cursed to be horny, and I wouldn't have it any other way."

—Ashley Poston, *New York Times* bestselling author of *A Novel Love Story*

"If the 1999 cinematic masterpiece *The Mummy* was an awakening for you, then get ready to be AWAKENED by Rosie Danan's *Do Your Worst*. I was transported to the Scottish Highlands; I was highly invested in Riley and Clark breaking this curse; and I was positively feral for them to BREAK THE CURSE, if you know what I mean. Anything Rosie Danan writes, I will devour whole and lick my lips afterward. I am a forever fan."

—Alicia Thompson, *USA Today* bestselling author of
The Art of Catching Feelings

"Rosie Danan's incandescently sexy *Do Your Worst* features a spooky Scottish castle, whip-smart prose, and the HOTTEST grumpy archaeologist since Indiana Jones. Watching Clark and Riley spar with one another, both while they are fighting and while they are . . . errr, *not* fighting . . . is a delight, as is the genuine sweetness Danan weaves throughout the story. In short, this book is everything I'm looking for in an enemies-to-lovers rom-com. Enjoyed every page!"

—Jenna Levine, *USA Today* bestselling author of *My Vampire Plus-One*

"*Do Your Worst* is the adventure romance of my dreams. The chemistry between Clark and Riley is explosive, and the story [Danan] weaves is a seamless blend of humor, spice, and page-turning fun that makes this book absolutely shine."

—Lana Ferguson, *USA Today* bestselling author of *Under Loch and Key*

"Jam-packed with [Danan's] signature wit, heat, and heart, *Do Your Worst* is the most fun I've had reading this year. Sexy characters, sizzling tension, and a delicious payoff. I can't wait for everyone to get their hands on this book." —B.K. Borison, author of *Lovelight Farms*

"This book had me under its spell from the very first page. Riley and Clark's connection is both melt-your-heart tender and singe-your-eyebrows hot. *Do Your Worst* is Rosie Danan at her best."

—Ava Wilder, author of *Will They or Won't They*

"[Danan's] ability to write romantic comedies that bring you through every emotion is unmatched. *Do Your Worst* is sneaky with its depth; hot, chest-clutching fun that lingers on long after you've finished!"

—Tarah DeWitt, *USA Today* bestselling author of *Funny Feelings*

"*Do Your Worst* is a romp of a book, as sexy as it is exciting and heartfelt. Riley is pure determined, charming chaos, and Clark is her intense, perfectly buttoned-up foil. Their battle of wills is a delight to read, and humor mixes with pathos as they confront not just the historic curse placed on Arden Castle but their own troubled histories. This is enemies to lovers at its most magical."

—Sarah Hawley, author of *A Witch's Guide to Fake Dating a Demon*

"*Do Your Worst* is a reminder of everything I love about romance novels. Hilarious, irreverent, and intoxicatingly steamy, this magically unique masterpiece is something I didn't know I desperately needed, but now can't stop thinking about. Rosie Danan has solidified herself as a top-tier name in the romance genre, and I will rabidly read everything she writes. With a plot just as juicy as the smoldering enemies-to-lovers romance, *Do Your Worst* was intricately crafted and perfectly executed. I couldn't stop turning the pages."

—Mazey Eddings, author of *Late Bloomer*

"Danan's signature bawdy humor and heart explode off every page in this enemies-to-lovers tale that captures *The Mummy* vibes."

—*Entertainment Weekly*

Praise for
THE INTIMACY EXPERIMENT

"Danan's book is at its very best when it's connecting faith, trust, strength, and desire in complex ways. . . . An ambitious and rewarding story." —*The New York Times Book Review*

"This follow-up to Danan's steamy 2020 debut, *The Roommate*, is filled with humor, healing, and heady good times (and yes, that is a naughty pun)." —Vulture

"Rosie Danan has a staggering gift for subverting expectations. . . . *The Intimacy Experiment*, on the whole, is a blessing of a book— tender, bruising, sexy, and transcendent." —*Entertainment Weekly*

"I could cry about how much I love Naomi and Ethan. Rosie Danan's writing brims with compassion and wit, and there's a tenderness that runs underneath everything—even when her characters are positive they're not falling for each other. A stunning, subversive romance that made me proud to be Jewish."

—Rachel Lynn Solomon, *New York Times* bestselling author of
Business or Pleasure

"*The Intimacy Experiment* by Rosie Danan is effervescent. It is the perfect combination of endearing vulnerability, swoonworthy romance, and scorching chemistry. Rosie Danan brings us a charming exploration of the intersections of sex, love, faith, and identity in a fiercely feminist novel that will leave you breathless."

—Denise Williams, author of *Technically Yours*

"Focusing on prejudices and preconceived notions people may have about both sex workers and Jewish folks, this book brings patience, love, understanding, and high heat to the budding relationship between two apparent opposites who find themselves extremely attracted to each other."   —Book and Film Globe

Praise for

THE ROOMMATE

"One of the steamiest romances of the year. . . . A downright revolutionary story about modern women owning their desire."

—PopSugar

"Rosie Danan's *The Roommate* is seriously sexy, seriously smart."

—Helen Hoang, *New York Times* bestselling author of
The Heart Principle

"Genuinely, swoonily romantic."

—Rachel Hawkins, *New York Times* bestselling author of *The Heiress*

"What an incredible debut! Danan gives us strangers to annoyed roommates to kinda friends to angsty pining to finally lovers with humor, wit, and just a hint of pathos. Josh and Clara are easily my favorite 'smash the patriarchy' couple, and *The Roommate* is easily one of my top romance reads of 2020!"

—Jen DeLuca, *USA Today* bestselling author of *Haunted Ever After*

"Rosie Danan not only created characters who you'll think about long after you're finished reading, but she wrote a powerful, feminist book that makes you laugh as hard as you cheer. *The Roommate* is sunshine in the form of a book. I can't wait to see what Danan brings us next!"

—Alexa Martin, author of *Next-Door Nemesis*

"*The Roommate* is laugh-out-loud funny, bananas sexy, and deeply romantic. Danan's voice is fresh and sharp, and the romance between Clara and Josh is both sizzling hot and heartwarming. Everything I want in a romance."

—Andie J. Christopher, *USA Today* bestselling author of
Unrealistic Expectations

"Nuanced, funny, super steamy, and surprisingly tender, *The Roommate* raises the bar for rom-coms in 2020—a smashing debut, and I can't wait for more by Rosie Danan!"

—Evie Dunmore, *USA Today* bestselling author of
The Gentleman's Gambit

"*The Roommate* is unapologetically sexy as hell. Danan's writing, like her characters, is funny, seductive, and full of heart. You're gonna love this book."

—Meryl Wilsner, *USA Today* bestselling author of *Cleat Cute*

"Fresh and different; a special, superbly written slow burn."

—Sarah Hogle, author of *Old Flames and New Fortunes*

"A deliciously fresh romance with strong characters and feminist themes." —*Kirkus Reviews* (starred review)

"Red-hot and fiercely feminist."

—*Publishers Weekly* (starred review)

"Incredibly sweet and romantic, *The Roommate* serves up a passionate but buoyant love story between two slightly lost people who figure out they have more to offer the world than they ever thought." —Shelf Awareness

FAN SERVICE

ROSIE DANAN

BERKLEY ROMANCE | NEW YORK

BERKLEY ROMANCE
Published by Berkley
An imprint of Penguin Random House LLC
1745 Broadway, New York, NY 10019
penguinrandomhouse.com

BERKLEY and the BERKLEY & B colophon are registered trademarks of
Penguin Random House LLC.

Book design by Alison Cnockaert

Library of Congress Cataloging-in-Publication Data

Names: Danan, Rosie, author.
Title: Fan service / Rosie Danan.
Description: First edition. | New York: Berkley Romance, 2025.
Identifiers: LCCN 2024029375 (print) | LCCN 2024029376 (ebook) |
ISBN 9780593437162 (trade paperback) | ISBN 9780593437179 (ebook)
Subjects: LCGFT: Paranormal fiction. | Romance fiction. | Novels.
Classification: LCC PS3604.A4745 F36 2025 (print) |
LCC PS3604.A4745 (ebook) | DDC 813/.6—dc23/eng/20230331
LC record available at https://lccn.loc.gov/2024029375
LC ebook record available at https://lccn.loc.gov/2024029376

First Edition: March 2025

Printed in the United States of America
1st Printing

The authorized representative in the EU for product safety and compliance is
Penguin Random House Ireland, Morrison Chambers, 32 Nassau Street,
Dublin D02 YH68, Ireland, https://eu-contact.penguin.ie.

This one goes out to all the fangirls
(gender-neutral)—the real unsung heroes.

FAN SERVICE

PROLOGUE

SEVENTEEN YEARS AGO . . .

ALEX LAWSON WAS infamous several times over.

Ask any of the polo-wearing, pearl-clutching WASPs in her small Florida hometown and they'd tell you her father—Dr. Isaac Lawson, conservation biologist—was a dangerous menace. His crime? Reintroducing a pack of red wolves to their native habitat in Ocala National Forest.

It didn't matter that he was trying to save a majestic species from extinction or that numerous safety measures separated his pack from their precious thoroughbreds. Tompkins, a tiny blip an hour and a half north of Orlando, boasted more Triple Crown winners to its name than anywhere else in the world, and rich people disliked the idea of beasts roaming the perimeter ready to sink their claws into two million dollars' worth of horseflesh. Was it any wonder that the first whisper of the word "wolf" sent every breeder and buyer in town reaching for their pitchfork?

In true lemming fashion, kids at school inherited their parents' prejudice. But obstinance ran in the Lawson blood. Alex met the taunting howls that greeted her on the school bus with a snap of her teeth and a snarling vow: *"I'd rather be wild than whipped."*

Then, one quiet morning, her mom left. And Alex quickly learned that dirty looks were a lot easier to swallow than pity.

"At least we managed to chase one of them out of town" followed her down the hall to English.

"I heard her sniffling in the bathroom" crawled across the back of her neck during lunch.

Alex always knew her mother, born and raised in New York City, hated Tompkins. That she saw its smallness, in every sense of the word, as a cage. But she didn't realize until she stood barefoot and bleary-eyed on the front porch watching her mom's Subaru pull away that Natalie Yates hated Tompkins more than she loved her family.

If *The Arcane Files* hadn't premiered that same night, maybe Alex wouldn't have fallen so hard or so fast into the fandom. But as it happened, the TW network's weird, experimental supernatural detective show found her at exactly the right (or wrong, depending on your views of a teenager forming an intense attachment to fictional characters) moment in time.

In Colby Southerland, chosen one, lone werewolf turned in a generation, Alex found a slice of hope. For Colby, there was power in otherness, strength born from trials, and purpose in isolation. And of course it didn't hurt that the actor who played him, Devin Ashwood, had tousled golden hair, eyes that glistened like emeralds in the sun, and, objectively, the world's most perfect mouth.

All it took was forty-seven minutes, not counting commercials, for Alex to fall into her most infamous identity to date. From that moment forward, she wasn't just an unwelcome outsider, or the girl whose mom bailed on her. No. Sitting in front of her ancient Dell desktop, in a small, inconspicuous corner of the Internet, Alex's passion for *The Arcane Files* and a natural aptitude for HTML turned her into the Mod.

Approximately two years and fifty-three episodes later, Alex attended her first and last fandom convention.

"I heard the Mod is gonna be here," the guy behind her in line whispered.

Alex subtly scratched at the back of her neck, where a seam of green face paint dipped below the collar of her velvet cape, turning just enough to catch a glimpse of the speaker in her periphery.

Tall, white, middle-aged, and wearing a decent approximation of Colby's signature leather-and-shearling bomber jacket.

"No way. Are you serious?" said his companion, the words coming out with a slight lisp around the fake fangs he sported. "The Mod's a living legend. The archive is my bible." His heavily makeup-emphasized dark brows mimicked those of Colby's frequent foe, the vampire, Nathaniel Van Lulen.

Alex's cheeks heated, threatening the glue that held on her papier-mâché facial wounds. It was nice to be appreciated for the embarrassing number of hours she spent meticulously cataloging the minute details of a television show *Entertainment Weekly* called "a poor man's *Twilight Zone* with excessive homoerotic tension."

"I know, but how are we gonna find him?" Cosplay Colby said. "No one knows who he is."

Yeah, that was by design. Alex doubted the Mod would command the same amount of respect and authority if people somehow found out the person behind their favorite episode summaries and character diagnostics was a gap-toothed high school student from bum-crack Florida. Still, she didn't appreciate the immediate insinuation that the Mod was a man.

Before today, Alex knew people appreciated the archive: her

site's hit count spoke for itself. And sure, the corresponding fo-rum's threads got a near constant flurry of activity from people discussing theories and debating ships. But these people were acting like the Mod was almost as big a deal as the actual celeb-rities they were standing in line to see.

Alex couldn't bring herself to be sorry that her birthday brought out the worst of Dad's divorce guilt. Not when he'd let her drive his precious Buick up here all by herself and shelled out for a con ticket that included an exclusive signing package that meant she got to meet her hero.

For once in her life, Alex was exactly where she belonged.

Miami's Supercon reminded her of a circus: the color, the costumes, the random intermittent screams. Excitement hung palpable in the air, along with the faint fragrance of sweat and hair gel. The convention center's vast domed ceiling might as well have been a cathedral, shimmering LEDs winking down as worshippers gathered to prostrate themselves at the altar of fiction.

From the unauthorized merch to the hand-drawn art to the people literally speaking to each other in invented tongues, one thing was clear: people here loved stories so much they wished they could abandon the real world to live inside them.

People here *were like her.*

After what felt like hours, the snaking line of ticket holders finally approached the photo-op room. A space as big as the school gym was split into thirds by long gray curtains strung up on metal rods and marshaled by con organizers wearing orange lanyards. Each of the show's main characters had their own line and photographer. To the right was Colby (werewolf detective), in the middle, Asher (Colby's human FBI partner), and on the left, Nathaniel (Colby's vampire archnemesis/queerbait pseudo love interest).

A pink-haired woman took names at the door and directed traffic based on people's preassigned time slots. While the Mod's admirers broke left, Alex joined Colby's line and got her first glimpse of Devin Ashwood through a slit between the curtains.

Only fear of asphyxiation from the stiff ruffled neckline of her Underworld Ambassador cosplay kept Alex breathing.

Devin's hair—naturally dirty blond with highlights of honey and amber—gleamed as he bent forward to sign what looked from here like a print from the 1999 "Back to School" photo shoot he did for Gap against his knee.

In person, he was even more handsome than in the twenty-seven-by-forty-inch print she had hanging beside the floor-length mirror in her bedroom. Her dad (unfairly!) hated the poster Alex had gotten as a foldout from a special edition of *Teen Beat*. He periodically mumbled, "Someone should tell that guy his T-shirt shrank in the wash," when he walked by her open bedroom door.

The thing about Devin Ashwood was that most people didn't take him seriously because he used to be a child star. Not Macaulay Culkin level, but he'd done a few family vacation movies and then a long-running stint on a daytime soap for the majority of his adolescence. Alex had never actually watched an episode of *Sands of Time*. But she knew he'd played Griffin Antonoff—son of Esmerelda Casablanca Antonoff, the series' beloved long-running heroine—from the ages of eight to eighteen.

Now twenty-five, Devin was playing Detective Colby Southerland, his first big breakout role as an adult. People who had never watched *TAF* often wanted to reduce Devin to a pretty face just because he had a roguish smile and washboard abs, but anyone who actually tuned in knew he was a once-in-a-generation talent.

Alex sighed with each step forward as the line dwindled, bringing her closer to the rays of his brilliance. It felt impossible that he was really standing there against that school-picture-day backdrop with a tiny rip in the pocket of his chambray shirt.

She pressed her fingernails into her palm. *You're seventeen years old. Get a grip.*

The funny thing was, Alex didn't want to like Colby when she first started watching *TAF*. It was so clear that he was the show-runner's self-insert—this paragon of heterosexual masculinity—nailing chicks and taking names. But Devin brought a vulnerability to the role that didn't come from the scripted lines. Even the goofy souped-up motorcycle they gave him couldn't cover the fact that his face sometimes looked as if someone had cracked him wide-open, right down the center like a walnut.

When a tall woman in a homemade T-shirt made Devin laugh, Alex almost passed out. God, why hadn't she brought a tape recorder? She wanted his voice in a seashell around her neck like Ursula the sea witch.

A few minutes later, he leaned forward to talk to an older woman stooped over a walker and took her hands in his. Alex's heart fluttered. She knew Devin would be just like his character, sensitive and sincere.

"You'll be the last one for Ashwood this morning," the volunteer gatekeeping his line said after verifying Alex's badge number on her clipboard.

Alex nodded, unhearing, as she mentally ran through her talking points one more time. She'd prepared various niche questions about the show's most ambiguous lore and discreet commendations on his craft choices.

For the few precious seconds that Devin Ashwood had his eyes on her, Alex wanted him to see that she wasn't some casual viewer. No. She'd been there since the beginning, rooting for him. Behind the cheap special effects and occasionally over-written dialogue, Alex saw the potential: all Colby and the show could be if only the network gave them the chance.

And then it happened. She was next. The last in line. For a few brief, spectacular moments, Devin Ashwood's brilliance was going to block out every bad thing in Alex's life.

"Hey," he said as she stepped in front of him, his voice some-how even deeper than it was on TV. "How's it going?"

Devin Ashwood held his arm out, inviting her to slide under for their prepaid picture.

Alex's brain turned static. Her feet grew roots.

Devin Ashwood wanted her to press her inferior mortal body to the chiseled marble of his chest.

And she just couldn't.

Her entire frame locked up.

All she could do was stand there and sweat.

The photographer, a middle-aged man with a goatee, huffed. "Let's go," he muttered. "You're the last thing standing between me and lunch."

When it became clear that Alex wasn't coming any closer, that she couldn't, Devin gave the bespectacled man a "one sec" gesture and slowly approached her until they stood almost toe to toe.

"My name's Devin," he said, low enough that his words wouldn't carry across the room.

Alex laughed; the sound punched out of her. It was so goofy, and so kind, for him to offer her his name.

His smile transitioned at her outburst, got toothier. "What's yours?"

"Alexandra," she managed, which was so formal, so not her.

A name she hadn't used since birth. Alexandra was a ballet dancer or a cheerleader. Student council president. Alex was a friendless dork who subsisted fifty percent on Cheetos.

"Nice to meet you, Alexandra." Devin Ashwood offered her his hand.

Alex extended hers, forgetting it was occupied.

He reached for the glossy print. "Is it cool if I sign this?"

His gleaming smile didn't falter, even when he had to tug a little to pull it loose. If anything, it softened.

Devin signed his name big and loopy, with emphasis on the *D* and the *A* and the double *o*'s of "Ashwood."

"I like your outfit." It was clear this man had experience managing hysterical fans, making small talk to put people at ease. "You're the Underworld Ambassador, right? From season two? Very niche."

"You noticed." The words came out mostly breath.

The Underworld Ambassador only appeared in three minutes and forty-eight seconds of the season's fourteenth episode.

"Of course." Devin returned the photo and shoved his hands in his pockets. "It was great to meet you." His eyes flickered to the door.

Oh no. It was over. Already. Alex's chance to make an impression was slipping through her fingers like sand. *Say something.* She mentally kicked herself. *Say ANYTHING.*

"Wrap it up," the photographer stage-whispered.

"Wait," Alex squeaked. "I have a question."

"Hit me," Devin said, still smiling.

Jesus. Six hours into this event, his cheeks must hurt.

"What's your deepest fear?"

The words flew out of Alex's mouth before she could stop them, with zero forethought, pulled from somewhere deep in her subconscious.

"Excuse me?" Devin's eyes went wide.

Holy shit. Why had she asked such an intrusive, weird question? One so obviously inappropriate for a fan at a staged photo op. Was this punishment for having zero real-life friends and a mild obsession with the Proust Questionnaire?

Any second now, Devin Ashwood was gonna tell her to get lost. Or call security.

Instead, he exhaled heavily through his mouth. "You don't pull your punches, do you?"

"I'm so sorry." Embarrassment seeped from her pores to drip at his feet.

This poor man had tried so hard to make her feel comfortable, telling her his name, making small talk. He'd been determined that Alex should get something nice out of this stiff paid interaction, and she'd ruined it.

Devin Ashwood opened his mouth and then closed it, shaking his head a little.

Alex witnessed the moment of resistance in him, how he winced and pushed through it, as if he owed her an answer for some impossible reason, and knew exactly how much it would cost him.

"The mask slips," he said finally, softly, ducking his chin, almost . . . sheepish. "From the outside, on a good day, I'm a decent stand-in for Colby Southerland. But underneath all this"— he gestured to his face—"trust me, it gets messy real quick."

The rawness of the confession made Alex's throat hurt. She didn't think as she followed her feet to slot herself against his side, slipping under his arm. The pipe cleaners on her headdress brushed his chin.

"Well, I think you're perfect," she swore solemnly.

Devin Ashwood laughed like it hurt as he squeezed her shoulder. "Thanks, kid. I try really hard."

A flash went off, accompanied by a loud pop that made them both jump. The photographer apparently had seen his chance for a candid and taken it.

Devin pulled back. "Take care of yourself, Alexandra."

"Alex," she said, voice only a little hoarse.

He raised his brows.

"Everyone calls me Alex, actually."

Devin Ashwood gave her a nod. "Alex it is."

In that moment, her crush grew into a mountain, a continent, a star.

Sure, she had loved him before, but that had been superficial. A child's crush. She'd loved Colby, really. A fictional character.

Now? Devin Ashwood had trusted her with his insecurities, had literally whispered his secret pain in Alex's ear. She would guard his tender heart as long as she lived.

She made it halfway to the food concourse before realizing she'd forgotten to grab the candid photo on her way out.

"Oh no." Alex sucked in a sharp breath. *No. No. No. No.* She couldn't lose the one memento she had from today. The one talisman she could take back with her, to ward against whatever came next.

She raced back, climbing the escalator like stairs even though her mom once told her more people died on them every year than in car crashes. The fates had aligned for her to see Devin Ashwood for a few extra seconds.

By the time Alex got back to the photo room, the place had totally emptied out. There was only Devin in the corner, chugging a bottle of water, and the hangry photographer packing his camera into a shoulder bag.

Having learned her lesson, Alex stepped behind the last curtain to collect herself for a moment before announcing her presence.

"Fancy seeing you again," she tried sotto voce before shaking herself. Ugh. No. That was horrible.

Alex would simply say, "Hey." Stick to single syllables. Nothing fancy.

"It ever weird you out?" a gruff voice with hints of a Boston accent—the photographer—asked. "Having all these strangers go to pieces over you?"

"Nah, man." There was Devin's mellifluous bass. "It's all part of the gig. You get used to it."

"You were really good with that last one, the mess. I thought she was gonna puke."

Devin laughed a little, hard, quick. Unkind.

The sound poured like ice water down Alex's spine.

"Tell me about it. I felt sorry for her. Did you see that costume? I figured the least I could do was show a little mercy. Grade A freak like that? Poor thing's gonna die alone."

Alex stumbled on limp noodle legs to the door, her ears ringing.

Screw the photograph. She didn't need it. Didn't want it.

A crowd from the lunch rush jostled her as she made her way to the bathroom. Alex rubbed at her stinging shoulder. *Don't you dare cry.*

Devin Ashwood's condemnation wasn't special. It came in the same pitch as the remarks from the people at the grocery store in Tompkins.

Colby Southerland. *The Arcane Files.* None of it existed.

In real life, being strange wasn't a virtue. Being rejected didn't make you strong.

It drove people away.

Alex thought about her dad, caught totally off guard by his wife leaving. Mom always said Alex took after him.

In front of the smudged bathroom mirror, she ripped her headdress off. Pins pulled at her scalp, but Alex welcomed the sting. She yanked one sleeve off her costume, then the other, shoving the cheap, synthetic material—all she'd been able to afford—into the metal trash can before bracing both hands on the porcelain sink.

Face paint and mascara bled down her cheeks. Tangled black hair hung limp around her shoulders. The person staring back at her was grotesque. A *grade A freak*.

Devin Ashwood agreed with every asshole in her hometown: Alex was doomed to be a social pariah.

The monster in the mirror broke into a terrible grin.

So be it.

About the Wiki

Hi and welcome to *Werewolf Support Group*, a free, fan-run online encyclopedia and message board dedicated to building a comprehensive and informative guide for *The Arcane Files*, an American supernatural detective television show that premiered on the TW network in 2006 and ran for 13 seasons.

The series, created by Brian Dempsey, follows FBI agent Colby Southerland (Devin Ashwood) as he learns to live with the gifts and gauntlets of being turned into the sole werewolf in a generation alongside his human partner, Asher Culpepper (Gus Rochester), while navigating a complex and charged relationship with his vampire archnemesis, Nathaniel Van Lulen (Anthony Mariano).

*Please note: Since the show went off air in 2018, forum moderation has been suspended and the database has been capped at 2,315 articles.

PRESENT DAY

DEVIN ASHWOOD WISHED he could say this was the first time he'd woken up butt naked in his backyard with no memory of the night before.

At least last time he'd been in his twenties. Call it a perk or a dangerous downside, but any former child star could tell you the consequences of mixing booze and benzos on an empty stomach.

Opening first one eye and then the other, he squinted up at the sky, trying to gauge the time based on the angle of the sun. Midday? Maybe? His parents never let him join the Boy Scouts.

Devin gingerly lifted his pounding head off the ground, wiping at dirt embedded in the surface of his scruffy cheek. His stomach rolled as he sat up. That, combined with his sour tongue, confirmed his suspicions: hangover.

Every muscle in his body ached. Was all this from working out? His personal trainer, Claude, had him on some new resistance-training program designed to keep his forty-two-year-old body from looking forty-two. It involved a lot of bungee cords.

Holy shit. Speaking of overworked glutes, he was ass to the

wind out here. Thank god he slept on his stomach or he'd probably have second-degree burns on his junk right now.

What in the world had he gotten up to last night?

He remembered most of yesterday. After hitting the gym in
the morning, he'd called his agent, gotten her voice mail, and
left a rude message.

Jade had been dodging him for weeks now. As if he didn't
pay her to take his calls. Which, okay, yeah, Devin hadn't
booked anything to write home about *lately*, but how was he
supposed to if he couldn't get his own representation on the
phone?

After hanging up, he Googled himself in a fit of self-loathing,
got predictably depressed by what he found, and then fucked
around playing *Call of Duty* until sunset. At that point he'd
been desperate enough to speak to someone, anyone, other than
the fourteen-year-olds on the other side of his headset who kept
threatening to "pwn" him.

He broke down and asked his publicist to find him a party.

That was how he ended up all the way out in the Palisades
for some cologne launch that was a total bust. If Devin wanted
to smell like a lemon fucking a pine tree, he would— Well, he
didn't was the point. The only thing that made the evening halfway worth putting on dress pants was the bacon-wrapped scallops they had going around on little trays.

Devin only managed to snag one of those before some
alleged former gaffer from the first season of *The Arcane Files*
started chatting his ear off. At first, the guy, Mitchell or Michael,
seemed decent. He told Devin his favorite episode was the one
told through the POV of Colby's beloved motorcycle, which did,
objectively, rule. But then he asked what Devin was up to now,
and when he explained he was actually trying to get the studio
on board for an *Arcane Files* reboot, the asshole laughed.

"Wait, seriously?"

Devin got pretty drunk after that. By midnight, he was slipping the bartender a couple hundred bucks to hand him a bottle of Blanton's and wandering off into the woods at the edge of the property.

After that? The rest of the night wasn't just hazy. It was missing.

Damn. It wasn't cute to black out. He was fucking middle-aged.

Devin got to his feet. He was filthy, his bare torso and legs covered in streaks of dried mud and scattered scrapes and shaded marks that promised to turn into full-on bruises. Running a hand through his hair, he pulled out a twig. *What in the Bear Grylls bullshit . . . ?*

Hobbling across his landscaper's "vision" of a "tranquil rock oasis," he let himself in the back door and went to put on boxer briefs. The question of whether or not he'd lost his phone in last night's mystery exploits was answered when it rang just as he managed to hike on a pair of sweats. Unearthing the thing from a potted plant next to his front door, Devin fumbled for the accept call button.

"Jade," he said, having seen her name on the home screen. "What the hell? I must've left you twenty messages. Next time you decide to go radio silent for a month, at least shoot me an email so I know you didn't get sucked into a sex cult."

His agent murmured some soothing excuses for her absence, something about a wellness retreat in Fiji, then suggested they meet for sushi later tonight.

Immediately, Devin's hackles rose. Jade hated sushi.

"Whatever, I heard it's good," she defended, when he said as much. "I'll order chicken teriyaki or something."

Bullshit, he wanted to say but didn't, too much of a coward to call her out twice in one phone call. He'd known Jade for almost twenty years; she sure as hell didn't make a habit out of compromise.

She must have bad news. Oh fuck. What if she was quitting the business? Or pregnant?

Between the state of his hangover and delays from construction on the freeway, Devin barely managed to shower and make himself presentable before he had to haul ass to Venice Beach. An investigation into what the fuck he'd done last night would have to wait until tomorrow. It was probably fine. His publicist would have called by now if he'd done something truly heinous.

At the sushi spot, Devin's pounding headache intensified despite the Advil he'd swallowed dry before handing his keys over to the valet.

He'd been in LA a long time. Fuck—he grimaced as he did the math—thirty-five years. Long enough to know that there were basically two kinds of places in this neighborhood: highly exclusive ones, where you needed your name on a list to see and be seen, and ones crowded enough with tourists that you could count on getting hustled out in an hour so the waitstaff could turn over the table.

This place fell squarely into the latter bucket.

By the time he was escorted to the table, Jade was already there, pounding away at her phone with a steaming mug of something aggressively herbal at her elbow.

Jade wasn't his first agent, but she was the first one Devin hired himself, a couple of years before he landed *The Arcane Files*. Thanks to what a judge called his parents' "questionable investment" with his paychecks, Devin was slumming it as a cater waiter in Pasadena between auditions, barely making enough to cover rent on a shitty studio. In those dark, lean months after *Sands of Time* had gone off the air, casting directors kept telling him he had a pretty mouth, then declining to actually book him.

At some benefit out on the water, Devin thought Jade—sleek and professional in her shiny black skirt suit—was a guest. It was only years later when they were sharing a joint in the back of a black car after the third-season wrap party that she admitted she'd snuck in a side door that night, just as hungry as he was.

"You an actor by any chance?" she asked him.

"How'd you know?" Devin had grown his hair out, paranoid about someone recognizing him working an industry event.

Looking back, that had been goofy. No one attending those galas fell into the demographic religiously watching daytime soaps.

Jade pointed to the headshot rolled up in the back pocket of his rented tux.

For some reason, she'd found that charming.

A few days later at her office—a single room rented in some warehouse out in Burbank—she offered him a contract.

"There's one thing you should know before you sign," she said, her pretty face guarded. "I'm a lesbian, and it's not something I'm willing to hide."

"Oh. Cool." Devin didn't actually know any lesbians, but Ellen DeGeneres seemed nice. "You got a pen?"

"You're late," Jade said now, standing as they exchanged pleasantries and air-kisses (god, sometimes he hated what LA had turned him into). "And you look like shit."

He supposed twenty-odd years of working together bred this kind of informality.

"Thanks." Devin took his seat and ordered a hot sake, hoping to take the edge off. Even the dim lighting in here made his eyes threaten to bleed.

Jade had the decency to let him order a shumai appetizer before she tucked her severe blond bob behind her ears and folded her hands in front of her.

Oh shit. Here it comes. His gut sank. Devin didn't want to hear whatever it was she wanted to tell him.

"I think we should pitch the reboot again," he spit out before she could break her bad news.

Jade's placid expression slipped, a flicker of irritation flaring around her mouth. "Devin, we've talked about this."

That was true. Jade had made her thoughts about reviving *The Arcane Files* clear. Her last words on the subject were something along the lines of "the dead should stay buried." Which, now that he thought about it, sounded like something Colby might say after stumbling upon a freshly disturbed grave. *Dun dun.* Fade to black. Cut to commercial.

Jade thought his starring role, the one that had made him if not a household name then at least someone regularly invited to the *Teen Choice Awards*, had grown stale. Come to think of it, had Jade ever liked Colby? Even after they'd renegotiated his contract between the third and fourth seasons and he'd started making good money? Was that the year she'd called his character "a maladjusted Hardy Boy with a tail"?

Devin didn't get it. Colby was smart and tough and cool. After thirteen years wearing his skin, Devin hadn't even had to think about how his character would react to a situation. It had become instinct, as natural as breathing.

"Come on, Jade." He gave her his most charming smile, the one *Seventeen* magazine had dedicated a whole column to before it went under. "Reboots are cool now. Kids today are obsessed with shit from the nineties and early aughts." He wasn't a hundo percent confident he'd pronounced that last word cor-

rectly, but Jade hadn't flinched, so probably "aughts" did rhyme
with "tots."

Jade took a sip of her tea. "How do you know what kids are
obsessed with?"

"I'm on the Internet," he said, defensive.

"Right." She put down her earthenware mug. "Listen."

Oh man. Devin hated that "listen." That was Jade's patented
"let you down easy" listen. The one he'd heard her use on Chad
Michael Murray at Jingle Ball in 2009.

"It's been almost seven years since *The Arcane Files* went off
the air. Even if I could get the network interested in a revival,
we'd never get the right people. Gus Rochester is in movies now.
He just did that big World War II epic where he cries beauti-
fully for like thirty minutes straight. And you know they gave
Brian Dempsey that series on HBO where they let him show
full frontal. He's happier than a pig in mud."

It was true. *The Arcane Files'* former showrunner kept giving
interviews where he talked about how his talent had finally been
"unleashed" on the premium channel's streaming platform.

Devin must have done something pathetic with his face, because Jade's tone softened.

"*TAF* had a good run. Thirteen seasons. That's the second-
longest fantasy series on cable. But it's over now," she said.
"Everyone's moved on."

Everyone—the rest of the sentence hung in the air alongside
the sweet smoke of incense—*except him.*

How had he let this happen?

When the show went off the air in 2018, Devin had been
excited to see what was next. He'd bulked up for the superhero
auditions that never panned out. After months of practicing
with a dialect coach to nail a British accent for consideration in

a period piece, he'd been told he "didn't look believable in a cravat." Whatever the fuck that meant.

Then COVID hit and everything dried up. Suddenly he was stuck in his big stupid house, alone. His ex-wife checked in once through an Instagram DM. Her profile picture was her and two ginger children.

As the months passed, he realized the only people he talked to regularly were on his payroll.

Devin had spent thirteen years on *The Arcane Files* seeing the same faces five days a week during filming months. The cast and crew had shared meals. Worked through long nights and holidays. He'd thought that had been, almost, like a family. But nobody hung around once he stopped being Colby. It had taken a global pandemic to make Devin realize how completely unlovable he was as himself.

"Jade, please, I need you to try."

His agent sighed.

She probably thought Devin meant from a financial perspective. That he had an online gambling problem or something. He didn't. She'd gotten him the fat paychecks all those years ago, and outside of his stupid car and the house, he'd barely touched them. Devin just felt useless—*used up*.

He needed to be Colby again: someone smart and good and brave. His character wasn't perfect. You could fill an ocean with his daddy issues, and his love interests had a tendency to end up dead on his watch. But Colby had a partner and a purpose.

"Please," he said again, hating himself even more for begging.

"Devin, I'm not just advising you as your agent. I'm telling you this as someone who's known you a long time and who genuinely cares about you." Jade's voice was firm, but her eyes were gentle. "I'm not gonna indulge this anymore. You gotta find something else that makes you feel good."

Pots and pans banging in the kitchen fifty feet away suddenly felt like they were colliding right inside his skull.

"Jade." What could he say to convince her? "Come on. Don't do this."

"Fuck." She reached for his hand across the tabletop, a gesture that was likely supposed to be comforting but missed the mark when she ended up nailing him in the knuckles with her chunky rings. "I'm sorry, but I'm also serious. If we can't agree on this, I think it's best if we call this business relationship and go our separate ways."

"You're firing me?" Devin couldn't believe it. For the first decade they'd worked together, they used to watch the Super Bowl every year. Jade would come over—she was from Texas and her family was big into football—and Devin would make dips. Taco dip. Buffalo chicken dip. Spinach and artichoke in a hollowed-out loaf of sourdough. Didn't that mean anything to her?

"I know this is difficult," Jade said carefully, all business. "But the timing is right for a new beginning. Did you see the moon last night?"

"Pardon?" She was always doing this, quoting powers-of-the-universe shit to him, telling Devin he was an air sign and they'd missed out on consideration for a role because something was wrong with Mercury.

"You subscribe to my newsletter, right?"

Devin did not.

"It was a once-in-a-lifetime event." Her brows folded down with displeasure. "A super blue blood moon eclipse occurs once every one hundred and fifty years."

"Wait, that's a real thing?" Devin had always assumed they'd made up "the wolf blood moon eclipse" for *The Arcane Files*.

Damn. He'd been too busy lost in the sauce last night to gaze up at the sky.

Jade got to her feet. "Order whatever you'd like. The bill's taken care of. My assistant will reach out to handle the partnership dissolution."

"Great," Devin muttered, staring down at his napkin. This was the most brutal dumping he'd ever experienced. And Erica asked for a divorce on Valentine's Day.

He rubbed a hand over his sandpapery jaw after Jade left. What the fuck was he supposed to do now? Sit here and order a spicy salmon roll?

"God damnit." He slammed his fist against the tiny circular table, drawing the attention of the surrounding patrons.

"Sorry," he muttered, shoving to stand without meeting their eyes.

Devin walked aimlessly down the boulevard, trying not to lose it completely. Passing headlights pierced his retinas. His vision was doing something funny, going blurry at the corners like a vignette as humiliation aggravated his hangover. God, what a shitty day.

Overhead, Jade's fancy moon taunted him, not quite full tonight but still glowing like a massive asshole in the sky.

He clenched his fists at his sides, the tension in his arms making his muscles sing. His hands felt weird, his nails pricking the insides of his palms. Had he forgotten to trim them?

Shoving mindlessly past selfie-snapping tourists, he walked faster, his body craving momentum.

There was a weird noise in the air—a kind of violent rumble—that Devin realized with a jolt was coming from his own throat.

Something was wrong with him. Was his airway closing? Had the smog in this city finally gotten so bad it actually took him out?

His life might be on the skids, but he didn't want to, like, die.

Would his obituary even make *Variety* at this point?

Devin patted his pockets for his cell phone, but his vision was too blurry to see the screen. He jabbed a finger, unseeing, at the device and heard rather than saw the screen splinter.

Shit. He growled in frustration as neon lights off the pier swirled together in his periphery. Disoriented, he followed his nose toward the beach, toward salt and sand, stumbling in the darkness toward the soothing shush of lapping waves.

Help. He needed to yell for help. An instinct he'd ignored for so long he almost didn't recognize it.

Vision black, panic clawing at his throat, Devin opened his mouth.

A harrowing howl cut through the night.

2

ALEX WAS IN the midst of getting peed on by a geriatric Doberman when her group chat exploded over the video.

It wasn't until after she changed into a fresh set of scrubs and took her lunch break (or rather breakfast break since she'd worked the solo overnight shift at the vet and it was currently four a.m.) that she had a moment to open iMessage.

To almost a hundred notifications.

Holy shit. Who died?

As it turned out, the deceased was Devin Ashwood's dignity.

> **CAM:** Do we think he lost a bet? Is this some kind of public degradation fetish we didn't know he had?

> **ELIZA:** idk but it's horrific and tragic and i can't look away

> **CAM:** I'm making the howl my ringtone. Idec

ELIZA: it's the part where he ripped off his own shirt like The Hulk for me

Though *The Arcane Files* had gone off the air years ago, the Internet friendships Alex had forged in that dumpster fire of a fandom outgrew their origins and remained ironclad to this day.

It was funny to think that Cam, Camila Adeoye, revered barrister who lived in South London with her wife and young daughter, had once been better known as NolbyGrl96, one of the most prolific fic writers in *The Arcane Files'* fandom.

For the record, Alex never wrote fic. Not for lack of interest; she just sucked at it. But she'd read it voraciously, even after Devin Ashwood read her for filth in 2008.

Her favorite fics had always been the ones where Colby helped Nathaniel accept that craving blood didn't make him inherently evil, coaxing him tenderly out of his shell. It was no wonder she'd been obsessed with Cam's *In My Veins*, a seminal work in the Colby/Nathaniel—shorthand Nolby—ship, and basically weaseled her way into being Cam's beta/best friend through shameless flattery.

Like every great *TAF* friend group, they needed a resident Asher bias. Enter Eliza Leonard, formerly dinosaurkitten, one of the most sought-after artists in the fandom. Alex and Cam blamed her being Canadian for the fact that she fell into the minority part of the fandom that preferred the "light" half of *The Arcane Files'* FBI partnership to Colby's tortured darkness. She'd since abandoned Toronto winters and was now an investment banker breaking hearts and taking names in New York City.

After Devin Ashwood labeled her pathetic all those years ago, maybe it would have been easier if Alex had abandoned *TAF* altogether. After all, she wasn't tuning in for the writing, and there were plenty of people who would have happily picked up her reins as mod for the archive. But when the rubber hit the road, she hadn't been able to part with the wiki.

It was her baby, and as things got messier with her parents' divorce, the archive became a kind of safe haven. She had built that tiny, nerdy corner of the Internet as a resource and meeting place for fellow fans. Why should she have to abandon a space where she felt good and powerful just because Devin Ashwood made her cry?

Even with her rose-colored glasses shattered, she still loved the ritual of watching the show every week. Sometimes waiting for Friday night at eight p.m. got her through an entire school week. The comforting experience transported her to a world where she always knew which side was good and which was evil. And if her previously unbiased reviews skewed a little snarkier starting midway through season 3, site traffic certainly didn't suffer.

Alex saw it as a personal fuck-you to Devin Ashwood that instead of dropping out of the fandom, she leaned in. Cam and Eliza were the only people she'd ever told about her crushing humiliation at Supercon '08. They were both discreet and petty enough to keep her shameful run-in with the series' star a secret while remaining ready to roast him at a moment's notice, even seventeen years later.

> **ELIZA:** OK WAIT we're ignoring the most obvious and important question—did he do his own makeup?? Because those claws and fangs look more realistic than anything the TW ever commissioned.

CAM:

CAM: Say whatever you want about the Arcane Files fandom, but seven years after the show goes off air Devin Ashwood is still feeding us.

ELIZA: I can't believe he waited for an actual super blue blood moon eclipse to pull a stunt like this—but then missed by one day.

CAM: I can. That messy bitch loves drama but he's simple.

ELIZA: Apparently there's a quote from some NASA scientist going around on Tumblr that says the sublunar point was—get this—twenty miles outside los angeles

CAM: how convenient!! I knew he was lurking on the remains of our patron hellsite along with all the p0rn bots.

ELIZA: The poor man's career was already in the toilet. I'm just glad we got to see his dick

CAM: . . . it was literally censored.

ELIZA: Yeah but unfortunately you could tell it's big 😣

ELIZA: Can you believe someone got paid to place that black box? And I'm over here slinging stocks . . .

Suddenly, what had been shaping up to be a pretty typical shitty Tuesday in the small Florida town Alex had never managed to escape took a turn for the better. She had to scroll back forever, through a veritable maelstrom of memes and all-caps exclamations, to find the actual article link.

The headline read, TV Werewolf Goes Feral.

A Pyrex full of tofu curry went cold at her elbow as Alex clicked through and read.

Assumed to be intoxicated . . .

. . . growling at a passerby . . .

. . . fully nude . . .

. . . allegedly did not attempt to bite any person or pets.

The actual words "Devin Ashwood" didn't appear until the second paragraph, but when they did, her stomach gave a sick little flip. You'd think after all these years she'd grow indifferent to seeing his name. You'd be wrong.

Alex no longer hated the man with the fire of a thousand burning suns. She was thirty-four years old and lacked the energy. But she didn't begrudge herself a little schadenfreude.

On that note, the video itself was . . . a lot.

At first she thought he was drunk. All that stumbling and squinting. The camera didn't have a great angle. It must have been security footage from one of the nearby storefronts. The capture was black and white, grainy. Ambient sounds dominated the audio. Outdoor diners at a neighboring restaurant. A guy playing saxophone on the corner with an open case at his feet. But the gossip site had added subtitles. At one point little white letters popped onscreen that read: [indecipherable growling].

He must have bought some kind of special contact lenses, because his eyes shone unnaturally bright, like they were backlit.

Alex knew what was coming. She'd read the article before hitting play. Still, it was wild to watch the "transformation" she'd seen so many times onscreen play out in real time.

Eyes, claws, jaws.

Devin's performance art followed *The Arcane Files'* formula exactly, with the end result being eerily similar to how Colby's partial shift had looked on TV. The transformation was in the same school of late nineties / early aughts paranormals like *Buffy* and *Teen Wolf*, where they kept the actors upright on two legs and used minimal prostheses on their faces and hands to make them look "monstrous" while still retaining plausible fuckability.

Couldn't he have at least added a tail?

The howl was by far the most convincing part. Alex spent plenty of hours in Ocala with her dad listening to real wolf pack communications. Somehow Devin had managed to nail something distinctly feral. A sound so deep and powerful, it seemed impossible for a human's vocal cords and diaphragm to achieve.

Goose bumps broke out across her arms as the clip continued.

God. The frustration in his long drawn-out cry was palpable.

He's scared, Alex thought. But that was silly. She didn't even have the volume on her phone turned all the way up. And besides, she had no business thinking she knew anything about Devin Ashwood.

He must have worked with a new vocal coach, because Colby never sounded that wounded.

When she got to the part of the video where he started ripping off his own clothes, Alex expected the tortured but tanta-
lizing choreography to be in the same vein as the shifts shown
on *The Arcane Files*. But Devin moved with surprising brutality.
It almost looked like he was scouring his own chest as he shred-
ded the fabric of his shirt with whatever kind of prosthetic claws
he'd managed to acquire.

By the time he fell into a naked crouch, Alex had to physically close her eyes against secondhand embarrassment.

"Morning."

Alex jumped when Seth, one of the vet practice's other techs,
came into the break room and picked up the ancient Mr. Coffee pot.

"Holy crap, Mizlansky." She pressed her palm to her racing
heart. "Make a little noise."

Was it time for him to clock in already? Sometimes he came
in a little early to catch Alex before her shift ended. Dr. Wronski's practice was small enough that she needed only one tech
on at a time, but Seth seemed to think that as coworkers it was
their sacred duty to exchange watercooler chitchat rather than
pass like ships in the night.

"Sorry." He smiled at her while filling the pot with water
from the sink on her right.

It was a nice smile. Genuine. Friendly. Seth kind of reminded
her of Shaggy from *Scooby-Doo*, all gangly limbs and unkempt
hair.

He slid into a seat across from her. "Did you hear they might
finally change the high school mascot?"

See, this was the problem with never leaving your hometown; people remembered your adolescent foibles.

She and Seth hadn't even been in the same grade. He was at
least three years younger than she was. But ask anyone in Tomp-

kins about Alex Lawson and you'd still get some combination of the same four words: "gay" "goth" "vegan" "bitch." The difference between Seth and the rest of the Tompkins population was he thought that made her cool.

The "gay" and "goth" pieces in particular weren't even accurate. Alex was bisexual with a preference for black clothing. Her local reputation was built on the aging pillars of a few select acts of teenage rebellion, the most memorable of which involved releasing the geriatric horse that their high school had kept (and mistreated) as part of their mascot, the Knights.

"It happened again?" In subsequent years, the story had turned into a bit of local legend. Other teenagers, role-playing as vigilantes, repeated Alex's midnight rescue with Cornflour's string of reluctant successors.

This town treated racehorses better than kings, but once stallions stopped being able to win, the ones who couldn't go on to stud became disposable.

"Oh yeah." Seth got up to retrieve his cup of coffee. "I think they're gonna go with something intangible this time. Apparently, 'lightning' was on the table."

Alex sighed. This part of her town legacy was also, coincidentally, Devin Ashwood's fault. At least indirectly. She'd walked out of that convention center all those years ago a ball of humiliated fury and remade herself in the shape of a rebel.

A normal person would have simply taken off the "freak" costume when they got home. Alex decided to make it permanent.

In the months that followed, she dyed her hair jet-black, pierced an eclectic array of holes in her body, and generally started dressing for school like she was going to a funeral. If the pearl-clutching conservatives of this town were going to hate her anyway, she might as well give them good reason.

As an adult she could see her teenage angst and acting out for what it was: all the stress and sadness and hormones bubbling over. But back then she'd just been mad. All the time. At Devin Ashwood. At her parents. At Tompkins.

Now she was mostly tired.

At the end of her shift Alex went home. The house was quiet, her dad at work. It always took a while for her to come down from the frenzy of the vet's office. She'd sleep for a few hours before going to pick up Rowen from school.

Alex first met the precocious nonbinary teen when they got matched through a queer youth mentorship program run out of Tompkins Community Center. Built when a pack of granola-crunching hippies had briefly infiltrated the WASPy confines of Tompkins in the late seventies, the TCC battled chronic underfunding and an increasingly crumbling exterior.

Along with all the other volunteers, Alex knew each day their doors opened might be the last. But until then, the TCC served as a haven for the town's outliers—the poor, the elderly, the queer.

Alex didn't actually believe she had much to offer Rowen in the way of life advice, as evidenced by *gestures helplessly at whole life.* But as long as the Florida legislature was determined to put queer and trans kids through hell, Alex wanted at least one of them to feel less unwanted in this town than she had.

She toed out of her sneakers at the rack by the door, then went to make herself some peppermint tea. In the kitchen, she found a reusable shopping bag with a new pair of windshield wipers inside on the counter, along with a hastily scrawled Post-it from her dad telling her to have a good day.

After setting the kettle to boil, Alex went out to get the mail. She flipped through the stack on the walk back, and sure enough—damnit. Another medical bill.

It had been more than a decade since her dad's first heart attack, but he'd spent a long time in and out of the hospital while doctors figured out what kind of treatment he needed. During COVID, he'd had an issue with his beta-blockers that led to arrhythmias and a pacemaker, and another long stint at Ocala General. That, plus his ongoing medication needs, meant his medical bills were like hydra heads: every time they paid one off, two more popped up in its place.

After assessing the damage, Alex hauled one of the sturdy wooden chairs from the table over in front of the fridge and then climbed atop it to place the letter in Nana's old bread box.

She did mental math while sipping her scalding tea. If she canceled her hair appointment for Friday, it wasn't enough, but it was better than nothing. At this rate, she'd spend the rest of her life living in the loft over her father's garage, their combined salaries barely enough to keep their heads above water.

It would help if she got a better-paying job, but Tompkins wasn't exactly bursting with gainful employment opportunities for a college dropout who'd spent most of her misbegotten youth antagonizing the people who controlled the town's commerce.

Besides, Alex would miss the animals. She'd grown attached to the regulars on the night shift. Even Snowball, who, thanks to his increasingly rheumy eyes, sometimes mistook her fingers for food. All the sleepy animal snores in chorus reminded her a bit of camping with her dad in Ocala as a kid, listening under the soft canopy of the tent as he named each forest creature by the sound of their night calls.

What could she say? Borderline pathetic empathy for animals ran in her family.

Later that afternoon, Rowen came out of play practice with a new turquoise stripe in their hair.

They ran up to Alex's beat-up old Honda and flung open the door before she'd come to a full stop.

"Did you see that the guy from that TV show you liked in high school thinks he's a dog now?"

Oh boy. Here we go.

She'd told Rowen about her youthful *TAF* obsession because the Nolby fandom had been a huge part of realizing her queer identity as a teen. While Alex purposefully never got into specifics about how her feelings toward Devin and his character Colby might have evolved, Rowen was too perceptive for their own good.

They knew, at the very least, that mentioning him riled Alex every time.

She fought not to flinch as she waited for Rowen to stow their bass in the trunk and buckle their seat belt. She hadn't willingly given Devin Ashwood this much airtime in her brain since Bob Barker was hosting *The Price Is Right.*

"Well?" Rowen said as Alex pulled away from the curb.

"Okay, fine." Alex broke. "Yes, I've seen the video. Obviously."

When her active attempts to appear unaffected by Devin Ashwood's latest antics went on a beat too long, Rowen rolled their eyes like Alex was a trial. "And? What do you think?"

She thought delighting in another human's public downfall seemed like bad mentor behavior.

"Maybe he's trying method acting," Alex offered generously.

"Seems like a cry for help if you ask me." Rowen folded their arms as Alex pulled onto the highway, heading east toward Ocala.

Alex snorted. What would Devin Ashwood need help with?

Help! I'm too rich. Help! Time has done nothing to dull the impact and intensity of my smolder.

When Alex's phone buzzed in the cup holder between them, Rowen picked it up.

"Taylor wants to know if you're free this Saturday."

"You can leave it on read," Alex said.

Rowen made a tsking sound as they put the phone back.

"Don't you think you're a little old to be playing games?"

"I'm not playing games," Alex huffed.

"I'm sixteen." Rowen leaned forward to fiddle with the notoriously fickle AC. "You think I don't know about ghosting? Therapists on TikTok say you have to make yourself vulnerable if you want to find love."

"Gross. Pass." Alex pulled a face and then, realizing once again that she wasn't setting a good example, added hastily, "I'm just busy right now."

"Are you?" they said skeptically. "I'm pretty sure I'm your only friend."

"That's not true. I have Internet friends."

Rowen shook their head. "Listen to yourself."

"Gen Z is so mean," Alex grumbled as she pulled into the parking lot at the preserve where they did their twice-weekly hot person hikes.

"We're not mean. We're honest." Rowen patted Alex's arm sympathetically before unhooking their seat belt.

Devin Ashwood had pronounced Alex a sad loser seventeen years ago, and despite her best efforts, he looked more like a soothsayer every day.

The Origin, wiki article #112

In the world of *The Arcane Files*, only one werewolf exists in every generation. Rather than being bitten or born, a werewolf must evolve during an ultrarare "Wolf Blood Moon Eclipse." This type of lunar event occurs approximately once every 150 years when a super blue blood moon eclipse passes within 200,000 miles of Earth's atmosphere.

Only this unique cosmic event generates a powerful enough energy exchange between the Earth and the moon to trigger the Change, during which the latent enzyme sitting dormant in all humans activates The One.

From that moment forward, whenever the full moon rises for the rest of their lives, The One werewolf will release their human form and take on the body of a wolf.

This type of transformation is referred to as a Full Shift, not to be confused with a Partial Shift, which is linked to a werewolf's emotions and occurs outside of the full moon.

3

"YOU'RE NOT LISTENING to me," Devin said into the speaker of his cell phone while pacing the confines of his home office. "I can't tell you how I got prosthetic claws to pop out because I don't remember any of it."

Three days into the worst PR news cycle of his career and his team was trying to triage. Ramona, his publicist, set up this conference call after Devin refused to meet in person.

"We understand you're under a tremendous amount of stress," she said, her voice corporate calm, "but we do have to ask these questions. The more details we have about the night in question, the better chance we have of regaining control of the narrative around the video."

Yeah, no kidding. Devin would love for her to grab the reins on the narrative. Page Six was calling him a deluded has-been. They had a live chat where makeup artists and VFX experts debated whether the fangs Devin sported in the video were made from organic materials or added in post.

The whole industry thought he'd torpedoed his reputation in one elaborate, desperate bid to retain Hollywood relevancy.

Fans of *TAF* had immediately made the connection with the super blue blood moon eclipse thingy from the show, and now everyone was making fun of him for orchestrating a fake transformation one night after the full moon.

And listen, Devin wouldn't claim to be above doing goofy shit for attention. He had once asked his barber for frosted tips *on his wedding day.* But even he didn't think it was a good idea to pretend to be a supernatural monster in public. Especially not the exact one he'd played on TV.

"So to confirm." He could hear Ramona's keyboard clicking in the background as she typed. "You were drinking prior to the performance and that's why you don't remember the details?"

"Uhhh . . . yeah." It seemed safer to let them think he'd done this on purpose (and likely also that he had a substance abuse problem) than to admit he had no idea what the fuck was going on.

Devin was scared shitless. Clearly something was medically wrong with him. It had been three days and his hangover symptoms had barely let up. Everything was too bright, too loud, too much.

He tried lowering his blackout shades and running a white noise machine 24/7. He wore sunglasses inside and ordered industrial-strength earplugs off Amazon. During last night's thunderstorm, he'd physically hidden in the closet.

Nothing changed the fact that he'd blacked out twice in the last week. And the second time whiskey wasn't even involved. Devin didn't know what triggered these . . . episodes, or whether it might happen again.

Just in case, he hadn't left the house since the footage went viral.

If he went to a doctor, they'd ask him the same questions as Ramona. Ones he didn't have answers to. What was he supposed to say? *Lately, every time someone hurts my feelings, I lose control and whip out my dick?* They'd send someone to arrest him.

If he did have a brain tumor, maybe it would go away naturally.

"I tried talking to a shrink," he confessed to his team. Dr. Palmindar Jaswal's initial assessment was that Devin had an acute anxiety disorder, the suppression of which had resulted in a nervous breakdown. "He gave me some breathing exercises to try."

Those helped a little when Devin remembered to do them. But then the guy started asking questions about Devin's "childhood trauma," which, yeah, hard pass.

"Hey, that's good, man." Devin's manager, Ellis, jumped in. "That's real good. Listen, this is not that big a deal. All the greats get into a little method acting now and then. Daniel Day-Lewis almost offed himself trying to live solely on almonds during filming for *The Last of the Mohicans*. And they nominated that guy for an Oscar. You just need to lie low for a little while. Keep your cool and let this blow over."

Right. Lie low. Devin could do that. Today's headline was tomorrow's hamster-cage liner or whatever.

He grabbed a pen off his desk and scribbled on a notepad: *Breathing good. Keep calm.* Then he underlined the word "calm" until the pen ripped through the paper.

His office made him feel stupid. It was full of books he'd never read, some of which didn't even have text printed inside. He'd gotten bored once and checked. Apparently even his interior designer never expected him to reach for one.

After making a bunch of promises to his team about how he wouldn't talk to any reporters and would consider cutting out gluten again, Devin hung up, feeling like a puppy that had pissed all over the carpet.

He reached over to his keyboard and unpaused the video that was still up on the screen of his laptop. Devin must have watched the security cam footage that the tabloids had gotten ahold of a hundred times over the last seventy-two hours, cycling through the stages of grief for his career.

The strangest part was, though he clearly recognized his face, his body, his clothes—Devin couldn't move like that. Thirteen years of playing Colby going into a shift and he'd never gotten his muscles to bulge and strain in that way. He'd never growled like that either, a vibration so deep it made his chest visibly rise and fall even from a security camera's vantage point.

A terrible shiver shot down his spine.

He wished he could call Jade. She was the one person in this town he truly trusted. He had other friends, sure, but no one he'd let see him like this—at his most pathetic. Jade had already abandoned him for being obsessed with Colby. Why would she believe now, when no one else did, that he hadn't orchestrated this whole thing?

Fuck. He was trying so hard not to go to pieces.

Every night, he went to bed hoping tomorrow he'd wake up normal.

Every morning, he didn't.

Eyes, claws, jaws.

Devin slammed his laptop shut.

It wasn't possible.

Except . . . what was the rational explanation for how he'd somehow managed to make his nails extend and turn gunmetal gray? How could he have lengthened his incisors in the span of a moment without touching his teeth?

He held his hands out in front of him. They looked normal, human.

For now.

He wished there was some way to check. Like a COVID test for werewolf germs.

Hell, maybe there was. His computer was right there . . .

Devin opened a web browser, then, on second thought, switched over to incognito mode.

how to know if you might be a werewolf, he typed into Google, with his tongue between his teeth.

The first returned hit was a webpage called Werewolf Support Group.

Holy shit. Devin's heartbeat began to pound. *Maybe there were others.*

What if this blackout / sinus pressure / possible animal-morphing thing had happened to more, less-famous people?

It would be kind of sick if he stumbled across a whole secret underground werewolf community forced to hide for fear of prosecution, like in the 2003 cinematic masterpiece *Underworld*. Devin's dick jumped a little at the mental image of Kate Beckinsale in that black leather catsuit.

Once the website finished loading—you couldn't get decent Wi-Fi in Topanga Canyon to save your life—the whole page looked janky as shit. On the banner stretching across the top of the page, someone with an entry-level understanding of Photoshop had overlaid tiny text in a script font on top of an overexposed picture of the moon. Normally Devin would need readers to make it out, but for some reason that wasn't an issue at the moment.

Hi and welcome to . . . Oh god damnit. Somehow he'd stumbled upon some kind of fan archive for his own show.

As Devin scrolled down, he saw widgets that linked off to episode guides, character summaries, and what looked like some kind of forum.

Great. People were probably talking about his latest exploits over there.

With his stomach in knots, Devin clicked through.

As it turned out, the comment section had been locked. There was a note at the top explaining that the forum had been frozen in 2018 but that previous queries would remain online as a resource until the site's web-hosting contract expired in 2026.

Can a werewolf get a vampire pregnant? the first question read. Apparently, user Nathaniel'sJuiceBox99 was writing a fic and wanted to feature something called "mpreg."

What the fuck was that?

Devin knew about fan fiction in the abstract. They were little stories people wrote about the characters. Occasionally someone brought a printed-out copy of one to a convention for him to sign. From what he gathered, most of them were real horny.

He kept scrolling. Man, these people had a lot of questions about werewolf dicks. And some of this stuff sounded painful.

Eventually Devin got nervous enough that he shoved down his sweatpants, just to check. But as far as he could tell, everything looked the same. Thank fuck.

At one point he noticed a search bar at the top of the site— aha!—and reentered his Google query, but no results came back. Apparently, the nerds who hung out on this thing had plenty of time to go back and forth about the finer details of self-lubricating assholes and male lactation but couldn't be bothered to dig into the basics.

Still, this was the closest he'd gotten to any kind of answers.

Before he knew it, Devin blinked and realized he'd been scrolling for almost four hours. Maybe it was because he was fraying at the seams, but the content on here was strangely fascinating.

He was about to click out of the browser when a little gray box at the bottom of the page caught his eye. Questions or concerns? it said. Email the mod, along with—he laughed—a Hotmail address.

Devin hovered his cursor over the link. What were the chances the person who ran this thing still checked that inbox?

As he'd read through the various user-generated questions and moderator responses, Devin found himself agreeing with the mod more often than not. First of all, they really knew their shit when it came to the show, but the best part was they would occasionally roast Brian Dempsey in a way that was objectively hilarious.

Whoever the mod was, they'd clearly once cared enough about *The Arcane Files* to spend countless hours of their life building this fan site. They would probably want to help out the actor who had carried the torch as the one and only Colby Southerland.

So yeah, Devin wrote the email. He made his request for assistance sound like a secret mission. *Our little secret*, he called it, figuring he might as well give the über-dork on the other end of the Internet a bit of a thrill.

He was already LA's latest laughingstock. At this point, what did he really have to lose?

Two hours later Devin awoke to the ping of a new email on his phone.

He fumbled blearily for it on his nightstand and then winced at the harsh glow of the backlight as he thumbed to his inbox.

The mod had written back!

Devin bolted upright.

They wanted to meet!

Whoever it was had sent a date, a time, and an address in . . . fucking Florida?

Well, his team had told him to lie low. Devin might as well hit rock bottom.

4

THE MOD WAS late.

Devin had been sitting at a sticky table with an honest-to-god newspaper and a ball cap pulled low over his brow trying to fly under the radar in this hick-town Dunkin' for almost thirty minutes.

Plenty of people had come and gone. MILFs in tennis skirts. An old guy who couldn't get the coupon on his app to work. Nobody looked twice at Devin.

Until her.

He didn't know what he'd expected from the mod. Maybe a dweeby mom's-basement kinda guy. Greasy, thinning hair. A stained graphic tee. Cargo pants.

This lady was . . . not that.

She looked like a witch fallen on hard times. With one of those rings in her nose that reminded him of Ferdinand the Bull and jet-black hair so dark it was almost purple pulled into a big sloppy bun on top of her head. Her milk-pale skin would have been hell in Hollywood. Those dark circles under her eyes a bitch to cover, not to mention the tattoos he could see peeking out from under the sleeves of the plastic-looking jacket she had on.

In purple scrubs and ratty tennis shoes, she was coming off a shift at some kind of hospital, Devin bet, maybe the ER. He perked up a little in his seat. It would be super convenient if the mod turned out to be a doctor. She could X-ray his brain.

The woman stretched her arms behind her back while she waited for her drink, the movement pulling up the hem of her scrub top just enough to reveal a sliver of creamy skin below her navel.

Devin's throat went dry.

The goth doctor was kinda hot, he realized with a jolt. In a cut-your-balls-off, too-young-for-him kinda way. Even if she did seem dead on her feet.

Her gaze passed over him after she paid, just someone scanning their surroundings on the way to the door, but almost immediately she did a double take, stopping her stride so fast the ice in her obnoxiously large coffee cup sloshed against the sides.

Who was still drinking iced coffee in January? This might be Florida, but it was still forty-six degrees out.

After a beat of awkward eye contact, Devin got to his feet and waved. If she wasn't the mod, she was probably a fan.

"Hey, how's it going?"

In the span of a moment, the woman's heavily lined eyes widened, then narrowed, then she burst out laughing. The sound was loud even over the rest of the noise in the busy coffee shop. The guy working behind the counter stopped to look on with concern, drawing the eyes of the entire line.

Uncaring, the might-be mod continued to crack up, clutching her coffee in one outstretched arm as her whole torso shook.

Devin wiped at his nose, feeling self-conscious. A quick scan confirmed his fly was closed.

Humiliation heated the back of his neck. Was this about the video?

Still laughing faintly, the lady approached his table.

"Hi." Devin made his smile toothpaste-commercial worthy. Maybe this was some kind of nervous fan reaction. Normally, he got criers. And that one lady who tried to trick him into signing a marriage certificate every couple of years at the cons. Uncontrollable laughter could be another symptom of the starstruck.

"This is a joke, right?" the woman said when she could finally speak. "Like a super-elaborate, weird, slightly mean joke?"

She had a naturally husky alto. Sort of a Scarlett Johansson–meets–Kathleen Turner thing. Like she needed a cough drop. To his surprise, Devin found he kinda wanted to give her one.

"Uh. What?" He blinked. "I mean, no." Why would his presence be a joke? "Listen, are you by any chance the moderator of an *Arcane Files* fan archive . . . ?" Devin's voice trailed off a bit at the end as he realized what a weird thing that was to say out loud.

The question set her off laughing again, though this time she nodded in confirmation while her shoulders shook.

"Is Eliza here?" She peered around the coffee shop like she expected someone to pop out from behind one of the tables. "This feels like an Eliza thing."

The next thing Devin knew, she had pulled her cell phone out.

"I didn't even know you were on Cameo," she said, mostly to herself.

Getting annoyed, Devin stood and put his hand over the top of her phone to get her attention.

"I'm not on Cameo. And you're not getting Punk'd either."

The lady wiped at the corner of her eye with her sleeve. "That show ended like twenty years ago."

At least she finally stopped laughing.

"Do you mind sitting down?" Devin had imagined this meeting as much more covert in his head.

After a brief hesitation, the lady took the seat opposite him.

As she scooted in her chair, Devin got a big whiff of her.

She smelled *horrible*. So harshly medicinal his eyes started to water. What'd she do? Get up this morning and bathe in a vat of Clorox?

Up close he had a better view of her hands too. She had "mind" and "body" tattooed across her dainty knuckles in a lowercase gothic font.

Jesus Christ. Devin couldn't give you any specifics, but this chick was one hundo percent worshipping the Darkness.

He pulled out the printed NDA he'd folded into his wallet and smoothed out the creases before passing the paper across the small round table to rest right side up in front of her.

"If you could just do me a favor and sign this before we get into anything delicate."

The mod leaned over the document. "Why does the watermark say 'Mile High Milk Bar'?"

"Oh, you can ignore that." Devin waved off the concern. "My lawyer added it back when I was thinking about investing in weed chocolate. The rest of the thing's boilerplate, I swear."

Several tense minutes passed in which she pored over the paperwork and Devin tried to breathe through his mouth.

At least the coffee here was decent, he thought, taking a sip of his latte. They'd definitely used half-and-half instead of oat as requested for his foam, but damn, he'd forgotten how much milk fat ruled.

Finally, the mod pulled a pen out of her pocket and scribbled a signature on the dotted line.

Alex Lawson.

"Do you have some kind of ID to validate that?" God, he sounded like a narc, but he'd promised the remains of his team that he'd keep the lid closed on this werewolf stuff.

Alex Lawson pursed her lips for a moment like she was thinking about telling him to shove it, but her curiosity must have won out because she dug around in her backpack and then flipped open her wallet to reveal a Florida driver's license.

Oh. According to her birthday, Devin was eight years older than her. She must have been in a retainer when *The Arcane Files* premiered. Meanwhile, last month's *People* magazine described him as "well-preserved."

Devin realized he was looking too long when she raised her eyebrow.

"If no one paid you, what are you doing here?"

"Shit. Yeah. Sorry." Devin straightened up. "So, you read my email, right?"

"Many times." Her mouth twitched like she still thought this whole thing was funny or maybe surreal.

He'd hoped the mod would take this situation a little more seriously, but Devin decided to push on. He'd flown all the way out here. And she'd shown up. He might as well lay out the situation.

"Okay, so then you should understand that I'm looking for some kind of test or assessment that would allow me to . . . you know, have peace of mind that I'm still . . ."

". . . human?"

"Well, yeah." Devin grimaced. It sounded more absurd coming out of someone else's mouth.

"Uh-huh." Alex took a long pull on her orange straw. "May I ask a question?"

"Sure, go ahead." The formal framing made him nervous, but what was he gonna do at this point, deny her?

"Why in the world would you think that I'm qualified to administer that particular exam?"

"What do you mean?" He felt his brows pull together. "You created that whole *Arcane Files* wiki. You spent over a decade detailing every aspect of the show's world-building and plot points. It's all hyperlinked and cross-referenced and categorized."

Devin didn't say, *You're clearly an obsessive weirdo*, but the truth of it still hung in the air between them.

"Okay." Alex folded her hands in front of her, and once again Devin found himself weirdly mesmerized by the contrast of the ink on her pale skin. "Let's say we accept that I have some degree of . . . authority"—she paused to wince—"on the werewolf lore of *The Arcane Files*. I would hope that you, as an actor on the show, would know as well as anyone that any archival expertise I may have *unwillingly* retained after all these years would be fictional. Since werewolves aren't real."

"Yeah, I know they're not real. Thanks." Unless he was turning into one. "That's why you're the closest thing to an expert I could find. On the forum, you used to answer all those questions that people wrote in. And tons of those went beyond the TV show. You were good at the—what do you all call them?—headcanons? Those hypothetical situations involving the characters."

Putting aside the glaring exception that for some reason she clearly thought Colby was having a ton of sex with Nathaniel.

There was no way Colby was gay. Devin would know.

"Wait . . . are you saying you read the forum?" Alex looked like her brain was breaking.

Devin tugged at his ear. "I mean, not all of it." *Pretty much all of it.*

"And you still came here," she said quietly to herself, picking up her drink again and sucking down, like, fifteen ounces in one huge gulp. "You know what? What the hell. Let's do it. Go ahead and try to transform." She started scooting back her chair, the metal legs screeching on vinyl in a way that made Devin wanna scream. "Do you want me to pull the table back too or . . . ?"

"Wait a second." He hooked his leg around the back of her chair so the horrible sound would stop. "I'm not going to"—he lowered his voice—"'transform' in this Dunkin'."

Alex frowned. "Why not? On the off chance you are . . . *mighty morphing* . . ." She giggled to herself. "You already did it on the Venice Boardwalk."

"Not intentionally," Devin grumbled under his breath.

God, this was all so confusing and stressful and embarrassing. And he still had a headache, so something was probably seriously wrong with his brain. At this rate, the most likely outcome of this whole fiasco was he had five more hours to live and he'd wasted his time flying out to Florida to meet some goth nerd and not even for sex.

"Wait . . . are you scared?" Alex looked like the thought made her a little sick.

"What? No," Devin said automatically. No one had asked him that.

But who was he kidding? He'd come all the way out here to ask a stranger for help.

He sighed, resting his elbows on the table. "Wouldn't you be?"

"Yeah," she said after a moment, though she didn't look particularly happy about it. "So, if you're not trying to shift, how do you suppose we determine whether or not you're afflicted?"

"I thought you might have an idea for some kind of test," Devin admitted.

Alex bit her lip, considering.

Devin found her teeth oddly fascinating. Everyone in Hollywood had veneers or at least braces. But hers were imperfect, with an obvious gap in the front. It was cute.

Could she stick her tongue through that thing?

"Is there any chance you might have enhanced senses?"

Devin knew what she meant. On the show, being a werewolf made Colby a low-key superhero. He had night vision, and he could track suspects by scent if he had a piece of their clothing or whatever.

"I've had a migraine for five days," he said. "You think that's something?"

Devin wasn't willing to commit to being a mutant just yet, but what if his sensitivity to light and sound and smells did come from some kind of wonky sensory overload?

Alex tapped her fingers on the tabletop while she thought. She had short nails poorly painted black.

He could tell she was intrigued by his hypothetical problem, even if she didn't like it. You could take the nerd off the Internet but you couldn't take the Internet out of the nerd.

"We could try the lie detector test."

"Oh shit." Devin had completely forgotten about the living lie detector thing Colby used to do with suspects. Basically he could zero in on their heartbeat and find irregularities in the rhythm to figure out if they were innocent or guilty when interrogating them.

"You think that's legit?"

Alex shrugged. "From what I've always heard, *The Arcane Files'* writers adopted werewolf characteristics on the show from the distributed folklore of cross-cultural and cross-generational accounts of lycanthropy."

"I'm sorry. *What?*"

"Werewolves aren't an invention of *The Arcane Files,*" she said slowly, as if worried Devin might not follow. "There have been accounts of them across history going as far back as a millennium. Stories of people growing claws and fangs and fur were especially prevalent across the Germanic regions during the early sixteenth to eighteenth centuries. If you look across the records and account for translations, there are certainly common parameters for the symptoms of the infection. Evolved senses, for example, are a pretty consistent marker."

Despite what this lady might think, Devin wasn't born yesterday. He knew werewolves existed prior to *The Arcane Files.* Hello, Michael J. Fox? But his particular "werewolf misadventures" had followed the world-building of *The Arcane Files* almost exactly.

Eyes, claws, jaws.

Maybe it was a coincidence?

"Let's try it." Devin cracked his neck, trying to psyche himself up.

The problem was he didn't know how to zero in on someone's heartbeat. He screwed up his face and closed his eyes and tried to listen, but he got everything all at once.

The highest pitches in the place slammed against his ear drums: the scream of the milk steamer, the whirling crunch of a bean grinder, acrylic nails scraping against a foam cup.

Devin's blood ran cold.

For days, he'd been working to actively suppress an onslaught of new and mostly unpleasant scents and sounds. Plus, he was still breathing through his mouth to keep the astringent smell of Alex out of his sinuses.

He rubbed at his temples, trying to push through, fumbling blindly, feeling like his head might crack down the center at any moment.

A loud slurping cut through the chaos.

Devin opened his eyes to find Alex with her mouth wrapped around her straw, going after the last of her iced coffee.

"You look like you're trying to poop," she observed.

"Thanks." Devin dragged his palm across his face.

"Is there a problem?"

"Everything's all jammed." Devin felt silly describing it, but he couldn't concentrate over all the screeching static. "My brain's like a radio getting too many signals at once."

Alex put aside her empty cup. She was looking at him like he was a puzzle to be solved.

"So try tuning it like a radio."

"What do you mean?"

"Colby needed a point of connection, remember? Start with eye contact," she said, bossy, excited. Whatever she might claim, Devin knew a superfan when he met one.

He fought not to smile a little as she stared him down, daring him to see through her.

Alex's irises were such a dark brown that even when she sat down across from him, Devin could barely distinguish any pupil. Locking eyes with her made him feel weird. Squirmy. A fish caught on a line.

But that sort of helped. It was a strong enough sensation that he could chase it.

Devin imagined himself zooming in as he let his gaze skip

down the pale column of her throat, as if checking for a pulse, the way he might with his fingers.

There—he swore he could feel it, the tiniest tremor a few inches south of her ear.

Devin put every ounce of energy he possessed into blocking out the rabble, removing everything in the room that wasn't this woman. He tried to breathe her in, chemicals and all. Tilting his head, he followed the rushing sound of blood pumping beneath her skin through the complicated archways of her arteries to her heart.

Thump thump. Thump thump.

He had it! Her heartbeat in his tenuous grip.

"What now?" he gritted out.

"Ask me a question," Alex said.

Oh, right. Devin went with the first thing that popped into his head.

"What's your middle name?"

"Kiley."

Thump thump. Thump thump.

That seemed normal. Honest.

Devin guessed he had his baseline. He knew there were other ways to tell if a person was lying. You watched for shifting eyes and flushing cheeks and sweat at the hairline. But with surprising urgency, Devin found he wanted Alex to believe what was happening to him was real. So he'd do it her way.

"What kind of car do you drive?"

Alex's cheek twitched like she was chewing on it.

"A 2007 Honda Civic."

"Oh god." Devin recoiled. "Really?"

Revulsion pulled him out of his concentration. He had to channel Colby to go back under, the way he used to pretend everything around him was moving in slow motion.

Thump thump. Thump thump.

Devin detected no spike. Nothing irregular. Was he missing the change?

"Where do you work?" He squinted, trying to double down on the link.

"The vet clinic on Clinton."

Thump thump. Thump thump.

"Dang," Devin said. "I was kinda hoping you were a doctor."

"You and my bank account both," she muttered.

Thump thump. Thump thump.

Her heartbeat held unwavering in his ears. Listening to it made Devin feel weird. Almost . . . calm. Like meditation, which he'd historically always sucked at.

"What's your favorite sports team?" He was running out of questions here.

"I don't like sports."

Thump thump. Thump thump.

"Jesus Christ." Devin slammed his palms down on the table. "The point of this whole thing is for you to lie."

Alex put her chin in her palm. "These are really boring questions."

"Excuse me?"

"I'm just saying, if this was an episode of *The Arcane Files*, the writing would be better." A note of petulance underscored her general air of ambivalence.

"Yeah, well, this isn't an episode of *The Arcane Files*." Devin spent so much of his life performing for other people's entertainment. And apparently it wasn't enough. "We're talking about my real life here." Besides, Brian Dempsey and the writers always turned up their noses at Devin's on-set ad-libs.

"Since this whole thing is ripped directly from the show, could you try to make it a little more exciting?" Alex had a twinkle in her eye, like she knew exactly how uncomfortable she was making him. "At the moment we're skewing bland."

Devin ground his back molars together. "You want me to ask you more interesting questions?"

She shrugged. "I mean, if you can manage."

"Okay, you know what? Fine." Devin leaned back and crossed his arms. "When was the last time you masturbated?"

To his surprise, a smile bloomed across Alex's face.

Apparently his outburst pleased her.

She took out her phone and checked the time. "Roughly fourteen hours ago."

Thump thump. Thump thump.

Devin's whole face heated. He'd expected her to balk. It was eight a.m. There was a little old lady next to them sneaking Sweet'N Lows into her handbag.

And she'd just . . .

"Oh no. Are you embarrassed?" Alex asked, mock sympathetic.

"No, you are," Devin snapped, and that was just gasoline on the fire.

She shook her head at him. "I'm really not."

Thump thump. Thump thump.

Great. She wasn't lying. And now Devin was picturing it. Her. Those pretty hands with the stupid tattoos, sliding down her stomach and between her legs. Had she used a toy? She looked like the kind of girl to have one of those bullet vibrators, something discreet and efficient. She probably hissed at the first press against her clit, her thighs flexing as she brought her knees up, feet pressing flat to her mattress, arching into it.

Devin grunted. Fuck. He was hard in Ben Affleck's favorite coffee chain.

He shifted in his seat, trying to subtly relieve the pressure.

Since when was his dick into goth girls? He didn't have a type exactly, but he probably hooked up with more blondes with big fake tits than not. To be fair, though, that was more LA demographics than Devin being picky.

Alex's eyes were laughing at him, even if her mouth stayed closed.

When was the last time anyone had been this openly mocking to his face? Especially a fan . . .

Wait a second. Alex was a fan. And not a casual fan. Everyone on that archive had been positively gagging for Colby's dick.

He narrowed his gaze.

This chick wanted tougher questions? Well, Devin had been raised to entertain an audience.

He had enough of a handle on this super-hearing thing that he could lean back in his chair and ask casually, "Did you ever have a crush on me?"

Alex choked on an ice cube she'd been crunching. Twin spots of scarlet appeared high on her cheekbones.

Gotcha. It was Devin's turn to smirk. Maybe he was being a little mean, but he hadn't slept in days and his head was killing him. Plus, she started it.

"Well?" He raised his eyebrows and waited.

"No," Alex finally said from between her teeth.

Thumpthumpthumpthump.

"Holy shit." Devin jolted in his chair.

She was lying. He could *hear* it.

"Are you attracted to me right now?" He didn't actually mean to antagonize her. The question was out of his mouth before Devin could consider the consequences.

"No," she said again, the word somehow drenched in loathing.

Thumpthumpthumpthump.

Upon later reflection, he realized he shouldn't have jumped to his feet, pointed straight at her, and shouted, "You're lying!" but Devin got swept up in the moment.

"This is ridiculous." Alex's chair clattered to the ground as she stood.

Whatever. He was a human lie detector, baby!

Devin indulged in a grin and realized he hadn't smiled in a week.

He didn't know why Alex was so worked up. She looked pretty cute, all flushed and flustered, storming out the— Shit.

"Hey, wait!" He followed her out into the humid Florida morning. "Where are you going?"

Alex fumbled in her backpack. "I'm late for work."

Thumpthumpthumpthump.

"No, you're not," he said, distracted. Now that he knew how to calibrate against a specific sound, it wasn't actually that hard. "I thought you said you were gonna help me."

She pulled out her keys and unlocked her car.

A few feet ahead of them, a 2007 Honda Civic beeped.

"I can't."

Thumpthumpthumpthump.

"Still lying," Devin said and then immediately winced.

"Fine. You're right." Alex opened the driver-side door. "I just don't want to."

Devin didn't need super senses to know that was the truth. He jumped in front of her bumper before she could get in and reverse.

"What if I pay you?"

He wasn't trying to be offensive, but she was wearing a patched jacket, driving a car that looked like it would break down at any moment, and she'd made that comment about her bank account inside.

By the way her face twisted up, Devin could tell immediately that Alex wanted to say no but that something held her back.

"What do you expect me to be able to do?"

"I need to figure out what's wrong with me. Maybe we could attempt to re-create the"—he swallowed thickly—"*shifting* thing in a controlled environment."

Alex raised her eyebrows. "So you really think—?"

"I don't know." Devin cut her off before either of them actually said the word. "But whatever is going on . . ." He swallowed thickly. "I don't think I can get through it on my own."

After a long moment, Alex sighed. "How much?"

5

ALEX NORMALLY AVOIDED both alcohol and social obligations, but considering the morning she'd had, she made an exception.

"Oh my god," Seth yelled from across the bar before rushing to throw himself into her arms. "I can't believe you showed up."

"Happy birthday," Alex said into his shirt. He smelled like rum and Irish Spring soap.

"Come meet everyone." Her coworker tugged her to the back of Ott's bar, where a small group had clustered on the sticky dance floor.

Ott's was an institution in Tompkins, the kind Alex normally wouldn't be caught dead in. It was a bar for rich people who enjoyed pretending to slum it. The pool hall was dark and artificially divey. They charged ten bucks for domestic bottles and played PGA tournaments on their flat-screens. But it was the only place in town if you wanted to dance on a Friday night without driving an hour and a half each way.

"This is my boyfriend, Matt." Seth looped his arm around a handsome Latino guy. "Matt, this is my grumpy coworker, Alex."

"Nice to meet you." Matt smiled and then said, sotto voce, "Sorry, he's a little drunk."

"No, it's okay," Alex assured him. "That description is accurate."

She gave Seth the little wrapped present she'd brought, a set of his favorite Muji pens.

"See," he told Matt, clutching them to his chest. "I told you we were friends."

Alex's heart twisted. She always chalked up Seth's offers to hang out after work to the kind of mandatory, insincere social niceties demanded among coworkers. That suddenly seemed really shitty and unfair.

Why couldn't she let Seth be her friend? According to Rowen, Alex needed more local ones.

They got along well enough, and she knew he was into nerd stuff. Comic books, Alex was pretty sure. She'd tuned out the last time he went on a rant about *Saga* in the break room.

Man, was she maybe an asshole?

Not forming attachments to people, places, or things in Tompkins had been a conscious choice in high school after her mom left, a sort of "I'll leave before anyone else can leave me" cheap teenage rebellion.

But ever since Alex had dropped out of Florida State and come back to take care of her dad, her self-imposed isolation felt more like an unintended side effect of working and worrying all the time.

Now that she'd made a deal with the devil for half up front, maybe that should change.

"Do you guys wanna do shots?" she yelled over the music. Alex needed to bury the memory of Devin Ashwood saying *Did you ever have a crush on me?* under about ten thousand layers of booze.

"Yes," Seth shouted, adding a lot of *S*'s at the end of the word.

Alex laughed. Yeah, they could definitely be friends.

Matt offered to come with her to the bar, but she waved him off, and he and Seth went back to dancing with a small crew of other locals Alex vaguely recognized.

The bar was packed, some big football game on the TV. People jostled for shoulder space to get their order in with the single harassed-looking bartender.

After serving a group of rowdy guys in Hawaiian shirts, he made his way over to Alex. "Hey. What's going on?"

"It's possible that I made a deal with a monster this morning."

The bartender held his hand up to his ear. "What was that?"

"Three shots of tequila, please," Alex shouted back, holding up the corresponding number of fingers.

He nodded and went to grab a bottle off the shelf.

Unfortunately, waiting for her drinks gave Alex what she'd been desperately trying to avoid—time alone with her thoughts.

Alex had spent an inordinate amount of time—half her life, really—diagnosing what was wrong with Devin Ashwood. Perhaps she was uniquely qualified for this bizarre job.

"That's a lot of money," she said after he made his offer, in case he didn't know. "Do I still get paid even if nothing happens?"

"Absolutely. If we go through this whole thing and it turns out I'm just having a nervous breakdown or something, no one's gonna be more grateful than me."

"Than I," she corrected instinctually.

"What?"

Alex shook her head. "Never mind."

When she got the auto-forwarded SOS email from her long-dormant mod account two nights ago and arranged to meet the sender, she never expected it to actually be him. Alex thought for sure she'd walk in to find Eliza pulling a prank while in town for a business trip. It would have been an elaborate setup, sure, but what was fandom if not people investing questionable amounts of time and energy into fictional stories?

Flesh-and-blood Devin Ashwood could never in a million years come to *Tompkins*. That should be, like, illegal, actually, Alex was pretty sure. Something they added to the town charter. *No celebrities. Especially ones with which residents once had intense, emotionally fraught interactions.*

Alex's tiny, embarrassing hometown was so sad and rural they didn't even have a real coffee shop. But in further evidence that the universe did not give a single shit about her mental stability, Devin Ashwood had shown up anyway. He sat across from her sipping from a foam cup, asking for her help. And he'd looked—Alex refused to think about how he'd looked for one-third of a Tide commercial on the TV across the bar.

Fine. He looked fucking good. Seventeen years older and somehow more handsome. He'd been almost too pretty when he was young, those full lips and high cheekbones, ridiculous cow eyelashes, and honest-to-god freckles in the summer.

Now he had that full tawny beard threaded with a few gray strands, fine lines at his eyes and across his forehead (despite the Botox rumors; nature must be healing). He was still the most beautiful man she'd ever seen, but this time he looked real.

Whatever. It wasn't news that Devin Ashwood was hot. *The face that launched a thousand ships* was Cam's favorite pun.

It didn't matter. Clearly, there was something wrong with him either physically or psychologically.

Alex didn't care about the results of a fictional lie detector simulation. In no way was she prepared to engage with the possibility that (1) werewolves might be real, and (2) Devin Ashwood might be turning into one.

So yes, she'd gotten herself into a huge mess. But that was a problem for tomorrow.

"Here you go." The bartender passed across four shot glasses—three full of liquor and another one full of limes—and Alex collected them in a square between her hands. She barely made it ten feet back toward the dance floor.

"Alex Lawson, as I live and breathe!"

Oh fuck.

She didn't turn around, just kept squeezing past people as tequila sloshed over her fingertips. Thanks to her morning run-in with Devin Ashwood, Alex was now uncomfortably aware of her own racing heartbeat.

"I thought that was you." Pete Calabasas pulled up in front of her with two of his friends. "Are those for us?" He plucked the shot glasses from her fingertips and then handed them back to his lurking buddies. "You shouldn't have."

"Seriously?" Alex said to no one in particular, since the Calabasas family got to do whatever they wanted in this town without consequences because they owned one of the racing facilities.

In boat shoes and a pink polo, Pete might as well have been a meme for a douchebag. Alex wanted to reach out and pop his collar so bad.

He raised one of her shot glasses in a toast. "You ruined our party. Seems only fair we ruin yours."

Ugh. Not this again.

Senior year of high school, Pete and the other rich kids started hosting illegal bonfires in Ocala. Alex didn't give a shit if they wanted to drink Natty Light and jerk each other off, but they left their trash everywhere and destroyed animal habitats, so she'd reported them to the forest rangers.

The rest of the story was simple: They got busted. It went on

Pete's permanent record. His parents paid some fines. And apparently, he'd never gotten over it.

"Listen, Pete, I know you peaked in high school, but sheesh. You really gotta let this one go. It was sixteen years ago."

"Yeah," he said, artificially white teeth gleaming in a leer. "And I'm still waiting for you to make it up to me."

Jesus Christ.

Alex moved to step around him but he shadowed her.

"Where are you going?"

"Some asshole stole my alcohol," she said, turning on her heel and shouting over her shoulder. "I'm going back to the bar to buy more."

Alex made the mistake of letting her guard down after that.

She danced with Seth and Matt after bringing back a fresh round of shots. They talked about Seth's manga collection and Matt's latest woodworking project. The DJ played some halfway-decent music. Alex thought about leaving an hour in, going home, and watching reruns of *The Good Wife*, and decided against it.

At closing, Seth and Matt had a sober friend willing to drive to an all-night karaoke place a few towns over, but Alex begged off. She'd stopped drinking hours ago and the day was catching up with her. Besides, she was at the end of a very long bathroom line and didn't want to make them wait.

By the time she got to the parking lot, it was mostly empty, her car at the very end under a fading yellow streetlamp. Her phone vibrated in her pocket.

> **CAM:** OOP, according to E! "sources close to Devin Ashwood" say he's spending time at a "Bali wellness retreat"

> **ELIZA:** I need a Bali wellness retreat.

> **CAM:** if the video was a public cry for help, does that mean we have to stop making fun of him?

Alex was in the middle of typing a reply when the screen went black, the battery dead. Shit. She'd forgotten to plug it in after work this morning, caught up in the whole Devin Ashwood of it all.

It was strange to have intel on him that she couldn't share. To be sitting on the ultimate *Arcane Files* gossip and have to swallow it. She hated keeping stuff from her friends.

Are you attracted to me right now?

Her skin heated all over again. Mortification and . . . something else.

Maybe it wasn't the worst thing that she'd signed an NDA.

This time, Alex smelled Pete before she saw him. Cologne and stale beer filled her nose right before he grabbed her arm.

"Where you going, Lawson?"

Alex slipped out of his hold, her free hand clenching into a fist instinctively, the other gripping her useless phone.

"Get away from me, Pete, or I'll call your wife and tell her about the lipstick on your collar." It was a poorly kept secret that he slid his wedding ring off when he went out drinking with the boys.

Alex lengthened her strides. Her car was fiftyish feet away. But she didn't want to run if she could help it.

"Aw, come on," Pete said as he and two friends slid into position, flanking her in a half-moon, cutting her off. "Don't be like that. Greg and Chip and I, we're just being friendly."

"Be friendly with each other." Alex was reasonably sure Pete didn't actually want to fuck her, but he'd always had some kind of fetish for the fact that she found him repugnant while everyone else in his life lay down on their bellies for his family's money.

She veered right, trying to go around them, but they moved with her.

"Get out of my way," she said, proud of herself that her voice didn't waver. They were big, a pack of former high school football players gone to seed after a decade. Her dad had given her pepper spray when she went to college, but it was at home in a drawer somewhere, forgotten like all her other best-laid plans.

Alex had the most absurd flash of Colby Southerland in her mind at that moment. He was good in a back-alley bar fight. A small, silly part of her wished he was real. That he'd show up to save her.

Compulsively, she looked around the parking lot again. It was still empty.

Her heart thundered rabbit fast. These men thought she was a nightmare, but apparently not enough to leave her alone. At least, *not yet*.

Once Alex accepted that there was no way out of this situation where she retained her dignity, the rest was easy. It was a strategy she'd invented one night during her freshman year of college, when she'd been walking home alone from the library after dark. The approach relied on a simple cultural truth: no one wants to mess with the weird girl.

The first time she barked, the three grown men just stared at her, uncomprehending. The second time, when the animal sound she made was louder, more urgent, they jumped back involuntarily.

"Dude, what is going on?" either Greg or Chip said, tripping over his loafers, looking to Pete for instruction.

It was always simpler than Alex thought to make the noise, to tap into something feral. Also, strangely, kind of fun. A little like learning to roll her *R*'s in Spanish class.

She barked a bunch of times in quick succession, pulling from her diaphragm to make the sound deeper.

"Stop it," Pete yelled, his face curled up in a mix of revulsion and discomfort.

Alex lunged forward, letting her hair fall into her face as she tilted her head at an unnatural angle. Her imitation of the dogs at work was pretty decent, she thought, snapping her jaws at the end of the noise, driving these assholes back.

"Man, this chick is nuts," the smaller of Pete's buddies said, holding up both his hands and backing away.

The other one took out his wallet and threw it at Alex's feet.

"Take what you need, lady," he said, before fleeing to his car on the other side of the lot.

Alone, Pete was no match for her. A few more barks—the key was to let your mind depart your body for another plane—and he immediately bailed.

Alex bolted for her car and locked herself inside.

Holy shit. She breathed hard through her nose, hoping she wasn't about to puke from adrenaline. Alex crossed her arms over the steering wheel and lowered her head onto them, trying to breathe.

The knock on her window a moment later made her scream and clutch her chest.

Devin fucking Ashwood crouched down and gave a little wave. "Hey—sorry to bother you. But are you, uh . . . good?"

No. She was not good. Public humiliation wasn't enough. *This guy* had to show up after the fact as a witness?

Alex rolled down the window. "Where the fuck did you come from?"

"I just got out of an Uber. I thought I'd grab a drink"—he thumbed toward Ott's—"but apparently the only bar in this town closes at nine thirty p.m." After a beat, he said, "I, uh, came back here because I thought someone might be hurting a dog."

"So . . . you caught the end of that, then?" Alex hadn't been this mortified since she got her period in the middle of chem class and Ryan Wellesley asked her why she didn't just "hold it in."

"Well, yeah." Devin looked a little embarrassed for her. "Got those . . . you know . . ."

"Super senses. Right." Alex nodded because, sure, why not. "How could I forget?"

The hysterical laugh that had been bubbling in her for the last few minutes finally bubbled over before taking an immediate dramatic nosedive into a sob.

"Oh holy—" Devin reached for her side door and set off her alarm.

"What are you doing?" she said, wiping at her eyes as she unlocked it.

"I don't know. You're crying," Devin said helplessly as he slid into her passenger seat, lifting his knees to avoid the small mountain of trash in her footwell.

As if that explained it.

He fumbled in his pockets and came up with half a Dunkin' napkin. "Do you want this? It has my gum in it but I folded it over."

Alex stared at him. But you know what? It was better than her sleeve.

"This is a low moment," she said, taking it and blowing her nose.

"For what it's worth, I thought that barking thing was cool."

Alex closed her eyes against a fresh wave of mortification. "Please do not condescend to me."

"No, it was honestly impressive. I mean, no offense, but look at you."

"Oh, no offense?" She blinked. "Okay."

"I just meant," Devin said, voice soft and almost gentle, "there were three big guys. You weren't gonna fight 'em." He shrugged. "So you did what you had to do."

"I guess." By tomorrow morning the story would be all over town. She'd probably spend the rest of her life with rich assholes barking at her. And the worst part of that was, Alex would have to figure out some other way of scaring off drunk assholes for next time.

"You're brave," Devin said, not like a platitude but like an observation.

Alex made a dismissive noise.

Her hands were clammy where she still had them in a death grip on the steering wheel. The scent of Pete's cologne lingered in her nose. Cloying. Overwhelming. She could still feel his hand on her arm, a phantom weight she couldn't shrug off.

"I'm serious," he said, Colby earnest, and the sincerity in his tone did something funny to her stomach.

Ask anyone in Tompkins not related to her by blood and they would tell you, Alex Lawson was a loser.

A menace.

A fuckup.

A nerd who spent her life fantasizing about other people's adventures.

No one called her brave. Ever.

"Brave" was a word for fictional protagonists on her favorite shows. Though Alex had to admit, the suggestion was flattering. Even when you considered the source.

"You're also scary as shit," Devin said, not without awe.

That compliment she would take.

Alex scrubbed her hand across her face. For seventeen years Devin Ashwood was the grudge she couldn't—wouldn't—shake. Now he was her best chance of getting her family out of debt.

"You want me to go find those guys and kick their asses?" To add insult to injury, his jawline looked marble-forged in the low light.

"Don't be ridiculous," Alex said, even though that was exactly what she'd wanted ten minutes ago.

She could pretend in less weak moments that she had killed and buried the version of Devin Ashwood that had served as her childhood hero, but reality was a lot more complicated. Part of her would always be that brokenhearted teenager who desperately wanted her favorite actor to make everything okay.

That was the trouble with fandom. Spend enough time thinking about a fictional character and you started to believe that your version of them was real. That they belonged to you in some small, private way. Devin Ashwood had Colby Southerland's face, and Alex still didn't know exactly how to parse them apart.

She wanted in that moment, foolishly, what she'd always wanted from Colby. What he'd given her for thirteen seasons despite the asshole actor behind the role—comfort. The ache was so strong, the longing for this person who didn't exist, that Alex had to wrap her hands around her knees to keep from reaching for him.

If she wasn't careful, Devin Ashwood would break her heart twice.

Partial Shift, wiki article #203

During a Partial Shift the werewolf retains a humanoid form with select beastly enhancements. The physical transformation of the Partial Shift always follows the same progression—<u>Eyes, Claws, Jaws</u>. First, the werewolf's eyes change from their human "resting" color to glowing silver. While it takes a while for the werewolf to adjust to their new sight (<u>1.02</u>), once they do, their silver eyes will provide superior vision, as evidenced when Colby uses his Partial Shift sight to navigate the depths of the ocean on a mission tracking <u>Merpeople</u> (<u>3.08</u>). Next, their fingernails harden and lengthen to produce steel-like claws of approximately 1 inch in length. These can be used as weapons or utility tools, depending on the situation. Finally, their incisors extend into fangs, which, while not poisonous, are sharp enough to easily punch through metal (<u>2.12</u>).

Partial Shifts are most often triggered when the werewolf experiences extreme emotions resulting in a loss of control (<u>1.15</u>, <u>5.10</u>, <u>12.20</u>, <u>15.04</u>).

> *"We wanted Colby to look like a monster, but still be hot enough that even as a human, you wouldn't kick him out of bed. Also, special effects are expensive."*
> —Timothy Winthroop, *The Arcane Files* writer, seasons 1–4

6

DEVIN CHECKED IN to the finest hotel within a ten-mile radius of Tompkins: a Hilton Garden Inn off the highway with three stars and stunning views of a neighboring bog. His executive suite featured a shitty little sitting room complete with a faux-leather beige couch, a kitchenette with an electric kettle, and a mattress that was sure to mess up his alignment.

When he gave his room info to his assistant and asked her to send clothes and his PS5, she used a soft, concerned voice because—oh yeah—his team had floated the story that he was in rehab. Well, that was less inflammatory than the truth.

The morning after they met, Alex suggested via text that he meet her that same evening at the vet clinic where she worked the overnight shift. Apparently they'd have the place to themselves and she'd have access to "supplies"—whatever that meant.

If Devin thought about anything too hard right now, he panicked, his breath coming short and shallow while he broke out in a clammy sweat. So he put up blinders and focused only two feet in front of his face. Despite rising concerns, he deemed himself innocent until proven guilty (human until proven were-wolf).

With the day to kill, he rented a vehicle since Uber barely worked out here. The souped-up truck felt appropriately backwoods, but in a fun way, and driving around Tompkins was a trip. The town clearly had money. Or at least parts of it did. But not the same kind of money Devin had grown up around in Los Angeles. These people were Old-Money Rich, aka boring as fuck.

Their quaint little Main Street looked like a set on the back lot. Pastel-twinset-clad townspeople might as well have been extras in another remake of *The Stepford Wives*. He saw several hand-painted signs announcing an upcoming county fair that were so twee they made Devin's teeth ache.

It was like an invisible line divided the haves and the have-nots around here. Or, more likely, considering the entire economy seemed to revolve around racehorses, the haves and the help. At least no one seemed to recognize him as he ran errands, which was good, all things considered. Even if it made his battered ego twinge.

He pulled into the vet clinic's small parking lot a little after eight p.m. As he stepped out of the truck, Devin tipped his head back to check out the night sky. The air was better here than in LA, cleaner, sweeter. His senses were still going haywire, everything too much all the time, but not right now. Not here in the quiet, in the darkness, with nothing moving for miles in any direction.

The inky blackness dotted with stars reminded him of Iowa, where he'd grown up—or, he amended, at least where he'd lived until he was seven and his parents first figured out a way for him to make them money. It was surprisingly nice.

When he tried the handle on the front door of the vet, it turned easily, even though the little wooden sign in the window had been flipped to *Closed*. The second he stepped into the front waiting room all the hairs on his arms stood up. Without conscious thought, Devin found himself sniffing at the air. It was heavy with the combined smell of dozens of animals.

As he stepped forward, a wild chorus of howls and screeching broke out from the animals contained in the rows of metal pens. Devin froze. The alarm felt strangely charged. Personal. Like the cats and dogs knew something he didn't. Before he could stop himself, a growl built in the back of his throat. Devin hurried farther into the facility, through a long hallway, and outside, where a single horse grazed within a fenced-in pen.

The stallion had a blondish coat and a dark brown mane. His ears drew back at Devin's approach, and he began to toe the ground nervously.

Not wanting to upset the poor guy any further, Devin went back inside and found Alex wielding a spray bottle of antiseptic near the front office.

Devin's nose itched. The smell he'd recognized on her at the coffee shop wafted from what looked like a homemade cleaning solution in a spray bottle.

"Oh thank god." Relief washed over him. She didn't smell bad naturally. He hadn't been able to tell last night when she was shrouded in stale beer and smoke.

Alex raised her eyebrows.

". . . you don't use Clorox," Devin supplied, lamely. "I'm very against that brand. Morally. Due to their impact on . . . fish."

"Uh-huh." She put away the bottle and crossed to the cages of animals to speak softly to one hound still whining, clearly agitated by Devin's presence.

Devin's cheeks warmed. "Do all visitors upset them this much?"

"No," she said grimly and led him out of the room and into the hall.

"I think I might have upset your horse," he confessed as they walked.

She made a dismissive noise. "Lou will be all right. He's jumpy around most people."

"Lou? Is that his name?"

"Yeah, it's short for Legacy's Outlaw."

Devin grinned. "Sick. Is he a racehorse?"

Something pulled tight around her mouth. "Former."

"What's he doing here?" The horse didn't look sick or anything.

"Someone abandoned him," Alex said tightly, opening the door outside but leading him in the opposite direction from Lou's pen. "It happens every few months. Owners don't want to pay to feed and house a racehorse that can't run anymore and won't take to stud, so we get them tied up out front."

"What the fuck? Someone just left him?" Devin didn't know why he felt so personally offended.

Alex stopped in front of a big garage and entered a code into the security pad outside the door.

"Racehorses are bred for one purpose, mentally as well as physically. Owners want them anxious, reactionary, 'spooky,' they call it. Once they can't run anymore for whatever reason, a lot of folks don't want to deal with the hassle of managing them."

"But it's not his fault," Devin said, too loud. "The horse, I mean." He cleared his throat. "He didn't ask to be raised for the limelight."

The security pad beeped, and the garage door groaned open.

"It's not his fault," Alex agreed, her eyes softening a little in a way that made Devin oddly self-conscious. "But it's hard to find them homes after they're left here. They're finicky. Misunderstood. Especially the older ones. They need a soft touch."

Devin followed Alex inside. "What happens if you don't find someone to take them?"

Alex flicked on a set of overhead lights that came on with an electric buzz.

"They get shot in the head."

"What?"

The garage had cement floors. To Devin's left were a couple of big white vans branded with the vet's name and to the right were rows and rows of industrial metal shelving full of boxes and plastic-wrapped medical supplies. In the middle of the floor, Alex laid out a huge black tarp.

"Nice setup. Very *Dexter.*"

She didn't smile.

Tough crowd.

On top of the tarp, Alex unfolded a small wooden table and laid out a laptop along with a series of vials and metal instruments, including a whole pack of big, violent-looking needles.

Devin gulped.

Taking out one of the syringes, Alex tapped the side to break up a series of bubbles in whatever clear liquid it contained.

"What is that stuff?"

"Horse tranquilizer," Alex said, mild as you please.

Fuck. "Could it kill me?"

She gave him a look that said, succinctly, *Grow up*, and replaced the vial on the tray.

"It's just a precaution. Worst-case scenario, it'll knock you out for a few hours."

The barest hint of a smirk tugged at her lips.

Whatever Alex expected to happen tonight, clearly she wasn't very scared.

That made one of them.

She cued up the video of him at the pier on her laptop.

"I thought we'd start by going over everything you remember about the last time you had an 'incident.'"

"Last time," Devin said, "or the first time?"

Alex furrowed her brow. "It's happened more than once?"

"I think so." He filled her in on everything he could remember, plus all that he couldn't, starting with waking up naked in his backyard the night of the actual full moon.

"Fading out at the pier felt like fainting," he finished, realizing he'd been talking for almost thirty minutes straight. "Like when they're gonna film a shirtless scene, so you can't eat or drink any water for like forty-eight hours."

"That's not a relatable analogy." Alex looked appalled.

"I'm just saying I got woozy and lost consciousness. My body was there, obviously"—he grimaced, thinking of the howling—"but my mind wasn't."

"Okay." Alex looked a little green around the gills. "Well, since you haven't been to a doctor, I'd like to at least establish a metabolic baseline. If you're cool with it, I can do a basic workup. Obviously I normally perform these assessments on animals, but we actually use a lot of the same devices. I can run a bit of blood work, take your temperature and BP, and establish a pulse rate. If anything comes back massively troubling, at least you'll know to go to the ER for follow-up."

"Oh." For some reason Devin had expected they'd just jump into provoking the shift. After all, that's what he'd asked for. The fact that Alex was taking his ridiculous situation seriously, treating Devin like he mattered, made him feel . . . odd.

"Sure," he said, then cleared his throat. "Thanks."

You're paying her, Devin reminded himself before he got carried away with the idea that Alex cared.

She drew blood first.

"Afraid of needles?" she guessed as she pricked his skin.

Devin nodded, sitting upright in the folding chair she'd produced for him, not wanting to admit that it was her gentle fingertips on the crook of his elbow making him shiver.

Never before in his life had a physical made him horny.

She took his temperature with a digital thermometer held an inch from his forehead. "You're running hot."

It was the scrubs, Devin decided. The way the thin royal blue material clung lovingly to Alex's ass as she bent over to put the device away.

"I'm gonna take your pulse next," she told him, her husky voice perfect for naughty-nurse porn. "Try to unclench."

Alex stepped close, until Devin's chin was practically nestled in her tits.

He took a deep breath and focused on letting go.

And then she touched his neck with two gentle fingertips, and it was all Devin could do to bite back a groan.

The urge to catch her wrist and bring her fingers into his mouth surged through him.

What the fuck?

He jumped to his feet, pulling in air like someone had outlawed it.

Alex frowned. "Is something wrong?"

"No," he said, glad she couldn't tell when *he* was lying. "Just . . . you've got cold hands."

"Oh." Alex made a fist and then *blew on it*, which, yeah, was not helping matters.

Devin had been coiled so tightly for the last week, terrified that the second he let his guard down something animal inside him would break free.

He took a step backward from Alex, then another. It was like trudging through quicksand. Fighting his own instincts. He'd never felt anything like this, a stark divide between his rational mind and his gut.

"What's going on?" Alex frowned.

Oh god. The last thing he needed right now was for her to suck on her bottom lip.

Colby fought his wolf's urges all the time. In the lore of *The Arcane Files*, your wolf was like an extra-feral version of your id, animal instincts kicked into turbogear, constantly oriented toward maximizing pleasure and minimizing pain. Your wolf wanted what you wanted deep down, only *more*.

Never in a million years would Devin have guessed that the terrible beast of his nightmares would want . . . her.

It was why Colby was abstinent (that, and the writers seemed to think all the bare-knuckle restraint increased the show's sexual tension). He never indulged himself in any creature comforts that might weaken his resolve—the poor guy slept on a threadbare mattress on the floor of a dingy walk-up.

"I need a minute," Devin said, bolting for the back door.

If he had turned into a werewolf (he really needed to remain in hypotheticals for as long as possible), his wolf shouldn't be this strong, not yet. Colby's instincts grew most powerful during the full moon, which, according to the Internet, wasn't for another three weeks.

This burst of attraction could still be a fluke, he told himself.

And the fact that he'd gotten hard talking to her over coffee? Well, that was probably a fluke too.

Alex Lawson was *not* his type. And besides, the last thing he needed was to fuck around with the one person who might be able to help him. Luckily, Devin had been working on a PhD in suppression ever since the first time he'd asked his parents if he could quit acting and go to real school and they flat out said, No ❤.

He took a few deep breaths, locked up whatever the fuck this was, and went back inside.

"Everything okay?" Alex said when he returned to the garage.

"Yep." Devin resumed his seat.

At least she still smelled like dog chemicals.

"Just had to water the roses."

Alex rolled her eyes. "Charming."

She took the rest of his vitals with minimal fanfare.

"How's it looking?" Devin asked while she typed the readings into her laptop.

"According to these stats, you're exceptionally healthy. Like maybe world-record healthy."

That didn't sound so bad. He paid enough trying to stay in shape.

"Okay." She closed the laptop. "Time to move on to the main event. You feel up to attempting the Change?"

"I don't actually know how to do it on command." It was, in his limited understanding, like sex. He had to be in the mood.

"Hmm." Alex tilted her head. "Well, what if I try to trigger it?"

"How?" Devin did not like the wild glint in her eye *at all*.

"Well, if we go by *The Arcane Files'* example, we've got a few choices. The most frequent trigger for Colby is pain."

Devin winced. The writers room had always seemed to have a kind of fetish for whips, chains, and other things Rihanna sang about.

"I'd really rather avoid flogging you," Alex said, "if at all possible."

"Agreed."

"The second-most frequent plot device used to bring forth Colby's transformation was the death of a loved one," Alex continued, counting on her fingers. "But that's not exactly viable, for obvious reasons."

Yeah, not least of all because Devin didn't really have anyone he cared about that much. His stomach twisted. He couldn't imagine telling this moody stranger his intimacy issues. *It all started when my parents thought I'd be more focused as a child actor if they actively discouraged me from making friends* . . .

Devin racked his brain. What else had happened on the show to force a shift?

"We could try making out," he suggested tentatively. *Wait, who said that?*

To be fair, lust was a massive trigger for Colby on the show, especially in the season 4 two-part special. But still.

Immediately, Alex pulled a face. "Absolutely not."

Christ. The ego hits just kept on coming.

"You know, for someone who used to have a crush on me, you're pretty rude."

"Listen, I did not— Wait." Her eyes grew wide. "That's actually a good idea."

"What is?" Her having a crush on him or . . . ?

"I could hurt your feelings," she said with palpable excitement. "You said that's what brought on the Change last time, right? That fight with your agent?"

The gleam in her eye made Devin squirm.

"You could at least pretend to feel conflicted at the prospect of berating me."

She shrugged. "What's the point in lying if I can't get away with it?"

He supposed it would be better to lose control now, with some degree of safety protocols and monitoring in place, rather than on some random, unknown future occasion. Colby sure as shit wouldn't have backed down from a challenge like this. As an FBI agent, he'd walked through hell and back—literally—to get answers.

"Okay, fine. I guess we can try it." Devin rolled his neck.

How bad could it be?

7

ALEX HAD FINALLY found the perfect opportunity to get revenge against Devin Ashwood. She set up her phone to record video and made sure the tranquilizers were within arm's reach.

Who knew all those takedown speeches she'd practiced in the shower as an angsty teen would actually come in handy one day? She used to imagine alternate versions of history where she marched around the curtain at that con and gave Devin Ashwood a piece of her mind instead of running away after he insulted her. And yet now that her time had come, she found herself hesitating, biting her pinky nail instead of delivering a verbal smackdown that was long overdue.

It was hard to enjoy herself, knowing this wasn't a fair fight. Alex had spent more than half her life analyzing him with a giant chip on her shoulder, bolstered by a veritable army of introverts on the Internet whose hyperfixated sleuthing skills would probably scandalize the actual FBI.

Over the years she'd gleefully consumed reports of Devin Ashwood's flaws and misadventures like so many BBQ kale chips, licking her fingers as she went. But standing face-to-face with him, Alex couldn't bring herself to mention his messy divorce or the rumors of adolescent drug abuse.

"You chickening out?" Devin gave her a half smile, a hint of teasing challenge from where he stood across the tarp. "Because I promise I can take it."

Fuck he was cute. A million times more potent in person. And just like when she was seventeen and starstruck, he'd picked up on her nerves and leaned in, trying to put her at ease.

Alex stiffened her resolve. She could not afford to like him.

She had at least five perfect setdowns she could've delivered in that moment easy, so of course she said, "Your performance in the season-six finale was really mediocre."

". . . Huh?" Devin seemed to have expected a better effort.

"I'm serious." Okay, this was not her best work, but she'd thrown the gauntlet and now there was nothing left to do but double down. "It was questionable the entire season whether you had any chemistry with Kennedy Roberts at all, but your response when she told you she loved you as Juliette? Completely wooden. Your face didn't move for a full nine seconds. Literally. People made a timer on Tumblr."

"Everyone loves that episode." A flicker of confusion passed over Devin's face. "It has one of the highest scores on IMDb of the entire series run."

"Okay, first of all, it's embarrassing that you know that." Alex didn't consider herself cruel, but maybe she was a little righteous. "Second of all, people like that episode because of *Gus*. That's the episode where he makes a deal with Death to visit his mother in the underworld. I cried so hard watching that scene I literally threw up."

Relying on critiques of the show felt safe, familiar. Artists, at least in theory, knew art once shared belonged to the audience to interpret and interrogate.

"Wait a second." Devin shook his head. "That was the B plot. Colby and Juliette were the main story arc. We laid the foundation for that romance for like sixteen episodes."

Holy shit. Did he really not know?

"Nobody likes that pairing."

"What do you mean?" Color climbed Devin's cheeks.

Rising body temp, Alex mentally recorded. They were on the right track.

"There's an entire tag on AO3 labeled 'no beta we die like my boner whenever Colby kisses Juliette.'"

"That's ridiculous." Devin's nostrils flared as he inhaled. "What are you saying? That I'm not compelling as a romantic lead?"

"Oh, no," Alex said, sunny, beginning to enjoy herself. "I fully believed Colby was in love with Nathaniel."

Devin pinched the bridge of his nose. "Why does everyone think that?"

"Are you kidding me?!" Despite herself, Alex's voice rose. "How else do you explain Colby whimpering while Nathaniel drank blood from his *femoral* vein?"

He rubbed the back of his neck. "I don't know . . . they were buddies?"

"Please!" They were in Alex's arena now. She could fight shipper wars for days. "Colby placed both of his hands on Nathaniel's bare abs in the middle of a supernatural street fight and bellowed, 'Tell me who hurt you!'"

"What was he supposed to do? Not avenge his—" Devin cut himself off. "Colby is not gay. And look, there's nothing wrong with being gay. I'm just saying Colby isn't."

"How can you be sure?"

Devin threw his hands in the air. "Because I'm not gay!"

Alex blinked. "Please tell me you realize—"

"Yes, okay, I heard it." Devin began pacing in a small circle. Alex noticed for the first time the dark circles under his eyes.

Had he not been sleeping? And if so, for how long? No wonder he seemed out of it, close to the edge.

Alex's breath stuttered as his eyes flashed silver under the garage's LEDs.

"Uhh. Devin—"

"Do you know how many people told me I was the reason they kept watching *The Arcane Files* for all those years?" He swung his arms in agitated slashes through the air. "And then after thirteen seasons, the thing finally ends and Gus, fucking Gus Rochester, who literally got discovered waiting tables at SUR, is the one to make the transition into movies?"

With a metallic-sounding click, like a lock sliding into place, Alex watched Devin's fingernails lengthen, darken, and turn to sharp black points.

Oh god. The baby-fine hairs on Alex's arms stood up. It was happening. The Change. For real.

And Devin was seemingly oblivious, lost in a self-loathing spiral that Alex had contributed to, even if he did a lot of the heavy lifting himself.

"Did you know that asshole couldn't even be bothered to thank me in his acceptance speech?" He kept pacing, his strides lengthening into something fluid, almost . . . a prowl.

Goose bumps broke out across Alex's arms. A primal fear response. Prey recognizing predator.

"I was supposed to be the breakout." His voice trembled with something more than anger.

Alex edged toward the syringe full of tranquilizer slowly, hoping to avoid notice.

It didn't matter that Devin had found her heartbeat in the middle of a crowded restaurant, that he'd caught her in lie after lie. Alex had written off his extraordinary metabolic readings as a fluke, perhaps an admin error. Who could blame her? The human brain found plenty of ways to justify the impossible.

Her heart clenched as she closed her fist around the syringe. Great. Now all she had to do was stab him in the neck.

"But no. Nope." As Devin closed his eyes and laughed without humor, his incisors extended, sharpened, forming into lethal-looking fangs.

Alex's every instinct screamed for her to *move, go, RUN*, but she didn't heed them.

As a vet tech, she regularly stuck her hands between the jaws of panicked, angry animals. Already she knew this was a thousand times more reckless. But it wasn't enough to take this experiment halfway.

Eyes, claws, jaws.

Devin seemed to be triggering a partial shift. If whatever was happening to him kept playing by the rules of *The Arcane Files* for whatever reason, he wouldn't be able to fully transform—to take the shape of an actual wolf—outside of the full moon, but they'd never know if they didn't test how far into the Change his body could progress. Because of the angle, the video on the pier hadn't shown his final form one way or another.

Devin bowed his head, his brow furrowed, and his mouth thinned, as if he were fighting a massive sudden-onset migraine.

"Here I am"—his voice dropped in pitch, taking his already gravelly tone into a growl—"an unemployed laughingstock stuck in the middle of Hicksville, USA, begging a complete stranger for help because I'm turning into some kind of half human, half dog."

As hurt bloomed like roses across his perfectly stubbled cheeks, Alex gave herself over to adrenaline. She shoved down the parts of herself that were soft, afraid.

This was her idea. Her responsibility. She'd told him they needed to do this, that it was the only way.

"Devin," she said tentatively once more, shivering because she no longer expected him to answer.

His eyelids sprang open. With a vicious snarl he dropped from his standing position into a crouch on all fours.

Alex gasped, stumbling backward a few steps.

As loath as she was to admit it, she was an expert in Devin Ashwood. The way he held himself, the way he moved. There was a time, as much as it physically pained her to recollect, when she'd literally spent hours cataloging all his different smiles. That was how she knew, *in her bones*, that the thing in front of her wasn't him.

The wolf—she didn't know what else to call it—raised his head, scenting the air. His startled gaze landed on her like gunmetal, white-hot and lethal, cutting down her form in wary assessment.

Alex forced herself to hold still. Not to flinch or make any sudden movements. She hadn't grown up Dr. Isaac Lawson's daughter without learning the safest way to respond when suddenly confronted with a wolf.

It was a total mindfuck how eerily similar Devin looked to how they'd made him up on the show. When they'd applied contacts, and prosthetics to his teeth and nails—just enough makeup to suggest "wolf" while still keeping his face and form mostly unchanged. Heaven forbid viewers forget for a moment that their hero was handsome.

Oh god. Now was *not* the time to start thinking about the 5K-comment thread on the archive discussing the prompt "be honest, would you fuck Colby in a partial shift?"

It didn't matter that he looked mostly human. Alex knew on a cellular level he wasn't. Not anymore.

The wolf held himself rigid as his eyes darted around the room. That type of limb locking, Alex knew from her father, meant the animal was afraid and ready to defend itself at any cost.

It was like she'd suspected when she first saw the video: he was scared.

He didn't seem any more comfortable with this transformation stuff than his human counterpart.

Devin had estimated that his previous shifts lasted for hours, but there was no way Alex was just gonna hang out, trapped here alone, waiting for nature to run its course.

She had the syringe in hand. But her plan had been poorly conceived, back when she'd still believed, deep down, that werewolves were fictional. She'd need to get close enough to administer the tranquilizer. Within maiming distance.

She forced herself to take a step forward, slowly.

The wolf growled, warning her back. He still seemed more wary than threatening, but instinctively, Alex lifted her hands like she was under arrest.

He immediately bared his teeth as if she'd challenged him.

Of course he doesn't recognize that type of surrender. Alex lowered her arms and dropped her gaze to the ground. She almost said *Easy there, good boy* in her best soothing vet-tech voice but stopped herself just in time.

The wolf's growling shifted, slowed.

Good. Alex needed him to think her submissive long enough to strike.

She reminded herself that Devin Ashwood had called her brave last night and, churlishly, she wanted to prove it.

That said, had the wire transfer even cleared yet? Who was going to make sure her dad went to his doctor's appointments if this all went south? He'd order Domino's for dinner every night, left to his own devices.

And what about Rowen? If Alex died, no one would be there to pick them up after band practice on Thursday. They'd call her cell, waiting in the rain, and it would just ring and ring.

Hopefully Cam and Eliza, at least, could eventually laugh at the irony of the circumstances of her death.

Against her will, Alex let out a whimper.

The noise seemed to give the wolf pause. He frowned at her, the gesture almost comically human against the monstrous blazing of his electric-silver eyes. Cautiously, he approached, prowling on all fours, sniffing the air. In some act of mercy from the universe, he seemed to like the way she smelled. His growl quieted, though it stayed in his throat, an engine idling, low, constant.

"Does that mean you wanna be friends?"

The wolf shifted back into a crouch to better study her, tilting his head as though intrigued by the sounds she was making.

Unsure she'd get another chance, Alex seized her opening and rushed to close the distance between them. She swung her arm in a descending arc that left no room for uncertainty as she plunged the needle into his neck.

The beast howled, the sound wounded this time, an accusation, his eyes flashing with betrayal.

To be fair, Alex knew the feeling.

"Sorry," she said inanely, as the cry died in his throat and his eyelids began to droop.

Devin's body listed to the side, the wolf throwing out a clawed hand to try to catch himself as he slumped to the ground.

Fully zonked, the beast began to snore with a force that moved his whole chest.

After much grunting effort, Alex managed to roll him over flat on his back. His breathing shifted in the new position, his mouth falling open so she could watch in real time as the fangs receded back into normal blunt incisors.

The shift definitely seemed tied to his emotional state. His claws went next, fading back into human fingernails with that metallic *snick* sound.

Alex leaned over and gently pushed up one of his eyelids to confirm his irises had gone back to their signature celery green.

With the immediate threat neutralized, she once again checked his vitals. His pulse was slightly elevated but remained steady, strong. Under her fingertips, his neck was warm, and sure enough, when she took his temp it was high—102. The wolf ran hot.

Up close she could make out the fine lines across his forehead and where they fanned out from his eyes. His skin was gorgeous, smooth, glowy—way better cared for than hers—but she could also see a very faint acne scar under his chin.

It was strange to find a spot on the topography of his face that she hadn't previously mapped. Alex had seen pictures of him from so many angles. Two decades' worth of gifs on her dashboard and in her DMs. When she was younger and more foolish, she'd pull them up to study, trying to diagnose the exact shade of his eyes, hunting for the perfect words to describe the dip of his upper lip. But she'd never seen him like this, lax in slumber. She noticed she was just resting her hand gently on his throat and shot, shakily, to her feet. Suddenly, this all felt strangely intimate.

Alex had been so sure werewolves were a myth. Fiction from the TV show she'd dedicated the greater part of her adolescence to archiving. Most fans would love the chance to slip into the world of their favorite story. To have the actor who played their beloved supernatural character adapt into him in front of their very eyes. But in practice, it felt more like a nightmare than her dream come true.

She pressed a hand to her racing heart, trying to ground herself with the facts.

Werewolves were real.

Devin Ashwood was turning into one.

Alex had agreed to help him.

"Shit." She forced herself to take a deep breath. This was fine. She could handle this. Stuff like this happened in fic all the time. She wiped her clammy palms down the front of her scrubs.

As much as she might want to pretend to be grown up, above it, her fangirl heart had always secretly hoped for something like this to happen. Who wouldn't want to be the one who was clever and brave enough to rescue the damsel in distress (in this case, Devin)?

Real life had been difficult at times, had called for sacrifice or courage, but taking care of her dad never once felt heroic. Maybe she deserved this, even if Devin didn't. One chance for adventure in her small, boring life. The opportunity to bring at least one man who'd once disparaged her to his knees.

All she needed was a plan.

Building the archive had seemed an overwhelming undertaking when Alex first had the idea, before she broke it down into small pieces.

Step one: watch the show obsessively.

Step two: take wildly detailed notes, explaining what she saw to herself.

Step three: ask her friends for help.

The same strategies might work here.

It was weird that Devin's werewolf stuff followed so closely to canon. Was it because it was him? Had he spent so many years playing Colby, falling so far into the role, that his body forgot where the character stopped and he began?

They had that in common, she realized; they both saw too much of themselves in Colby Southerland.

Even if she lost her nerve, Alex needed the money. For Dad's medical bills. For car repairs. For the roof that both of them had been pretending wasn't leaking all year. Like it or not, she was in this with Devin until they figured it out or he destroyed one or both of them. Whichever came first.

Alex jumped as her phone alarm went off. It was time to check on the (other) animals. Given the volume of horse tranquilizer Alex had given him, even with what appeared to be an evolved metabolic system, Devin would likely be out for a few hours. Alex promised both herself and his sleeping form that by the time he woke up she would have a plan for next steps.

The next time she called Devin Ashwood a monster, it would no longer be a metaphor.

The Trials, wiki article #227

The season 1 narrative arc revolves around Colby accepting
and adapting to life as a werewolf. His mentor, Bathalda, is part
of a centuries-old order called The Guild, a secret society
that exists to find and prepare The One to defend the world
against supernatural threat.

The Trials consist of three main tests, which Colby must
pass before The Guild will release him from captivity:
Endurance, Instinct, and Submission. Each test represents an
essential aspect of managing and wielding his wolf.

8

DEVIN WOKE UP groggy to orange dawn spilling in through the dusty windows of the vet's garage and someone singing Alanis Morissette off-key.

As he groaned and sat up slowly, a Florida State sweatshirt slid off his chest.

What the—? Without conscious thought, Devin brought the body-warm fabric to his nose. Oh. It was Alex's.

The same astringent he'd seen her holding earlier permeated the worn cotton and stung his nostrils, but underneath there was the familiar, soothing scent of detergent and something sweeter, more organic, that made him close his eyes and sigh. Devin took a deep inhale, trying to parse the mingling smells apart.

The only thing he could come up with to describe this new, nice scent was "fresh rain," which, cool, he was pretty sure that was the name of the fancy hand soap his housekeeper had once gotten for his second guest bathroom. So much for an evolved schnoz.

Alex seemed to have stuck what better not be a small rolled-up dog bed underneath him as a pillow. Leaning down, he sniffed that, too, but lucky for her, it just smelled plasticky and new.

Fuck his head hurt. He massaged his temples as another wave of tone-deaf wailing came from the corner. God, Alex was the worst singer he'd ever heard. And he'd once run into the Situation doing "I Will Survive" at karaoke on the Las Vegas strip.

For reasons he couldn't understand, waking up prone on Alex's murder tarp was less terrifying than the two times Devin had woken up after transforming at his own home. At least here, he wasn't alone. Devin made a half-hearted attempt to fold her sweatshirt, ignoring a funny warmth tucked somewhere behind his pecs.

He figured you just couldn't be that scared, scientifically, while held in the embrace of the finale refrain of "You Oughta Know."

Devin followed the sound of Alex's voice to the back corner and found her in a wheelie chair she must have dragged out here from the office, with her feet resting on a utility shelf. She had her laptop propped on her thighs, typing away while a huge honking set of headphones covered her ears. Every time the beat dropped, she tapped one foot against the metal, making the whole thing shake precariously.

Considering the lingering lethargy in his limbs, Devin would bet she'd had to use her horse drugs to take him down. A terrible sense of fear gripped him, and once again, he found himself instinctively following his nose for a diagnostic, trying to subtly sniff her for traces of injury. He heaved out a huge sigh of relief when he didn't get any traces of blood or battery polluting her scent. The idea of having hurt her made him so sick his vision wobbled.

Devin recognized that relying so heavily on his nose to

navigate the world wasn't normal, but somehow it felt natural. As if he'd always known how to isolate scents and use them for diagnosis and simply forgotten.

In *The Arcane Files*, the wolf lay dormant in everyone. It was the kind of power people tapped into during extraordinary moments: an athlete with a broken leg dragging himself over a finish line, a mother lifting a car off her baby—things headlines attributed to the grace of god. But only Colby experienced the Change that let him access those kinds of superior skills and inexhaustible resolve on the regular.

It was why he had to serve his fellow man, taking on the kind of supernatural foes that other agents couldn't. The skills and power the wolf granted were a gift, Colby's Guild handler told him, but only if he embraced them.

Honestly, Devin didn't give a shit about fighting crime or saving people, but he figured the better he understood what the fuck was happening to him, the greater chance he had of making sure no one else ever found out. So sure, he'd lean in like that Sheryl Sandberg lady said, even though he couldn't remember whether or not she'd gotten canceled.

Once, when Devin was ten and still pretty early in his tenure on the daytime soap, he got the flu during sweeps week. *Sands of Time* was recorded live, and his character, Griffin Antonoff, had a big scene where the man he thought was his father got shot in front of him. In hindsight, it was kind of a fucked-up simulation for a kid, but whatever, Devin hadn't considered that at the time.

His first agent, this guy named Clifford whom his dad had literally found in the yellow pages, said the scene was Devin's big chance to show range. He wanted him to burst into real tears during the live filming for the mid-season cliffhanger. Devin practiced making himself cry for a week in front of the dingy bathroom mirror in the walk-up his parents rented near the studio. He'd picture the worst stuff he could imagine over and over. His parents dying. His goldfish, Gilda, dying. This one commercial about starving children in Africa that came on whenever his parents fell asleep in front of the TV watching Nick at Nite.

Anyway, he got pretty good at calling forth waterworks and totally would have nailed the scene if he hadn't woken up on the day of filming with a fever and the shakes. It was the first time he remembered being really sick, the kind of hot where your brain feels like a fried egg someone accidentally left on the skillet to burn.

"I'm sorry," he told his mom when she came to wake him up to get dressed. He didn't know what they'd do, if they'd try to film without him or postpone the scene.

"What do you mean?" She went to the plastic dresser in the corner and started pulling out clean socks.

"I can't go in," Devin said. His voice even sounded painful, a muddy kind of croak. Was it possible she hadn't noticed?

His mother came over and pressed her cool hand to his forehead. "People don't care if you're falling apart. They care if you falling apart makes their lives harder."

You could be weak, Devin heard, as long as you didn't show it and inconvenience everyone else.

"A lot of kids wanna be on TV," his mother said, handing him the socks.

Devin got dressed and went to work.

Alex looked over and caught him standing there like a weirdo.

"Oh good. You're up," she said, apparently still not afraid of him despite whatever bad behavior he might have gotten into while his brain took a vacation.

She gave him a once-over, presumably because she felt guilty for having knocked him out cold.

"Are you hungry or nauseous? Those are the two outcomes I see most often when patients come off tranqs."

Devin almost laughed. By "patients" she meant pets.

He checked in with his stomach. The idea of a big, rare steak filled his mouth with saliva. He pictured sinking his teeth in, juice bursting in his mouth. Devin licked his chops, and okay, that was probably the wolf kicking in again. He needed to get a better handle on recognizing the impulses. Right now they were overwhelming, so vivid and powerful he mistook them for his own.

Separating what the wolf wanted from what he wanted was an intimidating prospect. Devin had trained himself almost his entire life to repress his desires. He'd lost track of the number of times he'd been sore and hungry and alone—*relentlessly focused*—in pursuit of his career.

"You don't have any meat here, do you?"

"Meat? Probably not." Alex got to her feet and gestured for him to follow her back inside the vet's office. "I'm vegan," she explained, leading him into what looked like a break room.

She opened the white refrigerator and peered inside. "Can I interest you in a coconut milk yogurt?"

Before he could help himself, Devin screwed up his face.

"I will take that as a no." Alex shut the fridge and climbed, surprisingly limberly, up onto the countertop to check a top shelf. "There might be some old beef jerky up here."

In addition to Alex's ass (which Devin was *not* looking at because he was a gentleman and also she was strange), the break room countertop supported a toaster oven, an ancient Mr. Coffee with a stack of foam cups, and the kind of honest-to-god watercooler Devin had never actually seen in real life. A schedule with different upcoming surgeries and shifts was listed on the whiteboard taped to the wall.

After a few awkward seconds of watching her balance on her knees, Devin decided he should go spot her. Just in case. He hovered behind her, not fully understanding this new protective impulse and scared that she'd ask him what the hell he thought he was doing if she turned around and found him directly beneath her.

"You gonna pull out a bully stick?"

Alex didn't bother to turn around. "You'd probably like it."

Devin huffed out a laugh. What the hell was with this woman?

And why was it working for him? His gaze kept sliding back to the curve of her ass, which, to be fair, she'd placed precisely at eye level. He kinda wanted to bite it . . .

Must be the wolf again. As Colby, Devin always played his wolf impulses like call-of-the-void stuff. He forgot where he'd first learned about that concept. Probably one of the makeup artists had a psych podcast on in her trailer or something. But apparently part of the age-old human survival instinct meant that when you stood at the top of a cliff and looked down, a tiny part of you thought about jumping. And while most people thought imagining such a thing, even for a second, meant there was something wrong with them, it was actually your brain's way of protecting itself. That shiver of revulsion at the suggestion taught your body *that would hurt* and so you cataloged the situation and ones like it as dangerous—do not enter.

The urge to make sure Alex Lawson was safe, as well as the one to caress her butt, felt exactly like that: strange, *other*, even though Devin knew he didn't have to follow through with them.

Maybe werewolves were abnormally horny? *It would certainly explain some of the fanfic.*

Devin made a mental note to do some follow-up research.

"Aha!" She leaned back from the cabinet holding an industrial-sized bag of cashews for his approval. "Okay, so it's not beef jerky, but it's got protein. You gym guys are obsessed with protein, right?"

"What's a gym guy?" He held up a hand, offering to help her down.

Alex stared at it, blinking.

"I just meant you have . . . you know." She raised her chin slightly toward the sleeve of his T-shirt.

". . . arms?"

"Muscles," she mumbled, placing her little tattooed hand in his.

Her palm was sweaty.

Devin grinned. He knew she wasn't *that* opposed to making out with him.

They both took seats at the little round table, sharing the bag of cashews between them.

"How long you been vegan?" Thanks to extensive dating experience in LA, Devin knew that question and the corresponding lecture were a guaranteed boner killer.

Alex closed one eye as she considered. "Little over a decade."

"Yeah?" Devin feigned interest while tossing back a handful of nuts. "You catch *Babe: Pig in the City* on Netflix or something?"

Alex looked very much like she wanted to knock the two legs of his chair that remained on the floor out from under him. "My dad got sick."

"Oh." Devin lowered his chair sheepishly back to the ground. "Mad cow?"

"What? No." She plucked out a cashew and threw it at him. Devin caught the nut in his mouth.

Alex traced the grain of the wood table with her finger. "He had a heart attack."

Oh fuck. Devin stopped chewing.

"Is he . . . okay now?" The answer better be yes or he was definitely gonna have to let her kick him in the balls for being insensitive.

"Yeah." Alex took her time selecting the perfect cashew. "They put in a few stents, and he's on medication and stuff."

"But you worry about him." It wasn't a question.

"Pretty much all the time," she agreed. "The doctor suggested the change in diet, and my dad made the switch but not quietly." Her eyes brightened with clear fondness for her father. "I thought he'd feel better if he wasn't the only one trying to swap out bacon for seitan. And it was something I could do."

"Ah." He found himself studying her in that moment, the way he might a choreographer outlining footwork. Devin often observed normal families when he had the chance, trying to collect pieces of what it meant to be loved so that he could better play a son in future roles. "Hence the cashews."

That made Alex smile a little, the sweetest little tilt of her taciturn mouth.

"Hence the cashews," she repeated.

"That makes sense." This was the closest Devin had ever come to agreeing with a vegan.

After a while, Alex got up and poured them big cups of water without asking Devin if he wanted any, which was a little pushy but also nice.

Devin decided to let her off the hook.

"You can just say it. You don't have to figure out the right way to break the news. The drugs are out of my system and I'm fed and watered."

Alex nodded. Devin got the feeling she was a woman who enjoyed directness.

"So," she said, holding his gaze and everything, "you're definitely a werewolf."

At this point Devin had gotten a little better at the whole tuning-in-to-her-heartbeat thing. He didn't even have to close his eyes. He just extended his breath and focused on tuning the radio the way she'd once instructed him, imagining the dial turning down ambient noises one by one.

The hum of the AC.

The chorus of soft snores from the animals in the other room.

The faint electric buzz of the overhead lights.

Until he found the beat of her heart, strong and steady. It was probably intrusive and weird, and Devin made a little vow to himself that he wouldn't do this all the time just because he could, but he found the particular metronome of her pulse soothing. How come they didn't put human heartbeats on white noise machines? Wait a second, should he go on *Shark Tank*?

Anyway, didn't the fact that he could hear her heartbeat from across the table already prove she was telling the truth?

At the grim confirmation, Devin expected to lose his cool. But all he found was a strange calm. A gratitude. At least someone was saying it out loud. Devin wasn't having a mental breakdown. He wasn't making things up for attention. Something impossible was really happening to him.

He drank a long sip of the water and found he was glad for that too.

"You're taking this surprisingly well," Alex said when he'd drained the cup.

Devin blew out a long breath. "I have been so shit-your-pants scared for the entirety of the last week, I think my system's fried. It's like, you know when you're on a real ugly crying jag but then all of a sudden you just stop. You hit a wall. And you're empty and exhausted and dehydrated as fuck but there's relief in being wrung out."

Alex gave him a look.

"What? You never watched *Titanic*? When that old couple gets in their bed at the end and they're just holding each other as the water rises?" Devin made a dismissive noise. "Grow up."

She folded her lips together like she wanted to say something but wouldn't let herself.

"I'm not saying I'm not scared," he clarified. "But being scared won't save me, will it? I'm a fucking actor. I can compartmentalize." He zipped closed the top of the discarded cashew bag for safekeeping. "So . . . what do we do now?" Alex was the brains of this operation, after all.

She went and grabbed her laptop from the garage and then set it up between them.

"Okay, so while you were sleeping—"

"Does being passed out from ketamine count as sleeping?"

"—I used Python to scrape the metadata of all the *Arcane Files* footage uploaded to YouTube."

On the screen some kind of software ran code he didn't understand.

"Whoa, what the hell? You're like Hugh Jackman in that hacker movie where Halle Berry gets her tits out."

She laughed, low and raspy like her voice.

"Thanks. I think? Anyway, remember how in the whole first season, Colby went through the Trials? He had his Guild handler guiding him through everything, right? Monitoring him as he made progress, watching his back."

"Yeah. Suzannah Jackson played Bathalda." Devin's heart

twisted painfully. He'd read that she'd passed away from complications of COVID. "She tried to teach me how to knit once when the power went down on set."

"Well, what if I did that?"

"Taught me to knit?"

"Made you some sort of werewolf trials. We've got three weeks until the next full moon. Here, look." She pulled a piece of paper out of her pocket and spread it out on the table. "It's a moon map."

"Did you draw this?"

"Yeah." She went pink around the ears. "It's not a big deal. I just wanted to be able to show you that we're at the last quarter moon right now, about fifty percent illumination." She moved her pen along the chart, tracking the days as the moon's illumination grew progressively dimmer. "You should have an easier time controlling the instincts and abilities for the next seven days, but after the new moon, things will ramp up relatively quickly."

"So, assuming this thing works the way we think it will, the cycle is gonna repeat every twenty-nine days," Devin counted. "No rest for the wicked, huh?"

"Now you know how people who menstruate feel."

Whoa. Devin never really thought about periods before, but dang, what a scam.

He considered Alex's offer. He'd trained for roles before. Combat training. Accent training, god help him, for when Colby went undercover. It had all sucked in different ways, but at the same time he found the exercise grounding, rewarding, progress broken down into bite-sized pieces when what people wanted for him to do—to be—seemed impossible.

"You don't think there's any chance we can reverse it? Make me human again?"

"Not according to *The Arcane Files*," Alex said, showing him another tab on her computer. "As I'm sure you remember, that was a major plot point in seasons one and two. Colby tried to reject the Change, but in the end he found the best he could do was control it."

"Fuck." This wasn't a short-term setback. Like the time he'd broken his leg skiing or that one year he'd tried Botox at the urging of his facialist.

"I could keep looking," Alex offered, "research werewolf lore outside of *The Arcane Files*. See if anything seems possible." She sounded doubtful about the effectiveness of alternative routes, and Devin got it. There had to be a reason his transformations followed the textbook of the series bible.

"But in the meantime, I've got three weeks to figure out how to shift without blacking out before the next full moon." Last time he'd gotten relatively lucky, finding his way back home with minimal bodily harm. There was no guarantee that next month, or the one after that, he wouldn't run into an innocent bystander. Or a mountain lion.

"I think finding a way to keep your wits about you is your safest bet," Alex confirmed. "You'll still be operating 'heavy machinery,' but at least you won't be under the influence."

Devin smirked. "Nice metaphor."

Mirroring *The Arcane Files* could work. At least they had a lot of reference material. At the very least Devin would go into the full moon with some mental and hopefully physical preparation. Besides, he had no fucking clue what he'd do otherwise.

If Colby could handle being a werewolf, Devin could too.

"All right. I'm in. You think of how to adapt the trials, and I'll do 'em."

He hoped Alex had the stomach to watch him suffer.

ALEX: okay I know we've moved on from the fandom, but do you guys ever randomly get headcanons for the Arcane Files?

ELIZA: alexandra kiley lawson, if you came here to tell us that after all these years you're finally gonna write Arcane Files fic I stg I will have no choice but to feed you to Frank the Goat

CAM: omg not frank!! RIP livejournal

CAM: but for real I toiled in the salt mines!! AO3 didn't even EXIST when I started writing Colby/Nathaniel. and now miss "i prefer to beta" is about to hit us with an idea for a 150K Soulmate AU

ELIZA: to be fair, Law betaed with an iron fist. She would always be like "actually Colby didn't have that scar until season 4"

ELIZA: you had the most canon-compliant fics on the internet 🙂

ALEX: if yall are DONE. Can I share my headcanon now?

ELIZA: you may.

CAM: we are benevolent.

CAM: but im not gonna write it for you

ELIZA: unless its like disgustingly horny

CAM: like go to jail levels

ALEX: 🙄

ALEX: no one has to write anything. I've just been thinking, ever since devin ashwood started acting up on the news, what if you could turn a werewolf back into a human?

ELIZA: . . . but you can't. Colby tried a bunch and failed, right?

CAM: oooh yes remember he went looking for a vampire to bite him and nathaniel was like "you haven't yet earned the privilege"

ELIZA: I know porn when I see it, yes

ALEX: okay but forget canon for a second

CAM: Law. That is one of those sentences were its like "you'll know I've been kidnapped when . . ."

ELIZA: say something hyper-specific so we know its you

ALEX: . . .

ALEX: Fine. my first sex dream was about Scar

CAM: LMAOOOO

ELIZA: I love that about you

ALEX: can we focus pls?

CAM: I mean, if you're done trying to become the dark queen of the pride lands

ELIZA: joking aside, why would you want to turn colby back into a human?

CAM: yeah are you trying to make him less fuckable? Is that the headcanon?

ALEX: assume its too scary and isolating. That colby's desperately clung to the idea that he's normal for his entire life despite mountains of evidence to the contrary

ELIZA: sounds more like Devin Ashwood than Colby

ELIZA: but fine, we'll bite. What if he has access to some kind of ancient amulet?

CAM: we need a call for this

ALEX: im wearing my pimple patches dont make fun of me.

INCOMING CALL FROM INDOOR GIRLIES

An incomplete list of all the ways it might be possible to turn a werewolf back into a human as brainstormed by Alex Lawson's fandom group chat using various pop culture and folklore methodologies:

- **Ancient Relic:** Discovering an ancient talisman that contains the essence of the first wolf, which can "reset" any lycanthropes who touch it.

- **Quantum Spell:** A wizard invents a spell based on quantum mechanics that can isolate the "lycanthropic" particles and neutralize them.

- **Virtual Reality:** A tech-savvy character designs a VR simulation that tricks the werewolf's brain into believing it's human again.

- **Celestial Alignment:** Wait for another super blue blood moon eclipse . . . in 150 years.

- **Alchemy:** Combine elements like gold, mercury, and rare herbs under a lunar eclipse to create an elixir that undoes the transformation.

- **Chronomancy:** Manipulate time to before the individual was cursed, allowing them a second chance to avoid it.

- **Symbiosis:** The human and werewolf aspects of the person reach an agreement or balance, allowing for willful transformation or even reversion to form.

- **Wolfsbane:** An herb often cited in folklore as a cure for lycanthropy.

- **Silver:** Silver bullets or silver blades are often depicted as the only way to kill a werewolf, thereby "curing" the condition.

- **Exorcism:** A religious ceremony intended to cast out the evil spirit causing the transformation.

- **Spells and Charms:** Magic words or rituals are sometimes said to reverse the affliction.

- **Love's Redemption:** In some stories, true love's sacrifice can lift the curse. *Note: sounds fake.*

- **Have a vampire bite them.**

9

IN DEVIN'S DEFENSE, he never meant to show up to Alex's house uninvited.

Last night—technically early this morning—after they'd agreed she would become his werewolf Obi-Wan Kenobi, he went back to his hotel, ordered four cheeseburgers from room service, and passed out on top of his scratchy duvet.

When he woke up the next day at two p.m., he had a bunch of texts from Alex, including a list of possible methods for turning a werewolf back into a human. Jesus, had she slept at all?

DEVIN: Lotta these involve magic or other supernatural creatures.

ALEX: Werewolves don't usually spontaneously appear in isolation

DEVIN: you saying I'm special?

ALEX: That's one word for it

ALEX: I still think using a version of The Trials in an effort to achieve symbiosis is our best bet

DEVIN: We're ruling exorcism out?

ALEX: I'm Jewish

DEVIN: 👍

DEVIN: Why is wolfsbane crossed out? Isn't that a real plant?

ALEX: It is. A subgenus of plants actually

ALEX: It's also a lethal poison

DEVIN: Oh.

DEVIN: Bummer.

DEVIN: What about true love? You think I should redownload Raya?

DEVIN: Taking your silence as encouragement.

DEVIN: Are gym selfies douchey? Be honest.

ALEX: Today is my day off.

Damn. That period was loud. Which, okay, fine. Devin under-stood boundaries. He could occupy himself for twenty-four hours. No problem. He had one of those sudoku puzzle book-lets that he'd impulse bought at the airport in his backpack. And the TV in his "executive suite" probably had pay-per-view porn. Unless hotels got rid of that stuff when they stopped paying for cable.

Alex had AirDropped the video footage from the garage onto his phone before he left yesterday, so he watched that a bunch of times. Even though he'd been trying to play it cool in front of her in the break room, in the harsh light of midafter-noon he was still pretty fucking alarmed.

The press tore him a new one when they thought he was faking being a werewolf. What would they do if they found out he was actually biologically some kind of supernatural creature? Well, they wouldn't believe him, obviously. It was ridiculous. Outrageous. Impossible.

Even Alex, who was primed to buy into this shit after spend-ing more than a decade in the fandom, hadn't believed him until she saw his fangs with her own eyes.

Devin still struggled to accept the truth, and he was fucking living it. All his life, he'd been told to make himself the perfect canvas for a character. To file down his sharp edges and kill the parts of himself that weren't palatable. His dad once threw out a pair of hot pink sneakers Devin had bought because they weren't "masculine" enough.

Flopped on his stomach on the bed, Devin swiped through Raya, but the closest matches were in Miami. Damn. This wolf shit certainly wasn't gonna make dating any easier.

Last Tuesday he'd been a middle-aged out-of-work actor. Now he was a middle-aged out-of-work actor with claws. He was like Lou and all the other racehorses that got abandoned at

Alex's vet—worthless without the next job. His parents and all those on-set handlers raised him to be looked at and hobbled him for everything else.

Devin's breathing grew painful, ragged, his vision starting to swim.

Shit. He could not afford to break down. Not again.

Being a werewolf was probably like doing mushrooms. If you let yourself lose it, you were definitely gonna have a bad time. Devin needed to focus on the plan, on taking action. He would do the trials and get a handle on himself. He'd book the next job. No matter how long it took, he always booked the next job.

No one would ever find out he was anything less than exactly what they wanted him to be. At the very least, outside of trying to sniff Alex, his wolf didn't seem particularly violent, thank god. Devin really didn't wanna hunger for human flesh. Though speaking of hunger . . .

He ordered room service again. Man, that menu was getting old fast. He might have to get wild and buy a hot plate off Amazon.

After eating, Devin stood and rolled his muscles. He felt less sore today than he had after the previous transformations, which seemed like progress. Maybe he should try going to the gym off the lobby. Actually, hold on a second. Devin didn't need to wait for Alex to start investigating his— God, the word "powers" sounded outrageous even in his own brain. The full moon was coming in twenty days whether he was ready or not. He might as well take advantage of every minute and try to hone his senses solo. (Also, he'd checked and the porn selection here was beneath him.)

He drove the truck out to Ocala Forest. Tapping into his inner animal in nature seemed like a better idea than trying to coax his wolf out in the back of the hotel's neighboring strip mall.

After hiking for about an hour, Devin managed to find a secluded clearing.

Okay. He pumped his arms back and forth. *You can do this. Become one with the beast.*

It was foolish to only be able to access his wolf senses unconsciously or when provoked. If Devin honed his awareness, figured out how to tap into these skills on demand, he would be less vulnerable to letting them overwhelm him.

Since he'd mastered his sense of hearing at least once, learning to listen to Alex's heartbeat, Devin decided to start there. He closed his eyes and let the sounds of the forest rush in, rather than using half his concentration to keep them out. It was getting a little easier to tune, as if his brain were building muscle memory for the skill. Devin started close.

A birdcall overhead, high and sharp, insistent.

To his left, a squirrel scurrying up a tree.

Downwind, the roar of a river rushing.

Devin tried to extend his sense, reaching, testing how far he could go.

A child's squeal of excitement.

The crunch of leaves under a hiker's boots.

The spray of an aerosol can.

Devin inhaled deeply. *Sunscreen.*

Now that his nose was in the game, he moved his focus there, raising his head to catch scents mingling on the breeze, employing the kind of deep breaths he'd learned from watching Yoga with Adriene during the pandemic.

My breath is my anchor. He mentally recited Adriene's mantra from one of the episodes. (Yes, he felt silly. His whole life had recently become silly as shit.) His nostrils flared as he took in a gulp of swampy Florida air.

My anchor is my breath.

Damp soil.

Composting leaves.

Sticky, sweet tree sap.

Dry and peeling bark.

Dew-dusted grass.

Salty human sweat.

The plasticky chemicals of synthetic workout wear.

Feathers.

Fur.

Devin opened his eyes and zeroed in on a white-tailed deer leaping across a fallen log miles in the distance.

The urge to run, to chase, swept through him. Devin followed his feet, cutting through undergrowth, picking up speed.

His heartbeat spiked, but not from exertion.

He was fucking *fast.* Lengthening his stride, he pushed himself, pumping his arms and legs harder, leaning forward, chin and chest into the run. Trees and shrubs blurred in his periphery, becoming smudges of green and brown and white.

His Apple Watch beeped—asking if he was driving.

Devin grinned into the wind, cataloging new scents.

A sweet-smelling flower.

Car exhaust from the highway.

But then, on a random inhale, he caught a new scent.

DarkBitterDelicate.

There was something almost familiar about the mingled notes, but Devin was too far away. The scent hung elusive in the air, just out of reach.

Devin skidded in the damp soil, kicking up dirt as he

switched directions, following the demands of his wolf to *Track-SeekFind*.

When Devin tried to pull the scent apart, he got memories.

Tipping his head back to stare at the ink-spill sky over the Grand Canyon.

His first sip of hot chocolate on the streets of Mexico City.

Climbing naked into bed after buying himself disgustingly decadent sheets.

He chased the trail to a house, dark red siding with white shutters and a blue door, tucked into the edge of the forest. On the porch sat two wooden rocking chairs.

He slowed to a stroll as he approached. After an extended sprint like that at his age, Devin should be winded, bent over, red-faced, huffing and puffing. But he hadn't even broken a sweat. Hey, if they did reboot *The Arcane Files*—no, *when*—he should totally offer to do his own stunts, like Tom Cruise.

There was no driveway to speak of at the house, but someone had inlaid big, flat stones into a little winding footpath. That same someone, he suspected, who had hand carved the mailbox to look like a mallard. Even at forty-two, Devin heard the siren song of the thing, beckoning vandalism. Evidently others agreed, because the beak was already chipped.

After thirty-odd years of living in LA, Devin couldn't believe how easily he could walk right up to the front door, no security, no gate. The scent he'd tracked wafted from a window above the garage, tantalizingly out of reach. He was hungry again. Starving, actually. For food and sex and adrenaline. To possess and protect. With the opposing urges to bare his teeth and show his belly.

Devin tilted his head and narrowed his gaze, trying to see through fluttery white curtains.

"Can I help you?" a tense voice asked, low and wary.

He'd been so focused on the trail, he hadn't noticed the man with slate hair perched on a ladder by the side of the house, his arms full of wet leaves as he cleared out the gutters.

Devin shifted his attention to the sweet smell of decay (the leaves) and Old Spice and exhaustion (the man).

Wait—*could Devin smell feelings now?* That was pretty sick, but he didn't have time to dive into it because the old guy was looking at him like he might call a forest ranger at any moment.

Shit. What could he say? *Hello, sir, sorry you found me loitering on your property but something above your garage smells really good and I'm pretty sure I want to eat and/or fuck it?*

This was why other people wrote his lines.

"Uhhh," Devin said. *Great start. Extremely eloquent.*

But then the guy saved him by squinting. "Wait a second. Aren't you that kid from that TV show?"

Kid? Really? This guy had maybe twenty-five years on Devin. But, Devin noticed now, he stood favoring one leg, listing a bit on the ladder. That plus the weariness coming off him in waves . . . Maybe he was older. His heartbeat was elevated, and there was something almost mechanical about his pulse.

"I'm Devin Ashwood. You might know me from a show called *The Arcane Files?*"

Recognition flickered and then settled in the older man's eyes.

"My daughter used to watch." While his pulse steadied, he was still frowning. "Is that why you're on my lawn? Did she win some kind of contest?"

Devin considered lying for a split second. That cover story seemed easier, less embarrassing. But something about the man's dark, clear-eyed gaze made him hesitate.

"No. I was just out for a run when I came across your house. It's very—" *Small. Old.* "—quaint."

The man rolled his eyes. "Yeah, thanks."

Apparently Devin was dismissed because the guy went back to work, getting down to move his ladder over to the next patch of gutter, wincing a little as he started climbing back up.

Devin wasn't normally a busybody. But this dude looked a little rough, climbing up and down over and over. And Devin didn't have anything better to do. He could spare an hour. His gaze fell back on the window over the garage, and once again the trail was in his nose: the best thing he'd ever inhaled. Maybe this old guy sold drugs.

"Do you, uh, need any help?" Devin called.

The man halted halfway up the ladder. "You wanna clean my gutters?"

It was a fair question. Luckily, Devin had studied improv as part of his lifelong commitment to acting, so he was able to turn around a smooth reply.

"Yes. I'm training for a top secret project and I could use the exercise."

"Uh-huh," the guy said, clearly unconvinced, but after a long moment of assessment, he sighed, then shrugged. "Some famous actor wants to clean my gutters, I'm not gonna stop 'em."

The guy's name was Isaac, Devin learned, as the man set to work clearing an herb garden bed in the front lawn of weeds while Devin took over the gutters. The kind of small talk Devin learned while still in braces revealed that Isaac was some kind of biologist working in wolf conservation. How convenient was that? Devin welcomed any and all resources that could prolong his survival.

"So," he said, real casual, as the sun dipped lower in the sky, "how does one conserve a wolf?"

Isaac's laugh carried from the garden bed below. "Well, red wolves are particularly tricky because they're so close to extinction. We started out introducing a mated pair to the forest in an area designated for their habitat."

"Not a lone wolf?" Devin scooped up an armful of leaves, determined to ignore the many types of bugs his nose was urging him to categorize. "Doesn't every pack need an alpha?"

"No," Isaac said, picking up a pair of shears and starting in on his shrubs. "That concept was introduced based on the behavioral patterns of wolves in captivity. Wolves in the wild are totally different animals."

"Yeah, tell me about it," Devin muttered under his breath. He'd unintentionally sprung from his cage and had never been more vulnerable.

"A mated pair leads the pack together."

"Mated? You mean like they're soulmates?" Devin had secretly watched *The Notebook* seven times.

"Something like that," Isaac allowed. "After our first pair got acclimated, we were able to slowly bring in pups born in captivity for them to foster. Now, after almost thirty years, we've worked our way up to a small population of twenty-five wolves."

Isaac's work gave him purpose. Devin knew because he spoke about it with the same determined passion that Devin recognized in himself when he spoke about *TAF*.

Why did everyone think he was such a loser for wanting to keep Colby alive? Isaac was living proof that it was fine, arguably noble, to build your life around one project, to plant seeds and spend a lifetime tending them. What was so bad about fighting to preserve the place where you belonged?

"The hardest part of my job these days is protecting the pack from humans," Isaac said grimly.

Devin stilled, his blood running cold. "People shoot 'em?"

The older man nodded. "Or they set traps, leave out poisoned food."

"That's fucked up." Devin dumped his next armful onto the tarp laid below with extra vigor.

"It is." Isaac let out a gruff sigh. "People don't like the idea of predators. They work themselves up out of fear. There was an incident over a decade ago where a couple of the wolves went beyond the borders of their habitat and took down some livestock. Now everyone's afraid they'll come after the horses. In case you haven't noticed, people around here are big into horses."

"You responsible for defending the pack all by yourself?" Devin wasn't trying to be a dick, but earlier the man looked about an inch from being bested by his gutters.

"I report in to the Florida Fish and Wildlife Conservation Commission," Isaac said with pride. "But yeah, I'm the only designated researcher responsible for this pack."

A newfound kinship with these wolves he'd never met seized Devin. For all he knew, someone would try hunting him one day. Maybe it was because he didn't really have a family that the idea of this pack losing an elder or a cub made him have to blink really hard. It just seemed evil, that a wolf fucked up one time, and now no one wanted them around anymore.

Before he knew it, he was opening his mouth, saying, "You take volunteers?"

Isaac paused his pruning. "You offering?"

Devin got that it must seem odd. First he insisted on doing the man's chores; now he wanted to follow him around at work. "I'm in the area for the next couple of weeks, and I've got a lot of free time during the day."

Isaac peered at him for a long moment. Jade would have said he was trying to get the measure of him. Devin's belly swooped. He'd rather not be found wanting.

"All right," Isaac said finally. "I'll give you my card and you can stop by. I'm sure I can find something for you to do."

Devin waited until he was facing the gutters again to grin.

Wait until he told Alex that he'd found such an awesome resource of wolf knowledge all on his own. She'd probably be proud of him.

To Devin's surprise, he enjoyed a bit of manual labor. Being outside, getting dirty. It was soothing to have a task that occupied his hands while asking nothing of his mind.

By the time they finished bagging and tagging everything, the sun had set, and Isaac insisted Devin come in for a beer.

Devin wasn't positive, but he had a feeling he might have made his first friend outside of the industry. At the very least, he and Isaac had potential.

Inside, the house was even smaller than it appeared from the yard. The Good Scent Devin had been tracking grew stronger as Isaac led him through a tidy living room with a decent TV and two big, slightly sagging plaid couches faded from sunlight.

Devin forced himself to breathe normally, not to pick up any of the throw pillows or that handmade quilt and bury his face in them. Everything here, from the wooden table spotted with water rings to the slightly fraying flat-weave rug, gave off the same wildly attractive scent along with the impression of being both loved and lived in.

Someone had painted the walls of the living room a cheerful yellow that reminded Devin of butter slathered on toast. Or maybe he was just hungry. All the walls he'd grown up with were taupe or gray, the kind found in motel rooms and crumbling short-term-rental condominiums. Now he lived in a mansion. A big white square that someone else had decorated.

Devin didn't know when he'd turned into such a sad sack. Maybe it was the whole creature-of-the-night thing. You didn't see a lot of happy werewolves.

Isaac put on the Dolphins game and handed Devin a Bud Light. "I gotta get dinner started, but make yourself at home."

Devin decided it wouldn't hurt to kick back and watch for a little while, listening to Isaac puttering around in the kitchen, telling Alexa to play the B-52s. Sinking into the couch kicked up a new wave of the Good Scent. Devin hugged a pillow to his chest and took a long swallow of beer.

The Dolphins were down by twelve and Devin had become one with the sofa when, out of nowhere, Alex Lawson walked through the front door wearing an oversized flannel and cupcake-patterned pajama pants.

"Devin?" Her eyes turned to saucers. "Oh my god." Her hands flew to her damp hair. "Why are you in my house?"

"This is your house?" Devin flopped around like a beached salmon, trying to escape the couch's clutches and get to his feet.

"My dad's," she said, a little sheepishly. "I live above the garage. Hello." She gestured aggressively at a wall behind him where—Devin turned—school photos of her from what looked like kindergarten to high school followed the ascension of the stairs, a study in disaffected youth.

Oh. No wonder Isaac smelled vaguely familiar.

"Wait." The puzzle pieces slotted together. "Isaac is your dad?"

"You talked to him?!" Alex sounded less shocked and more pissed by the minute. "Listen." She crossed her arms. "I agreed to help you out, but we need to have a hard conversation about boundaries right now."

"Okay, wait a second." Devin held up his hands. "I did not come here to stalk you. I was in the forest, trying to become one with my wolf—"

"Shhhh." Alex nodded meaningfully toward the kitchen, where Isaac was singing off-key. "We can't talk about this here."

She grabbed Devin's wrist and dragged him into a neighboring coat closet.

It wasn't until she had him trapped in a three-by-three room with the door shut and one dim light bulb overhead that he realized—

"Oh fuck. You don't smell bad at all." Mindlessly, he stepped forward, leaving barely an inch between their bodies as he inhaled the Good Scent straight from the source. Holy shit. It was Alex.

It wasn't conscious, the decision to step toward her until her back hit the wall, making a series of rain slickers quiver. He didn't mean to lean down, bracing one hand on the shelf just above her so he could brush his nose against the crown of her head and inhale her shower-damp hair.

Devin couldn't help the way her gasp at his sudden proximity (or what he belatedly realized was kind of an insult) made him shudder and grit his teeth. He'd done a lot of drugs in his life, and nothing held a candle to huffing Alex Lawson straight from the source.

Devin almost whimpered with the primal urge to shove his face into her neck and sniff her like a glue stick. Whatever chemicals she used at work must have covered up her natural scent the previous times they'd been around each other.

"You should quit your job," he said, closing his eyes and ignoring other, more feral instincts. "Become, like, an air freshener model."

"That's not a thing," Alex said, but her breath against his chest was uneven. Her heartbeat hectic in his ears.

When Devin opened his eyes, she was looking up at him. No—*she was looking at his mouth.*

Like a bolt of lightning down his spine, it occurred to Devin that he could probably kiss her. That she might let him. And fuck, he wanted so badly to know if she tasted as good as she smelled.

Normally fans having a crush on him was flattering but awkward. In a lot of ways, "object of desire" felt like just another part he'd been cast in, only no one told him his lines. Devin had to improvise the role of daydream made flesh and hope that he didn't miss his mark.

Alex's cheeks flushed from anger or embarrassment or something else. Devin tried to identify the difference in her scent, but he couldn't. The air in the closet was drenched in hunger. His definitely, but hers too. Except the notes of Alex's desire were a lot more complicated than his, as if she didn't want to want him.

Which, okay, yeah. He got it. People wanted Fun and Flirty Devin Ashwood. Not Devin Ashwood Faces Public Humiliation or Devin Ashwood with a Terrible Secret. Scared Shitless Devin Ashwood. Devin Ashwood Turning into a Glorified Dog.

"Sorry." He pulled back, even though he was pretty sure if he looked down he'd be able to see her nipples through her shirt. "Lost my head there for a second."

Kissing her was a bad idea, even if she'd changed her mind about making out with him for science. Devin shit where he ate once, metaphorically speaking, with his ex-wife, Erica. At first it was great. Convenient. Spending all your time with your favorite person. But then when the TW didn't pick up her contract for the next season, she started resenting every time Devin went to work. Mixing business and pleasure wasn't a mistake he was eager to repeat.

Devin couldn't afford to alienate Alex. Even if he could find someone else to train him for the upcoming full moon, what were the chances they'd be this smart or this stubborn? Devin was relying on Alex's abundance of both of those traits to keep his ass out of animal protective services. Or jail. Whichever came first.

He needed to get out of this closet. Swallowing her scent on every inhale wasn't fucking enough.

"What kind of conditioner do you use?" If it was nontoxic, he could buy some and use it as lube.

The non sequitur made her frown.

"It's homemade." She gathered her hair over one shoulder. "Unscented. I have sensitive skin."

Yeah, he bet. She was pale as moonlight and pinked up in seconds. Devin bet that pretty blush went all the way down her chest. Bet it matched her— *Okay, no. Rein it in.*

"There's a chance I may have accidentally tracked you," he confessed. Talk about a professional conflict of interest.

Alex shook her head. "What?"

"I feel like there's no normal way to explain this." Devin backed up as much as the coat closet would allow, almost disappearing behind a weather-resistant parka, and dragged his hand through his hair. He shouldn't tell her that her pheromones or whatever made him horny, right? Women didn't like that.

"Nothing about you is normal," Alex said, still looking dazed.

"Devin?" Isaac called from the kitchen. "You're not gluten-free or anything, are you?"

When Devin didn't answer right away, he heard footsteps.

"Oh god, my dad cannot find us alone in here," Alex whispered furiously. She pushed Devin toward the door with two hands and then proceeded to box him out in her own rush to get to the hall.

They both managed to exit before Isaac rounded the corner wearing a green canvas apron.

"I was just showing Devin here where to leave his shoes,"

Alex blurted out, even though no one had asked and Devin was in fact still wearing his shoes.

It didn't seem to matter. Isaac brightened at the sight of his daughter like the sun breaking above the horizon.

"Oh hey, Al. I was wondering when you'd be over." He waved dramatically at Devin as if Alex could have missed him standing right beside her. "Did you know your favorite actor was in town?"

Alex smiled bright and brittle. "He's not my favorite actor."

"Are you kidding?" Isaac looked between them. "You had such a huge crush on him when you were—"

"You're thinking of someone else." Alex tried to shake her head without actually moving her neck.

"What? No, I'm not. I was gonna ask him to take a picture to send to Cam and Eliza. Don't you think they'd go wild— Oh." Isaac seemed to finally clue in to his daughter's discomfort and held up his hands in defeat. "All right. Whatever. Chili's almost ready." He pivoted. "Devin, you're welcome to stay for dinner if you'd like. I'm gonna level with you. Food doesn't taste as good without meat or real cheese, but we do okay."

Regardless of the wolf's carnivorous preferences, the offer of a home-cooked meal made Devin's mouth water.

"I'd love to stay. Thanks," he said, trying to play it cool. He should care less. In Los Angeles he had a private chef, so technically he ate home-cooked meals all the time. But there was something about Isaac offering him food he'd prepared for himself, for his family, that made Devin's ears burn. "That sounds great."

"No." Alex stepped in front of him, tripping a little over the overlong hem of her PJs in her haste. "Devin can't stay."

"Why not?" Isaac, his one friend in this room, sounded genuinely put out.

"Well . . ." Sweat broke out on Alex's brow, which was momentarily distracting because it dialed up the salt in her scent and made Devin think of tequila and beaches and body heat.

"I am sure that as a famous actor"—Alex's tone was not complimentary—"Devin has more important things to do than eat dinner with us."

"How sweet of you to worry." Devin very gently chucked Alex under the chin. "But I can't imagine anything more important than a home-cooked meal with my biggest fan."

"You better go find them, then," she ground out between her teeth.

"Al," her dad said, clearly taken aback at the venom in her tone. "What's gotten into you? The man spent the last two hours cleaning out our gutters to save your old man's bad knees."

"He— What?" She stared at Devin like he'd suddenly sprouted wings.

"Yeah," Isaac said meaningfully. "So do me a favor and don't bite his entire head off, huh?"

"Don't worry. I'm used to fans getting nervous around me." He winked at Alex.

She made him feel like a kid, ready to pull her pigtails and push her down in the sandbox. Devin blamed the wolf for the instinct to play fight. To tussle.

Alex glared at him like she hoped it flayed the flesh from his bones.

Unfortunately for both of them, all that heat went straight to his dick.

"There's a really weird energy here." Isaac pointed between them as he started backing up to the kitchen. "Anyway, dinner's in five," he said without fully turning around.

Alex swiveled as soon as they were alone. "Did you really help my dad with yard work?"

"Well, yeah." Devin bent down to unlace his running shoes, since he was staying. "That would be a weird thing for him to lie about."

"Why would you do that?" Maybe it was the fuzzy pajama pants, but something gave Devin the impression that she was suddenly small, young.

"He looked a little unsteady," Devin admitted, collecting his discarded shoes and placing them on the rack by the door.

"I told him not to get up on that ladder." The new sharp note in Alex's scent—fear, his brain translated—made Devin's stomach twist.

Must be sympathy pains.

"He had barely started when I showed up. And I made him come right down." He explained because he didn't want Alex yakking on his socks. "He gave me orders from the ground. Seemed like he had a pretty good time, to be honest."

For the second time in their short acquaintance, Devin watched Alex Lawson pull herself back together in two deep breaths. As an actor, he was impressed.

"Okay," she said softly after a moment, looking up at him with something that wasn't anger or distrust. "Well. Thanks. Thank you."

Almost more than her scent, Devin was fascinated in that moment by the depth with which Alex cared about someone other than herself.

I live above the garage, she'd said. At thirty-four.

He had a feeling Alex had given up a lot more than meat to take care of her dad over the years. And sure, Devin had sacrificed plenty for his parents. Birthday parties, graduation ceremonies, several million dollars. But not by choice.

"I would have thought cleaning out gutters was beneath you, but I guess . . . I don't actually know you, and maybe I should give you a little more credit." Her dark brown eyes didn't look as strange in this low light. They were almost pretty. Like dark pools, he thought, deep enough for someone to get lost in.

"Maybe," she stressed when Devin gave her his toothiest grin.

His wolf instincts suggested he try scenting her again.

Dude. No. Read the room.

Man, he needed to learn some control. Stat.

At least he couldn't try to mount her in front of her dad. Well, probably.

To Devin's pleasant surprise, he enjoyed Isaac's vegan chili, and the jalapeño corn bread he served on the side was even better. He happily accepted offers of seconds and thirds.

Alex and Isaac's dinner table chat was like watching cats wrestle: hard to follow but entertaining. They lapsed in and out of stories, mentioning people he didn't know and would never meet, but the cadence and teasing tone delivered an easy kind of comfort, a borrowed familiarity that reminded Devin of the sitcom reruns he put on at home when his glass house rang hollow.

Isaac topped up his water from a fat-bellied pitcher. "Got your notes ready for Wednesday, Al?"

"Mostly." Alex crumbled the remainder of her corn bread into tiny pieces that didn't make it to her mouth.

"What's on Wednesday?" Devin wanted whatever gossip made her wilt like a wildflower.

"Town council meeting," her dad explained. "Al here goes every month to try and get donations for the old community center on Braintree despite the fact that the only kind of recreation people care about in Tompkins comes on hooves."

Getting to her feet abruptly, Alex gathered empty bowls. "I'm gonna get started on the dishes."

"I'll help," Devin offered. He saw a dinner guest do that once on *Mad Men*.

"Why are you embarrassed about advocating for a community center?" he asked in the kitchen as he grabbed the chili pot from the stove and brought it over to the sink. "Seems like an honorable cause."

Alex loaded the dishwasher, clanging ceramics together in her haste. "I'm not embarrassed."

Devin closed one eye and practiced tuning in to her heartbeat the way he had over coffee. Sure enough, it was erratic.

"It's weird that you lie so much when you're this bad at it."

She startled and then scowled. "I never should have taught you how to do that. It's rude."

Devin smiled and turned on the faucet, filling the empty pot with water.

He'd started to think her gruffness was a thin shell. This whole "I hate everything and everyone" shtick might work on those content to never look beyond her tattoos and piercings, but Devin was an actor—he couldn't help but be compelled by a character study in contradictions. As far as he could tell, Alex did care. A lot.

"What is it about this community center that makes you fight for them?"

Alex pulled detergent from a cabinet.

"I grew up going there with my mom," she said, uncapping and pouring it, not looking at him. "She used to say it was the only place in this town where she felt welcome."

Devin turned off the water. There were no signs of a third occupant in this house. No scent, no photographs.

"She left me and my dad when I was in high school, and I stopped going because it hurt too much." Alex closed the dishwasher with her hip and sighed. "I thought I was done with this town and everyone in it. But then my dad got sick my second year of college, and suddenly I found myself back in Tompkins without a job or a social life. No one would have me except the TCC. I started volunteering at the front desk, and then after a while they let me pilot a queer youth mentorship program."

She did look at Devin then, leaning back against the counter with the faintest trace of a smile.

"And the kids are just the best. They're funny and weird and smart and . . . the TCC reminds them they belong, even when other voices say they don't."

"That sounds really nice." Devin did not consider himself particularly woke, but he followed the news enough to know there was no bigot shortage in Florida. "I bet you're real good at fundraising on their behalf."

Alex laughed hollowly and shook her head. "I'm a disaster. I never get any donations. The whole thing's an exercise in futility."

"But . . . it's a community center. We're talking like indoor basketball? Pottery classes?" Didn't people in the suburbs go wild for that shit? Hell, if Devin wasn't careful, a couple more days of boredom in this town and he'd be signing up to get Swayzed there himself. "How hard of a sell can it be?"

Alex looked at him for a long moment, like she was trying to decide if he was making fun of her. Which, come on. His comedic timing wasn't that bad. She'd know.

"Local politics are a popularity contest." She came to stand next to him, pouring soap on a sponge and reaching for the pot. "And I don't know if you've noticed, but I'm not exactly well-liked around here."

"Yeah, I meant to ask you, what's the deal with those guys from the bar hassling you? Did you accidentally euthanize their dogs or . . ."

Devin's wolf still wanted vengeance for the way they'd made her heart race. It had taken everything in him to resist shifting in the parking lot knowing he had zero control, telling himself Alex didn't need him committing cold-blooded murder where she could be called to stand as a witness.

She finished with the pot and handed it to him, nodding toward a towel looped through the handle on the oven. "I guess you could say I 'raged against the machine' a little in my misbegotten youth, and people in this town have a long memory."

Devin dried. "So what if you make a bad first impression?" In that case it was simple. "You just need to get people to take a second look."

Alex scoffed. "Trust me. I have lived here almost my entire life. They've looked plenty. Half the guys I went to high school with still call me 'Casper, the Unfuckable Ghost.'"

Devin pressed his lips together. It wasn't funny.

"It's fine." She took the pot from him and hung it on a rack above the stove. "I have always cared too much about things people in this town think don't matter and not enough about the things they think do."

Devin should let it go. It wasn't his problem. Only . . .

"I can help you." And what was more surprising, he wanted to.

He'd been so lost, so useless, not just this last week but practically since *The Arcane Files* went off the air. But earning public approval? That was, like, his thing.

And if Devin was a little addicted to the way Alex had looked at him after she found out he'd helped her dad—like maybe, just maybe, he had the potential to be some sliver of Colby—well, no one else had to know.

She came to stand in front of him, a small chili stain on the collar of her flannel. "What do you mean?"

Devin stood up a little straighter. "I shouldn't have to tell you, of all people, but I happen to be very likable."

It was one of his skills, along with crying on demand and eating it from the back.

"All we need to do is put forth your greatest asset."

Alex frowned. "I'm not gonna take off my top."

"No." *But more on that later.* "I meant me. Obviously."

He might be terrible at making deep, abiding friendships, but he knew how to make people pant at a surface level.

"I can totally help you out."

Alex wrinkled her nose. "Help me out how, exactly?"

Maybe help you take out that nose ring for starters. Devin didn't say that.

"I can make you look good. Like, let's say everyone around here starts seeing us hanging out, right? They'd be like, 'Okay. Damn. This chick's spending time with Devin Ashwood? Must not be such a bitch after all.' To be clear, that was someone else talking, not me."

He'd barely known her a handful of days, but it was obvious just from being in their home, observing them together, that Alex was never gonna leave her dad. And based on the passion with which he spoke about wolves, her dad was never gonna leave his work here in Ocala. Devin might as well use his limited stint in town to make their lives a little more bearable.

"Are you . . ." Deep creases appeared on Alex's forehead. "Suggesting we 'fake date'?"

"Whoa. No. Jesus." Devin took an involuntary step back. "Who said anything about dating? I was offering to be your fake *friend.*" He didn't wanna be mean, but the two of them? As a couple? No one would buy it.

But friends? Sure, maybe. He was a seasoned actor after all. And this was kinda like a good deed. Almost as nice as one of those Make-A-Wish things. He'd always thought it was really cool how many times John Cena took kids to Disney World.

Alex still looked confused. "So you would, what, come with me to the town council meeting?"

"Yeah. Why not?" As he'd told her father earlier, Devin didn't exactly have plans outside of werewolf training. "Besides, it's probably a good idea to socialize my wolf around crowds. You're supposed to do that with dogs, right? To make them less likely to bite people."

"That is true." Alex sounded resigned.

"Great," Devin said. "It's settled. I'll escort you around town for the next week and make everyone think you're cool."

Alex's mouth twisted like she was sucking on a lemon.

"You know, if you want people to like you, you should really work on your resting face," Devin told her. "Do you know about 'smizing'?"

10

ALEX AND ROWEN both had homework on Monday after school let out, so they headed to the library. As they made their way to the second floor, Rowen's eyes flicked over to the teen section. They seemed to relax only after confirming the LGBTQ+ lit table was still there.

"You know Ms. Carlotta was on the news last week telling book banners to kick cans." Alex leaned down to nudge their jean jacket–clad arm.

"Yeah," Rowen said, casually fluffing their turquoise bangs. "I know."

Carlotta Jenkins was the lead librarian and one of the only out elder lesbians Alex knew in town. She'd been with the Tompkins Library since it opened in 1967. There were plenty of hateful people in this town, but Alex tried to identify and point out adults fighting the good fight for Rowen's sake.

Alex lowered her voice to a conspiratorial whisper. "You know she threatened to kick me out once in high school?"

Rowen's amber eyes went wide. "For what?"

Despite their own sterling school record, Rowen loved stories about Alex getting in trouble.

"For carving my initials under my favorite table in the back. In hindsight, I am deeply ashamed of defacing library property."

"Wow. You were such a nerd," Rowen said after insisting Alex show them.

Still am, Alex thought as they both crouched underneath the right corner table and Rowen pressed their fingertips against the paper clip—carved divots she'd once gouged in the wood.

How else did you explain staying up late last night watching her *Arcane Files* DVD box set like it was 2008?

Alex had conveniently forgotten just how dreamy Devin was when he was younger. He'd been so green in those early seasons. Almost innocent. As if helping her dad with yard work and pushing her up against the wall of her own coat closet last night wasn't offensive enough.

Her favorite thing about those early days of his playing Colby was that he clearly didn't think he was good yet. Any casual viewer could tell he was thrilled to be there, his performance all raw experimentation and commitment to the bit. And sure, sometimes it was over-the-top, but that had been the thing that made him great as Colby: he hadn't been afraid to look silly, running around growling at fictional criminals. He leaned into Colby's journey to accept and master himself as a werewolf like it was *Hamlet*.

Gus Rochester might have had a few standout episodes as Asher, but of course it was easier to play the straight-man co-pilot to the eccentric werewolf. Devin's belief in Colby and his struggle single-handedly kept the whole show from being a parody of itself. And now he was doing it again: selling the supernatural in a way that gave Alex no choice but to buy in.

While Rowen started a book report on *Animal Farm*, Alex tried to brainstorm ideas. The problem was that so much of Colby's trials on the show involved straight-up torture. Even more than Alex remembered. Brian Dempsey and the other writers really had a fetish for beating him up.

In theory, Devin Ashwood wasn't a stranger to the concept of "no pain, no gain." He graced the cover of *Men's Health* a few years back and talked ad nauseum about how he and his trainer ordered a replica cannon from Scotland so that Devin could push it up a hill.

Maybe Alex could look up some kind of Olympic training regime. Didn't Michael Phelps eat like fifteen pizzas a day? Devin would love that.

"Soooo." Rowen nudged Alex's knee under the table. "I heard Devin Ashwood is in Tompkins."

"What? Where?" Alex tensed as if Rowen had read her thoughts. Rookie mistake.

"Cassidy Nowicki was bragging at lunch about how he saw him in the checkout line at the grocery store."

"Sounds fake," Alex said, pretending to type on her computer like a movie extra.

"Apparently," Rowen continued, "when the cashier asked what he was doing in Tompkins, he said he's in town to work with *you* as preparation for some top secret movie project."

"He didn't." Alex understood wanting to give an alibi for being in town—but the racehorses were right there.

Rowen shrugged.

"I'm just relaying information . . . unless it's true." They narrowed their eyes, making their forehead freckles converge into one über-freckle in the center.

"Fine. We are working together." If she and Devin were gonna show up as "fake friends" around town, they'd need a passable origin story. This worked. Barely.

"Wait." Rowen slammed their book shut. "You're actually hanging out with a celebrity? What is he like?"

Well. In some ways, Devin Ashwood was exactly what she'd imagined. Thanks to his ego, Alex was now living her very own version of *She's All That*.

Except in this case, the popular guy didn't even pretend he found her fuckable.

It shouldn't matter that Devin Ashwood wouldn't deign to fake date her. But Alex's heart, built for yearning, had never cared about rationality.

Why did he have to go and win over her dad? Of course the man would find Alex's Achilles' heel without even trying. She'd never get over her dad's beaming while Devin devoured his "special recipe" vegan chili.

Alex couldn't believe all the ways she was still susceptible to him, like he'd been engineered in a lab to make her weak.

She groaned and settled on the only truth she could stomach revealing.

"He's a big dirtbag puppy."

"Interesting," Rowen said, narrowing their gaze.

"What's interesting?"

"Oh, nothing." They pretended to pick lint off their T-shirt. "It's just that puppies are cute."

"No." Alex sputtered, arguing with objective truth. "They keep you up all night and poop on the floor."

Rowen tapped two fingers against their lips. "Would you describe Devin Ashwood as adorable? Cuddly? Do you want to pet his head and let him lick your face?"

"I am a cat person," Alex said, with as much authority as she could muster.

She didn't want Rowen to know about any shameful, crush-like feelings she might harbor against her will. It was too embarrassing, too juvenile, too cliché.

Oh, being in forced proximity with the hot actor from your favorite television show made you squirm?

Oh, his voice is so deep in real life that when he stood close you swore you could feel it reverberating against your skin?

For a split second there, you imagined what it would be like to kiss him?

Absolutely mortifying.

Alex was already self-conscious enough about the kind of example she set. She was supposed to be a role model and mentor for Rowen. But why would they trust that she knew anything about being a successful adult when Alex had so little to show for her thirty-four years?

"So what are you guys working on?" Rowen leaned forward on their elbows. "Is it a movie? Is Kristen Stewart gonna play you?"

"Please, we look nothing alike." Alex flipped Rowen's copy of *Animal Farm* back open and handed it over. "And I seriously can't tell you what we're working on. I signed an NDA and everything." *Thank god.*

Rowen made a face. "What's an NDA?"

"A nondisclosure agreement. It means he can sue me if I tell you." Alex wouldn't have revealed Devin's secret anyway, even though she didn't like keeping stuff from Rowen. It was too big. Too personal. Too . . . raw.

Rowen tsked. "That's convenient."

Alex tapped the worn cover of *Animal Farm*. "If you go back to writing your thesis statement, I promise to draw some new merch designs for the band before your big show at the end of the month."

Rowen grinned. "Deal."

Once she'd confirmed they were actually working and not on YouTube, Alex went back to her own laptop.

Ever since that brainstorm session with Cam and Eliza yesterday, she couldn't stop thinking about how, and more importantly why, Devin's werewolf experience followed the same rules as Colby's.

All this would be so much easier if she could lay everything out for them. She'd thought about it the other night, her thumbs hovering over her phone. But while it was one thing to speculate about a celeb, Alex no longer had the same distance from Devin that she used to. Each day he became more real to her. Betraying his trust now would mean more than risking his payout by breaking the NDA.

She had to figure this out on her own.

Everything Devin had shared with her so far about the physical and mental manifestation of the wolf followed Brian Dempsey's vision to a T, starting with his one-of-a-kind origin. In every other werewolf story, they were either born or bitten. But no. Dempsey had to use a real, extremely rare scientific phenomenon.

As the archive's mod, Alex had spent decades of her life cataloging Brian Dempsey's pedantic monologuing. She wasn't proud of knowing all the tricks to finding his most obscure interviews. But being a fandom archivist was like riding a bike: strange and unnatural. Anyway, she remembered how to search.

Kids today didn't appreciate the art of creating a keyword bouillon.

"Brian Dempsey" + "Super Blue Blood Moon Eclipse" + "Origin"

Alex scanned the results page and recognized the titles of indie blogs that Brian and the other writers used to drop in on whenever there was a new season to promote. Taking a deep breath, Alex trudged forward into the bowels of Brian Dempsey's self-proclaimed genius.

Two hours and two bags of Rowen's homemade trail mix later, she began to despair. There were only so many times she

could read the ramblings of a cis het white guy before her eye-
balls started to bleed.

Scanning what felt like the millionth TV zine, Alex hit command F on autopilot.

Q: One of the things that sets *The Arcane Files* apart
from other werewolf stories is the origin. What made you
decide to tie Colby's transformation to a real but
exceptionally rare type of moon?

BD: I'm about to get a little personal here.

Alex rolled her eyes. If Brian Dempsey started talking about
how he hand sharpened all his writing pencils again, she was
bailing.

BD: Obsession with the moon runs in my family. It's a bit
of a folktale passed down across generations, but my
great-great-grandfather Zachariah Dempsey was
convinced he was a werewolf. I guess he somehow figured
out that his home was at the exact sublunar point of the
last super blue blood moon eclipse and he was adamant
that meant fate had chosen him.

Wait, what? Alex leaned forward, scrubbing at the screen
with the sleeve of her chambray, but the words didn't change.

Q: So you used your family folklore as inspiration for the
werewolf world-building on *The Arcane Files*?

BD: Yeah, exactly. I went home for Christmas break
during my senior year at NYU and I'm trying to write my

pilot, you know how it is, when down in my dad's
basement I find all these journals about my ancestor's
"werewolf powers" just sitting there. So I start going
through them, and the details are wild. I mean, they jump
off the page. It was so clearly nonsense, but at the same
time, I knew it would make a great TV show.

"Oh my god." Alex put her face in her hands. Bright lights
flashed behind her closed eyelids. Somehow the idea of the
werewolf lore of *The Arcane Files*, the rules of which she'd carefully cataloged over the course of decades, not being fictional
was harder to believe than Devin Ashwood standing in front of
her with claws and fangs.

Was it possible? That Devin's werewolf experience wasn't
simply mirroring Colby's, but that they were one and the same?

Anyone can be a werewolf, but there can only be one. The
voice-over that played at the end of the opening credits rang in
her ears.

The wolf blood moon eclipse came once every 150 years,
but the sublunar point would change every time.

Could the right set of coordinates rob you of your humanity?

With shaking hands, Alex pulled out her phone and texted
Devin for the address of the last place he remembered going on
the night of the full moon.

Once he replied, it was easy enough to put the address in
Google Maps and pull the coordinates. To Google for the last
full moon's sublunar point and confirm the match.

"Well, I'll be damned." It was wild that Brian Dempsey's
mining of his family history for world-building hadn't been a
bigger story in the fandom. That Alex herself hadn't cataloged it
at some point in her quest to compile a single source for show
lore. But scrolling further through the same interview, she found

the culprit. The reason she and so many others had likely glazed over Brian Dempsey's signature self-important rambling if they found themselves on this tiny, obscure blog littered in the detritus of the old web.

At the bottom of the interview, Dempsey heavily hinted that fans could expect to see a "culmination of the long-simmering tension between Colby and Nathaniel in season eight." Classic BD queer baiting. He knew how many fans tuned in every week hoping to see their favorite blatantly implied ship made canon.

The promised "culmination" never came to fruition, of course. But the fandom lived for those kinds of crumbs back in the day. It was a sick cycle and just one of the many reasons Alex had complex feelings about her love for *The Arcane Files*, even all these years after its demise.

"'Just when I think I'm out,'" Alex quoted under her breath, "'they pull me back in.'"

"You know," Rowen said, "for someone who brought me here to work on my English paper, you sure are randomly exclaiming a lot."

"Sorry," Alex said, sheepish. "It's been a really weird couple of days."

DEVIN: GREAT NEWS! I found an unscented cleaning solution for you to use at work. All-natural, never tested on animals!!

ALEX: . . .

DEVIN: I bought seven crates and had them rush shipped, so they should be there by the time you start your shift later.

ALEX: How am I supposed to explain this to my boss?

DEVIN: Mysterious benefactor?

ALEX: 😑

DEVIN: Okay, but you'll still use it, right?

DEVIN: Right???

11

WHEN ALEX INITIALLY told Devin that she'd found evidence of someone else turning into a werewolf 150 years ago, his first thought was *Damn, that fucker's definitely dead.*

"Wait, are they dead?" he asked Alex, who had driven over to his hotel directly from the library to break the news in person and was now perched on the couch in the "office area" of his suite.

Who knew how long werewolves lived? The show ended with Colby still alive.

"So, yes." Alex picked at the plate of fries he'd ordered for her from room service. "Public death records confirm Zachariah Dempsey died in Maine in 1927."

"Sucks." Devin rolled a little in the office chair he'd brought over to sit across from her. It would have been cool if being a werewolf made you immortal, even though in movies that always ended up making people miserable.

"Do you know how he died?" Devin didn't want to say the words "silver bullet," but he was thinking them.

"It might be best if I don't tell you. It's pretty unpleasant." Alex folded her hands in a gesture that seemed unnaturally prim. "Let's just say it makes sense that Brian Dempsey doesn't talk about him much."

"Come on. I can handle it." Her reluctance to offend him surprised Devin. This was the woman who upon hearing for the first time that he was either turning into a monster or having a mental breakdown basically said, "Sounds like a 'you' problem."

"Okay. Fine," Alex said. "He was caught feral in the woods behind his home, naked and covered in chicken blood, and later hanged . . ."

"Yikes." Devin swallowed.

". . . and then his corpse was stolen and put on display in a traveling circus, where people booed and threw rotten fruit at it."

"Right. Not ideal." When Devin pictured word getting out about his being a werewolf, he mostly imagined a flaying in the tabloids, followed by a quick and bitter descent into irrelevancy. But if people started hunting him . . . Shit. Was he the new most dangerous game?

Alex toed off her sneakers and slipped her socked feet up onto the couch beside her. "Do you think there's any chance Brian Dempsey believes his great-great-whatever really was a werewolf?"

"No." Devin didn't have to think about it. "I worked with the guy for thirteen years and he was completely bought in on the idea that *The Arcane Files* and everything that went with it was like a golden volcano erupting from his brain. He might reluctantly credit family folklore on some blog that only reaches people who are—what did you call it?—'extremely online,' but he absolutely convinced himself over the years that Colby's story belonged to him and him alone."

If a magazine or industry guild tried to recognize Devin's performance publicly, Brian always came into work sour the next day. It was almost funny. It got so bad near the end of the series run that he'd direct his notes over Devin's left shoulder.

"Brian Dempsey is one of those guys who isn't ugly but he's, like, forgettable-looking. You know how ugly guys can have rizz?"

Alex gaped. "Did you just say 'rizz'?"

"Did I use it wrong?" Devin thought he'd correctly identified the meaning using context clues, but you never knew what those kids really meant in their Reels.

"No . . . I think that's right." Alex looked like she wanted to laugh.

It was an expression Devin was starting to recognize on her. This withholding. Even though he'd never been invited to *SNL* and was still bitter about it, Alex made him want to be funny.

To earn the harsh huff of her breath. The shake of her shoulders. A glimpse of that gap in her teeth. But he couldn't just start spitting *That's what she said*s. Unlike the conveyor belt of women who petted his arm in Santa Monica, Alex wouldn't give it up for something cheap.

"I'm just saying"—he brought himself back to his point—"Brian Dempsey is the human equivalent of wallpaper. He might have an HBO contract now or whatever, but back when *TAF* first came out, he needed the world of *The Arcane Files* to be something he made up, because making it up was the only thing about him that was special.

"If he thought it was possible that being at the sublunar point during a wolf blood moon eclipse really turned you into a werewolf, I would've been stealing bacon-wrapped scallops off his plate at that perfume launch party."

Alex nodded, like that tracked with what she'd heard about the showrunner from the outside. "So we have confirmation, then. Or at least the closest to it we're likely to get before you, you know, go all hairy. The lore at the root of the show is real."

Even though evidence had been building since the wolf moon, Devin still couldn't quite believe it.

Looking back, he could see the seams where the show began branching out from this core story, expanding as the seasons went on and the narrative got bigger. They hadn't added Nathaniel, the first supernatural creature other than Colby, until the second season.

The original concept had been so zoomed in on Colby—one man's agonizing journey to accept and harness his werewolf identity.

Devin played it like the five stages of grief. Maybe that experience had primed him to accept what was happening to him in real life. All those months turned into years of using an emotional melon baller to hollow himself out and make room for the character.

In the narrative, the thing that saved Colby from falling to pieces was joining the FBI to solve crimes and battle evil in the way that only he could. Now more than ever, Devin needed to keep the flame of a reboot alive. If fate or destiny or whatever existed, they couldn't be sending him a clearer message about what he was supposed to do.

"Do you want to try contacting Brian anyway?" Alex said with about as much enthusiasm as someone might offer, *We could try contacting a giant pile of shit and see if that helps.* "If you show him the partial shift in person, he should be predisposed to believe you."

Devin immediately recoiled, sending his wheelie chair back a few inches.

"Absolutely not." He could practically hear his parents in his ear. *It's a liability. It's a weakness.*

In terms of unhealthy coping mechanisms post—series cancellation, turning into an actual werewolf was worse than getting a face tattoo. Devin couldn't imagine showing Brian, someone he'd worked so hard to please for so long, something so *wrong* about himself. Even if the showrunner thought it was fascinating, he'd never look at Devin the same way again.

Besides, according to Jade, Brian thought looking too tied to *TAF* at this point would tarnish his reputation with HBO.

No. Devin's only chance at coming back from the Venice video reputation massacre was getting the reboot green-lighted so he could play the whole thing off as an early PR stunt, making it look strategic rather than erratic.

"I don't want anyone else to know." He held Alex's gaze across the table. "Just you. I trust you."

"Oh," Alex said, small and surprised.

"I mean, you're nobody." He meant it neutrally; there were pros and cons to her anonymity. Sure, she was poor, but it also didn't get splashed all over the Internet every time she wore something unflattering or said the wrong thing or got her heart broken.

Alex's face fell. She leaned down and started tugging on her shoes.

"I should get out of your hair." Even with his werewolf senses powering in at less than twenty-five percent, he could smell the hurt and anger coming off her in waves as she headed for the door. "We have a plan to attempt the first trial tomorrow; let's stick to it. Hopefully by the full moon, you'll have this whole thing under lock and key."

"Right." That was the goal. On the show, Colby could curl up, docile, at home in his wolf form during the full shift. If Devin could get back to LA by the full moon, his expensive-ass security system should take care of making sure no one got in or out while he was in that state. With any luck, over time, his allergy to working during the full moon might just become a quirky little detail of his rider. Between Stevie Nicks and Lana Del Rey, someone was probably already doing that.

Only, Devin didn't want Alex to leave, especially not like this. He meant what he'd said about trusting her, but more than that, he found that he wanted her to trust him. He didn't kid himself that it would be easy, that he was anywhere close, but he could see the fragile thread of it building between them.

"Alex. Wait. I'm sorry."

The apology caught them both off guard. Alex stopped with her hand on the doorknob.

Devin had to dig deep to explain himself; he wasn't used to it.

"I'm starting to think LA is like an asshole trigger for me." One mention of Brian Dempsey and he'd panicked, reverted right back to being self-conscious and afraid. "I've felt better here these last few days." *Around you.* It was almost like . . . he could be better here. If he tried. "Must be because there's less smog, you know?"

She turned, a barely there smile behind her eyes. "Sure."

"You don't have to leave. We could . . ." What? Hang out? Was Devin really that lonely?

I mean, yeah.

"We could . . . ?" Alex surveyed the small hotel room, as if also trying to figure out why they'd spend time together if not to talk about werewolf stuff.

Hey—there was an idea.

"We could watch *The Arcane Files*. I can tell you all kinds of behind-the-scenes stuff," Devin said, trying to play to her old archive moderator interests.

And sure enough.

"Okay," she said after a beat, her heart rate speeding up. "I guess I have a few hours before work. But the gossip better be really juicy. I've already listened to the DVD commentary a hundred times."

The First Trial, wiki article #456

Endurance is the first of The Guild's trials to prepare Colby Southerland for the responsibility of being a werewolf. Because his werewolf transformations are linked to his emotions, both physical and emotional discomfort pose a risk to him. He must prove that he can withstand and overcome prolonged pain. During this trial, Colby must swim across a frozen lake underneath the ice before the top layer freezes.

Mod Note: Episode writer Josephine Schwarber revealed in a recent interview that Devin Ashwood sustained multiple rounds of frostbite on his toes as well as pneumonia while filming these scenes on location in Canada.

12

DEVIN DIDN'T KNOW what he'd expected when he walked into the vet's office for his first trial, but it definitely wasn't a forty-seven-slide PowerPoint presentation, he could tell you that much.

His eyes kept sliding from Alex and the laptop she'd propped up on a chair in the center of the garage to the industrial-sized metal tub looming in the corner.

"Okay, so obviously we can't submerge you in a frozen lake like they did for Colby's endurance trial, but I'm reasonably confident that I can simulate the sensory experience in a safe way using this bathing station." Alex pointed at the tub with an office laser pointer he suspected she'd purchased for this occasion. "Normally we wash the large dogs in there, but don't worry, I made sure it's thoroughly sanitized."

At least she'd accepted his donation of the cleaning solution. His schnoz was in heaven, even if his ass was starting to fall asleep in this folding chair. He'd gotten here twenty minutes ago, and they were still only on slide four.

"I researched cold water therapy," she continued, "like the

kind athletes do after a big game, and found some overarching safety guidelines."

The slide changed to display pictures of various sports stars across generations grimacing while up to their necks in ice baths. Damn, even Jeter looked uncomfy.

"As long as we keep the water between forty-eight and fifty-nine degrees, you should be able to remain submerged for twenty minutes. Most doctors recommend ten to fifteen, but experienced athletes can do twenty. Assuming that your body temperature remains stable, I think it's reasonable that we attempt that benchmark, since we're supposed to push your stamina to the limits."

Stamina, huh? Devin smirked.

Alex had on pale pink scrubs today, and he kept accidentally wondering whether they were lighter or darker than the color of her nipples.

He liked her in full archivist mode, including embedded sources. She was both nervous and bossy, the combination oddly charming.

"I'll consistently monitor the water and your body temp to make sure you're not in danger of hypothermia." Alex cleared her throat, so he was probably leering.

"Wait a second—hypothermia?" Devin gulped. "Is that, uh, a big concern here?"

When they shot the lake scenes for Colby's trial, he got to wear the bottom half of a wet suit, they'd put him in his own personal heated van after every shot, and he still almost lost pinky toes.

"Well." Alex clicked the slide. The words "medical risks" appeared in large, bright red type on the screen. "Messing with your body's core temp can be dangerous, obviously, but I did create a 'warming zone.'" She walked over to a metal cot with a thin mattress piled high with fluffy towels and a sleeping bag and held up her arms like Vanna White.

"Looks cozy." This was fine. Athletes did ice baths all the time. And Alex seemed more than prepared to monitor the situation closely.

"If at any point it seems like something might be going wonky, we'll stop. Colby failed his trials dozens of times. We can always think of something else." Alex came over and put her hand on his arm.

Devin stared down at her pretty tattooed fingers, premourning the loss of her gentle touch. He needed to tell her that from a timeline perspective they couldn't afford to get this wrong. She wasn't going to like it.

"Well, actually. I sorta need to nail it on the first try. I forgot until my publicist texted me this morning, but I agreed to play in the TW network's celebrity basketball game on February second." He winced as he finished the sentence.

For a long moment, Alex just stared. "Of this year?"

"Maybe?" he said sheepishly.

"Devin." Alex started pacing. "You can't be serious. You've never even been conscious for a full moon as a werewolf. You can't go out in front of a packed arena that same morning."

"We've got three weeks to practice." That gave him plenty of time to get back to his place in LA and put security measures into effect before the shift.

Alex thrust her hands onto her hips. "It took Colby almost six months to complete the trials. He failed 'submission' nine times." The furious fold of her mouth said, *It'll probably take you nine hundred.*

"No, listen, I know." Devin stood up so he'd stop feeling like a kid on the set of a principal's office. "But I've already sort of been through the trials once, you know? I played the part. That's like spiritual rehearsal. Besides, the risk is worth it."

He'd given up a childhood and arguably a marriage to be an actor. This wasn't that different. And in any case, there was no other option. He'd fallen too far from the video's bad press. His comeback clock was ticking, and at this rate, the charity event might be the last appearance he managed to book for the fore-seeable future.

He'd never been particularly well respected in the industry. His career track record was basically child actor stigma plus soap actor stigma plus long-running TW show stigma. Every role he'd played was in a part of the entertainment landscape that no one took seriously. Kids and families, housewives, nerds. The audiences that liked him were the ones that constantly got discounted or dismissed as unable to appreciate "real" art.

Devin couldn't afford to second-guess himself. Not when it came to his career. If he said he could get this werewolf thing under control in a matter of weeks, he would.

"I'm an actor. I've learned all sorts of stuff on the fly. I per-fected a French accent in five weeks."

Alex began to tap her foot against the concrete floor. "As someone who has extensively analyzed season eleven, I can as-sure you that you did not."

"Wait, really? No. Come on. Lots of people struggle with the r's, okay? At least admit that I pick up fight choreography super-fast." He did a roundhouse kick to demonstrate.

Alex sighed. "Even if that's true, in those circumstances you had a full team of experts with established training programs. May I remind you that I am a vet tech armed with a DVD box set and an archive I first built when I was *fifteen*."

She was trying to protect him, Devin realized, blinking against the shock of it. His parents, his team, everyone else in his life would have agreed "the show must go on" and fuck the cost, but here was Alex, trying to save him from himself. Devin didn't know how to process someone telling him that his well-being mattered more than his career. It felt impossible. And like a gift.

Devin held her steely gaze. "Can you trust me enough to let me try?"

He knew the answer would have been no yesterday. But there had been a moment in the hotel last night, after he'd gotten her hopped-up on room service root beer and catty cast gossip, that Devin had looked down at their knees almost but not quite touching on the couch and thought he'd done something right by asking her to stay.

"Fine," she said, guarded and begrudging, before stalking over to the tub and hauling out a huge green Coleman cooler full of what looked like gas station ice.

"You can go ahead and strip," she called over her shoulder, casual as you please.

"Uh, like, naked?" Devin wasn't a stranger to taking his clothes off in front of people, but usually he had a little more warning. And time to do some push-ups in his trailer so the veins on his biceps popped to their best advantage.

"You can leave your underwear on." Alex's voice was perfectly even as she reached for a hose hanging off the wall.

Devin began shucking his tracksuit, waiting for Alex's heartbeat to speed up, for her cheeks to turn pink. He loved her crush on him.

She didn't even bother looking up.

Devin told himself he wasn't disappointed. Alex must have come to the same conclusion he had: whatever attraction existed between them should be suppressed in favor of a professional working relationship that prioritized their shared mission. Damn. Sometimes being mature really bit the big one.

Together, they dumped bags of ice into the massive tub, and then Alex filled the basin within a few inches of the brim using the hose. Fuck. When Devin sat down, the water would go up to his chin.

Alex placed a battery-powered heart rate monitor on his finger. "You can get in whenever you're ready," she said, looking at the ice-clouded surface of the water. "But fair warning, whether or not this works, it's probably going to be really unpleasant."

"Oh, you mean different, then," Devin said, "from the blackouts, public humiliation, destruction of my career prospects, and the complete upending of my physical and mental health?"

"Good point." Alex brightened slightly. "Never mind. Should be par for the course."

The second Devin stepped into the basin, every muscle in his body pulled taut with shock.

He forced himself not to linger on one foot. Climbing in fully, he sank on his butt into the icy depths between one breath and the next.

Water sloshed, settling around him, lapping at his jaw and dampening his beard. Tingling needles stabbed every inch of submerged skin.

He shook his head, breathing through his nose. Somehow the cold was in his teeth, even though they remained above water.

Alex set the timer on her phone and pulled up a folding chair alongside the tub so they were at eye level.

The wolf howled inside his head like a car alarm going off, blaring, disorienting, drowning out his thoughts.

Devin gripped both sides of the basin, forcing himself to stay down while every instinct revolted.

"Breathe," Alex said, reminding him that he wasn't.

His vision flickered, the colors in the room going less saturated.

"Are my eyes—"

"Silver," she confirmed. The tranquilizers were on the table beside her again, in case Devin couldn't beat this thing back by himself.

The moon was only at fifteen percent illumination tonight. That was nothing. His wolf would grow exponentially stronger, more insistent, in the week before the full moon. Devin needed to fight right now like his livelihood depended on it.

He exhaled carefully through his mouth, focused on slowing down his ragged breath. The cold was so intense he couldn't think.

His wolf howled again. *PainBadWrong*.

Devin tried to ground himself, unconsciously reaching out for the thump of Alex's heartbeat. The soothing metronome became an anchor in his ears. The rest of the world didn't exist. There was just Alex and his breath.

He caught the impossibly good scent of her on each inhale, even underneath all the layers of competing scents in the clinic. Devin could narrow in on her now, could sort and sift and zoom with his senses.

Alex's smell wasn't just alluring; it was comforting somehow. Safe.

Slowly, Devin relaxed his muscles one by one. The cold became clarity, and he entered a state almost like meditation as his body gradually went numb.

Devin blinked as if against the wrong contact prescription, trying to pull the room back into focus. This was the first time he'd been fully aware of the change in his anatomy, observing as it happened in real time.

He knew he'd managed to reset his eyes against the first sign of the partial shift when the pink of Alex's scrubs stood in starker contrast to her skin.

"Impressive," she said, leaning over to check the temp of the water. "The first few minutes are supposed to be the hardest."

Yeah, we'll see.

After measuring the water, she used a different thermometer to check him. The electronic device beeped in her hand. "You're down four degrees, but since you've been running hot, that's okay for now."

Devin nodded. "The wolf is pissed."

Alex tilted her head. "How does he communicate with you?"

The question was a welcome distraction. Devin could think about how to explain instead of about the way his balls were trying to climb back up into his body.

"The physical stuff—eyes, claws, jaws—it's all involuntary. Like the way your heartbeat picks up without your permission. My body reacts and then my brain has to catch up. Closer to the full moon, I guess it's sort of like being drunk. My inhibitions lowered. I was more susceptible to what the wolf wanted and less aware of my body. I didn't lose fine motor control entirely, but it took me longer to notice when I slipped into something not strictly human."

When Devin looked over, Alex was taking notes on a little pad propped against her knee. She must have had it in her pocket.

He bit back a smile. *Once a nerd, always a nerd.*

"What?" Alex said when she caught him, defensive in a way Devin was increasingly finding delightful. "I'm not gonna update the archive or anything, but don't you think you should have some kind of record of your experience?"

Devin supposed that would be useful. Maybe someday he'd

write a memoir or at least a guidebook for the next sap caught at the wrong place under the wrong moon.

"The emotional communication with the wolf is almost like arguing with yourself." If she was gonna take notes, he might as well give her all the details he could. "You know how sometimes you pick up a pair of leather pants and part of you is like, *Hell yeah, my ass is gonna make 'em weep*, and then another part is like, *Am I too old for these?*"

Alex arched an eyebrow. "Do you own leather pants?"

"That was a hypothetical." He'd returned them.

"Of course." She leaned over to take his temp again.

Beep.

"Your vitals are holding steady but your temp is down to ninety-seven."

Devin grunted in acknowledgment. Every muscle in his body felt stretched to the breaking point with tension.

"Is it interesting getting to know your subconscious on a deeper level?" Alex asked. "Like, what does the wolf want?"

"Mostly food." Devin clenched his jaw. "He likes to run." It was getting harder to concentrate, the cold seeping into his bones through his skin. "And to be around you."

Alex flailed, almost dropping the digital thermometer in the water.

"Your wolf likes me?"

Devin lowered his chin to his chest and shifted his breathing, trying to take long inhales through his nose.

"Don't get so excited." He closed his eyes again as he lost control of his vision. "You're the only person he knows."

From the wolf's perspective, Alex was helping them, protecting their secret, ensuring their survival. He didn't understand the nuances of human relationships. Or the exchange of big wads of cash. As far as he was concerned, Alex smelled *GoodStrongSingle*. Homeboy's qualifications for a mate were pretty cheap.

Devin shifted in the water, trying to force himself to stay submerged. His movements sent waves pouring over the sides of the tub to land against the cement floor with a slap.

Something was off, strange, about his body's reaction to the cold. Alex had said that for most people, ice baths were uncomfortable, not unbearable. They'd done them on *The Bachelorette*, for crying out loud. But something in Devin's evolved physiology must make his body react differently to the temperature shift. It was getting harder to breathe. He had to work for it, his heartbeat racing into a sprint.

When Devin played this trial as Colby, he'd suffered stoically: all straining neck and fierce growls, a single tear after hours of near drowning in the freezing tundra. He didn't have that kind of dignity right now. His chattering teeth were the only thing preventing raw cries from escaping his mouth.

Claws sprang from his fingers, punching holes in the steel tub where he'd grasped the edge. Devin tipped his head back and groaned.

Beep.

"Okay, that's enough. You need to get out." Alex's heartbeat turned hectic in his ears. "Your body temp is down to ninety-six degrees." Panic began to bleed through her voice. "Hypothermia can set in at ninety-five."

"Give me a second." Devin needed to hold the line against the wolf. To make the claws recede and his vision revert once more. If he couldn't control the wolf this far from the full moon, what chance did he have as they got closer?

"Devin, get up. I'm serious." Alex must have leapt out of her chair and stepped behind him, because suddenly she was pushing ineffectually at his shoulders, trying to move him. "You could seriously hurt yourself."

"I'm fine," he said, the words jumbled by his inability to keep his teeth apart.

The metal sides of the tub crunched as Devin bore down on them, making more water spill and sending loose ice cubes skidding across the floor.

"You've proved you're tough, okay?" Alex was trying to placate him. "Are you prepared to go to the ER if your extremities start turning blue?"

Devin ignored her, grunting as his claws retracted and then reappeared. He could do this. He had to.

The digital thermometer beeped urgently.

"Ninety-five degrees," Alex read out, brittle with frustration.

Devin began to shiver violently all over.

"Almost." He could barely catch his breath to form the word.

"Please." Alex's voice had grown thin, desperate.

The scent of her fear cut through everything. *Make it stop*, the wolf demanded. A surge of strength erupted from somewhere in Devin's chest, and his claws receded with a metallic click.

He opened his eyes to find Alex trembling with fury.

"Get out of the fucking tub," she said. "Now."

Blue with cold and shocked silent, Devin obeyed, stumbling out onto the towel she'd laid on the floor.

"Take off your underwear and get in that sleeping bag," she ordered, giving him her back.

So much for bedside manner.

He lost his freezing boxer briefs and then climbed up onto the cot and into the sleeping bag. After a few minutes in there under Alex's hawklike supervision, Devin stopped shivering.

"I did it." He smiled at her. "I reversed the shift. Did you see?"

"I saw." Alex knelt down and pointed the electronic thermometer at his forehead.

Devin scowled at the obstacle between them. He was lightheaded and she was pretty. He extended his neck so he could look at her again full in the face.

The machine beeped and Alex exhaled.

"Ninety-seven degrees." Her shoulders relaxed away from her ears. "Looks like you might have avoided harrowing consequences, you lucky asshole."

Devin snuggled deeper into the sleeping bag. It smelled like the forest and woodsmoke and Alex. Like he was cocooned in her scent. Devin and the wolf agreed this was for the best.

"You did good too," he told her, sudden-onset drowsiness loosening his tongue.

Alex looked up from checking his pulse rate. "What?"

"You used your big brain to make up that test and it worked." Devin yawned, happy and sleepy and out of it.

"Shut up so I can take your temp again," Alex said, but her scent turned pleased.

He held still, docile, with his arm tucked under his head as she re-aimed the thermometer gun and clicked the button.

Beep.

"Shit." She frowned.

"What's wrong?"

Alex took another reading.

Beep.

"Your temp is falling again."

"Is that why I'm getting real dizzy?" Devin pressed his hand against his brow. "Good thing I'm already lying down, huh?"

"Fuck." Alex's good scent was tainted by a sudden spike of panic. Her face drained of color. "I read about this. I think you're going into afterdrop."

Black dots danced at the edges of his vision. "What's that?"

Alex bolted upright. "Sometimes, after the initial stages of rewarming following the onset of hypothermia, a patient's core temperature continues to fall. It happens most often when cold exposure is slow and prolonged."

"Oops?" Devin stuck a hand out of the sleeping bag and curled his palm around her wrist. "Wait, am I dying?"

"Not yet." Alex pulled free to yank off her shoes and then tugged down the zipper on the sleeping bag.

"Hey," Devin said, in what was supposed to be protest but came out weak and slightly slurred. "Why'd you do that? 'M cold."

Alex took a deep breath. "Whether or not this works, please know that I blame a lifetime of consuming truly reckless amounts of fan fiction."

The next thing Devin knew, she was crawling onto the cot and pressing her body against his.

"Don't be alarmed," she said as she pulled the sleeping bag around both of them and zipped it back up. "I'm trying to transfer some of my body heat."

"Why would I be alarmed?" Devin mumbled. Sounded like a great idea to him. He slid his bare legs between her clothed ones, tucked his chin into her neck, and wrapped his arms around her waist, even daring to sneak his chilly hands up under the front of the shirt of her scrubs.

Alex swore, goose bumps breaking out across her stomach. "Easy there, spider monkey."

Devin sighed, ruffling her hair. "You're so fucking warm."

"Right. That's the idea."

"Like a little furnace." He snuggled closer. "Feels incredible."

"I'm just hoping we don't bust the seams on the sleeping bag. This thing is a woman's single."

Alex still had the thermometer clutched in her fist. She twisted her wrist to point it at him at close range.

"Ninety-seven degrees!" She did a celebratory wiggle, pressing against him in new and inconvenient ways.

Devin groaned; his dick was cold, not dead.

"No, that's good!" Alex said, misunderstanding his reaction. "That means it's working. How do you feel?"

"It's, uh, hard . . . to say . . ." Was there, like, a medical term for "horny"?

Completely oblivious to his increasingly urgent problem, Alex took his temp again.

The device beeped.

"What's it say?" Why did she have to be so soft?

"Ninety-eight point eight," Alex read. "Practically human." Her body sagged against his. "I think we can relax."

Yeah, in about five seconds she was gonna find out how relaxed he wasn't. He didn't even have pants on.

Devin knew this was supposed to be a trial of endurance, but these circumstances were truly inhumane. The lingering water from his skin had dampened her scrubs, making the already thin fabric an even flimsier barrier between his naked body and her clothed one.

He tried to distract himself, thinking about taxes and AI and other things that normally killed his boner.

But Alex was so sweetly curved, and she smelled so delectable, and she was taking such good care of him— Oh god. Oh no. Since when was he aroused by emotional intimacy?

Sweat beaded at his hairline and behind his knees. There was nowhere to go, no way to twist his hips or put space between them.

"Oh," Alex said, growing warmer in his arms by the second as his hard-on proudly announced itself against her ass.

"Fuck, I'm sorry." Devin tried to reposition but only succeeded in rubbing against her. "Just ignore it."

"Sure." Her voice sounded strangled and her heartbeat went nuclear. "No problem."

"It's an involuntary response," Devin rushed to assure her. He didn't want Alex thinking he was trying to take advantage of her saving him from cardiac arrest or whatever. He respected her boundaries around their relationship, hand to god.

She stiffened minutely in his arms, her scent shifting. *DesireEmbarrassmentGuilt.*

Devin hated that he'd made her feel bad after she'd so resolutely ignored the blatant opportunity to ogle him presented by today's trial.

"I haven't had sex in like sixteen months," he revealed, providing a helpful new layer of plausible deniability to the way he obviously wanted to fuck her six ways from Sunday. "Sometimes the rumble of driving my rental truck over a particularly large grate excites me."

"Got it," Alex said tightly.

They lay there for several more minutes, intimately pressed together, both silently agreeing not to talk about it.

And Devin had thought the ice bath was painful.

13

"IT'S ENORMOUS," ALEX complained the second she saw the F-150 Raptor he'd rented parked in her driveway on Wednesday night.

Devin could tell that was a milder descriptor than the one she wanted to use.

"Exactly." He smacked the hood cheerfully. "We want people to notice us hanging out at the town council meeting, right? To win you some points in the court of public opinion. That's the whole idea."

Alex grumbled under her breath and ignored his attempt to help her up into the passenger seat.

He found himself staring at her smooth, pale calves as she tried to hitch herself in. The knee-length black dress she had on revealed the most skin she'd shown since they met. She looked nice. Even if she was ruining the dress's softening effect by pairing it with the scariest pair of dick-stomping boots he'd ever seen.

With her hands full of a Tupperware of muffins labeled *VEGAN* in big block letters, plus the ugly knit bag strapped across her torso making her lean dangerously, Devin ended up having to grab her elbow anyway to save her from eating shit in her own driveway.

He would blame admiring her legs on the wolf if he could. But he was starting to register those impulses. It was like his thoughts were keys on a piano and the wolf's always came from the bottom register. They were part of him but bolder, simpler.

The wolf didn't understand that objectifying people was bad. Rules and rationality meant nothing to him. He released Devin's most primal responses from wherever his subconscious had previously held them hostage.

Good thing Devin was aces at repression. When he was growing up, it was the name of the game. Not just so he could wear the face of a character, but because his survival in the industry demanded that he be docile. He wasn't talented enough to be difficult. Especially when he was a child actor, his parents and colleagues had expected him to rein in his needs and emotions. To be professional even through puberty.

Devin had played keep-away between himself and what he really wanted for so long that having all these impulses suddenly unleashed felt both reckless and fun. Everything was lower stakes tonight. The moon was only at eight percent illumination. The angry hive of bees in his brain had faded to a low whirr.

Devin could finally relax, knowing his chances of transforming tonight were almost nil. Which, thank god, because Alex was squirming out of her skin next to him: smoothing her skirt, crossing and uncrossing her legs, flipping down the visor twice to check her teeth. But it was okay. Devin could be the one in charge this time, helping her navigate her own version of being the thing people feared in the night.

"Wanna guess the horsepower on this thing?" He smacked the wheel, giving her the layup on purpose.

Hook, line, and sinker, Alex launched into a lecture about

the environmental impact of the truck's fuel consumption. She really worked herself up, even got a little pink in the cheeks, totally forgetting her nerves.

Good thing he'd offered to be her fake friend. She clearly needed one.

By the time they walked through the front doors of Tompkins Middle School, Devin felt optimistic. Normally when he wanted to go incognito around normos he wore a uniform of jeans, dark T-shirt, and baseball cap, but for tonight he'd opted for a slick western-style button-up that brought out the dark green in his eyes and slacks that said, *I respect civil service*, while still being tight enough to give people a thrill.

He'd even trimmed his beard so everyone could get a good look at the moneymaker.

The lobby of the middle school was dingier than the ones he'd filmed in, with cracks in the tile floor and one of the lights over the receptionist desk burned out. Someone had set up high-top tables in the lobby, and a crowd of what must have been more than fifty people formed little pods, clucking at one another, catching up with neighbors, glomming around those with perceived power.

It wasn't that different from Hollywood parties, only everyone here dressed worse and there was no booze. Most people seemed to be moseying around with small plastic cups of juice and toothpick-pierced cheese cubes.

"Are we here early?" A sign on the wall said the actual meeting would take place in the auditorium at seven p.m.

Alex set up her muffins on one of the open tables. "This is the part where everyone plays politician, trying to secure support for whatever they're going to propose. Basically, it's thirty minutes of gossip and snacks."

The crowd filled out further, but as Devin had predicted,

Alex's muffins went untouched. A few people came over to look at them with interest, but the vegan label might as well have read *formaldehyde-laced* given the way they immediately pivoted after clocking the block letters.

Alex, standing stalwart behind her lemon–poppy seed children, might as well have been a potted fern for all the attention people paid her.

"We could take off the label," Devin suggested.

"No," she said vehemently. "These are the only vegan-friendly option here. Do you know how often I show up to an event and the only thing I can eat is ice?"

Devin could not say that he did. So he shut up.

A few men came over wanting to talk to him about his truck—"That your Raptor out there? Cool, man. I got the King Ranch"—and then a pack of older women wanted to know if Devin was single "for their college-aged daughters."

"Yeah, but I'm not opposed to MILFs either," he told them, to a round of pleased titters and Alex elbowing him in the ribs.

"I thought you were here to help me fit in," she said when her scowling scared the old biddies away.

"I am. That MILF thing was a conversation starter. I know you've got Gillian Anderson in a silk shirt as your phone lock screen."

Alex's first instinct was to tell him to fuck off—he could tell by the way she snapped her head around and opened her mouth—but then she seemed to remember she needed him.

"I can't just say whatever I want and assume that it'll be met with approval." Her voice came out pitched with forced calm. "Even if not all of these people recognize you're famous, I don't look like a fucking cowboy on the cover of a romance novel."

Pure pleasure exploded in his chest.

"You think I'm handsome." It wasn't as if he hadn't suspected as much, but man did he still like hearing it. "Rugged." He fingered the pearl buttons on his shirt. "I can go one lower if you want."

"Focus, Narcissus," Alex said, but not before her eyes flicked down to the glimpse of clavicle he'd revealed.

"Okay, not to mansplain, but you seriously gotta relax. Outside of straight-up flipping everyone in the room the bird, you've got the least inviting body language of anyone I've ever seen."

Alex stared down at her own arms folded across her chest, and Devin resisted the impulse to press his thumb to the divot between her furrowed brows.

She tried putting her hands on her hips . . .

"Nope, now you look like a prison guard."

. . . and then let them hang limply at her sides while morphing her facial expression into something placid.

"A prison guard on poppers."

Devin had never met someone so bad at acting like a human.

"We're just gonna grab a little fresh air," he announced to no one in particular and then directed her toward a side door.

"Okay, shake it off," he said once they'd escaped out into the muggy dusk of the parking lot.

Alex wrinkled her nose, which had the surprisingly charming impact of making her nose ring glint in the low light.

"Shake what off?"

"Whatever's going on in your head that's making you all stiff and scowly."

"My personality?" she said helplessly.

Yeah, quips aside, Devin didn't actually buy that. He'd seen her in there, scared out of her skin.

"You know, disaffection only works if you don't care about anything."

He looked at her, really looked at her, maybe for the first

time since they'd met. It wasn't just her body language keeping the world at bay. So much of Alex, from the hair to the makeup to the nose ring to the tattoos to the clothes, had so clearly been chosen to close her off from all the WASPs around here.

It was funny, not in a ha-ha way, how much effort she'd put into making herself fit the mold of a misfit—when if he dropped her in Silver Lake, no one would bat an eye. Everything about her was daring someone to say something.

Those guys hassling her in the parking lot at the bar took on new meaning. What he'd assumed was a one-off occurrence— a shitty booze-fueled fluke—he now realized likely wasn't.

Alex and her father had literally lived on the periphery of this small, tight-knit community, never quite earning acceptance for most of her life. She must be exhausted, constantly walking around spoiling for a fight.

It made sense that now, when she needed to, Alex couldn't undo a lifetime of conditioning. She was completely clueless about how to make people she didn't like, like her.

"Okay, first things first," Devin said. "You gotta convey approachability. Try lowering your shoulders."

Alex rolled them up and then back into the same exact position, succeeding in little beyond making her tits move.

There was nothing for it; he'd have to show her.

"Can I, like, touch you?" Devin figured it was best to employ intimacy coordinator guidelines for explicit consent at the moment, given that so far this evening neither of them had acknowledged he'd had his bare dick wedged against her ass for medical purposes twenty-four hours ago.

"Just your arms," he clarified. All the actors he knew were super tactile, always in each other's space. Acting was a physical art form. He didn't know how to explain what he meant in words.

"Okay," Alex said, looking a little pale at the prospect.

It was on the tip of Devin's tongue to tell her people literally paid for the privilege of touching him at cons. But instead, he gripped her upper arms, not too tightly but firm enough that he could use the hold to direct her body into motion. In a warm-up exercise straight out of the first shitty acting workshop he'd enrolled in at nineteen, Devin bent his knees and rocked them both until they could move together in a kind of shimmy.

Even as her body fell into the rhythm, Alex's face contorted into a painful expression.

"You can laugh," he said. It might help.

She did, the sound harsh at first, punched out, before flowing into something lighter, sweeter.

"I feel goofy."

"You look it," Devin assured her. "Like a rag doll from Hot Topic."

That only made her laugh harder.

The skin of her bare upper arms was soft and warm under his hands. The wolf thought this was playing. Devin felt a sudden urge to nip at her neck, to nudge her ass with his— *Okay, nope, that's enough touching.*

He stepped back suddenly.

Alex looked marginally more relaxed at least; blood flow must have returned to her previously clenched limbs. With her face flushed, her lips bitten pink, her beauty was striking, a sock to his solar plexus.

"All right," he said, his voice rough in ways he refused to examine. "Now we're gonna go back in there, and this time you need to go up to people and show them you're friendly."

"How?" The breeze blew a strand of Alex's midnight hair into her mouth. "I'm bad at small talk," she said, whiny in a way that made the wolf suggest nipping her again.

Devin really needed to figure out a better filtering system, now that he'd opened the gate to these weird impulses.

"Just ask people about their lives."

"I don't care about their lives." She wrapped her arms around herself and glared at the door. "I hate them."

"Yeah," Devin said between his teeth, trying to maintain his red-carpet smile as a man in a tie got out of his car and walked toward them. "That's your problem. *They can tell.*"

That took Alex aback somehow.

"Fuck," she said very softly, pressing her hand to her throat.

Devin got it, he really did. These people weren't vapid in the same way as Hollywood, but they clearly traded on status and wealth. Two things Alex didn't have.

"You don't have to give them everything. I'm not asking you to make friends. Most people want a blank canvas to project onto. Soften yourself just enough to make them consider your cause."

Alex narrowed her eyes at him. "You sure know a lot about people for someone who claims to not have any real friends."

"Gaining approval is my livelihood. It's a different skill set. I've had it ingrained in me since childhood: be whatever they want. To actually get close to people, I'm pretty sure you have to show them all your gross weakness and stuff." Devin made a face at the idea.

"The mask slips," Alex said, almost to herself.

"What?"

"Nothing." She dropped her gaze to the pavement. "That was unexpectedly profound."

"Yeah? Well, don't worry, I won't let it happen again." He nudged her shoulder gently. "You ready to get back out there?"

"No," she said, but then took a deep breath and led him back inside.

Devin grabbed them two cups of lemonade off the reception

desk. He could tell from the smell that the neon-yellow liquid would be sickeningly sweet, but whatever, they needed props. He was getting slightly more used to Alex's own scent untainted by cleaning chemicals. It was easier not to drool all over her when there were other people around, competing for his sensory attention.

"Okay, let's try letting people see us talking." As subtly as possible, Devin nudged Alex with his knee until she entered a pose that passably resembled someone casually leaning against the desk, then moved so he faced her with his back to the crowd.

"Pretend to tell me a joke or something."

"Knock-knock," Alex said woodenly.

"Try harder," Devin said between his smile.

She took a tiny sip of the lemonade.

"What do you call an out-of-work actor with a receding hairline?"

Devin ignored the obviously false jab—he had amazing hair, thicker than hers—and focused on trying to tune his sense of hearing to eavesdrop.

It was harder with the moon this dim. He had to strain himself to extend the range of his hearing beyond those directly beside them.

He didn't get much of note.

". . . heard he's sleeping with his dental hygienist."

"I need a new accountant or a new lawyer. I can't tell which yet, but I'll let you know."

"Every time Marcy picks the Book of the Month, I end up crying."

"Isn't that guy over there famous?"

"Do you think that Lawson girl is paying him? Like as an escort?"

"She'd have to."

"Aw, man. Come on. Haven't you ever wondered if she's got anything pierced below her neck?"

"Devin." Alex grabbed the front of his shirt, whispering urgently in his ear. "You're growling."

"What?" He stopped staring at the group of guys to their right long enough to look down at her and realized the low vibration in his ears was coming from inside his chest.

Shit. He didn't actually know how to stop it. The wolf was *pissed* at the disgusting display of disrespect. A wave of animal possessiveness surged through Devin's gut. Apparently eight percent illumination wasn't enough to fully dilute his desire to rip those dudes' throats out with his teeth.

Alex, seemingly at a loss, ran her fingernails gently down the hair at the nape of Devin's neck, a sort of soothing scritch, until the noise in his throat changed register, turned into something softer, needier—not exactly a better option.

Luckily, someone shouted out a five-minute warning for the meeting, and the crowd narrowed into the auditorium.

As soon as they took seats near the front, Alex's knee started bobbing.

Devin used to get like that before auditions sometimes, all the nervous energy in his body desperate for somewhere to go. If he knew her better, if they were actually friends, he'd have put his hand over her kneecap to try and settle her. Letting her know he was there. That she wasn't in this alone. But given the whole inconvenient-erection fiasco, Devin figured he should avoid any and all overtures that might be mistaken for solicitation.

An older Latino man took the stage and asked everyone still standing to find a seat; they'd be starting soon.

Alex rifled around in her hideous purse, pulled out a big pile of turquoise pamphlets, and then started counting them.

Devin snagged one off her lap, curious. But then he flipped it over and *whoa*. She'd covered the paper in tiny, barely legible type. His eyes glazed over. This thing was a goddamn treatise, outlining her "save the community center proposition" with no less than *nineteen* bullet points.

"Alex." Devin spoke out of the corner of his mouth, trying to avoid the middle-aged ladies behind them who had leaned forward, blatantly looking to eavesdrop. "This is too much," he said, not without some pity. "Can't you just pass around pictures of old people smiling or cute kids or something?" On second thought: "Maybe that's not cool unless you get permission from a parent or guardian. I don't know anything about children."

Alex shoved the stack of pamphlets into her bag and then fell back in her chair, shoulders slumped. "I know I'm trying too hard, but it's a community center that supports marginalized people in a rich, conservative pocket of Florida. I need to prepare for any kind of opposition, no matter how unfounded."

Devin felt bad. She looked all deflated and pathetic.

"It's admirable," he said, "what you're doing." Not to him exactly, but to someone, surely. "You're obviously real passionate about giving old folks and poor people and queer kids and stuff a nice, safe place to go. Where they can feel like they belong." He repeated back one of her bullets that had actually made sense. "And *clearly*"—Devin touched a toe to the bulging bag at her feet, where flyers now stuck out haphazardly—"you put in the legwork. Even snobs like these people should appreciate your hustle."

"Yeah?" Under the pound of eyeliner, she looked fragile.

"Yeah," Devin said, and found that he meant it.

Alex nodded in acknowledgment of his praise and then sat up a little straighter. Like he'd helped.

The town hall meeting itself was pretty fucking boring. Lots of pointless procedure and fifteen whole minutes spent debating whether or not they should install a new water fountain downtown. *What kind of jerk voted against water?*

Since he knew he still had curious eyes on him and he didn't want to make Alex look bad, Devin worked to pay attention, using the active-listening face he'd perfected for whenever Colby got case briefings on *TAF*. Still, his eyelids had started to droop, despite his best efforts. When it finally came time for Alex to speak, he shook himself as she gathered her note cards.

Holy shit, she'd gone pale, even more than normal.

As her fake friend, Devin had to do something.

He leaned over.

"You got this, champ." It was what his agent used to say to him before a big call, back when he had an agent.

Alex gave him a bemused half smile, but she looked slightly rosier as she got to her feet.

"Hello," she said, after taking the mic on stage. "I'm Alex Lawson, and I'm here tonight on behalf of the Tompkins Community Center. I run our volunteer fundraising committee and I'd like to, once again, invite any individuals or local businesses to consider supporting our nonprofit work through a onetime donation or seasonal sponsorship," Alex began in a rote, memorized cadence that made her sound like C-3PO.

"The community center is a hub of social, recreational, and educational programming, especially for underserved communities in our area."

Devin winced as she fiddled with her note cards, redirecting attention from her mouth to her hands.

A pair of guys in the back started chatting about last night's basketball game, not even bothering to lower their voices.

Devin turned to glare. But then, while he had his back to them, a cluster of women to his left started whispering behind their hands, making rude comments about Alex's nose ring.

Had people always been this garbage and he'd only now noticed because of his enhanced werewolf ears? Or did this town in particular attract assholes?

At least what Alex had to say was interesting, outlining the community center's programming and dedicated membership. Plus, there was conviction in her words, which was more than Devin could say for the rest of these chuckleheads.

He needed to do something.

Rising out of his seat, he projected from his diaphragm. "I'd like to make a donation."

Alex stared at him. "You would?"

"Yeah." He smiled first at her and then at the gaping audience. "I just got into town from LA," he said and winked at an old lady up front. "But I can already tell the TCC provides really special and essential services for Tompkins. So, uh, yeah, put me down for"—what was reasonable?—"five hundred K? Do you need me to go get one of those big checks?"

"Holy shit," Alex whispered, but the sound carried through the mic.

Devin hadn't intended to set off a kind of cascade, but it must have seemed like a cool thing to do, donating after he did. Because some car dealership guy jumped in on it. Then a lady from the local real estate firm.

It wasn't everyone. Some folks still gave Alex the stink eye as she came back to her seat, but she didn't seem to notice.

She spent the whole car ride home telling him in painstaking detail all about the programs and people he was supporting. Glassblowing and fiber arts, Krav Maga and affordable childcare.

Devin literally grew up with people taking money from him, but it turned out that giving it away felt different.

His insides went all warm and gooey, like a half-baked cookie.

"You didn't have to do that," Alex said, when he pulled up to drop her off outside her dad's garage.

He raised a single shoulder. "It's just money."

"No. It's not. Not to me," Alex said softly. There was something new in her scent, a flavor of fondness that Devin didn't recognize.

He felt like blushing. Thank god they were sitting in shadow.

"Yeah, well, don't go thinking I donated just because we're fake friends." He pulled one of the pamphlets out of his back pocket and flapped it at her. "Because I'm super passionate about seniors' pickleball. I can't get enough of those old guys running around with sweaty jocks." He flipped open the pamphlet and chose a word at random. "And Zumba? Don't get me started on Zumba. Did you know the health benefits start at—"

Alex cut him off by pressing her lips to his cheek, just for a second.

Devin stopped breathing.

He'd been thinking about her so much; there was nothing else to do in this town.

"Alex—" He didn't know what to say.

"Thank you," she whispered and then hopped out, taking the still-full container of vegan muffins with her.

Devin drove down the block before he pulled over and pressed his hand against his cheek.

His heart beat like the wings of a hummingbird. He felt *like a virgin*.

Was kissing someone on the cheek a friendly brush-off or, like, an invitation to physical intimacy?

There had been a degree of safety knowing that she was the one who wouldn't let anything happen between them. If Devin was suddenly responsible for keeping them from ruining their professional relationship by fucking . . . Shit, they were totally gonna ruin their professional relationship by fucking.

ALEX: good morning. if you kiss a straight man on the cheek what are the chances he does NOT interpret that as flirting

ELIZA: did you make skin-to-skin contact? Or was it like one of those French air kisses

ALEX: contact but dry and very brief

CAM: as opposed to a WET cheek kiss?? Thanks for clarifying it wasn't sloppy

ALEX: idk!! I'm just providing details in case they're relevant

ELIZA: what was his reaction

CAM: yeah did he start heavy breathing

ALEX: so

ALEX: I don't actually know how he reacted because I did it and then immediately ran away

ELIZA: that tracks

ALEX: He was parked in front of my dad's house! I didn't wanna get caught lingering on those weird little cameras he installed!!

CAM: what is your relationship to this straight man

ALEX: . . . coworker-ish?

ELIZA: GIRL

ELIZA: WHAT

CAM: brb calling HR

ALEX: no, wait. It's not that bad. he doesn't work at the vet.

ALEX: he's just this random rich guy who's in town for a few weeks so he hired me to show him around

CAM: okay Pretty Woman!!

ALEX: omg dont start

ELIZA: is the rich stranger hot?

ALEX: objectively, yes

CAM: Oh objectively, huh?

CAM: *whoopigoldbergyouindangergirl.gif*

ELIZA: what prompted the spontaneous cheek kissing?

ALEX: he was being sweet and funny and idk it was dark?

CAM: Are you trying to [redacted] this man?

ALEX: no. He would never.

ELIZA: wtf why not? He should be so lucky!

ALEX: im pretty sure he considered kissing me one time and then the idea immediately filled him with terror and/or revulsion

ALEX: so do I bring it up the next time I see him? Like do I apologize?

CAM: I think you have to wait and gauge his response. You dont want to make a huge deal out of this and then find out he wrote it off as friendly. Or European. If he pretends it didn't happen you should too

ELIZA: when are you seeing him next?

ALEX: day after tomorrow. Pre-kiss I told him I was volunteering at the county fair this weekend and he got REALLY excited about cotton candy

CAM: only in Florida would you have a fair in January

ALEX: they're catering to snowbirds

ELIZA: is it possible the county fair will have . . . a kissing booth

CAM: Jacob Elordi hive rise up

14

THE COUNTY FAIR wasn't really Alex's scene. Even without Devin's enhanced werewolf hearing, her ears hurt from the combination of screaming children, dinging bells from rigged ring-toss games, and the constantly looping melody of a parked Mister Softee truck.

Riotously colored tents and food stalls sprouted across Meyer's Field overnight like so many magic mushrooms. The scent of fry oil and spun sugar hung heavy in the air. From funnel cakes to fun houses, everywhere Alex looked promised thrills or chills, but thanks to spontaneously kissing Devin Ashwood a few days ago, she was still full up on both those fronts.

Alex was only here because Rowen heard they needed someone to run the face-painting booth and begged Alex to sign up. They'd set her up at the far end of the field among local vendor stalls selling crocheted coasters and hand-stamped greeting cards.

The booth was simple: a couple of folding camp chairs and a card table for her materials and cleaning supplies. At least the organizing committee, in an act of uncharacteristic benevolence, had provided a white canopy to keep the sun off her back.

A couple of hours in, Alex found herself having a surprisingly nice time. The kids' excitement was infectious. Her cold, black heart warmed by a degree every time she put her hand over their eyes so she could sprinkle glitter across their freshly decorated cheeks.

Parents stood at her shoulder, monitoring her services rendered with varying degrees of curiosity and trepidation. Despite the side-eyed glances at her tattoos and piercings, Alex was pretty sure she won some of them over when they heard their kids giggle and gasp in wonder as she held up a small mirror to reveal their reflections sporting unicorn horns and tiger stripes.

She hadn't painted anything in ages, and it was nice to dust off the cobwebs, using her skills to make something simple and delightful. It was impossible to stay grouchy while painting kittens and dragons and rainbows. Her favorites were the kids who wanted to be something they'd made up themselves, a "ghost collector" or a "snow shark." A few gangly teenagers even stopped by asking for fake tattoos on their biceps, hearts that said *Mom*.

The word didn't make Alex's belly flip anymore. It had been so long since her own mother left. As a child she sometimes tried to imagine a parallel universe where her family stayed together, but she could never quite get there. Natalie Lawson had never belonged to her. Not really. At thirty-four, it was a fact rather than a tragedy.

By noon her line ebbed as most folks headed toward the food stalls. Alex had just finished turning a little boy into a starfish when out of the corner of her eye she caught Devin walking toward her.

Even though he'd been here more than a week, her heart still flew into her throat every time she saw him against the backdrop of her hometown. It was still so strange. Jarring. She always felt like she'd conjured him, like he had stepped, somehow, as a mirage out of her mind.

He was dressed for the unusually crisp air in jeans and a long-sleeved baseball tee; she was still getting used to the way he was slighter in person, narrower hips and a tighter waist, than he appeared on TV. Alex knew from the ice bath incident exactly how that body felt against hers. How warm.

She shook her head, refusing to let herself linger on the feeling of his legs on either side of hers, his arms caging her in. Thanks to the new moon, he should be fully human tonight. Or as close to it as he could now get.

For some reason that made Alex more nervous. As if his being a werewolf had blotted out the fact that he was first and foremost famous. And someone who'd once hurt her.

She'd just started outlining butterfly wings on a little girl with ribboned pigtails who proudly introduced herself as Manuela when Devin took up a spot behind her shoulder, apparently settling in to watch.

Manuela was unwilling to be observed without comment.

"There's a man behind you," she informed Alex, not bothering to lower her voice.

"It's okay," Alex said as she swirled indigo paint over the little girl's brow. "I know him."

"Is he your boyfriend?" Manuela, tiny investigator, prodded.

"No," Alex said evenly, glad he couldn't see her face.

Manuela squinted at him, considering this input.

"Is he your dad?"

Alex barked out a laugh; Devin choked.

"My dad's over there." Alex pulled back her paintbrush and pointed over Manuela's shoulder to where her dad stood corralling a small petting zoo that included goats, lambs, and a very old, very grumpy-looking pony.

Manuela turned back and threw up her hands, exasperated. "Well then, why is he here?"

"I'm her friend," Devin said, and Alex had to nod and smile and pretend that word didn't somehow feel like both too much and not enough.

Manuela had turned her inquiry over to Devin. "Are you gonna get your face painted?"

"Oh, I don't think he wants—" Alex said, but Devin crouched down until he and Manuela were at eye level.

"Do you think I should?"

"Yes," the little girl declared with all the gravity of a formal deliberation.

"Then I will," Devin said, tone equally serious.

Watching him be sweet sent a pang through Alex. At fifteen, she'd thought him unimpeachably benevolent. At thirty, hopelessly self-centered. She was beginning to suspect reality was somewhere in the middle.

He was human, even if he was a werewolf.

Alex placed the final touches on her butterfly design and invited her giggling subject to choose a glitter. After the big mirror reveal moment, when Manuela's grandmother generously thanked Alex in Spanish she could mostly understand, the little girl happily hopped down from her stool.

Devin helped himself to her abandoned seat.

"Seriously?" Alex dunked her brushes to clean them.

"Why not?" He gave her half a grin and gestured toward her palette. "Dealer's choice."

"The face-painting stall isn't really for adults," she said, even as a dangerous kind of curiosity had her considering his features, thinking about colors that would complement the pink undertones in his skin. "You'll look silly."

"With this bone structure?" He had an impish glint in his eye that Alex recognized. "Never gonna happen."

God, how much of Colby was just him, completely unfiltered?

Alex picked up her damp brushes and wiped them dry on a clean rag.

"Is that a dare?"

She was surprised. She'd always heard that Devin subscribed to the same macho bullshit as *The Arcane Files'* showrunner. Well, here was one way to put that theory to the test.

Leaning forward, she gripped Devin's chin lightly between her thumb and forefinger.

He didn't flinch as she adjusted the angle of his face to make it easier for her to paint, just looked up at her from under those long, dark lashes.

With her opposite hand, Alex brushed a strand of hair back off his forehead, out of her way. He'd let it grow; in the back it brushed his collar. Up this close, she could see a few strands of gray glinting in the sunlight amid the sandy brown, shining like woven silver.

God, Alex, it's called aging. Did she have to be so romantic about it?

His face had changed over the years, gotten slimmer, the skin tighter against his cheekbones and across his forehead. He'd always had a slutty mouth, lips too pink, the bottom one overfull. The beard he'd grown after *TAF* balanced things out, made him less pretty. It also cut her canvas in half and would make the contrast between the bright colors even more ridiculous.

Alex started with black, to sketch the outline.

"That's cold," Devin complained as the bristles touched the tip of his nose. He wrinkled the offended area, smearing paint toward his cheek. He had tiny veins on the sides of his nostrils that they must cover with makeup for press events. Seeing them made Alex feel strangely protective, almost tender.

She made intense eye contact with her palette.

He ducked to catch her eye. "Am I making you nervous?"

"No." She dipped a cotton ball in water and cleaned up the smudge.

His breath fanned across her wrist.

Devin narrowed his gaze, trying to read her. His eyes were so pretty. Alex could stare at him for hours for no reason other than the selfish pleasure of it. But she wouldn't. Obviously.

It was fine that she didn't really dislike him anymore. She'd known he was charismatic since the first time she'd watched the pilot. That wasn't news. He wouldn't have lasted three decades in Hollywood if he hadn't learned, at some point, how to make people want him. And the fact that he'd actively put those skills to work on her behalf, curling his finger and goading her out of her shell? Well, Alex felt totally normal about that. Obviously.

"You paint stuff other than faces," Devin said, not a question, as she brushed across his cheeks and up onto his forehead.

"Yeah," Alex said, taken aback at the observation. "Mostly oils, sometimes watercolors—I mean, I used to. All my canvases have been languishing in my dad's garage under dusty tarps for years."

She shouldn't be so surprised that he was watching her while she watched him. There couldn't have been more than a handful of inches between their mouths. Observation at this range was practically inevitable.

"How come?" She could tell he was trying to keep his face still, not to throw her off, even though he clearly wanted to raise his eyebrows.

Alex rinsed the brush before switching from black paint to pale pink.

"Shelling out seventy bucks for a tiny tube of oil paint when we were drowning in bills always seemed too selfish. Painting isn't a poor-person hobby." Her mouth quirked. "Though thanks to you, I've recently come into significantly more disposable income."

"Have you decided what you'll do with it?" He didn't seem perturbed that she'd managed to part him from not one but two sizable chunks of his money since they met.

"You mean after I pay off all the bills?" Alex paused, looking over his shoulder to where her dad was working. "I don't know. I've never had the luxury of choice before."

They should have enough left over that she could rent a bigger place, maybe turn the loft into a studio. She could go down to part-time at the vet, finally have enough hours and energy to accept the community center's long-standing offer to make her the director of programming. The monthly subscription model she'd worked on in her head for years, adding hybrid and online classes to modernize their income streams, could go from a pipe dream to reality.

Alex hadn't slowed down long enough to consider how massively Devin Ashwood had changed her life. Twice.

She switched to white paint for the finishing touches. When she held up the hand mirror, he didn't bat an eye, even though she hadn't held back at all. Had gone full Pixar. Cloudlike white wool and rosy pink cheeks.

"A wolf in sheep's clothing," he said, getting the joke immediately and smiling. "Very clever."

He blinked when she offered him a tub of makeup-removing wipes.

"What are those for?"

And you know what? Alex couldn't even in good faith say he looked bad.

The motherfucker was right—some combination of good genes and comfort in his own skin made him look endearing, inviting, underneath the paint. *Like a hot dad*, her mind supplied, and then Alex wanted to *die*.

Despite their obvious age gap, she'd never had this particular lurid thought about him before. Though she couldn't imagine she was the first. Devin Ashwood was an actor of a certain age. He had that whole "distinguished" thing that happened when former pretty boys lose the last traces of baby fat plumping their cheeks.

"Are people calling you a zaddy?" Alex slapped her hand over her mouth the second the words fell out.

It was something she'd text the group chat. Before she'd met one, Alex used to indulge in all kinds of harmless speculation about her celebrity crushes. This felt decidedly different. Decidedly dangerous.

He's a real person. That shouldn't be so hard to remember.

Instead of going pale or red with indignation, Devin merely looked confused.

"Are people calling me what?"

Oh god. He didn't know what it meant.

This was worst-case scenario. Now Alex had to *explain*.

Could she lie? Say it meant, like . . . someone with good fashion sense? Anything but the truth.

Her mind was a cauldron of filth, bubbling over.

Good girl, bend over for me, in his gruff voice.

NO. Absolutely not!

Devin sat, in the middle of the fair, waiting for her answer.

"Ummm." The face paint made this worse somehow, she decided.

He looked both prettier—her design drawing attention to the absurd luxury of his eyelashes—and more rugged—the dark beard jumping out in contrast, his jawline practically squared off.

"It's like a sex thing," Alex said finally, spitting out the words like she was allergic to them.

That took him aback. He looked over both shoulders.

Oh yeah, Alex remembered, mortified, there were kids everywhere.

Fuck. She was a degenerate.

Devin lowered his voice, but his eyes sparked with interest. "It is?"

"Yeah, maybe Google it." Desperately searching for a distraction, Alex threw up the *On Lunch Break* sign they'd given her and pointed toward the only ride that didn't make her actively sick. "Wanna go on the Ferris wheel?"

She'd dug her own grave. Any second now, Devin would smirk and ask, *What kind of sex thing?* with a full-body leer. He was well aware what he did to her. In the haze of looking into his eyes, she'd forgotten herself and handed him a ripe opportunity to crow.

Her crush was a cyclone, ready to swallow her whole.

He seemed to sense her embarrassment and didn't press the issue. Devin Ashwood put his hand on her elbow to pull her gently aside so a kid coming toward them on a scooter didn't barrel right into her.

"Sure," he said, his touch gone from her arm before she could focus on it.

They made their way to the line for the ride.

"Is it okay to give children that much sugar, like, legally?" He looked on with concern as a kid a few places ahead of them gobbled a snow cone, smearing red food dye 40 across his lips until he resembled the Joker.

"I think on special occasions." Alex thought about how contained his world must be in LA. The youngest person he saw on a regular basis was probably some twenty-one-year-old ingenue brought into auditions to read for the role of his wife.

Wait— On the show, Colby had (briefly) a long-lost younger sister. That actress must have been thirteen or fourteen. She'd been a series regular in seasons 3 and 4 before they wrote her off. God forbid she start to display any character growth independent of a man.

What was one more death on the already heaping pile of Colby's tragic backstory? There was a specific fix-it fic she'd read back in 2016 that was just sixty thousand words of Colby moving to a cottage in a coastal Maine town where all he did was go to therapy and learn to knit.

"Have you ever been in therapy?" Alex realized as the words left her mouth that she'd done it again, extended a conversation from her head out into the world without a proper setup. All her closest friendships lived online in group chats with no rules about non sequiturs.

At least this question seemed to throw him less than the last one.

"Yeah, I went for a little while with my ex-wife. We were sort of past the point of no return, though. Therapy ended up speeding up the divorce. I guess that proves it's effective, just, you know, in the other direction."

Alex was glad they were walking side by side so she didn't have to look at him. Even though Devin was being casual, didn't look hurt or offended that she'd asked him a second inappropriate question in a row, she still felt like a slimeball. He wouldn't be revealing stuff like this to her if he knew how much pleasure she'd gotten over the years from mocking him with her friends.

"Sorry, I didn't mean to pry."

"You didn't." Devin gave her a look again, like he was trying to figure her out. "Anyone who wants to can read about my failed marriage online. Fun fact—*People* magazine keeps their archives from the late aughts onward linked on their website."

Alex had, in fact, read the article he was talking about—a "what doesn't kill you makes you stronger" cover story his soap opera actress ex did, not long after they'd filed. Unfairly but unsurprisingly, Erica Ashwood (née Trevain) had been unpopular in the fandom from the moment she and Devin had started dating while working together in season 6 of *The Arcane Files*. You could tell she'd tried to use the divorce press to set up her singer/songwriter career—posing with a horse at the sprawling Nashville farm she'd bought "to get away from all her ghosts."

Alex had been twenty-five and still holding her big Devin Ashwood grudge.

He was her nemesis, the perfect imaginary outlet for all her seething frustration with her life. She'd savored the sense of schadenfreude. Had let every ugly, mean feeling her parents' divorce had inspired fall all those years later on these beautiful famous people she didn't know as the group chat took turns copy/pasting passages and sending Crying Colby memes.

Now she felt like an asshole. She really didn't want to feel bad for him. Alex preferred to feel bad about herself, exclusively, in peace.

"That must suck, having your private life splashed all over as entertainment for strangers." *For me.*

Devin gazed pensively into the middle distance. "I'm sure it would if I could read."

Alex startled, and he cracked, his mouth shifting into a closed-mouth smile.

She'd never seen or even heard of Devin Ashwood making fun of himself. Of the way people, perhaps ungenerously, saw him as less than bright. It was a level of self-awareness she would never have given him credit for before she met him. Alex savored the ways she'd been wrong about him, devouring every revelation that made him real and somehow winding up hungrier after the fact.

"The truth is boring compared to the headlines," he said. "Erica thought she'd married a bigger star or at least someone with ambition bigger and badder than a career-defining role on the TW network. We would fight every time I signed a new contract. After the tenth season, she said I was selfish staying with a 'sinking ship,' even though she wasn't even working at that point. Erica always said she married me for my potential. And I guess I ended up being a bad bet."

Alex felt a childish impulse to rush in, to say that Erica Trevain was a talentless hack. It was a strange reaction, to feel protective of a younger version of this man she didn't know, not really.

"I'm sorry," she said, meaning it in more ways than one.

"What about you?" he said as they reached the front of the line. "Ever been to therapy?"

Alex watched the ride, all those people going up, up, up, none of them worried about the fall.

"When I was in high school. For a while. My dad thought it would be a good idea, after my parents got divorced." Her throat constricted as she skirted within grazing distance of their brief, one-sided history.

"And was it?" Devin shielded his eyes against the sun.

"Eh." Alex pulled a few tickets out of her back pocket and handed them to the attendant, who ripped the orange paper in half and pointed to one of the gently swinging carts.

"I think I was too good at telling the therapist what she wanted to hear. Or she wasn't good enough at getting me to not do that? I don't know."

"That makes sense." Devin led the way to one of the bobbing

carts. He held the little metal gate open for her. "That you'd find a way to keep even a professional at arm's length."

"You think I'm ice-cold?" The metal bench was hard under her butt as she took a seat.

"No." Devin dropped himself next to her with a grin. "I think you wish you were."

The space wasn't that tight—she watched four teenagers squeeze into one cart behind them—but Devin manspread spectacularly, so their thighs ended up pressed together when they didn't have to be. Alex couldn't ignore the heat of him, the heavy slab of muscle in his thigh. She could reach out, place her hand on his knee, slide up across the rough denim.

He was looking at her, smiling, hair stuck to his cheek. Without thinking, Alex reached to brush it back.

Devin turned his nose into her wrist, brushing the sensitive skin there like he couldn't help himself.

Oh god—was the Ferris wheel the most romantic ride at the carnival? From a pop culture perspective, objectively, *yes*.

This was the only place in the whole fair that created a degree of sequestered privacy. It moved slow enough that no one was likely to get motion sick and yak. The sides of the cart kind of obscured them from any potential viewers from the ground. You could hold hands or make out or do whatever it was that Reese Witherspoon got up to in that one movie that Alex had never seen but that she did sometimes come across gifs of on Tumblr.

She recognized the way her whole body buzzed with electricity. Before she knew better, Alex used to think a crush couldn't hurt you if you didn't act on it. Locked safely behind the boundaries of her own mind, Alex lived out a thousand fantasies without ever risking her heart.

She'd told her friends plenty of times that a crush was bootleg love: all the endorphins, none of the risk. A crush on a celebrity was best. Because it was impossible, you could fantasize about anything, unburdened by pesky details of reality. You could live out whole relationships like that, daydreams where you were always in control. Fictional lovers couldn't leave you.

It would be so easy to fall into the same trap she'd missed as a teenager. To let a single spark catch in the kindling of weakness for Devin Ashwood that somehow still ran in infinite supply inside her chest. To go up in flames for him.

She had to do something to fuck up the vibe.

"I actually met you once, before you came to Tompkins." Confessing the origin story of why she'd hated him for almost twenty years ought to do it.

Devin startled beside her, dragging his gaze from the sky to her face. "What do you mean?"

Alex swallowed. "You came to Florida's Supercon in 2008, and I had one of those passes for a meet-and-greet photo."

Devin winced. "Oh man, I did so many cons back then. I'm really sorry but I don't remember."

"No. God no. It's fine. I didn't expect you to."

"Somehow I have a feeling it's not fine." Devin held himself very still. "Did I forget to put on deodorant?"

"No." Alex laughed. "I distinctly remember you smelled expensive and kinda spicy." She chipped at her already half-ruined nail polish. "It's just . . ." She took a deep breath.

This was silly. She could say it. Even though she never had before.

"I made this really intense costume. It was— You know the Underworld Ambassador—with, like, the green facial wounds and the neck spikes?"

"Oh shit, really?" He looked genuinely impressed. "Damn.

That thing was elaborate. And you made it yourself? When you were like, what—sixteen?"

"Seventeen. The con was on my birthday." The rocking motion of the ride was making her sick.

"I wish I'd known," Devin said. "I would have sung to you, no problem."

Alex could only imagine the tizzy that would have sent her into. She'd seen YouTube videos of him playing Hanson covers on an acoustic guitar.

"That would have been a relief for me, actually. Sometimes you get out there under the lights and it's just, like, *How do I use a pen? How do I spell my last name?*" He pulled a face.

"No, I—I didn't tell you it was my birthday." And it was like Alex was back there in that convention center room, the world walled off by curtains. "I was super nervous and weird, and I'm sure a lot of people are weird about you, but I really . . ." Her chest hurt, the cage of her ribs suddenly too tight. "I cared so much. This may come as a surprise to you, but I was not a cool child. Not well-liked. And my mom had quit on us not that long before that and I just . . ."

"You wanted me to fix it." Devin looked crushed, his whole face sinking.

Alex exhaled. "Yeah."

He knew. Of course he knew. So many strangers must put their problems on him.

"And I didn't," he said.

"You almost did." Alex smiled at the memory for maybe the first time. "You were sweet at first. My crush was *a problem*."

"But then . . ." he prompted.

"But then"—Alex exhaled heavily—"when I left I overheard you saying to the photographer that the reason you were so nice to me was because I was"—she made herself say it—"a grade A freak that was gonna die alone."

It was such a child's wound. Alex had nursed so many hurts since then.

Her dad calling from the hospital.

Packing the car to leave school in the middle of the semester.

She'd had her heart broken many ways. But you never forget your first.

"Alex. Fuck." Devin lowered his face into his hands. "That is so awful. I want you to, like, punch me in the face."

"It's not all your fault." She hit him on the leg gently to coax him to look at her. "No one could have lived up to my idea of you."

He swallowed thickly. "You were just a kid."

"Yeah, but I'm not anymore." Alex could see environmental factors now. The stress of the situation, the goading photographer.

He looked so miserable; his face drained of color. "'Freak' is on the list of ableist words my agent gave me in 2020 during that brief window when it seemed like white men in Hollywood might actually get canceled."

Alex laughed, the sound shocking in her own ears.

Devin had been right the other night at the town council meeting: she didn't treat most people, including him, like they were real. Multifaceted and capable of depth she might not immediately clock.

Blanket disdain had served her as a powerful weapon of self-defense, or so she'd always thought. What had it saved her from, really? What did she have to show for it? She was a bitter hag at thirty-four. It took a lot of gall to maintain a superiority complex when you'd accomplished nothing. When the only person you liked less than everyone else was yourself.

It stung that Devin Ashwood had clocked her coping mechanisms in a handful of days. He was the world's least self-aware man—he had a tattoo on his own thigh of a fan-favorite line he'd once ad-libbed—but somehow he saw through Alex like cellophane.

The thing about getting an apology from him all these years later was, Alex didn't need it, not really. Devin wasn't the one she needed to forgive.

Poor thing's gonna die alone. She was the one who kept repeating it.

"I never stopped to ask myself what might have been going on in your life." It was a realization as much as a confession.

He blinked. "Are you asking me now?"

Alex was. She had the capacity for it. Finally. "I think it might make us both feel better."

Devin squinted. "Summer 2008, right?"

"June," she confirmed.

He scrubbed his hand over his face. "My parents were going to jail."

"Devin, what?" Alex had followed every story on him back then. She'd heard that his parents had managed his money when he was growing up, that it had caused tension, that he'd filed legal paperwork when he was sixteen to get control of his own assets. But this?

She thought she'd known the whole story. Because she was an archivist. Because she was his biggest fan. Alex realized now that none of that meant shit.

His voice was tight when he spoke. "My agent—my former agent—Jade, kept it out of the press through some miraculous feat. I'd cut them off almost a decade before that. And the sickest part is, I thought that would make them love me. Like, they'd miss the money, sure, but they'd realize what they really wanted in their lives was our family."

He laughed bitterly, staring down at his hands clenched white across the metal lap bar.

"But no. They refused to change their lifestyle when the cash stopped flowing and I guess burned through whatever they took pretty quickly. They must have wanted to keep up appearances badly enough that they committed tax evasion and fraud. I'm not sure if it was pride or what, but I didn't even find out about what happened until after they were sentenced. Their lawyer called my lawyer. Professional courtesy, he said."

Alex knew what it meant to have a parent put their own interests above hers, but she'd always had her dad leaning in, loving her enough that her mom's absence faded to a dull ache. She couldn't imagine suffering the betrayal twice. The lack without the abundance.

"I, ah . . ." Devin shook his head. "I really thought it was my fault. You know, like I should have kept supporting them, kept it from coming to that. Anyway, in the end, no one asked me."

Alex had always thought parasocial relationships were a victimless crime. But she could see now the way the lines blurred when you met your heroes. How Devin took on everyone else's expectations, the way the weight of them crushed him when he could no longer carry it.

There were no words to reflect their parallel hurt, the betrayals they'd both held back then, hidden beneath their skin.

Devin tried and failed to give her a smile, the curve crooked.

"Probably for the best that they never called again and asked me for help," he said, so low Alex almost missed it. "I would have given them another chance."

When he turned to face her, his eyes were the clearest green she'd ever seen, the sun on sea glass.

"It's not an excuse. I still wish I'd been better. That I'd been what you needed on your birthday."

"I know." Alex could see how hard Devin tried, how hard he was still trying, to give people what they wanted. To please them, if he could. "It took me a long time to be mad at my mom. As a kid, it felt like if I was mad at her, that was such a big, all-consuming hurt that it would wipe out everything. I'd lose all the good memories of her tucking me in or making spaghetti. I think, even then, I knew those good memories were all I was ever gonna get of her."

Alex had to fight to push the words out. But she wanted to. She wanted Devin to know this part of her. She wanted him to understand.

"It was a lot easier to be mad at you. Not the real you. But, you know, the cardboard-cutout version that had said the same thing I was hearing at school and around town. The kind of thing I heard in my mom's voice even though she never said it."

Her eyes stung, and in the few seconds she had to make the choice to stop talking or start crying, she chose the latter.

"That I wasn't good enough. Wasn't wanted." And Alex felt like her ribs had come apart. Like all the soft parts of her were out in the open air.

"You can still be mad at me," Devin said, quiet and gravely serious as he reached over and swiped at her tear tracks with his warm thumb. "If it's easier. If it helps."

Alex threaded her arm through Devin's and leaned her head on his warm, sturdy shoulder.

"I couldn't," she said honestly, "even if I wanted to. And I don't."

From the top of the Ferris wheel, together they watched clouds drift lazily across a sea of flawless blue. No moon in sight.

15

"DO YOU WANNA get a drink?" Alex said when they finally got off the Ferris wheel. Alcohol seemed like the best antidote for the volume of shared trauma they'd just exchanged. "There's a beer garden thing on the other side of the field."

"Yes, please," Devin said, following her eagerly.

They made their way through the throngs of families and clusters of rowdy friends strung out on sugar and grease.

At the taped-off entrance to the beer garden, a volunteer checked their IDs before giving them wristbands for the "twenty-one plus" area.

Devin was oddly quiet as they made their way across the hay-strewn dirt, passing crowded wooden picnic tables and several games of cornhole to get to the pop-up bar.

"You okay?" Alex asked.

"Fine," Devin said, staring out into the crowd, looking lost.

So, Alex's plan to put distance between them had worked, just not on her side.

She'd believed that if she revealed to Devin the truth about exactly how he'd hurt her, she could stop thinking about him naked. Instead, she'd accidentally given herself closure. She finally had the full story from both sides.

After Devin revealed what had happened with his parents, his voice saturated with hurt even all these years later, he was more human to her now than he'd ever been.

At seventeen, she'd wanted him to trust her with his secret pain, and now she had it for real. Alex thought she had changed so much from that starstruck teenager, but just like back then, his confession made her feel tender and protective toward him. He was still the asshole who had insulted her, but he was also sensitive and wounded and trying so, so hard to keep it together.

Devin thought no one wanted to see his "gross weakness." Alex couldn't tell him that she found his aura of tragedy hot.

She ordered two pints of whatever light beer the place had on tap and received foam-topped plastic cups. She'd just passed Devin his when a commotion from the back corner grabbed her attention. Snickers and hollering carried over on the wind. Maybe it was conditioning after a lifetime of being bullied, but the combination of sounds made her blood run cold.

Alex went up on her tiptoes, craning her neck to try to see. "What's going on over there?"

Devin followed her gaze. "Looks like some kind of dunk tank."

"Oh god." She rushed through the crowd, stepping around people, while Devin trailed her.

Seth had said something a few weeks back about wanting to volunteer at the fair. When Alex told him Rowen had already roped her into face painting, he'd mentioned he might do the dunk tank.

"No skills required," he'd said, with that easy smile.

Again, maybe it was trauma speaking, but Alex would never have signed up to be a fish in a barrel for this town.

She and Devin made their way to a cluster of people standing in a semicircle. The air over here smelled different. Worse. Of sweat and spilled beer and too many kinds of cologne mingling. Alex's stomach swooped.

Immediately she clocked Pete Calabasas in the center of the group, holding court. Of course if there was an opportunity to harass someone, Pete would be there with bells on. He had a beer in one hand—complete with a koozie that he must have brought from home—and a softball in the other. Beside him were the same two cronies from the bar.

Despite herself, Alex got a little dizzy, thinking about them following her, closing in like jackals. She tore her gaze away to find Seth behind the bars of the dunk-tank cage in a swimsuit and T-shirt.

He'd clearly been in the tank at least once, and if the forced cheerfulness he'd pasted on his face was anything to go by— more. It was chilly out here, the sun now lost behind a pack of clouds.

It wasn't just Pete talking trash. Various spectators had joined in, their taunting voices loud and sloppy from the open bar. Pete and the other guys were goofing around with the ball, tossing it to one another, intentionally aiming at the cage rather than the target. Even though the ball was bigger than the gaps in the metal bars on the cage, the crack of the impact still made a sickening rattle that shook the attached seat.

"Hey!" a pimple-faced college kid acting as attendant yelled. "Watch it."

Pete waved him off, yelling an excuse about how his aim got worse after a few beers.

The next time he pulled back his arm to throw, Seth flinched.

All the meatheads cracked up, hanging on one another as beer sloshed in their plastic cups.

"What's going on?" Devin asked from beside her. "Why are they singing Lady Gaga at the guy with the Buddy Holly glasses?"

Alex opened her mouth to explain homophobia, but Devin was narrowing his gaze, his lip curling in disgust.

"Wait a second, is this, like, a gay thing? Are those guys harassing that dude because he's gay? Because that's fucked up."

"Yeah," Alex said, rushing forward as the ball smacked the target and Seth went under. "It is."

This time the fall made Seth lose his glasses. He fumbled blindly for them in the water, his long hair plastered to his forehead.

Of course the shitheads loved that.

Why on earth he hadn't taken them off beforehand, Alex didn't know. The glasses sank to the bottom like a stone, and Seth had to open his eyes under the gross water, groping, trying to find them while the crowd roared their approval, mob mentality making them unambiguously cruel. The whole structure of this town bred attitudes of superiority, the haves and the have-nots.

People weren't outright shouting slurs here, so they probably thought they were just being funny. Giving the guy a hard time.

When Seth finally climbed out, waterlogged and dripping, Alex rushed forward to speak to him, positioning herself with her back to the assembled dickwads, as if she could block him from their view with her body.

"Oh hey," Seth said, breathing heavily from the time underwater. He tried to offer her a smile that didn't reach his eyes. "You stop by to watch?"

"Seth, don't go back up there." Alex caught his goose bump— covered arm. "Those guys are jerks and they're harassing you. You don't have to sit there and listen just because you signed up to volunteer."

"It's for charity," he said, shrugging miserably. "I've had worse."

Seth was underestimating Pete Calabasas's capacity for cruelty. The look in that jerk's eyes wasn't half as mean or booze-foggy as when he'd followed Alex out into the parking lot. She couldn't stand by and watch Seth, who'd called her his friend, on the receiving end of that kind of darkness.

"Let me take the rest of the shift," she offered desperately, even as she could feel a shudder coming on at the prospect of putting herself directly in the line of fire. "There's nothing these jabronies can say that I haven't already heard a million times."

Seth paused on the stairs. Alex could tell he didn't want to give up.

"No, I can't let you do that." He was going blue in the lips. The water must be freezing. "You don't even have a bathing suit on," Seth protested, wrapping his arms across his skinny chest.

"So? I'll just wear this." She plucked at the paint-spattered bib of her overalls. "It's not like they're precious."

"Excuse us a second." Devin pulled Alex aside by the criss-cross of fabric at her back.

"Are you some kind of masochist?" he whispered furiously.

"No?" At least, not on purpose.

A muscle in his jaw jumped. "Well, then let the nice man finish his own shift."

Devin didn't understand. This wasn't bad press coverage that would pass with the news cycle. Alex was living proof that towns as small as Tompkins had long memories. She didn't want

Seth to have to walk around his hometown scared and shut down the way she did.

Alex shoved past Devin to explain the switch to the attendant.

The guy shrugged at the end of her rambling. "I don't care who gets in the tank as long as it's not me."

"See?" Alex told Seth. "This guy says it's fine."

When he still looked on the fence about letting her take the literal fall, Alex had no choice but to pull out the big guns. "Please?" She reached for Seth's hand. "Since we're friends?"

Seth laughed a little, his shaking shoulders sprinkling water droplets on the rapidly muddying ground.

"Leave it to you to turn that into a threat." But he stepped back. "You're sure?"

Alex sighed with relief. "Totally. Give me the chance to pay you back for half a year of being a withholding bitch."

"You weren't—"

"I was," Alex cut him off. She'd been so busy trying to protect herself from this town that she'd failed to see that not everyone here was out to get her.

"Maybe a little," Seth conceded, his eyes flicking over to where his boyfriend, Matt, was waiting, anxiously wringing a towel between his hands.

Alex gave his arm a light shove. "Please get out of here."

Seth gave her a grin, shaking his head a little as he started walking backward. "You've always been a sucker for an underdog."

Her eyes found Devin. *You have no idea.*

Alex toed off her sneakers and then reached down to peel off her socks.

When the crowd caught wind of what was happening, their faces lit up like it was Christmas morning.

"Oh, Alex, aren't you sweet, taking over for your little friend," Pete singsonged. "And it's not even my birthday."

Here we fucking go.

She was halfway up the ladder when the whispering started.

All of a sudden someone shouted, "She can't go in like that."

What the hell?

"There's metal buckles on those overalls and she could pierce the tank," Pete's friend, the tall one—Chip, she was pretty sure—said.

The attendant went white. "Okay, hold up. I cannot have an insurance claim on my hands. This rental costs like eight thousand bucks."

Alex threw up her hands. "What do you expect me to do?"

"She could take the overalls off," Pete yelled back. "You've got a T-shirt on under there, right?"

Alex closed her eyes. Yeah. A white T-shirt.

"Absolutely not." The next thing she knew Devin had his arms around her waist, hauling her off the ladder and placing her gently on the ground behind him. His eyes flashed, but not silver. His hands curled into fists, blunt tipped and human.

"It's fine," Alex said. "So they see my bra and underwear. It's not that different from a bathing suit."

"Like hell it isn't." Apparently even his human voice could hit a register that sounded closer to thunder than human speech.

Devin wheeled on the attendant. "Tell them to go fuck themselves."

"Uh. No, thanks?" The guy held up his hands. "There are many of them and one of you."

"It's fine," Alex said again. She'd done plenty of unpleasant shit in her life. She reached for the metal snap at her left shoulder.

The crowd whooped.

Pete started clapping. "This game just turned into a wet T-shirt contest!"

"Wait." Devin reached for Alex's wrist. "I'll go in."

"What?" She froze. "Why?"

It was one thing for Devin to offer to be her fake friend; another for him to donate money to the community center when he, admittedly, had plenty. But for him to endure public ridicule? For her? No way.

Maybe he thought this was a chance to bolster his command over his werewolf senses. He must have forgotten it was the new moon.

"This won't work as an endurance test."

His nostrils flared. "It's not a test."

"If you're doing this because you feel sorry for me because of what happened when I was seventeen—"

"Alex." He exhaled, exasperated. "I don't feel sorry for you. You've been busting my balls for a week. I think we're even."

She lowered her voice. "Those guys are gonna be assholes to you."

"I'm gonna let you in on a little secret." Devin leaned down and kissed the top of her head in a way clearly designed to shut her up. "You can't out-asshole an asshole, baby."

And with that, he reached both hands behind his head and yanked off his shirt.

For a moment Alex's head was just static.

How many times had she seen those abs? A thousand? Ten thousand?

Alex couldn't tear her eyes away from the shadows underneath his collarbones, the slopes of his pecs, the divot of his belly button, the sharp V of his hip bones.

She swallowed, her throat suddenly parched.

"I couldn't be a hero for you when you were seventeen. Let

me give it a shot now." He unbuttoned and then unzipped his jeans.

Holy shit.

"Besides," he said, low, right against her ear, "if anyone here gets to see you in your fucking underwear, it's gonna be me."

Alex shivered.

By the time she closed her mouth, she was watching his perfect ass inside black boxer briefs climb the stairs.

Pete and his crew did not enjoy this substitution. They grumbled among themselves and debated abandoning the game. Devin didn't make for an easy target in the same way Alex and Seth had, but then Pete's eyes lasered in on her again.

"You're that actor, right? From that show she used to be obsessed with when we were kids." He turned to his short friend— by process of elimination, Greg. "Remember, she wore that ugly-ass T-shirt all the time?"

The guy shrugged. Alex was Pete's favorite target, and he wasn't gonna give up the chance to make her suffer, not if he thought he could use Devin to get to her.

"What are you doing here, man? Lawson's not the caliber of pussy you fly all the way across the country for."

Alex's cheeks heated. She shouldn't have bothered trying to push Devin away. Pete Calabasas was about to list every flaw she had for him and the gathered crowd.

Devin just stared him down. "That's rich, considering how hard you were bending over backward for an excuse to see her nipples."

Probably-Chip burst out laughing, punching Pete on the arm.

Pete's nostrils flared. "She's a loser," he declared. "She scoops dog poop for a living."

"Oh, and you're so much better, right?" Devin leaned forward, his elbows on his knees. "I bet you've got a big job. Corner office. But wait a second. What's that koozie say, man? 'Calabasas and Son'? That you? The son? Because having Daddy hand you a job on a silver platter is way more impressive."

Pete chucked the ball and missed, half a foot wide of the target.

"Uh-oh. You getting mad, bud?" Devin grinned, sitting back and widening his legs a little, drawing attention to his bulge.

Which, okay, was extremely immature, but also . . . fuck. Hot.

It wasn't that she'd never stood up to Pete before, but he saw Devin as an equal, maybe even his better. It wasn't fair, but Devin's blows landed in ways Alex's never could.

"Everyone in town hates her." The vehemence in Pete's tone was almost chilling. "She doesn't have a single friend here."

A much larger crowd had gathered since Devin got in the booth. Presumably because word had spread that someone famous was over here in his underwear.

"Yeah, see, I don't think that's true." Devin shook his head. "Because I'm up here taking your weak heat on her behalf, but as soon as your henchmen saw all these nice people"—he waved at his audience—"gathered round to laugh at you, they abandoned your goofy ass for the bar."

Pete turned in a circle, glaring in the direction of his cowardly friends, who had indeed turned traitor.

He chucked the ball again, this time landing even farther from the target.

The crowd snickered.

"Yeah, well. Alex Lawson is a vegan!" Pete spat desperately.

Devin blinked. "Seriously? That's it? That's the best you've got. The woman likes to eat vegetables? She cares too much about animals and the environment? Her cholesterol's better than yours and you don't like it?" He huffed out an exhale. "Time to put down the ball, tiger. You're embarrassing yourself."

Pete Calabasas's face turned an alarming shade of puce.

"Who the fuck are you anyway? Some old has-been."

Devin laughed. "Yeah, dude, I'm old as hell. But I'm pretty sure that woman over there, the one with the koozie that matches yours . . . Is she with you?"

"That's my wife." Pete's eyes flashed.

"That's your wife?" Devin raised his eyebrows. "Okay, well, please let her know it's totally fine that she's been using her cell phone to take photos of me in my underwear for the last ten minutes." He waved. "No, don't worry about it, sweetheart. You're good. Enjoy."

"I'm gonna kick your ass." Pete dropped the ball and rushed toward the cage, rattling the bars.

Devin grinned. "Oh, you're gonna kick my ass? In front of all these people." He made a tsking sound. "That's assault, my man. I don't care how much money your daddy has; you do so much as raise that scrawny little arm in my direction, and my stone-cold-killer bitch of a lawyer is gonna tear you a new asshole."

Alex wasn't the first person in the crowd to start cheering, but she was in fact the loudest.

Devin looked over at the attendant, who was holding an overflowing bucket of cash donations from spectators who had apparently been waiting their whole life to see Pete Calabasas publicly dressed down.

"We're good here, right?"

The kid nodded.

Devin jumped down, landing with an animal grace that

betrayed the fact that even at the new moon, he wasn't quite human.

He came to stand in front of Alex, and with a shit-eating grin he put his hands on his hips, fully preening. "Well. How'd I do?"

She shook her head in wonder. "You made every bad thing anyone's ever said about me seem ridiculous."

"Alex," he said softly. "That stuff is ridiculous."

"I owe you one." This town would never look at her the same way.

"One what?" Devin was looking at her lips.

Alex swayed toward him a little. "Whatever you want."

"Yeah?" He brushed her cheek with his thumb and then let the pad linger at the corner of her mouth. "You sure about that?"

Alex nodded. Fuck. Devin Ashwood was a lesson she'd never learn.

The Second Trial, wiki article #519

Instinct is <u>The Guild's</u> second trial to prepare Colby
Southerland for the responsibility of being a werewolf. To
bring Colby and his wolf closer together, <u>The Guild</u> sets him up
to track his mentor, <u>Bathalda</u>, across the Andes Mountains
during a storm using only his enhanced senses.

Mod Note: Rather than use the real Andes, this episode's mountain
footage was shot in California.

16

IT WAS GOLDEN hour when Alex pulled into the parking lot above her favorite secluded glen in Ocala. She sat on the hood of her car to wait for Devin, hugging her knees and gazing out at where the sun crowned the tops of the trees in hazy orange.

In some ways, bringing Devin here was more personal than having him at work or even in her home. This lookout point used to be her angst spot. The place she'd run to every time she felt tethered to Tompkins against her will.

At fifteen when her mom left.

At nineteen when her dad got sick.

At twenty-four when debt pinned her in place like a boulder.

Every time resentment built in her throat until she thought she'd choke on it, Alex came here, where the lush green tapestry of the foliage spread out for miles and miles in every direction. She closed her eyes and listened to the call and response of the birds, breathing with the forest, and for a few minutes at least, she was (almost) free.

"Nice night for a chase," Devin called out his rolled-down window as he pulled up beside her in that horrible behemoth of a rental truck.

Alex's heart leapt. She hated how giddy she was to see him after only a few days. She'd been willing the clock to move faster all afternoon, unlocking her phone every five minutes, hoping for one of the inane updates he sent her on his daily routine when they were apart.

He'd taken to visiting the vet even in her off-hours. Somehow he'd conned Seth into letting him spend time out back with Lou, where he fed the horse apples and carrots procured from the farmers' market.

In the afternoon, he volunteered with her dad, who couldn't say enough over dinner about how helpful Devin was—and such a good listener—also funny—did Alex know he was that funny?

Tonight, Devin looked ready for another *Men's Health* spread, stepping down from the cab in black athleisure and the cleanest white sneakers she'd ever seen.

Alex's gym clothes—swishy running shorts and a faded white tank top under a hoodie—seemed too dressed down in comparison. She should have tried harder to find something that matched. It didn't help that the only sports bra she owned flattened her tits like pancakes.

She got to her feet, brushing pollen from the car hood off her butt.

Devin's gaze lingered on the bare expanse of her legs.

Oh, right. He'd never seen her thigh tattoos. These shorts were cut high, especially on the sides, revealing the lacewing butterfly and black widow spider, a siren and Medusa on her other leg.

"Hey," he said, still staring where the curl of snakes disappeared underneath the hem of her shorts. "I mean—hey," he said louder, dragging his eyes to her face. "Sorry. Shit. I like your . . ." He waved rather than finishing the sentence.

"Thanks." Alex brushed her thumb over the ink and watched his Adam's apple bob roughly. So maybe her outfit didn't matter that much.

It was funny—she'd first gotten the tattoos because she'd been insecure about how pale she was. Even if everyone knew how bad tanning was for you now, back when she was in high school and college, "fake and bake" had been all the rage, especially the closer you got to Miami. In contrast, Alex had been almost translucent, a sick Victorian child.

But the designs were beautiful, bold American traditional lines. She'd hand-picked creatures people overlooked or underestimated to their peril. When she got naked now, she saw the art first, and her body made her feel the way the designs did: powerful and ethereal. Like she, too, was something to be admired, even revered.

She flushed to think that maybe, secretly, she'd known what she was doing a little when she got dressed. For the second trial, Devin would track her, chase her. So what if instead of prey, she wanted to be something alluring, elusive, someone worthy of his pursuit?

Bringing herself back to earth, Alex put on her best professional voice. "Did you do the prep work I suggested?"

Devin rolled his eyes. "Yes, I watched the second trial episode and reviewed your copious notes. I am now uncomfortably aware of the fact that I move my arms funny when I run."

"Only when you're trying to look fast."

They went over the plan.

"The idea is for you to let the wolf out little by little in order to find me. Wolves are endurance predators. They chase their prey over huge distances in order to learn about them. Tracking isn't just physically engaging; it's cerebral. The point of this trial is for you to be able to tap into the wolf's instincts to find me, but the key is that you stay in control mentally. Don't fall under, if you can help it. If you can halt the partial shift at your eyes, this should actually get easier as it gets darker. You'll be able to use the wolf's night vision. Any questions?"

"No, I'm ready." Devin bounced on his toes a little. "You realize this is basically grown-up hide-and-seek?"

"Pretty much," Alex admitted. She could see a bit of scientific rationale behind the trial—or as close to it as they could really get, considering the circumstances. But she still felt a little self-conscious, being the one championing using the show as a map. Was this all goofy? Playing at preparation for something impossible to control?

"Finally, we get to do something *fucking fun*." His grin hit her like a sucker punch. There was something wolfish in his teeth. The glint of the falling sun set off his slightly long incisors. Had they always looked like that, and she'd never noticed?

At their collective best guess, his transformation was an accident. An anomaly that could have happened to anyone in the right place at the right time. But suddenly Alex wondered if that was true. What if Devin Ashwood had been born just a little bit wild and the universe took advantage?

He stepped toward her.

"I think I need to, um . . . get your scent to start," he said, with only a hint of sheepishness.

"Oh. Right." Alex immediately tensed. "Of course."

This was how Colby prepared to track. Still, the idea of Devin sniffing her, on purpose, was simultaneously awkward and intimate. Especially because she knew her scent did something to him. That he liked it. Or at least his wolf did.

Alex knew the wolf was supposed to be your gut—your soul, even. But people overrode those kinds of instincts all the time.

Just because Devin was attracted to her on some primal level, that didn't mean his rational mind would ever want to indulge.

She pulled her hair over one shoulder, exposing her nape, and tried to stand still despite the urge to fidget. "Ready when you are."

Despite her invitation, Devin didn't move forward. In fact, he closed his eyes and screwed up his face like her words had given him a head rush.

"You okay?"

"Yeah." He relaxed his features with obvious effort, breathing slightly laboriously through his nose. "It's just, uh"—he covered his eyes with his palm—"where the wolf wants to . . . Let's just say some of the instincts are impolite."

"Oh," Alex said, suddenly remembering that the episode she'd made Devin rewatch featured an "erotic" dream sequence in which Colby imagined scenting Juliette, his always-out-of-reach lady love. It was one of those black-and-white montages that film school bros thought were the height of erotic cinematography: flashes of Kennedy Roberts's cleavage, her bare hip, the shadow of her belly button, her lower back right before the swell of her ass, the seam of her thighs.

If Devin was picturing *that*, only with Alex . . . Heat filled her cheeks, then raced down her spine.

His breath shifted, and Devin tilted his head, like he could *tell*.

Fuck. It was entirely possible that he could. Even if his fledgling werewolf skills couldn't fully interpret the cause of the changes in her scent and temperature, he could probably guess.

He rushed forward like he'd made an executive decision to get it over with.

"I'll just stick to your head, yeah?"

After pausing in front of her for a moment, he ducked around so he stood at her back.

Alex exhaled. It was a good call, avoiding eye contact.

He'd left a foot or so of space between them. She could feel the absence, the air between them humming like it held a charge.

"I gotta get a little closer. There's a lot of competing smells," he explained, closing in by degrees until his nose was almost pressed into her hair.

"Is this all right?" His voice was a gentle rumble at her back, the first notes of a summer storm.

"Yes," Alex said, shamefully breathy.

Devin nosed at her temple, then along her hairline toward her ear.

It felt like a trust fall, her belly roiling with nerves, anticipation.

The heat of him behind her beckoned. What if she just let herself lean back against his chest? She could reach up and thread her fingers through his hair, keep him close. If she tilted her head a few degrees, their mouths would brush. Alex wasn't supposed to be scenting anyone, but her own inhales deepened, grew more urgent, her lips parting.

Just when she felt like she couldn't resist temptation a second longer—she had to kiss him, had to know—he dipped his chin, moving lower, inhaling against her nape, his breath warmer than the breeze.

It was all Alex could do to keep her knees from buckling. She ached for him to touch her. To make the promise of his proximity real. How was she supposed to run when this was over?

All of a sudden, Devin groaned like he'd caught something new in her scent. He surged forward, crowding against her, his big hand curling around her hip, holding her steady, holding her up as he traced her pulse point first with his nose and then with the flat of his tongue.

Alex moaned, openly needy.

He answered with the barest scrape of teeth against her throat, the soft suction of his lips, but in the next second the warmth of him was gone. Devin pulled back, panting, turning away to face the forest.

"Shit." He covered his face with his hands. "Sorry. Fuck."

Alex could tell by his voice, rough and guttural, that his fangs had descended.

She was grateful for the minute or two it took him to wrestle back control, to reset the shift, because it meant she could work to slow her own heart rate. This was supposed to be a challenge.

You can't just lie down and let him have you.

She had to run, to hide, to make him work.

"Alex," Devin said, returning to her with green eyes and blunt teeth, "can I ask you for something?"

"Like, a favor?"

He nodded.

"Sure, what is it?"

His face was serious, pained. "When we get down there and I find you, even if you're scared, don't run."

Alex swallowed against the connotations of that. Of getting captured. Surrendering her body as his hard-won prize.

She almost said *Never mind, I can't do this. At least not well.* Not when she wanted to be beneath him, arched in offering. For him to slice through her clothes with his claws and claim her in the dirt.

Reading so many E-rated werewolf fics in her formative years was really coming back to bite her in the ass.

Alex wasn't the one called by the moon's wild thrall. What was it about Devin Ashwood that constantly took a battering ram to her dignity?

"No problem." Her voice rang with false confidence. "I've got this." Alex cleared her throat. "You forget, I deal with animals all the time."

Devin laughed, the sound rough, brutal. "Trust me. It's not the same."

Before she could ask what he meant, he nodded at her pocket.

"You got that Taser?"

"Yes." Alex took out the device he'd ordered for her online, so he could see.

"Good." A vein in his forehead pulsed. "How much of a head start do you want?"

They decided on five minutes. Alex knew she couldn't afford to waste a second.

She broke off from the entrance to the glen at a full sprint, legs pumping, belly button sucked toward her spine like she'd learned from the Nike Run Club coach.

She was far from a seasoned athlete, but she'd discovered in high school that running made her brain feel better. She'd done enough turkey trots and charity 5Ks that she should be able to avoid completely embarrassing herself. At least for the first few rounds.

Normally, Alex wouldn't call herself a particularly competitive person. But something about Devin always made her want to show off.

Despite the fact that she was puny and human, she tried to think like a wolf. They took down prey larger and faster than themselves by leaning into every advantage they could find. Outside of the head start, Alex's best weapon was that she knew these woods. Along with her dad, these birch trees had practically raised her.

Following a bend in the dirt path, she cut for the shallowest part of the brook that intersected the glen. Alex slowed to navigate the slippery rocks as she forged the waterline, following the rushing water deeper into the forest. The cool stream lapped at her ankles, covering her tracks.

They'd agreed that she'd run, not that she'd make it easy on him.

The gentle roar of the stream covered Alex's hectic breath. She checked her watch. Barely a minute left before Devin came after her.

She lengthened her strides to match the growing shadows as the sun set. Up here, just a little farther, should be—yes, the remains of an abandoned handmade dam. Its stacked logs and branches had been systematically woven together with the bushes that kissed the shoreline, creating a natural wall. Alex knew the weak parts, where there was a rough hole small enough for her to push through and slip to the other side without going around. She leaned over to catch her breath, pressing her hand against the spongy surface of a moss-covered log.

It took only a handful of minutes: she heard Devin before she saw him. No animal crashed through undergrowth like that, not even a bear.

Alex crouched down, curling in on herself, grinning because there was no one to see. For all the ceremony she'd tried to bring to these trials, they were still playing a game, and the anticipation of getting caught evoked the same response as when she'd been young and less inhibited: a hectic heart, a light-headed giddiness, the dueling desires to evade and be found.

On her watch, the seconds ticked by, proof positive of her cleverness.

Devin's clomping footfalls splashed from behind her. God, at this rate he'd be soaked up to his knees. Was he making his presence known on purpose, worried about scaring her with his approach? He needn't have bothered. Alex trusted him, as irresponsible as that might seem. Besides, his wolf liked her.

She pulled up the hood of the sweatshirt she'd chosen specifically for this occasion until her head was covered, her face cast in shadow. Now they were really Little Red Riding Hood and the Big Bad Wolf. She smothered the threat of hysterical giggles with her fist. Hopefully Devin appreciated camp.

On the other side of the dam, she heard him skid to a halt, water slapping the shore in a small wave caused by his wake.

Even if he saw the hole she'd climbed through, there was no way for him to fit his hulking body in the same space. He'd have to go around to tag her, costing him more time.

Alex did not account for the wolf's ability to leap.

Devin landed in front of her with glowing eyes and claws, grinning around rapidly receding fangs. Before her eyes he reversed the shift, his teeth and hands and eyes all reverting to their human form as easily as someone might pull off a pair of sunglasses.

His control had gotten better since the ice bath. Much better.

"Did you see that?" His smile was the wildest part of his face.

"Yeah, well, don't get too cocky. We're just getting started." Alex dropped her eyes to her watch again, avoiding the way he made her warm all over.

"I know," Devin said—soft, eager, holding out a hand to help her climb out of her hiding place.

For the next chase, Alex switched strategies.

Halfway through her head start, she peeled off the trail and sacrificed precious seconds shrugging out of her sweatshirt and pulling off the tank top that clung to her slick skin. Zipping the sweatshirt back over her sports bra, she hid the tank among the leaves of a sword fern before gunning it in the opposite direction.

As she ran, the sun slipped beyond the horizon. Darkness fell rapidly, making each step more precarious, leaving the crescent moon as the sky's only beacon. Alex headed into a grove of tupelo trees. She pressed her back against the rough bark of a particularly wide trunk, listening for sounds of Devin's approach. All she heard was cricket song, cut by the occasional croak of frogs. She rested her palm over her own racing heart.

A slight breeze came from the east, deliciously cool against her sweaty neck. It was so good to get out of her head for a little while, to pretend she was something wild that belonged to the forest. She never would have guessed that she could have this much fun with Devin Ashwood. That he'd bring out parts of her—silly and soft—that she barely recognized.

Alex knew the exact moment that Devin found her tank top. Because he *howled*. The sound was deep and round, beautiful and haunting, caught somewhere between wolfish despair and human admonishment. The forest seemed to shiver, the night air holding its breath.

For a moment, Alex arched her neck, her own throat aching with the foolish wish that she had the ability to answer his call.

She pictured Devin bringing her shirt to his face and smothering himself in the fabric of the garment. The soft cotton still warm from the heat of her body. His eyes falling closed in concentration as he drenched himself in her scent, his entire body strung tight with urgency.

Another howl cut the air. This one louder. Closer. A warning. *He was coming for her.* A promise. *He would always come for her.*

It got harder to stay still.

She could hear Devin whipping through branches at the entrance to the grove; any second now he'd spot her. Alex drummed her fingers against her bare thigh.

Her mistake was looking over her shoulder, locking eyes with him on his approach. His irises flashed silver in the blue-black dark.

Alex's breath caught.

Predator, her body said, flooding her nervous system with a cocktail of cortisol and adrenaline.

Squirrels clamored up trees to avoid him. Overhead, birds abandoned their nests.

It wasn't conscious, what came next.

Bracing one hand on the tree, she shifted into a sprinter's lunge.

"Alex," Devin shouted, and there was panic in his voice, his glowing eyes blown wide. "Don't."

It was too late. She pushed off the tree, kicking up dirt under her well-worn running shoes.

Her screaming instincts refused to be denied. Fight or flight, and she'd chosen the latter.

Alex pumped her arms and legs as fast as she could. Her heart thrashed in her chest.

Don't run. He'd warned her. Like a monster in a fable.

There was a rush of air as he picked up speed behind her, closing the distance.

A fluttery anticipation filled her belly—she was about to be caught.

Devin crashed into her, the force enough to send them both tumbling to the ground. He cradled her head as they fell but she still went down hard, her back hitting the grass with teeth-rattling force. Alex gasped in a breath, her nose full of the damp musk of churned earth.

Devin had her pinned before she could blink, both her wrists collected and held over her head, his claws scraping in the dirt. His thighs pinned hers on either side, the weight of him immovable. Inevitable.

"Sorry," he said around his fangs. "God—just—give me a minute."

His nose was in her hair again, but this time there was nothing controlled about it. He took great, greedy gulps of her scent. Like she'd long denied him something he needed to survive.

Heat stoked the fire behind Alex's already flushed cheeks. She should be afraid. He was still in the partial shift, his eyes glowing unnaturally, but all she wanted to do was wrap her legs around his waist and let him have her.

She must have read a hundred fics where Colby was feral for his mate, driven out of his mind with the urge to mount and mark. Leave it to Alex to confuse fantasy for reality.

"It's okay." She had done this to herself. Primed whatever wires had crossed in her brain to make this objectively terrifying development sexy.

"Is it?" Devin's voice was hoarse, laced with self-loathing.

But that wasn't fair. He'd warned her not to run. Alex was the one who had broken the rules. She didn't blame him for doing what his body demanded.

"Hey," she said, sharp enough to make him look at her. "I know you won't hurt me." At least, not like this.

Devin's eyes cleared, the silver evaporating like so much smoke, giving way to familiar and equally impossible green.

"I'm not worried about *hurting* you." He sounded appalled.

What? "Then why are you apologizing?"

"Alex," Devin choked, shifting his hips like he was terrified he might press against her.

"You can tell me." She'd spent her whole life greedy for him. His body, sure, but also his secrets.

"I can't." He shook his head. "You don't understand. The way you smell to me." Devin clenched his jaw, making the muscles twitch. "It's unreal."

"What does it smell like?" Alex bit her lip. She didn't wear fragrances, so what could there be? Salt and warm skin?

"You'll think it's weird." Devin dropped his gaze, but his thumb ghosted absently over the inside of her wrist where her pulse beat, the edge of a claw whispering across her skin. "I don't want you to get the wrong idea."

Alex softened at his obvious embarrassment. "I won't."

"Fine." Devin sighed. "You smell . . ." he began, then mumbled, "like you were made for me."

Her breath stuttered. He shouldn't be allowed to say things like that. Not to her.

She'd learned from her mother at fifteen that neither vows nor blood made people belong to each other.

But Alex was weak. The whole stoic apathy thing she had going on externally had always been a flimsy front. You couldn't offer someone something like this—a fantasy so vividly brought to life—and expect them to turn it down.

"Devin." Alex barely recognized her own voice, pitched below her normal alto with desire. "Tell me why you're holding my wrists."

He winced. "Uh. No. It's not very *gentlemanly*."

"You're not a gentleman." It wasn't an admonishment.

Devin laughed, the sound filled with relief. His body relaxed enough for the fangs to recede.

He let go of her wrists and leaned back until he was balanced on his knees, giving her space to get out from under him if she wanted to.

Alex didn't. She propped herself up on her elbows, closing some of the distance between them once again.

He dragged his hand through his hair, his nails returned to normal.

"You wanna hear that it's all I can do right now not to flip you over in the dirt and ride you until your knees buckle?" Devin closed his eyes like the words cost him. "That I've never wanted anything in my entire goddamn life more than I wanna shove aside those goofy little shorts you've got on and eat you out until you're writhing, whimpering, because the only word you can remember is my name?"

"Yes," Alex said, desperate and defiant, pressing her thighs together.

Devin's eyes snapped open. "What do you mean 'yes'?"

There was so much danger here. Alex felt it in the air, in the stillness. The sun had set while they played. And now there was only the moon to see by, a silver specter in this grove of shadows. It was easy to pretend she was somewhere else in that darkness. The glen was as black as her bedroom with the curtains closed. As black as the back of her eyelids when she closed her eyes.

"I mean I want that. You." She could be brave right now because he believed she was. Besides . . . "You can tell, can't you?"

Devin swallowed thickly, his nostrils flaring. "It's not the first time you've smelled like you want me. I don't assume that just because you're—"

She reached up and cupped his jaw, half-terrified of her own impulse to be soft with him.

"You're not assuming. I'm telling you."

"I'm a lot bigger than you." He leaned down to nuzzle her throat, his nose brushing her dewy skin.

Alex fought a shiver at the hint of danger in his voice, the trace of the beast. She wanted his tongue against her tendons again, his teeth on her tender nerves.

"A lot stronger." He kissed just behind her ear. "I could bend you in half before you could blink."

"I'm trying to get you to." Alex groaned. "Will you please shut up and kiss me?"

"Yeah?" He pulled back to check her face. "Oh, thank fuck."

He nosed at her clavicle, then down her sternum, pushing up her sweatshirt to rub his cheek against her belly. Devin nipped at her hip through her shorts, working his way toward— *Oh.*

That wasn't what she'd meant by "kiss," but Alex readily accepted the substitution.

He closed blunt teeth against the sensitive skin of her inner thigh, scraping across the tattooed skin, teasing, before ducking to place a hot, openmouthed kiss over her cloth-covered entrance, his nose pressing hard against her pubic bone.

Alex's hips jumped without her permission. She was half-terrified she'd give him a concussion, but he just moaned.

"Can I take these off?" He tugged at the waistband of her shorts. "They're in my way."

"Yeah." Alex was trying so hard not to say, *Whatever you want.*

She pressed her feet flat on the grass and pushed up onto her shoulder blades.

"Nice." He still had the goofiest grin.

Devin reached behind his neck and pulled his T-shirt over his head, then spread the fabric out below her ass.

"Thanks." Alex laughed, the sound high-pitched and semi-

hysterical, at the unexpected consideration. The ripple of muscles across his abdomen was falsely familiar and strangely dear.

Devin grunted. He didn't bother to try to take her shorts
and underwear all the way off, just yanked until the fabric
bunched at her ankles and she had to toe them off herself.

He hauled her forward, cupping her bare ass in both of his
big hands and pushing her knees toward her ears so he could
slide his head between her thighs and hook her legs over his
shoulders.

"Oh my god." Alex covered her face with her forearm as
Devin licked a broad stripe from her entrance to her clit.

Who did she think she was—lying half-naked in the middle
of the forest with Devin Ashwood between her legs and nothing
but a thin barrier of sweat-soaked cotton between her and the
dirt? Things like this didn't happen in real life. But then again,
she supposed, neither did werewolves.

"Fuck." He leaned against her thigh and looked up at her, his
pretty pink lips wet. "How have you been running around like
this?"

Before she could answer, he put his whole face back in her
cunt. Alex was honestly shocked. Werewolf or not, this man was
famous. He looked like a Pre-Raphaelite angel. He didn't have
to work this hard, dragging his tongue slow and precise around
her clit.

Alex slumped back in the dirt, spreading her legs wider in
his grip.

"Do you like—" he came up to ask.

"Yes—god." Alex shoved him back down. She did not want
him looking at her fucking face right now.

She kept her palm on the back of his head, cupping the base
of his skull, the silky strands of his hair brushing her knuckles
while his mouth worked.

Every time she made a sound for him—a gasp, a sigh, a mortifying little whimper—he'd say, "That's it, baby. You're doing so good."

Alex wasn't doing anything. She was lying here, letting him lick her pussy. She should tell him to stop calling her baby. The problem was she liked it. She liked all of it.

The way he kept groaning and taking little breaks to breathe against her thigh, like getting to do this, to touch her, taste her, was too good. Too much. The way he kept tracing his tongue around her clit made Alex forget to breathe, until the constellations overhead began to blur and spin. God, she was already close, her thighs shaking, her stomach clenched.

At this rate she was gonna come in like two minutes. Which, yeah, was not an option. Devin would never let her live it down. She swore if he brought up her crush on him after this—

He teased her entrance with his fingertips. "Can I?"

"Yes."

He kept making her say yes like he got off on it. Like he needed the confirmation almost as much as she did that this was real.

Alex trembled when he slid inside her, clenching so hard around his finger he gave her another almost immediately.

"You look so sweet like this, all slick and open for me." Devin sounded wrecked, his voice low and rough.

God, he was good. *Fuck*—she arched her back as he altered the angle. Good at paying attention, finding her weaknesses and exploiting them. It probably helped that he could hear her heartbeat.

But it was also just that it was him. Devin Ashwood kissing her. Devin Ashwood pressing his tongue inside her. Devin Ashwood closing his plump lips over her clit.

The slick sound of him working her over was almost as loud as her desperate breath in her ears.

He made her so hot. His earnestness and his grin and the way he was so proud of himself for pleasing her. Despite all her better instincts, Alex liked him. So much. She could admit it now, in the dark, silently to herself, only after he'd pinned her thighs to the ground.

I don't want you to get the wrong idea, he'd said.

And she wouldn't. This was sex. Just sex. If they both knew that, why should Alex hold back? Why couldn't she have this, have him, for at least a little while?

She lost track of time while Devin stretched her out on his fingers. His hands were maybe more possessive than his mouth, the way he held her up, held her close.

Pleasure built, bright and insistent, in her core until she was coming in a sweaty shock, clenching, making desperate little noises she would absolutely deny on her deathbed.

That was what did it for her in the end, not the perfect pressure or the way he curled just right inside of her. It was him saying "yes" and "baby" and "Alex, *god*, Alex."

Devin eased her through the aftershocks, softening his lips and stilling his hand.

Only when she'd caught her breath did he ease out and lower her back onto his T-shirt.

He wiped his mouth on his bare forearm and then, on second thought, licked that too.

"*Devin.*" Alex was scandalized even with her thighs still trembling.

He grinned at her. "What's up?"

What's up? Jesus Christ. Alex wriggled back into her underwear and shorts.

"Do you want me to . . ." She inclined her chin toward his hard-on.

"Fuck." He shivered and reached down to palm himself before yanking his hand away and sitting back on his heels. "No. I—I don't think we should."

"Oh." A wave of embarrassment washed over her. "Okay, sorry." She guessed the heat of the moment had passed?

"No, wait, it's not that I don't want to," Devin rushed to say. "Trust me. I've been fantasizing all week about doing stuff with you I can't even spell."

Oh. Alex could still feel her heartbeat between her legs.

"But I'm already close." He gritted his teeth.

"To orgasm?" That didn't seem like a bad thing.

He nodded. "But to shifting too." He gazed at her lips. "I want you so much. It feels compulsive. Untamable."

Even though his eyes were back to their human green color now, his pupils were totally blown. Had Alex ever seen anyone this cunt drunk?

He swiped at the corner of his mouth with his thumb and then brought that digit into his mouth. "Right now, after getting to touch you and taste you, I just—I don't trust myself not to shift."

"No, I understand." It made sense, even if Alex was disappointed.

"I think I could work myself up to it. To letting go without losing myself completely. Assuming you ever wanna do this again . . . ?"

Alex laughed. "I wanna do it again." The understatement of the year. Of the century. "It's gonna get harder, the closer we get to the full moon," she warned him.

"That's good though, right? That's the point of the trials. To test my resolve."

"Yeah. That's the point." Somehow these trials had become tests for both of them.

And the thing was, in any fantasy she'd ever had about Devin Ashwood, she'd never bothered to imagine what came after the orgasm. And if she had, it wouldn't have been this: pulling him down next to her until both of them lay on their backs in the dark forest, a few minutes of comfortable stillness before he very quietly said, "Thanks."

"For letting you . . ." Alex turned on her side to look at him and sort of waved below her waist.

"No." Devin laughed, the corners of his eyes crinkling. "I mean, yes, for that too." His eyes turned darker, dirtier, for a second. "Don't get me wrong. I'm grateful." He sucked his bottom lip into his mouth. "But I meant for helping me figure out how to live as a werewolf. For the first time in a long time, I'm starting to feel like I might be okay."

Alex didn't know what to do with that. The significance of the moment caught somewhere in her chest.

"You know this part of the forest really well," he said, covering for her hitch of breath by changing the subject. "I would have caught anyone else a hell of a lot quicker. But you knew exactly where to turn, where to step, how to muffle your scent."

Alex couldn't help smiling at besting him, even if it had been short-lived. "I grew up coming here with my dad."

She stared up at the canopy of dark leaves rustling overhead.

"I used to think this forest was the most magical place in the world. Our town is small and pretty pedestrian obviously, but this place? Anyone could be a heroine here." She held her breath and listened to the symphony of animal night song. The croaking *ribbets* and the crinkling of wings. "I used to run around pretending I was being chased by bandits or discovering mysterious magical herbs."

"Oh, I see." Devin's gaze warmed with something Alex could only call affection.

"What?" She patted ineffectually at her tangled hair.

"You've always been a huge nerd."

"Okay. Shut up." Alex nudged him gently with her elbow.

She was glad for the lightness of him, the way he made talking about her childhood not only possible but somehow easy. Even the parts she would have sworn were rusted over.

"I used to come out here because I felt caged in Tompkins, but I don't feel like that anymore. I know this place is small and messy. For a long time, I couldn't look past all the same flaws my mother saw, but it's been a while since I was here against my will." She couldn't pinpoint when the transition occurred exactly. It might have been when she met Rowen. Or when Seth decided he was her friend. "For better or worse, I chose this. All of it." Home.

"There's a lot more to Tompkins than I thought," Devin said in a way that made Alex think he didn't just mean the town. "I like it."

"All right. You don't have to lie."

"No, really. When you were a kid, you used to pretend you were running around with magical elves or whatever—"

"I did not say anything about elves!"

"—but I always wanted to know what it would be like to have a lemonade stand or go to a high school football game."

"Both of those things are boring." This man went to awards shows and partied on yachts.

"Okay, but hear me out." He propped himself up on his elbow. "Your town, the people in it, yeah, they've got problems. But they're average, relatable, real. It's like my close, personal acquaintance Matthew McConaughey is always saying, 'Hollywood is *The Matrix*.' I was basically born plugged in."

Alex had never really thought about that. The way his parents had brought him out there so young. How he'd never known anything else.

Devin ducked his chin so his hair fell into his eyes, hiding them from Alex's view. "I always wished I knew what it felt like to be normal." His voice was rough and almost a whisper. "I guess now I'll never know."

17

DEVIN DESERVED A fucking medal. He'd followed a "moral compass" for the first time in his life last night and—heads up—it sucked ass. Not only did he go home with a lethal-level case of blue balls, but then he got up the next day to do community service. The worst part was, he wasn't even mad.

He caught himself humming on his way to the community center. At first he thought it was just because the truck was still sexy as hell. But no. He was excited. Like he had bugs in his stomach or whatever, just because he got to see this place Alex cared about so much.

It was probably because she was discerning, hard to win over. She didn't get worked up over just anything. But also, it was nice to have plans for one night that didn't revolve around trying to keep the monster inside him at bay.

The closer he got to the address in his GPS, the sweatier his hands felt on the steering wheel. He would have wiped them off on his pants, but they were linen. For no particular reason. It wasn't because today was a no-scrubs day.

Devin liked Alex in scrubs. They had a lot of engineering

advantages. Elastic waistband for easy access (up until now this only factored in his imagination, but considering recent developments he felt it was still worth noting). No back pockets obstructing his view. But no-scrubs day meant he might get to see more of Alex's tattoos.

He'd been so distracted last night he hadn't even gotten it together long enough to unzip her sweatshirt. He shook his head. Rookie mistake.

He didn't have to wait long to be disappointed. Almost as soon as he walked through the double front doors, Alex made a beeline for him. God, she was wearing loose fucking cargo pants and a ratty Joni Mitchell T-shirt and he still wanted to pin her down and lick her neck. Unbelievable.

Devin gave her his best panty-melting grin until he clocked the harried expression on her face plus the turquoise-haired teenager at her side. He quickly rearranged his features into something less lecherous.

"Devin, this is my friend Rowen." She gestured at the teen in the sick distressed leather jacket with a neon pin that read *they/them.*

"Rowen, this is Devin Ashwood, and he'd love to help you check in guests and pass out their bingo cards."

"Uhh . . . I would?" He thought his appearance here tonight was an act of service in and of itself.

"Yes," Alex said firmly, "because thanks to your very generous donation last week, we have triple the turnout we were expecting and not enough volunteers."

"Oh." You'd think giving away a bunch of money would make people nicer to you.

Alex rushed off, abandoning him to spontaneous labor.

"You think she's avoiding me because she likes me?" he asked Rowen, watching her go.

They shrugged. "I don't pretend to understand the mating rituals of millennials."

"I'm actually Gen X."

Rowen stared at him blankly. "Never heard of it."

They led Devin to a big open gymnasium space with one of those old-school wooden podiums by the door. There, they showed him how to check people's tickets and find their corresponding table on the floor from the array of matching brown folding ones set up in long rows.

"I like your pin," he said, by way of making conversation. "Did you make it yourself?"

Rowen looked up from the seating chart. "Alex got it for me. I usually only wear it in places where I feel safe, like here or band practice, but a few of my friends have made their own now, so sometimes we wear them at school. It's easier when more people wear them."

"Oh yeah?" Using a Post-it and a paper clip, Devin fashioned himself a *he/him* pin to match Rowen's.

"Is this okay?" he asked, sticking it to his shirt through a buttonhole.

The teen nodded, smiling a little at his shitty handwriting before returning to their work.

Looking around, Devin could see, weirdly, why people liked this place. It was kinda dated—with orangey seventies hardwood floors and a ceiling made of those soft porous-looking square panels—but it was obviously well loved. Someone had hand-painted a mural on all four walls.

It might have been Ocala Forest, but instead of using dark greens and browns and grays—the colors Devin would have chosen—the artist had mostly worked in shades of blue and violet; soft, warm corals; and minty greens. On one side, a mas sive violet black bear climbed a tree so large the leaves bled onto the ceiling.

The wolf *loved* it. The art—like most things, to be fair—made him want to run, to feel the wind in his face. Devin found himself agreeing with his wild side more and more. Having these impulses fed to him was almost like having a creative collaborator—he got bursts of inspiration, feedback to his ideas. It reminded him a little of being on set. Only unlike the writers room, the wolf often approved of what Devin suggested.

Alex had definitely been right: suppression actively made his condition worse. Right after the first change, the wolf constantly barreled against Devin's mind, trying to get out, to get through. Since he'd added daily yoga and meditation into his morning routine, the early onslaught of impulses had faded, even as the full moon approached. Now the wolf mostly only showed up when coaxed. Devin almost felt comfortable in his own skin again. Like the wolf had settled. Made himself at home.

Devin still worried about the risks of shifting at the wrong time, and the prospect of the physical changes promised by the full moon hung, no pun intended, over his head. But he'd gotten so much better at controlling himself. *Well, mostly.* He'd worked himself into a sore jaw last night. He smirked. *Worth it.*

Rowen flipped a pen back and forth across their knuckles while they waited for the first attendees to arrive.

"So what's your deal?" They looked up at him from behind their bangs. "It's pretty random that you'd come to Tompkins for a month to prepare for a role."

Devin tugged at the collar of his shirt. The local dry cleaner must have used starch. "Well, you know, this place has a lot to offer."

"Like . . ." Rowen raised their eyebrows.

He looked frantically out the window and saw one of those ridiculous yellow *Hooves Crossing* signs.

". . . Horses."

"Horses," they repeated skeptically. "You been spending a lot of time at the track?"

"Well, no." Man, this kid was making him sweat. "But I have been kinda bonding with this older horse, Lou, at Alex's vet."

"Oh." Rowen stopped spinning the pen. "Is your next project something to do with rehabbing former racehorses? Because we could really use more awareness about how many of them get discarded by the system."

Damn. Now, there was a good cover story. Specific with a heartstrings-tugging hook. He should have used that from the beginning. Rowen was a genius.

"Uh, yeah," Devin said, guilt gnawing a little on his vocal cords. "That's exactly right." Lou wouldn't mind covering for him.

The idea that Devin might somehow help Tompkins's abandoned horse population made Rowen warm to him. They even said they thought Colby was "an early aughts bisexual icon."

It just made sense, once people started flooding in for bingo, for Devin to keep up the same cover story when locals tried to make small talk. He was surprised to find he was good at volunteering, at least the chitchatting portion. Obviously being a celebrity smoothed the way. It made people want to talk to him.

The residents of Tompkins seemed to relish this clearly delineated window where they could ask what he was doing in town, especially after his antics at the fair.

There was an easy assumption that he was interested in horse racing. Apparently quite a few Hollywood types had brought their cash to Tompkins over the years to try to invest or go big on a bet. As Devin checked tickets, passed out cards, and escorted little old ladies to their tables, his retired racehorse rescue story grew in detail like a massive ball of yarn.

By the time they rang the bell for the first game to start, he'd concocted a whole saga about his plans to buy farmland and set up an equine therapy program. People kept slapping his back and patting his arm and generally telling him what a welcome addition he was to town. They called him a "great guy" and thanked him for using his money and influence to do "such important work."

A lady who apparently worked on one of the local farms offered to cut him a deal on feed, and another couple gave him a card, said to call when he started looking for ranch hands.

Devin's throat got tight for a little while at the idea of being a contributing member of society beyond entertainment. In a pollen-allergy kinda way.

So what if he kinda wanted to play this new role, Devin Ashwood With Good Intentions? Sure, it was gonna be shitty when he went back to LA and they all found out he was just another rich asshole blowing smoke, but that was still a week away.

"You're pretty good at service work for a celebrity," Isaac Lawson said, coming to stand next to him at one point between rounds.

"Thanks." Devin shoved his hands into his pockets. "I did a stint in my twenties as one of those shirtless guys standing outside Abercrombie & Fitch at the mall."

"Right." Isaac's mouth twitched. "Well, I know Alex will be grateful. It's rare that she asks for help. You know what they say, 'The lone wolf dies but the pack survives.'"

Whoa. "That's deep." Devin felt like he should take notes. "Is that a finding from your conservation research?"

"Uh, no." Isaac gave him a look. "It's a quote from *Game of Thrones*."

"Oh. Right. Cool." Devin wouldn't tell anyone, but he felt a swell of pride at contributing. At almost belonging somewhere again. He'd been out of work long enough that he'd started to wonder if maybe he was no longer useful. What if the Internet was right: he was washed-up, a has-been?

Alex had a real job, plus she volunteered here at the community center, mentored Rowen, and looked after her dad. Devin didn't think he was lazy or anything. He'd worked long hours shooting, plus, especially in the early and latest seasons, he'd always hustled on promotion and PR. He worked out like a second full-time job. But he'd always had help.

When he was a kid, his parents were constantly around, until they weren't. But even in their absence he'd had a team of people, some of them better than others, looking after him, making tough calls on his behalf.

Alex took care of everyone, but as far as he could tell, no one really took care of her. Someone should get on that. Of course, they'd have to get past her walls before she let them.

The director of the community center, a tiny, angular woman named Beatriz, swung by his podium to thank him personally for his donation. "Would you ever consider teaching a course here? We do a summer stage program for ages five through eighteen."

"Oh, um, maybe." Devin couldn't bring himself to come out and say he wasn't staying in town long enough to see the seasons change.

Beatriz was telling him about last summer's production of *The Music Man* when Devin heard it—a change in Alex's heartbeat.

He hadn't realized, but the wolf must have kept an ear out.

Because Devin felt the sudden spike in her pulse rate echo in his own blood.

She didn't look any different, at least by the time he whipped his head around to check. Her expression was neutral as she handed out cups of punch on the other side of the room. But Devin followed the wolf's urging to end his conversation, to get closer to her, to investigate.

"You're sweaty," he observed when he got within a few feet of Alex. And not in the good way, like when he'd had her writhing beneath him.

She frowned at him. "Great, thanks."

He squeezed himself between the table where she'd set up the big punch bowl—its contents electric red with sherbet icebergs floating on top—and the wall, so he could stand beside her.

"What's wrong?" He lowered his voice. "Did someone insult your nose ring?"

"What? No." She glared at him but then brought her hand to her septum. "What's wrong with my nose ring?"

"Nothing. I like it," he said quickly and then found he wasn't lying.

First of all, it was subtler than he'd assumed, or at least he'd gotten used to it. But when he stopped to really look, the gold set off the dark coffee color of her eyes. Also, it made her look kinda naughty. Like a vampire or someone in a punk band. Alex would look hot playing bass. Or biting his neck. *Wait, what?*

"Don't come over here. Don't come over here," Alex said under her breath, looking toward some guy over by the door.

"Who is that?" Devin forcibly took the ladle from her; she'd been stirring so hard she'd splashed juice in a macabre spatter across the front of her flannel.

"His name's Taylor Chapman." Alex noticed the damage

spilled down her front—"Shit!"—and grabbed a rag. "He's this guy from Tampa I slept with a few times," she hissed.

"*You* slept with *that guy*?!" Devin supposed he was sort of handsome. In a Brooks Brothers kinda way. "He looks like he was breastfed until he was five."

"Oh my god." Alex slapped him on the arm.

"Here." He unbuttoned and shrugged out of his denim over-shirt. "You can put this on."

Alex stared at him like he'd stripped off and started whirling the thing like a lasso over his head.

"I can't wear your shirt."

"Why?"

She lowered her voice. "It's intimate."

Was she fucking kidding?

"Alex, I had your come dripping down my chin, like, twelve hours ago."

"*That's different.*" She covered his mouth with her palm, which, yeah, did not have the impact she thought it would. He took a big slutty inhale and then had to stop so he didn't go half-chub within ten feet of a bunch of grandmas.

Different how? Like he was good enough for sex but not some small gesture of familiarity?

"You're being unreasonable." He gestured to her chest—er, to the splotch—and felt his ears heat. "You look like you stabbed someone."

That much was true, but it wasn't the whole story. The wolf, poor confused bastard, mistakenly saw Taylor Chapman and his boat shoes as a threat. It would be best, he suggested, if Alex wore the protection of Devin's scent. So, whatever, they could kill two birds with one stone.

Alex peered down at the mess and then out of the corner of her eye at Captain Yacht Club and then sighed.

"Fine."

Devin stepped behind her, holding out the shirt like a jacket for her to slip into.

"What are you doing?" Alex tried to talk out of the side of her mouth. "I don't need you to put it on me."

This communication choice was completely ineffective as far as making their conversation incognito. In fact, it had the opposite impact, drawing attention to her lips, which, yeah, there weren't enough grandmas in the world; he was gonna have a situation.

"I'm being *nice.*" Also, his wolf had some possessive instincts Devin was going to have to work on when he got back to the hotel.

Alex looked over her shoulder at the shirt, then at Devin's face.

"Are you trying to scent me?"

"What? No. *You are.*" Shit. Why did she have to know so much about werewolves?

"Give me that." She tugged the shirt out of his hands, gently, and put it on.

His dick thought the mingling of his scent and hers in public was—uh, Something. When Alex turned back to the punch, Devin gripped the edge of the table and didn't stop until he heard the metal legs groan.

"Hey." Taylor Chapman definitely had veneers. Cheap ones. "You know where a guy can get some punch?"

To her credit, Alex didn't indulge this dopey joke. She handed him a cup, and not even one of the fuller ones. Though her heartbeat hadn't returned to a resting rate. "What are you doing all the way over here?"

"You mentioned you guys were doing this fundraiser a while back, and you seemed worried about attendance. Since I had the night off from the bar, I thought I'd come over. I know how much this place means to you."

So what? Devin wanted to say. Everyone knew how much this place meant to Alex. This guy thought he could play the hero, huh? *Chump.*

"Anyway." Taylor smiled, closemouthed and self-deprecating as he looked out at the crowd. "Guess you didn't need me. Nice work. And hey, isn't this the room where you did the mural?"

Alex nodded. Modest.

Devin ground his molars. He knew the brushstrokes felt familiar. Why hadn't he said something to her about the art when he'd first admired it? The wolf demanded to know every part of her. Now if Devin paid Alex a compliment on her work, she'd think he stole the idea from this finance bro.

The guy finally looked over at Devin, who might have, through no fault of his own, been glowering a little.

"Hey, man. I'm Taylor." He held out a tan hand.

Devin took it and did not let the wolf squeeze any harder than normal.

"Devin Ashwood." Okay, maybe a little harder than normal.

"Oh. Wait." Taylor leaned back to look at him. "Like, the actor?"

"Yeah." Devin, remembering he had a public persona to uphold, stood up a little straighter. He didn't always get recognized after he'd grown out his hair and beard during the pandemic, but it happened often enough, especially in context.

"I thought you were in rehab."

Alex stepped in front of him before he could work himself into a growl. "There's a good seat up front. You might want to snag it." She pointed and Taylor Chapman went.

Devin glowered. "Why that guy?"

"I don't know." Alex shook her head. "We met at a bar. He's

hot and rich. Guys like that aren't usually interested in me. When he asked me out, it seemed exotic. Interesting. You know. The chance to see how the other half fucked."

The wolf receded, deciding the perceived threat had been neutralized. Devin didn't agree. He kept his eyes on Taylor even as Alex passed out punch to other, nonthreatening guests.

In some ways, he liked when the wolf took the wheel on his emotions. Those impulses were always clear, strong, singular. Devin's own feelings? They were murkier and harder to pull apart.

He knew he didn't like Taylor Chapman and his easy smiles. But why, exactly?

It might be because he looked like he was actually six feet tall, unlike Devin, who was five ten, despite what it claimed on his IMDb page.

Grabbing a glass of punch, Devin downed it in one gulp.

It had been easy, these past couple of weeks, to pretend any sense of attraction he felt toward Alex came from somewhere inside him that was feral, other, wrong. But this feeling? This dizzy desperation? There was no denying that it was all him.

Maybe this draw to Alex wasn't just a sex thing. Maybe it was, like . . . a feelings thing? Where he didn't want her to be with anyone else because—

No. That couldn't be right.

Rowen called him over to help gather more chairs.

"Nice job today," Alex said later, brushing his forearm when they were folding up tables.

Devin beamed.

18

"YOU'RE IN A good mood," Seth said the next day at work during their overlap hour between shifts.

"What do you mean?" Alex whipped around, feeling caught for no good reason. She certainly hadn't been daydreaming about Possessive!Devin at the community center. The way his eyes went hot when she slipped on his shirt. It wasn't her fault. It was a beloved werewolf trope.

"You're humming while trimming Toast's nails," Seth pointed out.

Toast, the forty-pound Chihuahua-beagle mix on the exam table, grinned at her, his tongue flopping slightly out of his mouth.

Seth got up from where he'd been editing Toast's file on the exam room's ancient computer to come over and nudge her arm. "I recognize the signs of new love."

"Oh no. No, no, no." Alex winced. *That was too many nos.* "I've just been drinking more water."

Besides, it wouldn't be new love anyway. More like zombie love, brought back from the dead.

"Sure," Seth said in the voice of someone who very much didn't believe her. "Well, listen, I brought you something."

He dipped out of the room for a moment, then returned to hand her a brown paper envelope.

Alex opened the parcel to find a manga titled *One Piece*, the bright, playful illustration on the front immediately making her smile.

Seth pushed his hair out of his eyes. "It's the first volume of one of the greatest series of all time. I figured you needed an accessible entry point."

"Thank you." Alex hugged the gift to her chest, a piece of himself that Seth wanted to share with her. This was the deepest kind of friendship, in her opinion. Sharing stuff you loved, the stuff you got weird over, with someone else. Hoping they might get weird over it too.

"Does this mean I get to compile some of my favorite Kirk/Spock fanfic for you?" Alex considered herself an expert curator.

"Kirk/Spock, really?" Seth wrinkled his nose. "I always shipped the captain and Bones."

Alex smiled. "I can work with that."

It was the strangest thing in the world, that somehow Devin Ashwood visiting her hometown made her see it with new eyes. That his liking her made her like herself more. Enough to stop hiding in plain sight.

Seth gathered his stuff to head out but popped his head back in one last time to say good night.

"Hey, you know the guy you're definitely not falling for is outside, right?"

"What?" Alex looked up from where she was finishing with Toast.

"He stopped over a little while ago to hang out with Lou.

That horse is skittish around almost everyone, but for some reason he's calm around Devin."

"Probably because they're both high-strung and too pretty for their own good."

"For what it's worth"—Seth rapped on the doorway with his knuckles—"I always think it's a good sign when an animal likes someone."

Alex couldn't help thinking about Devin saying his wolf wanted to be around her.

"I've always thought that too," she said softly.

A bit later, after making sure Toast and the other patients were squared away, Alex headed out back.

She found Devin outside the fenced-in pasture, petting Lou's nose, their heads pressed together like coconspirators. They were quite the pair: beautiful, anxious, extraordinary, discarded.

Devin must have had prior exposure to horses. He moved around Lou too easily for the experience to be completely new. Alex knew he rode the same stunt horse for at least a few episodes when Colby went undercover as a Montana forest ranger in season 5, before, like everyone else that character loved, Brian Dempsey killed him off.

"Oh hey," Devin said when she approached. "Your face looks different."

Alex immediately thought he must see something revealing on her features. Some of her conflicted crush bleeding through.

But no. He squinted. "Did you move your eyebrows?"

Alex ignored him. It was possible that she'd put on a little more makeup than normal, some mascara and a few flicks of brow tint. Clearly, she shouldn't have bothered.

Their odd-couple friendship and even the sex might work against all odds, but every time she let herself think that maybe

Devin liked her—in a real, grown-up romantic way—he reminded her that was impossible.

"You hungry?" he asked somewhere around midnight when they sat in the office together: Alex catching up on data entry while Devin swiveled in Seth's chair, tossing a rubber-band ball from his desk in the air. "I bought food."

"Takeout?" She looked over eagerly.

"Better." He got up and grabbed a brown paper shopping bag from the break room. "I'm gonna cook."

"You realize we only have a microwave here, right?"

"Not a problem." Devin rooted around in the bag and came up with some kind of metal appliance. "Brought my own hot plate."

"Wow," Alex said. "What inspired this?"

"You always get hangry halfway through the shift."

"No, I—" Except, she did. Usually she started rooting around in her purse for dried mango around now. He'd noticed? *Wait—he cared?*

"I can hear your stomach," he reminded her.

Oh. Well, that was decidedly less sexy than listening to her heartbeat.

Devin began unloading several containers of Very Veggie Cup Noodles, a jar of crunchy peanut butter, and a bottle of hot sauce onto Seth's desk.

"Don't worry, recipe's vegan. I checked."

And so she watched in some combination of shock and awe as Devin Ashwood cooked for her.

He painstakingly used scissors to cut up scallions and squeezed lime on top before handing her a doctored foam cup of steaming noodle soup.

Alex sniffed a little, stirring the mixture and getting warm spice and nuttiness.

It might be glorified college dorm room food, but she couldn't help but be charmed by how nervous he looked waiting for her to take a bite.

"Well?" He had his hands on his hips, braced for her verdict.

Alex blew on a forkful and then took a bite. The flavors actually played together perfectly, sweet and salty with a bright acid pop.

"Pretty good." She hummed.

Devin finally pulled out a chair at the break room table and grabbed his own cup. "My mom used to make this for me."

"Oh?" The little he'd mentioned his parents since they met made Alex assume he didn't have any positive associations.

But of course that was never the whole story. As a child of divorce she knew better. Even after all these years, sometimes when she was sick or overtired, Alex fell asleep imagining her mom's hand in her hair, pushing back the wispy bangs she'd had as a preteen, her perfume like a field of wildflowers.

"Do you miss them? Your parents?" Alex held very still, not wanting to disturb whatever made him feel like sharing.

Devin stirred his noodles for a moment.

"I don't even know where they are. They could be dead. But I think I miss the idea of them. Not the parents they were but the parents I wish they'd been, ya know?"

Alex nodded. "I haven't spoken to my mom in over a decade," she said, the weight of it heavy and somehow shared.

"As a kid I got jealous watching *The Fresh Prince of Bel-Air*." Devin smiled ruefully. "Like, why didn't I have an Uncle Phil and Aunt Viv to take me in?"

The conversation shifted to lighter topics as they finished their meal. When Alex asked what Devin did during his downtime at the hotel, he admitted to watching *Wheel of Fortune* reruns when he wasn't working out or practicing meditation.

As she went back to updating patient files, he pulled up an episode on his laptop, scooting over in Seth's chair so they could both see.

"You're good," she accused, several rounds in. He kept solving the puzzles before the contestants.

He knuckled at his eyebrow sheepishly. "I used to watch a lot in my trailer on set."

Alex felt herself tucking this tiny detail away in the hope chest of her heart. This inconsequential fact about Devin Ashwood that would never make it into a magazine profile. That she could never tell her friends.

The group chat this morning was abuzz with the kind of daily life updates they shared like bulletins, knowing they'd get read at some point in their separate time zones. Cam's daughter was starting swimming lessons this week. Eliza secretly hooked up with her coworker on a business trip.

Alex's updates were stilted, edited around a huge Devin-shaped hole. The more time she spent with Devin, the more she wanted them to know, and the less Alex felt like she could tell them. The closer she got to him, the more distant she felt from her former self, the one that had once been a fan, then a hater. She was now somehow a friend . . . with benefits.

For so long, fangirl was the group chat's shared identity, the part that brought them together across time zones and space. By getting close to Devin, the real him, Alex forfeited that kind of relationship and in turn robbed her friends of some of the distance that made speculating about celebrities feel harmless and safe.

If Cam and Eliza knew how much time she spent with Devin, how he'd touched her, they'd be mortified. Cam had written in detail about a fictional version of him. Eliza probably still had sketches of his face saved in old notebooks. The NDA was a scapegoat keeping Alex from having to make the choice about whether to embarrass or hurt them.

Alex had underestimated the depths of this secret when she signed on to help Devin in that Dunkin' parking lot. She'd assumed this would be a fleeting interaction. That eventually it would become a story she could share without too extravagant an emotional cost. She thought she knew the narrative. *Devin Ashwood is eccentric. Devin Ashwood is obsessed with Colby.* She always assumed that video of him on the Venice Boardwalk would be the start of a great story, but Alex never imagined her role in it would be so . . . complicated.

At least hanging out with a werewolf who could sense changes in your core temp was convenient. Devin grabbed her sweatshirt off the hook by the door when the AC got a little carried away, draping it over her shoulders in the same moment that her arms broke out in goose bumps.

"Thanks," she said, turning and finding him closer than she'd anticipated, his hands braced on the back of her chair.

Spending time with him, trying to train him, it was all simultaneously harder and easier than she'd anticipated. She could rewatch and research and try to prepare herself a hundred different ways not to fall for him, but Alex had no defenses for the sweet swell of his cheeks when he smiled at her. For the way the heat he gave off made her want to curl around him.

While Devin harnessed his control, Alex was unraveling. And if he agreed to her idea for this last trial, she'd be going so much further.

"We should talk about the act of submission." She took pains not to whisper.

They'd both been avoiding the subject of the final test from the show. It was obviously the hardest to replicate. On *The Arcane Files*, Colby battled his mentor in a duel with wooden staffs. Despite every werewolf advantage, he'd had to learn to yield. To show respect. Humility.

Not exactly Devin's natural strengths.

"I know the most obvious replication would be for you to fight someone, but I don't actually think that's necessary," Alex said.

He came around to sit on her desk, facing her. "What do you mean?"

To buy herself time, Alex started twisting her hair into a bun.

Devin was distracted by the movement, tracking the flicks of her fingers against her nape.

"Well." She swallowed. "It's the submission that matters, right?"

"I mean, yeah, I guess. But what other type of submission is there?"

Alex stared at the ceiling.

"Seriously? Weren't you *People*'s Sexiest Man 2009?"

His green eyes widened as the full impact of what she was saying descended. He shifted a little, crinkling the papers under his butt.

"You want me to wear a collar?"

"Not necessarily." Alex fought a smirk. He really was an innocent Iowa farm boy deep down. "There are plenty of ways to explore that particular type of engagement."

"Okay." He blew out a long breath. "But who the hell am I gonna submit to?"

"Me, obviously."

He'd said he was too worried about provoking the shift if he lost control the other night, so this would be, like, an effective exercise to evaluate.

"You?" Devin blinked.

Cold dread raced down Alex's spine. Had she read something here completely wrong?

She thought this was a controlled way for them to pick up where they'd left off the other night in the forest. This took the explosive chemistry between them and shoved it in a neatly labeled box, making it useful. Professional, even. But if he didn't want to . . .

"Or we could find someone else," Alex offered.

"No." The word was out of his mouth so quickly it seemed like a reflex, like the doctor tapping your knee and making you kick. "It's just"—he ducked his chin—"are you sure you're up for it? No offense, but you were pretty . . . accommodating the other night."

"Excuse me." Her unease burned up in a flash of mortified indignation. "Are you calling me easy?"

Just because she'd spread her thighs for him in the woods didn't mean she couldn't also bring him to his knees.

"We're talking about power exchange here." Devin held up his hands. "I won't pretend to be an expert, but I've seen enough porn to know that shit requires a certain, you know"—he pounded his fist into his palm—"authority."

Alex crossed her arms. "I assure you I can handle myself."

She might have been born weak for Devin Ashwood, but she didn't have to let him know that.

"All right." He still sounded doubtful. "I'm in. Letting you boss me around the bedroom sounds way better than getting my ass kicked."

"To be clear, we both need to take the objectives of the trial seriously. This is about you giving up control. My participation will be purely as a facilitator."

"Whatever you say, boss." Devin smirked.

"I'm serious." Alex found herself on her feet, her face hot. "This is a professional arrangement. I might not even get off."

And then Devin did the worst thing he could have possibly done. He laughed.

"Sure."

"I don't see why I would." The tops of Alex's ears were on fire. "You, on the other hand, should prepare to be put through the ringer."

"Alex," he said, like she was being silly.

"Devin," she replied, like the word tasted sour.

He shook his head as he got to his feet. "Are we really doing this?"

Alex raised her chin. "Unless you don't think you can handle it."

"Oh, I can handle it." His eyes sparkled.

"We'll see," Alex said. She was taking great care not to think about him naked, his neck straining as he panted while she denied him over and over and over.

"Yeah, we will," Devin said, closing the meager distance between their mouths until their lips barely brushed. "Because you know I can smell you." He closed his eyes and inhaled. "I can hear your heartbeat."

Like a call and response, her pulse sped up.

"I can taste every emotion you don't want me to know." Devin lowered his mouth to the hollow of her throat, flicking his tongue against her skin.

Alex made a small, high sound through her nose.

His eyes flashed silver for just a second. "You think you can stay coolly detached while you fuck me? Try it."

Alex's cheap bralette did nothing to hide the fact that her nipples went tight at the gravel in his voice.

"You're real tough, aren't you, baby? So goddamn hard to please." Devin traced the shell of her ear with his lips. "But my face does it for you, my voice."

He placed a featherlight kiss on her nape. "You know I'd fuck you until you cried if you let me."

Alex closed her eyes, leaned into it.

"So go ahead," he said, mouth against her skin. "Put me on my knees and make me edge myself for hours. Suck my dick until I'm begging. Maybe, when you get really needy, you'll decide to ride me. But just so we're on the same page, *when* you come—the second that pretty cunt starts to flutter—I'm gonna fucking know."

The Third Trial, wiki article #608

An act of submission is the third of <u>The Guild's</u> trials to prepare Colby Southerland for the responsibility of being a werewolf. In order to prove that <u>The One</u> will not use his powers in reckless self-interest and instead always be mindful of his gifts, he must fight and lose to his mentor in a physical battle.

19

DEVIN HAD A plan. Alex wanted to keep him at arm's length? She wanted to pretend there was nothing between them but some not-so-sacred mission? Clearly, this woman was afraid of her feelings. Well, tough nuts, honey, because he was gonna woo the shit out of her. There was something between them. Something good. He was gonna be romantic as fuck until she saw him as more than a passing amusement. Because Alex made him want to be someone real. The kind of guy who drove her to work during storm season because her shitty little car couldn't handle wet roads.

Except, once you've sponsored a girl's favorite nonprofit and publicly defended her honor in a dunk tank, renting a cabin on the lake for the long weekend felt like pretty small potatoes.

Devin did it anyway. There was nothing romantic about his hotel room with adjoining conference suite, and no offense to Isaac, but Devin would really rather rail Alex without her dad fifty feet away.

He knew he'd need a different approach to make her see that he actually cared about her, not just what she could do for him. A few hours before they headed out of town for their third trial, aka marathon sex session (because let's be real, while he did want to prepare as much as possible for the full moon, they probably could have skipped this one once they decided they were against the more violent options for re-creation), he made himself a list.

- Listen to her when she talks.
- Ask her questions.
- Let her pick the music in the car.

It was the little things that mattered, he'd decided. Grand gestures were kinda cheap, especially since he was rich and famous.

Devin picked her up in the truck. Alex looked a little surprised when he took her bag, but carrying it made him feel like boyfriend material.

Overall, he could mostly resist the urge to press his nose against her skin and simply content himself to be near her, hooked up to a steady stream of the feel-good pheromones he got from her scent. Only occasionally did an extra-strong whiff make him go jelly-kneed.

Her bag smelled of her, warm and dark. As he brought it toward his face, trying to sneak a subtle sniff, the weight of it made his forearms pull. What did she have in here? Whips? Chains? It didn't clank when he shook it.

"What are you doing back there?" Alex called, twisting around in the passenger seat.

"Nothing." He tossed the thing in and closed the truck lid.

Everything was going according to plan until about fifteen minutes into the hour-long drive when Alex brought up safe words and Devin almost drove off the side of the road.

"Guess I need one of those, huh?" He'd seen *Fifty Shades of Grey*. That dude had a whole contract.

"Yes, definitely." Alex leaned down and pulled out a note-book from the backpack at her feet. "Let's talk through what we're comfortable trying and what we're not."

"I'm really not into pain," Devin admitted, "giving or re-ceiving."

His ex had brought home a pair of nipple clamps at one point near the end of their marriage. He tried the tiny metal device on himself before agreeing to use them on her and ended up biting his tongue so hard from the pain that he couldn't eat spicy food for a week.

"Me neither," Alex said. "I think we can just focus on con-trol, making sure you can give it up."

"Do you have, like . . . *scenarios* in mind?" Man, he was too old to be this sheepish discussing sex, but Alex was nearly a de-cade younger and she had all those tattoos. She probably liked stuff he'd never even heard of.

The air in the cab filled with the metallic scent of Alex's nerves as her pulse elevated. Her knee bobbed a few inches from the hem of her skirt. Devin didn't tease her for dressing up, but he damn sure noticed.

She tapped the pen against her mouth. "How do you feel about being restrained?"

"Uh . . ." His dick pressed against his zipper just from hear-ing her say it. "Positive?"

Maybe she did have ropes in that bag. Devin tried to create the vision in his head and met an instinctual resistance to the physical vulnerability, especially in an unfamiliar environment with unknown threats.

"My wolf might be a baby about it," he warned her.

Devin's primal side didn't like the idea of leaving Alex un-guarded. He didn't realize how well she could fend for herself.

Alex nodded. "That means we're on the right track from a trial perspective."

Right. The trial. Alex always managed to sew their intimacy up with tight little boundaries.

I might not even get off.

Yeah, not if he had anything to say about it.

They spent the rest of the ride discussing everything from STI status (negative) and birth control (Alex's IUD plus condoms) to aftercare preferences (Devin's: cheese). Even the nonsexy stuff was somehow sexy in Alex's husky voice, trapped in the car with the scent of their mutual desire.

Who knew discussions of consent could be like foreplay? Listening to Alex talk about what she wanted to do to him, telling her what he liked in increasingly breathless detail. By the time they pulled up to the Airbnb, Devin's dick was leaking in his jeans.

He opened the car door and gulped fresh air, trying to clear his head enough to enter the house's security access code.

Aside from the advantage of being set on forty desolate acres with an electrified perimeter fence originally built to keep out (other) wild animals, the place they currently occupied had sixteen-foot wood-beam ceilings, a giant stone fireplace, and plenty of cozy, if rustic, furniture in shades of cream and forest green.

Too bad Devin couldn't stop pacing long enough to appreciate any of it. He kept picking up things—candlesticks, the remote, a coffee-table book on elk—and putting them back down in different places.

His skin felt too tight, the air blowing across it too much. How was he supposed to prove himself to Alex when he was already this close to the edge?

He went for a run at noon, trying to exhaust himself. Devin didn't bother measuring in minutes or miles, just kept cutting through the trees until his muscles burned and he couldn't catch his breath.

After a shower, during which he took great pains not to think too hard about Alex getting up close and personal with certain parts of his anatomy, Devin threw on a new clean pair of jeans and a T-shirt that stretched across his chest and biceps.

On second thought, he added underwear. Alex mentioned orgasm denial in the car, and he didn't need his hard-on getting cheese grated against his zipper.

He wandered into the kitchen to find her laying out a big salad and opening a bottle of red wine at the massive dining table.

"Good thinking keeping things light," he said a few bites in, crunching Tuscan kale and crisp, tart apple. "I don't feel sexy after I eat a lot of carbs."

Alex's mouth twisted up around the rim of her wineglass.

She watched him wash the dishes with a similar note of amusement.

"What, you think just because I can afford housekeeping, I don't know how to be polite?"

"I didn't say anything," she said, leaning back against the counter and openly admiring his ass.

"Mm-hmm. Pass me that dish towel."

After, Alex led him into the lodge-style living room. She'd placed a heavy-looking armless wooden chair with a wide, smooth seat and thick block legs in the center of the room's woven rug. A length of nylon rope sat innocently coiled on the seat.

She picked it up and slipped her forearm through the center.

"Have a seat."

Devin's heartbeat broke into a sprint.

He was going to lose control tonight, one way or another. Worse, he wanted it.

Once he followed her directions, Alex knelt before him holding his gaze, her little skirt keeping her thighs pressed tight.

Okay, the size-medium T-shirt he'd picked for tonight might have been a mistake; he was basically a bosom-heaving pirate wench over here.

With someone else, this would have been weird. The squirming anticipation, the chance for the power exchange to fall flat. But because it was Alex, Devin forgot to be self-conscious. He was too caught up in her proximity. In the shiny sheet of her hair as she pushed it behind her shoulder.

The flimsy silk top she was wearing left her back exposed, slipping down past the wings of her shoulder blades. His palms itched with the urge to slide across the warm, naked skin there, tantalized by the fact that he couldn't, not until she said so.

With deft, confident movements, she tied his ankles to the front legs of the wooden chair using complex knots, explaining as she went about different methods involving columns and squares. Either Alex had a sailing background he didn't know about, or she'd done her homework. He wanted to ask if she'd tried this kind of thing before with other partners, but the wolf didn't want to know the answer. Possessive animal.

Alex paused before moving on to securing his arms, tilting her head as her gaze raked over him.

"Take off your shirt," she said, only a hint of hesitation undercutting the casual command.

He looked down at her with his chin lowered, mock innocent.

"You don't want to do it yourself?"

Alex huffed through her nostrils but reached for his hem. She let her fingertips graze beneath his navel, teasing the coarse hair above his waistband until he sucked in a rough gasp, contracting the muscles.

She leaned across him, letting her hair brush his neck, giving him a heady whiff of her scent *on purpose.* "I don't need to."

Touché. Devin chewed the inside of his cheek and reached to do her bidding.

He threw his T-shirt onto the overstuffed leather sofa across the room. Cool air from the AC raised goose bumps on his bare chest. He let his arms fall backward and flexed his fingers in invitation.

Alex moved to kneel behind him. The tease of not being able to see her but having her scent so close, her breath against his neck, somehow got him even harder than watching her bend over. He'd been so worried about the wolf getting skittish, but the beast trusted Alex. He was content, as Devin was, to sit and let her lead.

Alex looped each of his wrists several times in the coarse rope, then knotted between them so they were held neatly in place without chafing together. Devin almost swooned. She was so fucking competent.

"How does that feel?" Alex got to her feet when she was done, backing up to examine him from different angles.

Devin tested the knots, tensing his muscles and trying to force his body up, straining, until finally he slumped back in his bonds.

"Impressive," he said, proud that his voice didn't shake. Whatever she'd done was strong enough to hold a werewolf a week out from the full moon and yet still remarkably comfortable. He could probably break the chair by slamming it against the ground if he really wanted to get out of this thing, but not without giving himself some serious injuries.

After spending so much of this month half-convinced he

was about to shatter into a million pieces, suddenly he felt secure, safe, the physical sensation of being tethered and completely in Alex's care kinda blowing his mind.

Alex walked back toward him, more than the usual sway in her hips. He braced himself for her to touch him. His whole body pulled taut like an arrow, and she was due north. Devin zeroed in on her scent, her pulse, all the signals that told him she was alive, here, wanting him.

In the seconds while she closed the distance between them, he had time for a thousand different fantasies.

Alex on her knees, taking him into her sweet, mean mouth.

Alex kissing him, biting at his lower lip.

Alex sinking down on him with her arms around his neck, her eyes closed and his name rolling across her tongue.

She didn't do any of that.

Alex stood between his legs and reached back to unzip her skirt. The purr of the metal teeth parting was enough to make Devin dizzy.

She bent forward, her mouth coming *almost* within kissing distance as she shoved the material down toward her bare feet. Until she stood before him in nothing but that tiny top and a very pretty pair of panties. If Devin had his hands, he would have reached up to thumb across the thin black lace at her hip. He would have grabbed her ass and hauled her toward him, burying himself in the sweet V of her thighs so he could lick her through the fabric. Instead, all he could do was groan.

The word "trial" took on new meaning. It felt carved into his skin. He'd withstood pain, had leaned into his instincts, but this was about denial, about waiting, accepting scraps when he wanted to feast.

"Show me your tits," he said, flashing her his best "fuck me" eyes and trying to sound coaxing.

"Sorry." Alex shook her head. "You don't get to give orders right now."

She was not sorry. Devin could smell how not sorry she was.

"Fine." He clenched his jaw, counted to seven. "Show me your tits, *please*?"

At least he made her laugh. Alex straightened up so he was at eye level with her breasts as she reached for the bottom of her top, pushing it up to show a sliver of her stomach.

Devin swallowed, tight and painful, his throat raw with wanting, tensing and releasing against the urge to howl.

He expected a strip tease, the delicious agony of having to wait while she revealed herself in millimeters. She didn't seem to have the patience for that. Alex's cheeks were flushed, her brown eyes consumed by pupil as she tossed her shirt behind her in one smooth movement. Her bra—which, like every other piece of her clothing, was black—followed suit with a deft twist of her fingers.

Blood roared in Devin's ears.

His vision wavered.

He bit his tongue and tasted salt.

"Have you had your fucking nipples pierced this whole time?"

Alex gave the cruelest little nod he'd ever seen.

His gaze flickered between the lush curve of each of her breasts, the tight pink buds of her nipples, the shiny metal bars begging for his mouth: he immediately got a head rush.

She pushed her arms together and leaned over him until her tits almost brushed his chin. "Do you like it?"

"Oh fuuuuck you." If Devin liked it any more, he was gonna pass out. He strained against the bonds, knowing that wouldn't give him the distance he needed to get his mouth on her.

Alex grinned. She looked fucking wicked, so damn pleased with herself.

Devin's dick was gonna get sawed in half at this rate, and he didn't care. He loved making her happy.

She brought her thumb to her mouth and bit it. "Should I sit in your lap?"

Devin made a noise that he was not proud of.

"I swear to god you're asking me these questions just to make me an accessory to my own suffering."

"No." She straddled him, her thighs over his, the weight of her warm and soft and so fucking fragrant. He could taste her in the air on every inhale. "Not just."

She brushed her nipples across his lips, the petal-soft flesh, the cool metal, but pulled back before he could open his mouth.

Devin had never begged before. Had never wanted to.

"Please." The word ground out of him.

Was this weakness? For once he didn't care.

The wolf buzzed under his skin, but to Devin's surprise, he didn't struggle for control. He was a guard dog, his power held in check for a singular purpose, a beast built to serve one master.

Alex combed her fingers through his hair, brushing it back and away from his face, trailing her nails gently down his neck. She leaned forward, rocking herself against the line of his aching dick until Devin could just barely nose at the ripe curve of her breast, could extend his tongue and lick at the seam of her cleavage.

Her breathing was hectic, uneasy, like it was taking all her control not to give him what he wanted.

Devin traced his bottom lip, made it wet in invitation while she sat looking down on him. His cruel queen.

She gasped at the sight, shuddering a little, the tiny vibrations from her legs to his lap an exquisite agony.

"Let me," Devin said, straining his neck for her. Because his desire made her feverish, squirming and dark-eyed in his lap.

His arms ached with the need to hold her, to keep her close, but the bonds held true. He already needed to come so bad his body hurt all the way to his molars, but the pain was good. Bright and sharp and vital.

Alex arched her back so he could get his lips around her nipples. She was so sweet in his mouth, sensitive to every swipe of his tongue. He closed his lips and found the pressure she liked, following the rolling motion of her hips until Alex writhed in his lap, her hands fisting in his hair.

"Sorry," she said again, this time earnest, when she realized she was pulling, a tight, tingling pressure against his scalp.

"I'm not." Devin leaned back to blow across her damp, heated skin, watching her tighten for him around the shiny silver bar.

"Alex," he said, pressing his damp forehead to her sternum, closing his eyes and trying not to lose it.

What are we doing? he wanted to ask. *What is this? What's happening between us?*

She'd been no one to him when they met. Nothing more than a means to an end.

But now?

She had the power to make or unravel him. It was more than he'd ever allowed. Ever felt safe to hand over.

There were many things Devin didn't know. If he'd work again. What would happen if he didn't. How to be a real person instead of a character brought to life in carefully crafted vignettes.

How to love someone. How to ask them to love you back.

But he knew he could be good for her. That he wanted to be. Tonight. For as long as she let him.

He grew woozy off her pleasure, the scent and taste of her damp skin, the frantic movement of her in his lap. It was everything he'd ever wanted, the way she let him nuzzle her neck, bite gently at the underside of her chin.

Not having his hands free meant Devin had to work harder, dialing in further to her fervent gasps, her hungry little mewls as she rode his denim-clad lap. He made himself go slow, listening to the staccato of her heart as he gave her pleasure, calibrating his lips and teeth and tongue against her breasts by degrees.

"I've never seen anyone get as worked up as you do for me," he said against her throat. "You're gonna come just from me playing with your tits, aren't you?"

Devin meant it as a compliment. He fucking loved how sensitive Alex was, how she responded to him.

Her wide-open face shuttered. She stumbled off his lap on shaking legs.

"This is supposed to be a trial," she said, breathless, rough. Like she was reminding herself.

"I know." Devin couldn't make sense of her shift in mood. She'd been close; he'd felt it. God, her tits were shiny from his mouth.

Alex reached for his zipper.

"Whoa, hey—what—" But she was flicking open his button, pulling his dick out, and, "Oh fuck, Jesus, Alex—"

After the friction of her grinding against him for so long, he was beyond sensitive.

She slid to her knees between his legs.

"Oh god, you're not really gonna—"

She was.

His world narrowed to hot, wet suction as Alex wrapped her hand around his root and took him into his mouth.

"Baby, don't." Devin didn't know what he meant. *Don't tease me. Don't stop.*

But he had a safe word—"motorcycle"—and this wasn't that. Wasn't "no."

Even though the sensation was so much and he couldn't do anything, couldn't pull back or twist away.

As Alex traced her tongue around his head, featherlight and mean, Devin's vision wavered, colors dimming by degrees.

Oh god. Not this. Not now.

"Alex—" he said, tight, desperate, trying to warn her that he couldn't fight off the shift when he was this close to the edge.

But she just looked up at him from under her lashes and took him deeper between her slick lips.

Devin's hips bucked involuntarily, sliding him half an inch farther, the movement halted by his bonds.

The push and pull was perfect torture, exactly what he wanted held just out of reach. He could hope, be patient—but, god, he was shit at both of those things.

Alex's dark hair swung gently around the bare caps of her shoulders, brushing the tops of her perfect tits, still pink with his beard burn.

His wolf went feral at that, his mark on her skin.

Devin clenched his hands into fists, straining across his shoulders and chest as his claws popped.

Fuck fuck fuck.

"It's too good." Sweat slid down his collarbones, across his pecs. "You're too good at this." It didn't matter how many times he'd gotten himself off before they got here; he was hanging on by a thread. "You gotta slow down."

Alex sat back on her heels and blew across the damp head of

his dick, the cool air across his heated skin a clear call back to how he'd teased her tits.

"I don't think so."

He could feel the phantom weight of her in his lap again, how her thighs clenched around his hips as she rode him, getting closer and closer—

He could taste her in the woods, falling apart for him on his fingers, his tongue.

It was good that he couldn't reach down and rub at the seam of her lips where her mouth stretched around him. He was so close. Too close. He was the wolf in that moment, in feeling if not in form. Wild. Caught in her trap.

The scent of her desire spiked in the air as she bobbed her head in his lap.

Devin could deny himself almost anything, but the beacon of Alex's pleasure was impossible to resist—his fangs dropped.

God damnit.

She'd stop now: she'd have to. The eyes were subtle, his claws behind him, but Alex was watching his face so closely. No chance would she miss the final piece of the partial shift. He braced himself to see the revulsion in her eyes.

Devin Ashwood made her hot, not the monster inside him.

But Alex didn't pull back, didn't look away.

She held his gaze and reached down to rub herself over her panties.

"Oh fuck." He curled forward against the ropes, making a guttural animal noise as his orgasm punched out of him. The restraints meant there was nothing he could do but sit there and spill for her.

Alex swallowed around him, her throat working as she brought herself off with her fingers. The scent of her pleasure made his better, sharper, sweeter.

He'd assumed submission would be another battle, like fighting the Change, only more foreign. But there was freedom in this, and a choice. A power in not just letting go but choosing to surrender. To Alex. For Alex.

When he played Colby undergoing this trial, his submission had been nothing but rage and tension. An indignity to be withstood.

But what if submission wasn't about sacrifice, not really? This—Alex reaching over to carefully undo his bonds—this was about trust. He'd made himself vulnerable because he trusted Alex, but also, in some part, because he trusted himself.

And that, more than turning into a werewolf, made him feel newly made.

20

DEVIN AND ALEX might have awkwardly slunk off to their separate rooms after hooking up if they hadn't had salad for dinner and worked up quite the appetite. Instead, at midnight, they found themselves in the kitchen, making pancakes.

"I don't think I've spent this much time with anyone since I was married," Devin said contemplatively when they were both sitting at the carved wooden table in the rental house's kitchen, him back in his jeans and Alex in a set of flannel PJs from her suitcase.

"I'm not sure I understand that," she said, pouring maple syrup across her stack. "I might be an outcast and self-proclaimed cunt, but people like you—why don't you have more friends?"

It was a great question and one Devin had thought about a lot, especially lately. *Nothing like turning into a supernatural creature to make you question your social circle.*

"I think it's a combination of things," he admitted, keeping his eyes downcast on his plate as he cut his midnight snack into smaller and smaller squares. "My parents actively discouraged me from making friends when I was young. I don't think they wanted me to care about anyone besides them."

Other people were a distraction, obstacles to their ultimate goal of using Devin to make money.

"They told me I was different a lot, in a way that made me think I wouldn't fit in even if I got the chance. On the rare occasions when I met another child actor or someone's kid on set or whatever, I never really knew how to behave. I was used to talking to grown-ups or repeating lines that an adult had written for me. I knew how to act like a child but not how to actually be one."

Devin chanced a look at Alex's face, ready to see pity or disappointment at his revelation that he'd always been strange, alien, well before the Change.

Instead, he found her gripping her fork like a spear.

"I hate them," she said.

When he looked pointedly at her fork, she lowered the utensil/weapon sheepishly.

"Sorry." Alex shook her head. "I know that's not helpful."

Devin laughed.

"Actually, it kind of is. Makes me feel less messed up." He never really talked about his family at length like this. Jade knew pieces of what had happened over the years, more of the recent stuff with the lawsuits. But Devin mostly kept the stories of his childhood to himself. They were embarrassing. Sad. Even Erica, his ex-wife, hadn't liked hearing about it. The few times he'd tried to talk to her about his parents she started crying, and Devin ended up being the one comforting her.

Keeping this stuff from the press was an obvious choice. It would hurt his career. He couldn't be the blank slate for a character if people were thinking about his own "tragic" backstory.

It was nice to finally have someone else say, in so many

words, that it wasn't his fault he'd spent so much of his life isolated, near people but not with them.

Alex took a long sip from her glass of water like she was trying to calm herself down.

The wolf liked her anger, her fierceness. He read it as an overture of protection. Alex couldn't save him from his past, but every part of Devin liked that she wanted to.

"Weren't there any adults that looked out for you?" Alex asked a little desperately.

He tried to think back. It had been a while. His adolescence was mostly a blur of cheap apartments and auditions, of long days on set and wearing clothes that didn't belong to him.

"There were a couple of people on the soap crew that were nice, doting, I guess. The ladies in the hair and makeup trailer wouldn't let me drink too many cans of Coke. But it was such an awkward period of my life. I worked on *Sands of Time* from eight to eighteen, went from being a freckle-faced kid to a gawky teen to a"—he did air quotes—"'heartthrob' in front of those people. As my storylines changed, got romantic, even people I'd known for years started treating me differently. They went from pinching my cheeks to, well, *pinching my cheeks*." He grimaced.

"What the fuck? Devin, that's . . . I don't even have words for how messed up that is."

Alex put both elbows up on the table and scrubbed her hands across her face, and then she did something that completely threw him: she reached across the tabletop and took his hand, the one not currently occupied with eating, and just : . . held it.

She smelled like sugar and affection. Devin thought he could happily sit there in the semi-dark with her forever, just like this, talking about things that still hurt but somehow less than they used to.

He didn't know if it was the physical connection point or the trial they'd done earlier—the way his body felt loose and sated and safe—that encouraged him to keep talking. He hardly ever spoke this much when his words didn't belong to someone else. Maybe it was just that Alex didn't seem like she expected anything from him in that moment.

"*The Arcane Files* was the first place I knew that I belonged. From that first read of Colby, I just felt it in my bones that I was where I was supposed to be."

"Like fate?" Alex said, a mix of gentle and teasing. "Like you were chosen?"

And Devin had wondered. How could he become the only werewolf in a generation and not? But so far he didn't feel any great calling to public service.

"Colby was chosen to save people." Devin's accomplishments, even the bad stuff that happened to him, always felt flimsy in comparison to his heroic character.

Alex held his gaze. "Who says you won't?"

He wanted to say that he didn't know how. That if he could have, he'd have saved himself a long time ago. But Devin also wanted Alex to understand that he'd tried to form bonds during *TAF* and couldn't. It felt like unearthing something, showing her exactly where it hurt.

"I convinced myself it was just show business, all the relationship land mines on set. Gus and I got along okay at first, but there was always this unspoken competition. Our characters were partners, but I was the special one. And it didn't help that Brian Dempsey treated me differently from the jump. He was always more interested in Colby—which I guess makes sense given what we know about his family ties. Nothing I did was ever quite good enough. The more I chased his approval, the more Gus resented me."

"It probably didn't help that the audience divided into team Colby and team Asher." Alex bit her lip in a way that made Devin think she was considering the role of the fandom, maybe even her role as an archive moderator, in a new light. "And on that note, I can imagine it was awkward for you and Anthony that so many people shipped Colby/Nathaniel."

"It never bothered me the way it seemed to bother Anthony. I got the impression he read more about it online or maybe people were weirder with him in person—asking him to bite them and stuff? But yeah, I remember this picture of us at a cast dinner got circulated in a way that felt really strange. People diagramming the inches between our thighs under the table or something."

"Yeah, I know which one you mean," she said, not without a note of self-loathing.

"Look, I'm not gonna pretend there weren't fans who crossed the line, but the network was intentionally manipulative. They wanted to have their cake and eat it too when it came to Colby getting horizontal with dudes. They'd deny romance rumors at the upfronts every year until they were blue in the face, but even I picked up on subtext in some of the promos they had me and Anthony read. I'm pretty sure I said at one point that I could 'feel Nathaniel—'"

"—up your ass," Alex finished. "Yeah, there's a quote that will live forever in infamy."

Devin traced his thumb across the tattoos on her knuckles as she laughed. He'd been wanting to do that for so long that it felt illicit.

"Real-life speculating about me and Anthony stopped a little bit when I married Erica. It wasn't why I married her, obviously, but I remember the change. He got less jumpy about posing together at conventions and stuff."

Alex pulled her legs up onto the seat of her chair, curling in like a pretzel. "Why did you marry her?"

Devin fought against an immediate, instinctual shuttering at the bald question, two decades of media training kicking in on autopilot. But Alex wasn't a reporter. She wasn't even the Mod anymore, not really. She was the woman he'd trusted enough to let her tie him up. The one who'd seen the basest parts of him and still found him hot.

The truth still felt intensely vulnerable. He had to take two bites of sticky-sweet pancake for courage. He'd liked plenty about Erica. She was pretty and ambitious and warm. But really, he knew why he'd bought the ring.

"She had this huge Southern family and tons of friends, and from the very beginning, she just kinda folded me in."

Parties and BBQs, glasses of rosé on someone's fancy terrace for no good reason except the weather was nice. She'd treated them like a unit, and sure, sometimes he'd been bored or exhausted and wished he could skip out on plans, but for the first time in his life he'd had people slapping his back and calling him "Big Man," which he half hated, but that wasn't the point.

"When we got divorced, she took everyone with her."

The fall was swift and jarring. He went from having a packed social calendar to spending Thanksgiving alone on his couch with KFC.

"But through all of it, all those years, I never really noticed how lonely I was because there were always people around. My agent, my manager, my publicist, my trainer. It wasn't until Jade—my agent—dumped me that I realized, my whole life the only people that stuck around were the ones that I paid."

Devin got a bit of a head rush, finishing that sentence. It was the kind of quote that could have killed his career or what was left of it. Alex simply sat still, her empty plate in front of her, shadows from the window playing across her cheeks and chin, making it hard for him to read her.

"Do you think of me like that?" Her voice was barely loud enough to rise above the hum of the refrigerator. "As one more person you paid?"

"No." He wanted to reach for her, to hold more than her hand, but didn't dare.

The obvious question floated between them. Devin held his breath, waiting for her to ask.

She didn't.

"You stopped being someone I paid a long time ago."

Alex turned her head toward the window, hiding part of her reaction from him.

"We've only known each other a couple of weeks."

"I think"—Devin swallowed, unused to making philosophical declarations even when the moment demanded it—"sometimes getting close to someone has less to do with time and more to do with them letting you."

Even in his periphery, he could see the flash of fear in her eyes a few seconds before her scent changed.

"I'm not good at this kind of intimacy," she said, her voice wavering but determined. "Even the people I love the most—my dad, Rowen—I don't like for them to know when I'm struggling. I tell myself I'm protecting them. I'm supposed to be the strong one. The one with the answers."

The girl who became the Mod at fifteen. The same year her mom left.

"What about your friends? The ones your dad mentioned from the fandom?"

"Cam and Eliza."

All of a sudden, Alex pulled her hand from his.

"They've seen my messy parts. They know every mean thing

anyone's ever said about me. They were there when my dad got sick. The last time I spoke to my mom. But I think part of the reason our relationship works has always been that they're far away. It's easier, in some ways, to lay your heart on the line when most of your communication comes through a screen. You can hide when you need to."

She got up and dropped her dish into the sink with a clang.

"They trust me, so they give me a lot of leeway, but there's things that I've kept from them too."

Devin came up behind her and gently turned on the faucet. The rushing water was loud after so much stillness.

Alex turned to look at him over her shoulder, something lost in her eyes.

"When you decide to give someone everything, whoever that person is, they're gonna be really lucky," he said, gently nudging her aside to put their plates in the dishwasher.

What he meant was, *Let it be me.*

21

BETWEEN THE FORAY into BDSM and the emotional confessions last night, Alex was prepared for things to be different between her and Devin when she came downstairs the next morning for coffee.

She was not prepared for his first words to be "For the record, don't think I didn't notice that you cheated last night."

Several long seconds passed before her sleep-hazy brain figured out what he meant. When she caught on, her cheeks betrayed her by heating.

"I don't know that we have to call it cheating." Hunting in the fridge for almond milk had the dual benefit of hiding her face and cooling her down. "I came, didn't I? I thought you'd be smug."

Objectively, Alex should feel good about the success of last night's trial. She'd topped. Devin came without blacking out. By all accounts, the humble girl from the village helped the strapping prince tame the wild beast. Unfortunately, she couldn't help hating every minute that brought her time with Devin closer to an end. He'd been clear from the beginning—as soon as he got the werewolf stuff under control, he was leaving. The full moon was in five days, and he planned to be in LA when it happened; the end of her fandom fairy tale was rapidly approaching.

They'd gone to their separate rooms last night, but she still woke up with her palm pressed to the wall that divided them.

Alex took a seat at the island countertop and tried not to look morose.

Devin narrowed his eyes at her, steam from his own cup making the hair at his temples curl gently.

"Are you punishing me for something?"

"What?" Alex took a scalding sip. "No."

"You sure?" He leaned against the doorframe. A criminal offense against her ovaries. "Because if you tell me what I did to piss you off so bad that you won't let me make you come, I'll apologize."

"I'm not mad." Alex sighed, pushing her mug away. "These trials were for you. To help you manage your wolf. You don't owe me orgasms."

How could she explain that it hadn't felt fair to indulge herself when she was supposed to be the one in control last night? Wasn't it true that if she gave it up in that moment—was exactly as *agreeable* as he'd suggested—the whole guise of a trial would fall apart? Leaving all her plans, all her pride, unraveled like so much unspooled thread.

Back when they'd been together in the forest, Devin, a Hollywood heartthrob notoriously lacking in self-control, had been able to forgo his own orgasm entirely on the off chance he might lose his head and let something bad happen. Shouldn't Alex be able to do the same?

She was terrified of what would be left if they dropped the pretense that getting naked together helped Devin harness his supernatural abilities. That agreement was the only thing protecting her from ending up right back where she'd been seventeen years ago: hopelessly pining for Devin Ashwood.

"You don't seriously believe—" Devin shook his head. "You know what? It doesn't matter. We finished the trials last night. We did it. I passed. Professional engagement over." He swiped his arms in a definitive X motion. "The next time we have sex can be about you."

Alex froze. He said "next time" with such authority.

She could have replied with a whole host of reasons that "next time" was a bad idea.

I'm not sure we should make this any more complicated than it already is.

I'm falling for you, despite my best efforts. Despite knowing better. Despite the fact that I loved you once already and can still feel the burn of your indifference all these years later.

She could have said, *What if you only want me because I'm keeping your secrets? Because you think you're a monster and no one else could ever know and still leave their door open at night, inviting you in.*

But she didn't say any of that.

"Okay," Alex said. To sex with Devin Ashwood without pretense.

"Yeah?" He nudged her mug back toward her hand. "You want to?"

"I want to." Falling for him again was simultaneously the most mortifying thing Alex had ever done and somehow the nicest she'd ever been to herself.

Because there was healing in this—

In him making a mess of the Airbnb kitchen trying to serve her avocado toast.

In the way he leaned over to intrude on her crossword with

wildly incorrect suggestions. ("Why can't eight down be 'water-melon'?" "Because the space is four letters!")

In learning that he folded his socks (!!) and talked around his toothbrush, poking his head into the living room, bristles still working, to ask her if she wanted to go for a walk or maybe fishing later (and in his subsequent apology for inadvertently offending her "vegan morals").

Any plans she might have had for the rest of the day went out the window when she discovered the giant stack of fan fiction he'd printed out and packed in a three-ring binder.

"Who are you?" she demanded, positively brimming with glee.

"It's comforting," Devin said, chasing her around the kitchen island in his (no longer folded) socks, trying to get the binder back. "I'm nervous, okay? About the full moon. But it turns out a lot of people have explored that beyond the show, and Colby always ends up okay in these versions. He usually gets to be in love."

Alex could tease him for almost anything, but not that. He deserved to find comfort in Colby fix-it fic as much as the next person. Maybe more.

They ended up on the couch, with Alex showing him advanced search features on AO3.

He kept asking her stuff. Like first-date questions from someone who had never been on a first date. *Could she play any instruments? Did she own scrubs in every color? Who was in charge of clearing her porn cache when she died?*

Not everything she learned about him was flattering.

He took forever to blow-dry his hair and left an army of beauty products littering the double vanity shared between their rooms.

"Stand there and judge all you want, but you could use a vitamin C serum," he said when she commented on this.

"Excuse me?"

But she let him rub the obscenely expensive product across her cheekbones, down her nose.

"This is the first time I've given a woman a facial," he said, smirking like a dirtbag.

Alex scowled. *"Do not start."*

All in all, though, spending time with him without work or an agenda wasn't as strange as it should have been.

By the time the sun set, Alex's whole body was liquid from being around him all day. From the casual touches they'd both allowed themselves: arm grazes, his hand on her lower back, her foot wedged below his thigh on the couch.

One minute she was opening the fridge, saying, "Are you hungry? I brought some stuff for tacos, or if you want we could try to order—" and the next Devin was gripping her chin, firm but gentle, and kissing her—Devin Ashwood was kissing her!—and the fridge was still open, cold air all down her right side, but it didn't matter. Nothing mattered but the soft coaxing of his lips, the way his hand found the dip of her waist as he hauled her against him, taking the kiss deeper, claiming her mouth like something precious he'd thought he'd lost.

And it was good he was so strong, had all those extra senses working for him, because somehow he managed to close the fridge with his knee and push her up against it while Alex clung to him, both of her hands in his hair, her whole body pulling forward, succumbing, finally, to the undertow of him.

Arguably, they'd touched each other in ways more personal than this—more explicit—but suddenly Alex could appreciate how back in Regency days one kiss was enough to ruin a reputation. This was sharing a breath. What was more vital, more intimate, than that?

Then Devin's pleased little groan when she opened her mouth, the way he pressed his thumb exactly over her pulse point, like he wanted to mark the spot where her heart raced for him.

"I wanna give you whatever you want," he said, low and urgent and earnest. "Whatever you like."

Alex didn't know how to say *It's just this. It's just you. More than any other fantasy.*

So she said, "Can you maybe—" and he was looking at her, green eyes and blown pupils, his mouth already red from kissing her, saying, "Yeah," before she'd even finished the sentence.

"—touch yourself?"

His brows rose a little, and then a brilliant shit-eating grin broke across his face and Alex was hiding against the warm, spicy scent of his neck saying, "Forget it—"

"Oh no," Devin said, rubbing her back and then grabbing her ass—groping, really—like she belonged to him. "You want me to stroke my cock for you?"

In this, more than almost anything else, Alex saw the split between him and Colby. His character, for all his sterling virtues, would have balked at such a flagrant request. But Devin bloomed under attention, *shameless.*

He used the hand that wasn't on her ass to circle around her nipple, teasing, strumming across her piercing in a way that zapped like an electric current between Alex's legs.

"What else do you want, baby?" he said, mouth on her neck. "You want me to lick my palm, make it wet so you can hear it?"

"Devin," Alex gasped, genuinely scandalized. In a thousand lifetimes, she never would have imagined the mouth on this man.

But he just picked her up and tossed her over his shoulder in a fireman's carry, marching her out of the room.

"Where are we going?"

"I'm not kneeling on the fucking tile, Alex. I'm forty-two." He swatted her ass. "Think of my knees."

Devin took her into his room. To the big wooden canopy bed with soft cotton sheets.

He tossed her on top of the comforter, not particularly gently, and followed her down, both of them bouncing a little, rolling in, already reaching for each other.

He crawled on top of her. God, he was strong, solid, hot like a furnace, like a fever. Alex didn't have super senses, but she liked the way he smelled too. Like salt and sweat and sex. And the way he sounded—gruff and frustrated as he tried to get her clothes off without ripping the flimsy lace of her panties.

"Devin," she said, half to get his attention and half because she'd secretly always liked his name, before shimmying out of them herself, giving him what he wanted, like it was easy. Like it cost her nothing.

He kissed her again, dirty, grabbing under her thighs and hauling her closer, so she could wrap her legs around his waist, dig her heels into his lower back.

Alex nipped at his bottom lip, not totally prepared to abandon her previous request. "I thought you were gonna—"

"I am." Devin swore, breathing hard, tearing himself away. "Sorry, it's hard not to touch you when I have permission."

He already looked mauled, the neck of his T-shirt hanging wide from where she'd tugged on it, hair mussed in every direction, a warm-honey strand flopping in front of his brow. While Alex scooted back to recline against the pillows that smelled like him, he made quick work of his own clothes and then knelt on the bed.

Alex couldn't believe this was happening, that he was doing this *for her*. That thought alone made her dizzy, desperate.

Moonbeams spilling in from the window painted him in contrast, light and shadows, as he wrapped a hand around himself, set a loose, easy pace.

Up close he had some sun damage on his shoulders. He was both leaner and softer in the middle than he looked on TV, still muscular but not washboard ripped like Colby. There was a jagged pink scar under his left pec, shiny and new. The brown hair across his chest and down his stomach had the faintest sprinkling of gray.

He was the most beautiful thing she'd ever seen.

Devin's eyes trailed across her skin, from her mouth to her neck to her breasts to the V between her thighs. "I love looking at you."

Alex pressed her thighs together. It was as if somehow the way she felt about him was so big, so all-consuming, he'd caught it like a cold.

"It makes me fucking feral, thinking about you watching the show, reading all that filthy little fan fiction—"

"Hey," Alex protested, "it's not all filthy!"

"It's filthy enough." Devin laughed, warm and pleased. "Open your thighs for me."

Alex bit her lip. It was one thing to look, another to be seen. In the forest they'd both been frenzied, half-afraid of him losing control. A bed felt more personal. More real. Alex knew Devin better now. She liked him, impossibly, better now.

She'd felt less unmoored last night when she'd been the only one making demands.

But Alex did what he asked, let her legs splay open even though it felt outrageous while holding his gaze.

Devin was so close, kneeling less than a foot from her feet, concentrating his caresses on the head of his cock, his abs clenching, throat bobbing with each ragged breath.

He groaned at the sight of her, which was so mortifying it felt like swallowing a sun. She could feel how damp she was just from looking at him, from having him want her.

"You're embarrassed," he panted, not a question, and oh right, he could smell her feelings. "Don't be." He looked unabashedly at the place between her legs as he got himself off. "Alex, I've come from the scent of you lingering on my shirt."

He thrust a little into his hand, his grip tight enough that Alex wondered if it hurt. "Whatever's happened to me, whatever I am now, I want you more than any human ever could."

She watched him work himself over with this new knowledge: that Devin Ashwood had done this before, gotten off fantasizing about her. The role reversal was wild. A reckless, woozy happiness spiked in her blood.

It wasn't conscious, pushing herself off the pillows and grabbing his face, kissing him with both of them on their knees.

"Now," Alex said against his lips, reaching for his hand and redirecting it between her legs. "Please, now."

He grunted at the feel of her, curling two fingers inside, watching her face as she took them, her mouth falling open, her eyes closing at the stretch.

"Fuck the moon," Devin said, kissing her cheek, her neck, the hollow of her throat. "I'd like to spend the rest of my life howling at your door."

Before Alex could call him out for hyperbole, for the kind of promises that could give a girl the wrong idea, he pulled himself away, fumbling in his suitcase for a condom, coming back with his fingers in his mouth.

Alex rolled her eyes. "You're incorrigible."

"I don't know what that means." He smiled lasciviously, sitting down and then taking her hands, urging her to straddle him.

"What happened to all that werewolf super strength?" she complained, climbing into his lap anyway, her thighs twinging at the breadth of his hips.

"Alex, please." He rolled the condom on, holding his cock at the base for her to mount him. "What am I supposed to do? *Not* play with your nipple rings while I fuck you? Be serious."

She didn't have a good argument for that, so she braced herself with her hands on his shoulders as she took him in inch by inch.

There was a difference between knowing intellectually that Devin had a big dick—between riding him through layers of fabric—and this. The way he held still, letting her adjust to him by degrees. Alex held her breath until her ass met his thighs.

Devin ducked his head to kiss across her breasts, tender and then, when she leaned into him, just the right side of rough.

Alex fought to keep her eyes open. Devin Ashwood was inside her, and it was better than anything she'd ever had, anything she could have imagined. He rocked into her slow and deep, like he wanted—impossibly—to be closer. The feeling of fullness, the way he was looking at her like she was something precious, something amazing, it was so good. Too much. His mouth on her breasts, his hands curling around to her ass, gripping, guiding her against him.

He was the only werewolf in the world and he could read her from the inside out. Every movement of his hips, every smooth, deep thrust, was calibrated to her heartbeat, the flush of her skin, the scent of her desire.

Alex arched her back, winding her hand into a fist in the pretty, sweat-damp waves of Devin's hair.

She tightened her knees around his waist as he sped up his

thrusts, pinning her lips together so she wouldn't moan anything she couldn't take back.

Sitting back slightly, Devin sucked his thumb into his mouth, making it slick before slipping his hand between them to wind her up with small, quick circles across her clit.

That was it for Alex. Her whole body bucked as her orgasm crested. Devin wove his fingers into the hair at the base of her neck, kissing her to capture each whimper as it fell from her lips.

He murmured against her neck as his strokes inside her grew more frenzied, more wild. *How beautiful she was, how sexy, how he'd never wanted anyone the way he wanted her.* But when he came, it was her name on his tongue, over and over, a groan that shifted, suspiciously, into something like a growl.

People said don't meet your heroes, and for seventeen years, Alex thought she knew what they meant. Don't meet your heroes because they'll never live up to this perfect ideal you've built in your head. The version of them you crafted, collecting scraps of stories, knitting them together into a single malleable fantasy.

Meeting your heroes was a recipe for disappointment Alex had experienced firsthand.

Nobody said don't meet your heroes because they'll ruin you for everyone else. The truth was, Devin Ashwood didn't measure up to her expectations. He was more, in every sense of the word. Flawed in ways she never imagined, perfect in ways she didn't anticipate. And whatever falling in love with him smelled like—juniper or pink pepper or cedar—Alex hoped, as they lay there together in bed, that he couldn't parse it apart from all the other ways she wanted him.

22

THE NEXT SEVENTEEN hours at the cabin were everything Devin craved and everything he knew couldn't last. He got to hold Alex, see her grumpy morning face, lie in the grass with her while the sun was shining, listening to her rant about the "dearth of twenty-two-episode season orders and the impact on television as a narrative art form" as she knit him a daisy crown that he wore, indulgently, all afternoon.

On paper, they might seem like opposites. Him—charming, shallow, ripped. Her—bleeding heart with the personality of a feral alley cat. But they both lost themselves in stories. Devin had played Colby for more than a decade, and he was still constantly thrown by the details about the show that Alex could recall. She and her fandom friends had found deep wells of meaning hidden in plain sight. They'd crafted an epic love story for Colby and Nathaniel, weaving together pieces of canon with infinite threads. Devin found this simultaneously massive weirdo behavior and strangely humbling.

Alex might have moved on from the *TAF* fandom, but Devin and the trials took her back to that place; he could see her visiting it in her mind, remembering where she'd lived during certain seasons, what hair color she'd had. *The Arcane Files* was almost as big a part of her life as it was for Devin. After years of hungering for someone else to care about the show like he did, he couldn't get enough.

They packed up Wednesday morning and headed back to Tompkins. The full moon loomed closer on Devin's app, reminding him that they'd been doing all this werewolf training specifically so he could leave in a few days.

The end of his time in Florida seemed to have arrived all of a sudden. He'd been so focused on each of the trials, anxious about passing them, that the thought of how he'd leave Alex never really crossed his mind. Now it felt like an unexpected fourth test. One he'd never seen coming and had no frame of reference for how to navigate.

The wolf was getting stronger each day, sitting closer to the surface like an itch under his skin. Devin could control the shift, could still filter the wolf's impulses from his own, but his days of forgetting for a little while that he was more than a man lived in a different part of the calendar. The prospect of abandoning Alex was not something his other half enjoyed or even really seemed to understand. The wolf liked having Alex close in their own private space at the cabin, where Devin could monitor for threats or disruption.

Of course he couldn't explain any of this to Alex directly without scaring her. Devin had to act normal. Like one weekend of sex was enough to get it out of his system. *What a load of bullshit.*

Some asshole once said it was better to have loved and lost, but Devin didn't believe them. How could he when he already missed Alex even while she sat next to him in the passenger seat of the truck?

She has a job to do, he told the wolf when faced with the

sudden urge to push the child lock after they pulled up to her place. *She has family here, community, commitments. What do you want? To drag her back to LA? Have her life be a shadow of mine?* Yeah, that had worked real well with his ex-wife.

Devin managed to stay away for a full twenty-four hours, occupying himself with packing and visiting Lou, trying to explain to him that they might not see each other for a while.

But then he figured, Why shouldn't he spend the rest of his measly time in Tompkins following Alex around like a puppy? He'd obviously done way worse, dignity-wise.

Only, when he showed up at the community center, Alex wasn't there. He knew immediately—not by sight, though clearly it was only Rowen behind the sign-in desk in the lobby squinting down at a textbook. No, he knew by smell. Or rather by the lack of it. He should probably worry that he'd gotten attuned to Alex to the point that he could detect her absence through his nostrils alone. But Devin wasn't exactly well-versed in interrogating his emotions.

"Hey. How's it going?" He leaned against the reception desk, trying to look casual.

"Alex isn't here," Rowen said without looking up from whatever they were typing into their calculator.

Which, okay, yeah, he could see that. But he knew she normally volunteered for this shift on Thursdays. She'd texted him her schedule back when they'd started planning out times to meet for training, and he might have, accidentally, memorized it.

"She's not feeling so hot." Rowen circled a line in their notes. "I'm covering so she can lay down in her car out back."

In her car? What, that shitty tin can? If Alex was sick, she should be at home in bed, or in a hospital, maybe, depending on what was wrong with her.

Devin turned on his heel to go have words with her, but then it occurred to him.

"You okay here by yourself? You need help?" The wolf had a vague idea that Rowen was part of Alex's pack and in need of looking after.

"I'm sixteen," Rowen said, like that meant something.

"Yeah?" When Devin was sixteen, he had about ten different people taking advantage of him and, if that therapist he spoke to was right, an undiagnosed case of anxiety.

"I'm good," they said with authority. "Beatriz comes in to relieve me at five."

"Okay, cool." Devin did a quick scan but didn't see any immediate teenager-sized threats. "Just, like, yell if you need something."

He could hear within a couple of miles; he'd been testing it. The parking lot shouldn't be a problem. Maybe he could get them a bell?

"Uh-huh." Rowen returned to their homework; Devin was dismissed.

Outside, white rock gravel crunched under his heels. Alex's piece-of-shit Honda was parked under the shade of a giant palm tree. He swore there were new scratches on the fender since he'd last seen it, but at least Alex was inside. She'd curled up in the back seat like a pill bug, her little sneakers kicked off and her head pillowed on her arm.

When he knocked on the window, she shot up and banged her head on the ceiling.

"Shit!" they said in tandem, him sympathetic, her accusatory.

"Sorry, sorry." Devin tried the door, which turned out to be open, so he guessed he could have woken her more gently, but knocking seemed polite. "Why didn't you lock this?"

"I don't know. I thought I did." Her face flushed from either embarrassment or sitting up too fast. This was grumpier than he'd ever seen her. "What are you doing here?"

"Rowen said you're sick." He picked her calves up off the seat so he could slide in next to her and then put them back down over his thighs.

Alex made a noncommittal sound caught somewhere between a grunt and a groan.

Her frown was so deep as she rubbed at her eyes.

"What's wrong?" The impulse to put his hand on her bare ankle to see if she had a fever struck him, but he wasn't sure that would work. Was the forehead, like, a special place for that kind of thing?

While waiting for her to answer, half because he anticipated that she wouldn't, Devin inhaled, assessing.

Something very faintly metallic set off her normal scent.

His stomach sank to his ass.

"You're bleeding." He started scanning her body, turning her on her side to check her back, then her front—Alex protested loudly, swatting at his arm—but he couldn't find any open wounds.

What if the bleeding was internal? Like her organs. Someone died from that shit in the episode of *ER* where he'd played Male Nurse #2.

He opened the door, debating whether he could trust her junky car to get her to a hospital fast enough or whether he should just pick her up and start running.

"Devin"—Alex grabbed his sleeve from where she still lay half-prone—"what the hell are you doing?"

"Hospital," he said. *No time for full sentences.* What had she been planning to do—just lie here and wait for death?

"I got my period," Alex said through clenched teeth.

Oh. That . . . that made sense.

He sat back down. Shut the door. They both stared straight ahead.

Alex had a wintergreen air freshener that Devin wanted to throw out the window real bad.

"I don't know how to fix that." Erica mostly avoided him while surfing the crimson wave.

One corner of Alex's mouth lifted. "You pretty much just have to grin and bear it."

Devin winced. That sounded horrible. "Why don't you go home?"

Alex let her head fall gently against the window. "I can't really drive right now."

He remembered the parallel she'd made when they first met. Moon cycles. That time of the month. Devin didn't bring it up. He doubted Alex would appreciate any kind of comparison at the moment.

"It hurts that bad?" He knew, abstractly, that some people got cramps.

"It hurts that bad." She wrapped both arms around her lower abdomen. "I have endometriosis."

Devin didn't know what that meant, but he'd look it up later. It seemed like talking was painful. "You need medicine?"

Alex shook her head. "I took some."

"Chocolate?" He'd seen that in a *Cathy* cartoon once. He wanted, *needed*, to find a way to help.

She turned to scowl at him, the corner of her forehead still pressed against the glass.

"Is that a no?"

"No," she muttered, and then, her voice very small: "Would you—could you maybe take me home?"

Devin felt like he could tear the world in half for her, right now, if it would have made a difference.

"Yeah, of course."

He went back to the front desk quickly to make sure Rowen knew where they'd gone, then pushed the protesting Honda five miles over the speed limit on the way back to Alex's.

"Can I carry you inside?" he asked when they got there.

She'd slumped down so far in the seat she was practically horizontal; the seat belt cut just under her chin.

The wolf kinda wanted to just do it without asking, head off any potential protest before it started, but Devin knew that wasn't respecting her bodily autonomy and shit, so he waited for her reply.

Alex chewed her lower lip.

God, her front teeth made him lose it. *That fucking gap.* Devin felt like if he didn't get to stick his tongue in her mouth at least once a day, he might die.

"No," she decided after a moment, "I'm fine." She pushed open the door and got out but then immediately doubled over, wincing. His stubborn, brave girl.

"Okay," she said very softly, knowing he could hear. Her voice had gone brittle with pain.

Devin's vision ebbed, the wolf fighting to surface. He didn't fully understand what was going on. He wanted to attack whatever was hurting her.

Not what she needs, Devin scolded, wrestling back control and hustling around to get her.

When he got around to her side, Alex held up one arm to go around his neck. "Can you try to be gentle?"

"Yeah, baby." He bent down so she didn't have to reach, and then moved slowly once he had her gathered up against him, cradling the back of her head against his chest.

The wolf yipped approvingly when she tucked her nose against his shirt.

Devin swallowed. AO3 had recently introduced him to the concept of Fated Mates.

He didn't need to turn the lights on to get around Alex's loft over the garage. He could see without them, and Alex had her eyes closed anyway. A quick inhale told Devin that Isaac wasn't home from work yet.

"Bed or couch?"

When Alex didn't respond for a beat, seemed to be weighing what she wanted to say again, he made an executive decision.

Her bedroom smelled so fucking good, everything drenched in her scent, so rich and layered it was almost like a multisensory experience. Like he could taste her in the air. His knees threatened to buckle. Even spending all that time with her close at the cabin hadn't prepared him for this. It took all his concentration to shove the wolf back. He wanted to roll around on her rug.

Once Devin got her on the bed, Alex curled up again with her face mashed into her pillow. As much as he'd tried to make the transition in from the car as smooth as possible, Devin knew her body hadn't enjoyed the ride.

He felt panicky about the pain on her face, her eyes squeezed shut, her nose scrunched in a grimace as she kicked off her sneakers with two thunks.

The urge to howl strained the back of his throat.

"At the risk of truly forfeiting my dignity," Alex said, "could you maybe help me take off my pants?"

Devin gulped. "No problem."

This isn't sexy, he told his body. *She's weak and vulnerable. Be cool.*

His mouth still went dry as he undid the button on her jeans, as he slid down the zipper and guided the material over the warm, smooth skin of her thighs, revealing all that pretty ink as he tugged her pants past her calves and ankles all the way to her feet.

"I think I've got a heating pad in my closet." Alex pointed. "Could you check?"

Opening her closet was another ordeal, with Devin fighting the urge to smother himself in all her laundry. Luckily, he found the heating thing with minimal fuss, plugging it in and then going to get her some water from her tiny kitchenette.

When he came back, she'd gotten under the covers. Devin checked the pad and found the soft terry cloth warm enough to the touch.

"Alex," he said softly, setting the water down on the nightstand.

She opened her eyes but didn't turn. "Hmm?"

"You want this heating pad?"

Alex curled her chin toward her chest, once, twice, then shoved the covers down below her belly button and pulled up her shirt. "Can you?"

"Oh, uh, sure." Devin cleared his throat at the expanse of exposed skin above the band of her plain cotton panties.

Her skin was so soft against the backs of his fingers as he placed the heating pad on her abdomen. He did it as quickly as he could, trying to minimize contact, like he was playing Operation or defusing a bomb.

Afterward, he turned away from her and counted backward from five, willing his erection down. He was fucking embarrassed. But he couldn't help it. She was almost naked. In her bed. She had a freckle beside her navel that he valiantly did not try to stroke. He felt lightheaded.

"I'm gonna go," he announced. "You need anything else?"

Alex didn't answer, but she reached back and got ahold of his pant leg in her fist.

Her eyes were still closed, her other hand folded over the heating pad.

"Will you sit with me for a little? Just until this thing kicks in?" Her voice didn't have the same belligerent confidence as when she told him what to do in the bedroom.

This kind of vulnerability felt infinitely more rare from her. *It's rare that she asks for help*, Isaac had said. But here she was, letting Devin take care of her, wanting something from him that no one else did.

"I'll stay as long as you want," he said and toed off his shoes.

Devin climbed up into bed beside her and leaned back against her headboard.

He didn't know anything about comfort. When he tried to recall a model, a guide for this kind of thing, what came to mind was on-set handlers; PAs; his housekeeper, Teresa. He once gave her three hundred dollars to go buy him Gatorade during a particularly nasty hangover.

"Thanks." Alex wiggled a little so her knees curled into a position that was almost but not quite touching his leg.

Usually when people wanted him to make something better, he gave them money. Alex wanted him close because his presence felt good to her. Because something about him made her hurt a little less.

He still didn't really know what to do. Where should he put his hands?

But then he recalled the way Alex had climbed into that sleeping bag with him after his ice bath, urging him to hold her, using the warmth of her body to soothe him. To save him.

Slowly, like he was approaching a skittish animal, Devin reached up and brushed her dark hair back off her cheek. Alex leaned into his palm a little, so he kept his hand on her, sliding it up to scritch lightly at her scalp.

When she hummed approvingly, Devin went further, massaging her neck, her shoulders, until his wrist ached. Until her breathing had gone low and even.

The idea of not being here in a few days, not being able to provide comfort when she needed it, made him want to gnaw off his own arm.

She had paintings all over her bedroom. Landscapes and portraits and abstract watercolors. She'd hung dried flowers above her scratched wooden dresser, and her desk had a calamity of odds and ends, haphazard highlighters and scraps of notebook paper like she'd spilled ideas all over it. Her laptop, left open but sleeping, was covered in goofy stickers of cartoon cats.

Her space was so personal. So private. Compared to his bare, stark hotel room. To his big glass house in the California hills.

Every second in this room made his stomach twist with longing. Being here, close to Alex, knowing he had to leave, was torture.

He took the heating pad off after thirty minutes—the package had said to—and set it on the ground. But then, even when he knew he could get up and go, or at least go downstairs and watch TV, he didn't move.

Devin closed his eyes, matched his inhales to Alex's, and fell asleep sitting up.

23

ALEX WOKE WITH a start to a terrible growl.

Devin crouched over her with claws, fangs, and silver eyes—the whole shebang—his attention fixed on the closed door to her loft.

"Uhh . . . Al." Her dad's voice carried through the plywood. "Did you bring home a dog again?"

The mortifying reality of the situation rained down on her. She'd asked Devin Ashwood to lie in bed with her, fully clothed, because her body had begun its monthly betrayal and his presence had become a source of comfort.

"Just, uh, give me a second." She had to raise her voice to be heard over the menacing rumble radiating from Devin's chest.

"Hey." She put her hand on his nape, her voice soft but firm. "Stop that."

The wolf's growling halted, but he stayed in the crouch, looking back and forth between her and the door with his nose in the air, sniffing.

Devin might have gotten much better at controlling the impulse to shift, but it appeared they'd stumbled upon a vulnerability. Judging by the setting sun, they both must have fallen asleep in her bed. That meant the wolf had awoken in a strange place, to the sound of a potential threat intruding. This close to the full moon, his instincts must be particularly powerful.

"It's my dad." Alex petted along the strained tendons of his neck. "You know him."

Every time she saw Devin in the shift, Alex was taken aback by the way she didn't fear him. Even without all the lethal trappings, her body should have recognized the threat in his posture, in the snarl of his lip. But he felt familiar to her in every form, even this one. She didn't believe in soulmates, but she'd grown up around the idea of Devin Ashwood; his shape and voice were spliced into her memories.

He once said she smelled like she was made for him; maybe in some small way that was true. The way a tree grew around stone.

"It's okay," Alex said, low and even, keeping his eyes on her, trusting him to trust her. "We're safe."

Devin seemed to force his way back from the shift following the sound of her voice. He shook his head, his eyes returning to their normal green as he blinked in awareness of his position over her. He sheepishly bear-crawled off the bed to a standing position.

"Sorry about that," he said, shoving his hands in his jean pockets. "I didn't mean to fall asleep."

After hastily pulling on some pajama pants and smoothing her hair, Alex finally opened her door.

"Hey, Dad," she said, trying to strike a casual pose against the doorframe that somehow also blocked Devin from view. "What's up?"

"What's up," he repeated, holding two brown paper bags with the logo of their favorite Thai takeout place. "So we're just gonna ignore all the growling?"

"Oh that?" Alex gave a flippant little wave. "That was just the TV. You know I've been watching *TAF* reruns."

Isaac frowned. "Sounded awful loud."

"Was it? I didn't notice. I was napping." She yawned massively in illustration.

"Uh-huh," her dad said, using his superior height to peer around her. "Hey, Devin."

Alex turned to see him pink-cheeked and incriminatingly bed-headed.

"Hello, sir."

Isaac shook his head. "Well, I'm gonna take this food down into the kitchen. You're welcome to join me if you two are done 'napping.'"

Once the humiliation had sufficiently passed, she and Devin made themselves presentable and went over to the other side of the house for food. After they all ate, her dad took Devin into his office to "give him some new research around wolves" and probably also some vague "don't hurt my daughter" warning.

He came out with an armful of textbooks, looking slightly poleaxed.

"You don't have to worry about me," Alex said, once Devin had made a break for the safety of the loft. She leaned down to kiss her dad's cheek as he sank into his favorite armchair and reached for the remote.

"I always worry about you," Isaac said, uncharacteristically grave. "You've already given up so much to take care of me— leaving school, sticking around this town when I know it hasn't been easy. I just want to make sure you don't jump into putting someone else's needs above your own again."

Alex's heart flopped around like a fish caught on a line. "What do you mean?"

He turned to look over his shoulder. "I mean you had that

poster of him hanging on your wall for a long time. You sure you know what you're doing here—heartwise?"

Right. Alex used to be *The Arcane Files'* ultimate fangirl, and now here she was with Devin Ashwood in her bed.

When they met, she thought that meant she had this odd, uncomfortable advantage—knowing so much more about him than he knew about her. But having spent all this time with Devin now, Alex realized those surface-level details didn't matter. His birthday and his favorite food. They were nothing more than the parts of himself he'd been forced to sell.

No. It was much more intimate to let someone see your faded striped sheets. To have them eat dinner with your dad. To show them where you worked. To let them talk to the people in your life who both loved and despised you. Alex had given Devin back the advantage. Or at least they'd evened the playing field.

"I can see him a lot more clearly now." Alex could admit she'd miscalculated, underestimating Devin's capacity for tenderness. Realizing that he was—underneath all that handsome—surprisingly sweet rendered her weak. Weaker than she'd ever meant to get for him again.

One by one he'd dismantled her defenses. She could feel the heartbreak waiting like the promise of a bruise under her skin.

"He's going back to LA in a few days. Whatever's between us, it's ending. There's no future." She'd cut herself off cold turkey from Devin Ashwood once. Maybe it was like riding a bike.

Her dad stared at her for a long moment. "Does he know that?"

Alex opened her mouth, but no words came. Had Devin somehow suggested otherwise?

"For the record, I like him," her dad said. "He's funny. Good at chores." His face grew somber. "But I think you and I both know that sometimes you can really care for someone, really want to make it work, and still not be able to make your lives fit together."

The parallel to her parents' divorce sat between them, a dormant live wire. It was true, of course, that Alex had roots planted here and Devin would never willingly leave LA for Tompkins. But Alex wasn't her father. She would never ask him.

When she got back to the loft, Devin was on her tiny two-seater couch, reading one of the books her dad had lent him. He'd arranged himself so casually, one leg crossed over the other, a deep furrow of concentration between his brows, that she almost wondered if he hadn't overheard some of her dad's well-meaning intervention.

"Hey," she said.

"Hey." He looked up at her over the pages. "I've been thinking. What if you came with me? To LA."

Alex's heart stopped. "What?"

"Just for the long weekend," he rushed to clarify. As if Alex might think he was asking her to move in with him or something.

"You could come to the charity basketball game and stay for the full moon. My publicist texted that Brian Dempsey's back in town and rumored to make an appearance. I thought maybe I could try to get time with him, introduce you. We'd have a little more time together at least, to talk about, well, everything." He looked so transparently eager.

"You don't really need me anymore," Alex said, her brain still trying to process this conversation through the slight haze of her endo pain meds.

Was he trying to say that he wanted them to be something more? Was this a forty-two-year-old man's soft-launch proposal of a long-distance relationship? Because Alex really didn't think she had the self-esteem or stamina to pull off that kind of thing, especially with him.

"I don't know about that. I think this evening proved I'm still working out the werewolf kinks." Devin shoved back his hair. "I'm doing okay here in Florida, but that's small potatoes compared to being back under the spotlight around all the industry people I care about impressing."

Right. Because there was no one like that around here.

"If you came with me, you'd be a kind of . . . constant. Plus"—he smiled at her, one she recognized from the covers of *Teen Beat*—"that way I'll know there's at least one person in the stadium who doesn't think I'm a huge joke."

Alex saw the irony. No one in the world had made Devin Ashwood a punch line more times than she had. But he trusted her. He kept trusting her. In ways that felt precious and fragile and new.

"Come on." He nudged her arm like they were locker room buddies. "I've got like a million airline miles, and we can stay at my place. It's just one more weekend."

Well, that was certainly a finite expiration point. It would be so easy to say yes. To indulge in the fantasy one more time.

"Are you sure you want to expose me to all those rich and famous Hollywood people? As you've experienced, I'm not great with small talk." Alex didn't want to embarrass him or herself. She had never been to a city bigger than Tampa. And LA was like . . . cool? Wasn't everyone there engineered for Maximum Hotness? Did they even let losers like Alex cross city lines?

"Don't be silly," Devin said, all stalwart conviction and pretty eyelashes. "You learned from the master."

Alex bit the inside of her cheek, deliberating. This was the part of the fairy tale that would be harder to reconcile. Devin was asking her to see his real life, all the glitz and glamour, and experience firsthand every way she didn't fit.

But he looked so hopeful. And going to LA could be fun. At least she knew there would be plenty of stuff she could eat.

They'd spent all these weeks training so that he could withstand the full shift without winding up on TMZ or in jail. Alex might as well see this werewolf stuff through to its natural conclusion on the full moon. Would the airline let her put the Taser in a checked bag?

She let out a big sigh. "Fine."

Seth would cover her shifts if she asked him nicely, and she had all the extra money Devin had paid her, plenty to take a little more time off.

"Really?" Devin grinned so big.

It was impossible not to mirror him.

He picked her up around the thighs and swung her around in a circle.

It was horrible. She hated it.

(Mostly, she hated it.)

"Stop." She whacked him on the shoulder. "I'm in a delicate condition."

"Oops." He lowered her carefully. But then, as if he couldn't help it, he picked up her arm and raised it in the air, pantomiming like she was cheering. "Whooooo."

"No whoos, please." Where was his dignity? "Has anyone ever told you you're easy to please?"

"Nope." Devin popped the P.

He was painfully beautiful. His perfect teeth too big for his face.

Devin pulled her back into his arms, hugging her gently, and said into her hair, "Just you."

Somehow, despite a lifetime of avidly consuming supernatural fiction, Alex didn't see the edge of the cliff coming.

24

THE SIMPLE ACT of packing for LA triggered all of Devin's insecurities.

His acting career was over.

He had nothing else of value to contribute.

Pretty soon he'd once again find himself all alone in a big empty house without even a cat to eat his face after he died.

Except this time, he had a secret weapon.

Somewhere between ice baths and dunk tanks (was it kinda strange that he had spent so much of this trip wet and in his underwear?), Alex had become Devin's emotional support human. He'd never had one of those before. Someone he could tell about his fears and regrets, his big goofy dreams.

She didn't find his werewolf stuff gross or terrifying. In fact, Devin was beginning to suspect she might be sort of into it.

They had common interests and made each other laugh. Mostly on purpose.

Even her "caring about stuff other than yourself" thing had started rubbing off on him. He'd accidentally stayed up all night reading those wolf books from Isaac. Even the super-dry one translated from German. Isaac's annotations ran across most of the pages, the ink fading in certain volumes from black to time-weathered gray.

Devin didn't read much, as a rule, beyond scripts and online sports coverage. When he was growing up, books had always felt like busywork on top of his real job. His mom tutoring him on set. Having to highlight stuff and make flash cards while his adult costars smiled at him indulgently over their craft service salads.

But he had a real stake in wolves now, for obvious reasons. It was fucked up that people had hunted and trapped them almost to the point of extinction as part of a "government-sanctioned extermination plan to domesticate the landscape and expand grazing ranges" (Isaac's words, but Devin got the gist).

Devin got so worked up reading last night that he'd howled and woken his neighbors in the nearby rooms. Hotel staff called to scold him.

How did Alex handle caring about so much all the time? It was exhausting.

He needed to shift back into focus mode. To channel Colby. If he had any chance of turning around his reputation and convincing Brian Dempsey that a reboot was not only smart but essential, he'd need to be in perfect form at the basketball game. The stress and stimuli of going back in front of a stadium full of industry decision-makers and fans, not to mention cameras, on the morning of the full moon would push his control over his wolf to the limit, but as long as he had Alex, Devin knew he'd be fine.

Was it weird that he'd grown this attached to her in a number of weeks?

No. Wanting to stick together was normal after bonding during a traumatic occurrence. And trust him, sprouting claws counted.

Devin pulled into the driveway at her house and texted Alex that he was outside.

He scrolled through Instagram while he waited.

The Tompkins Community Center had tagged him in a gallery of images thanking him for his "incredibly generous donation and volunteer time" at the org last week.

Damn. That sort of blew his "mindfulness retreat" cover, but hey, maybe Page Six would write him up as charitable. He looked good in the photos, happy, with Alex's mural in the background.

While weighing the choice between playlists and podcasts for the ride to the airport—which would Alex hate less?—it occurred to him he could go in and help her with her bags. Show a little chivalry.

He tried the front door and found it unlocked. Alex appeared at the top of the stairs just as he stepped across the threshold. His breath caught.

She'd changed her hair, styled it, he guessed, the long dark locks flowing straight and smooth around her shoulders. Her makeup was different too, less. Lighter colors. Peaches and pinks across her cheeks and lips and eyes, where previously he'd only seen the colors of midnight.

Her clothes must be new. A matching set in drapey white linen. The top cut low, the sleeves hanging down, exposing the pretty curves of her shoulders, the line of her collarbones, and the top of her tits flushed slightly pink.

"What do you think?" She did a little twirl that sent the thin skirt floating around her ankles, then paused in a pose for his appraisal with one sandaled foot thrust forward. When had she painted her toenails shell pink instead of emerald?

Devin answered honestly. He didn't even think about it. He couldn't.

"I fucking hate it."

She smelled *wrong*. The clothes were new and chemical treated, lingering traces of plastic and metal from hangers. Worse, he could smell strangers' hands on her. Whoever had done her hair had touched the nape of her neck. Devin fought back a snarl.

The scent of each new product mingling with her skin assaulted his nostrils, all of them intolerable because they diluted his favorite smell in the world. Devin clenched his fists, trying to fight the shift. The wolf was a mess. He wanted his claws so he could tear her clothes off and then shred them. Why—he demanded—wasn't Devin rushing forward to rub himself all over Alex until the offensive scents were covered?

"Are you serious?" She relaxed out of the strange model pose and kind of slumped against the railing. "I drove, like, two hours to Nordstrom." Alex brushed her hand down the skirt, which, in classic linen fashion, already had wrinkles. "I thought this was how rich people dressed in LA."

"There's not a universal uniform." Where had she gotten that idea? Watching reruns of *The OC*?

Devin eyed the duffel bag slung over her shoulder. What if all she'd packed was this new stuff? Where were all her stupid threadbare T-shirts and those faded jeans with holes he knew came from years of real wear and tear because their placement wasn't strategically slutty?

"I was making an effort to fit in." Alex crossed her arms.

"Why would you try to fit in?" She didn't do that. Her entire MO was prolonged rebellion against the majority.

"For you." Her voice took on a hard, sharp note. "In case we're out together and someone's looking."

The wolf was so close to the surface, Devin could barely concentrate. He squeezed his eyes shut and tried to breathe through his mouth.

"No one's gonna be looking at you," he said fiercely. *They better not.* If any aggressive paparazzi or Weinstein-style studio creeps tried getting close to Alex, he would rip their arms off.

She huffed out a breath. "Okay. Fine."

When he looked next, the blush from her chest had spread to a hot red in her cheeks.

She waved at the door, which Devin was blocking with his body.

"Can we just go, please?"

He looked at his watch. They didn't have much time before the flight, but this was an emergency. His head hurt. And his heart was pounding out of control. Devin hadn't realized how much he relied on the constant comfort of her scent. How uniquely it made him feel happy and safe and, okay, fine, horny. But that wasn't the point right now.

"Do you think you could undo all that?" He waved at her hair and face and outfit, resisting the urge to pick her up and march back upstairs. If they just rolled around naked together in her bed for a while, everything would be better. After Googling "endometriosis" last night, he understood she'd likely want to avoid penetration for the duration of her period. But they could still make out, and Devin was pretty sure he'd get her to come with his mouth on her nipples.

"Can I undo—" Alex repeated, then stopped. Her eyes turned murderous. "I almost forgot what an asshole you are."

She stormed back up the stairs, the wooden heels on those sandals clopping like Lou's hooves at a gallop.

Devin followed her to her bedroom. Just being inside, breathing the air that smelled good, right, made him relax by degrees. He flopped onto the crisp white comforter atop her neatly made bed. This ordeal had taken a lot out of him.

Alex started flinging clothes out of the closet haphazardly. A pair of pilling sweatpants hit him in the face. He inhaled; *bliss*.

"Any other aesthetic preferences of yours I should keep in mind ahead of this trip?" Each word dripped acid.

It was a bummer that telling her how hot she looked when she got mad wouldn't do him any favors right now.

Devin got why she smelled so angry right now. Changing was annoying. And obviously she'd put in effort getting ready. Plus, she was probably nervous about the trip. LA had about a billion more people than Tompkins. And she'd be accompanying him to a big celebrity-packed event.

"Don't worry about impressing anyone." She didn't need to win approval in LA the way he did.

Devin had spent his whole life hungry, most of it literally as well as figuratively, waiting with baited breath for the day everyone realized the only interesting things he'd ever done happened onscreen. Alex was so much better than him. In so many ways. He had one thing he was good at. He needed to ride it until the wheels fell off.

The basketball game was the perfect rebrand event. Brian Dempsey would be there. Devin had enhanced speed and hand-eye coordination. He could go all Michael J. Fox on the court, play amazing, raise a buttload of cash for charity, and wind up back on top.

If he nailed this, the viral video of him in Venice would suddenly look like smart marketing versus a breakdown / cry for attention from an aging actor.

Devin could do it. He knew he could. Because Alex would be there, cheering him on.

The lone wolf dies but the pack survives. That George R. R. Martin guy was really onto something.

CAM: 🚨 🚨 Batten down the hatches, Law. Devin Ashwood is in your hometown!! https://www.instagram.com/TompkinsCommunityCenter/

ELIZA: OMG what the HELL is he doing in Florida??

CAM: IDK!! But that's her community center, right? She sent us pics when she was working on that mural.

ELIZA: Can you imagine if Law saw Devin Ashwood and didn't tell us?

CAM: lmao no. Like they're hanging out right now and that's why she hasn't responded.

ELIZA: Our mod would never! Fandom bond is sacred.

CAM: She's being suspiciously quiet.

ELIZA: Did Devin Ashwood capture you and drag you back to his werewolf den? Send a moon emoji if you've been Taken.

25

IN THE BACK of Devin Ashwood's private town car, Alex brought her phone so close to her face she almost hit herself in the nose.

Fuck.

Her stomach twisted as her cell continued to chirp with new texts from the group chat. She fumbled open the leather pocket on the back of the seat in front of her but found it empty. A fancy car like this should have motion-sick bags back here like on airplanes.

What could she possibly reply?

So. Funny story. I have actually been hanging out with Devin Ashwood for a month, but I couldn't tell you guys because he made me sign an NDA.

The truth sounded flimsy even to her. The NDA might forbid her from discussing all his werewolf stuff—which, fair. That was a liability. But she probably could have mentioned he was in town, maybe even that they'd spent time together, especially if she'd checked with Devin first to suss out his comfort level with external comms.

If Alex was honest with herself, it wasn't just legal documents keeping him her dirty little secret.

It felt like her life had split in half that day in the Dunkin' parking lot. On one hand was the Devin Ashwood she'd thought she'd known from a distance. That idea of a person, an amalgamation of trivia and daydreams, belonged collectively to the fandom and to her friends. Almost like a mascot. They'd always shared everything they knew about that Devin Ashwood. Every photo, every random fact or scrap of a quote. But then she'd met him. In real life. And he'd gotten up on a ladder and cleaned out her gutters so her dad wouldn't fall.

She didn't know how to reconcile these two versions of him. Alex hovered covetously over *her* Devin. The one who was still infuriating but also sweet and scared, in some ways she'd anticipated and in some she hadn't.

Sharing Devin wasn't a big deal when she hated him, but Alex couldn't stop herself from being covetous now. She wanted him in private ways, for parts of him to belong to her and only her. It was a fundamental shift. A betrayal.

Devin with his face painted.

Devin reading fanfic, curled up on the couch.

Devin with his head between her legs, mouth wet, calling her "baby."

She never meant to get in this deep, to hide so much from her best friends. Worse, Alex had been selfish enough to willfully mislead them so she could still benefit from their advice without disclosing something that was objectively huge.

They'd turned on Devin Ashwood for her all those years ago without blinking, but now Alex's disdain had evaporated like so much fog, only to be replaced by—

"Everything okay?" Devin put his hand on her knee. "We're almost at the stadium."

Because of flight delays, they had to go directly from the airport to the basketball game.

"I'm good." Alex shoved the device back into her purse, deciding it was better to say nothing to her friends than to keep lying.

She'd figure out what to tell them when she got back to Tompkins in a few days. When she'd managed to swim clear of the riptide of Devin's attention. When everything went back to normal.

At the stadium, a man with massive shoulders and a security badge that read *Rahul* stopped them at the side door.

"Name?"

A muscle in Devin's jaw ticked. "Devin Ashwood."

Rahul stared down at his clipboard. "I'm sorry, Mr. Ashwood, was it? I'm not seeing that name."

"I'm sure it's there." Devin had on his press smile, but sweat beaded at his hairline. "Can you check again, please?"

He'd been a ball of nerves since they'd landed on the tarmac at LAX, obsessing over what he ate on the plane, how his hair looked, who would be at the event. Was all this anxiety a consequence of the full moon agitating his wolf?

Alex subtly put her hand on his elbow, trying to soothe him while Rahul scanned the list once more.

They were taking such a huge, foolish risk putting Devin in front of a massive crowd and a live televised audience. This was his first public appearance since the video and, allegedly, a stint in rehab. Even an industry outsider like Alex knew there would be extra eyes on him today. If he lost control for a moment on that court, the first hint of the partial shift would blow his chances of shrugging last month's bad press off as a onetime fluke.

She'd tried to talk him out of playing, but Devin insisted this was exactly what he'd trained for: the chance to live his normal life despite the Change. Still, the last thing they needed was for him to get worked up before the game.

"Sorry, buddy," Rahul said with a grimace. "Not on here."

"That's impossible." A familiar low rumble sounded from Devin's chest, the prelude to a growl.

"Would you excuse us for just a second?" Alex tugged Devin into a patch of sunlight to the side of the entrance.

He wouldn't meet her eyes. "This never happens to me."

She almost laughed. Was he really embarrassed right now? Alex had never been on any list. In her life. Unless you counted honor roll at Tompkins High.

"Hey." She kept her hand on his arm and lowered her voice. "None of this celebrity stuff matters to me. At all. Let's blow the whole game off and go eat tacos."

Devin's mouth twitched and his shoulders relaxed. "You're the only person in my life who's ever encouraged me to play hooky."

Alex brightened. Maybe she did have something to offer him besides werewolf training.

"I'll tell Billy to bring the car around." Devin took out his phone but swore when he saw the screen.

"What is it?"

The tension was back in his face, in his limbs. "Brian Dempsey's here."

Alex held back a groan. So much for tacos.

A *TAF* reboot promised Devin everything he craved: purpose, security, adoration, even—she guessed—a way to give meaning to his ability to transform.

Someone else would have called him out for caring too much about a TV show. Alex couldn't.

If Brian Dempsey has no haters, that means I'm dead.

Devin was on the phone, pacing in a tight circle, trying to

clear up the list situation, when a woman in a bright jumpsuit and incredible gold Jordans walked up and tapped him on the shoulder.

"Jade?" Devin's face went on a journey from relieved to guarded in the span of seconds.

The woman gave him a fond closemouthed smile. "Need some help?"

With a few whispered words to Rahul and the flash of some kind of printed pass, all three of them were swept through the door a few moments later.

"You're a lifesaver." Devin squeezed Jade's hand. "I owe you one."

"You owe me several," Jade said with the kind of indulgence Alex recognized as someone else who knew better than to care about Devin Ashwood and did it anyway.

"I gotta get changed. Alex, you good?" he said, jogging backward down the hall to the locker room.

"Yeah, don't worry about me." She tugged at her simple black T-shirt dress. She'd gone out and bought all those new clothes, had made a huge effort to show Devin she could fit in here, and still somehow ended up back in something three years old from Goodwill. Unvarnished. There was probably a metaphor there. You can take the girl out of the small town . . . Oh well. Alex had plenty of practice being snubbed.

"We missed proper introductions." Jade extended her hand. "I'm Jade Nelson. Devin's former agent."

Alex accepted the handshake. "Alex Lawson. I'm his—" Oh god.

Acquaintance? Sex partner? Hired help? Charity case?

"Friend," she settled on.

"Nice to meet you." Jade's grip was firm, assured. "Devin could use more friends."

She led the way to some kind of VIP box with plush reclining seats, full catering, and an open bar. Weirdly, no one here seemed interested in sitting. A group of fifteen or so people, all in suits, lingered near the buffet, where elaborate trays of food remained untouched.

Alex gulped.

"Don't worry. They're sheep in sharkskin," Jade whispered, steering Alex over to the group and introducing her around.

To Alex's immense surprise, the cluster of moguls seemed to find it both endearing and fascinating that she worked as a small-town vet tech. She barely had time to explain what she did before they started launching into stories about their own pets, wanting her opinion on whether such and such behavior was normal or not. After a half hour, Alex had one woman trying to convince her to move to Malibu and become a live-in pet sitter.

For a moment after they parted ways, Alex found herself considering it, this sister life where she walked dogs in the California sunshine, where she had ties to nothing and no one, except maybe Devin Ashwood.

Her heart yearned in more ways than one.

The freedom and anonymity presented by the size and scale of LA were everything Alex thought she'd always wanted. Her mother had given her up to chase this kind of life, one where each day was filled with strangers and limitless potential.

I should want this, she thought at the same time she realized she didn't.

Sticking out in Tompkins might suck sometimes, but at least her presence made a difference. She was a pebble in the machine, a divergence in the brook. Alex had always considered herself an outcast, a misfit, but getting to know Devin, learning about how, slowly, everyone had left him—his parents, his ex-wife, his costars, his team—she finally saw how much community she had in comparison.

"Wait, I'm sorry. Excuse me, but were you a member of Werewolf Support Group?" A strawberry-blond woman, who belatedly introduced herself as a publicist named Viola, pointed frantically to the sticker on the back of Alex's phone, which rested next to her purse on the bar top.

Alex started, staring at the cartoon werewolf reclining on a chaise lounge with the caption *Shift Happens*.

She'd forgotten about the faded and peeling image of the archive mascot. That sticker, a gift from Cam, had weathered almost two decades on Alex's desk before, on a whim, she stuck it on the back of her boring black case earlier this year.

"Uhh, yes." She blushed. Of all the places to get called out for fandom involvement . . .

They chatted for a while. It turned out Viola used to be active on the forums. Sometimes it felt like that site, this fandom, was the scaffolding of her life, guiding Alex, shaping her as much as she'd shaped it.

"Holy shit, you're the Mod? No way. I lived for Mod Notes. No one could tear down Brian Dempsey quite like you." Viola reached into her giant leather purse and passed Alex a crumpled purple flyer. "I'm having a party later in Silver Lake. You should come."

Alex smiled. "Maybe." She doubted she'd be able to leave Devin during the full moon.

The conversation wrapped naturally when music blared and an announcer clad in an incongruous tuxedo came out to kick off the game.

Alex and Jade made their way toward the plexiglass partition that overlooked the stadium floor, taking seats in the front row.

The host, a white man Alex vaguely recognized from

Entertainment Tonight, introduced the lineup for both sides one by one. Most of the names on the backs of the jerseys belonged to C- and D-list network talent, supporting characters literally and figuratively. The few higher-caliber stars were either very young or very old, bookends of a career in this business.

With a jolt, Alex realized Devin, jogging in place while he waited his turn, likely fell into the latter category, at least in the network's eyes. Hopefully he didn't realize.

"You're worried about him." Jade caught her staring, one hand pressed to the glass as Devin did some drills, passing the ball back and forth with a former *Grey's Anatomy* lead.

"I just know he's nervous," Alex said, as discreetly as she could, since the other guests in the suite had begun to make their way down to the seats.

"All right, folks," the announcer's voice boomed. "Up next"—he paused for dramatic effect—"we've got a man who thinks he's a werewolf."

Titters from the suite echoed across the rest of the crowd, along with a few hollers and howls.

Devin faltered a little as he ran out, his sneakers skidding on the shiny wooden floor. Obviously, this jab hadn't been cleared with him ahead of time. To his credit, his smile didn't falter.

"Ah, I'm sorry." The announcer pretended to peer down at invisible note cards. "This says he used to *play a werewolf.* My mistake." He flashed a smarmy grin. "Sports fans, please give it up for Devinnnnn Ashwooooood."

"What a shithead." Jade sighed, then downed the rest of her cappuccino in one long swallow. "Hopefully that's the worst of it."

It wasn't.

Devin played well through the first period—making interceptions and impossible-looking three-pointers. Alex didn't watch sports, but her dad did. She recognized this performance toed the line between exceptional and outrageous.

"Did you know Devin was this good at basketball?" Jade had the look of someone who rarely found herself surprised and did not enjoy the sensation.

"I think he's been practicing." Alex sucked at lying, but Devin wasn't giving her much choice right now.

Her stomach swooped. Did he really think this showboating behavior—during a charity game—made him look cool? While he hadn't shown any signs of transformation, he did seem agitated, his gaze constantly sliding to the sidelines.

Alex followed his line of sight and caught a glimpse of Brian Dempsey's red hair at the same time Devin did.

"Oh, that's not good."

Devin's play got more aggressive immediately. He stole the ball and didn't pass, even when the volunteer coach, a beloved veteran of the WNBA, threw up her hands in exasperation.

"Did he just—" Jade bit her lip.

"Foul a geriatric game show host?" Alex wiped at the nervous sweat that had gathered at her hairline. "Yep."

Devin had many good qualities. Self-awareness was not among them.

He'll do anything. He thinks this is his last chance.

Jade took off her glasses and pinched the bridge of her nose. "People are starting to boo."

A few seats down, two gray-haired execs feigned handwringing. Lines of their commentary cut through the high-pitched alarm of the buzzer.

"Desperate."

"Sad, really."

"Never did know when to quit."

Alex gave them a dirty look. She had said all those things

and more about Devin Ashwood. But that was different. He might be a pathetic try-hard, but he was *her* pathetic try-hard.

"Can you get me down there?" Alex thumbed at the court. "I might be able to calm him down."

Jade nodded. "Worth a shot."

It took some sweet-talking, but they got onto the court just as the second period ended.

Devin missed his mouth with his water bottle when they came up behind him on the bench. "What the hell are you two doing down here?"

Had he seriously not clocked the hostile environment brewing around him? His teammates were squeezed together on the other side of the bench, obviously trying to put as much physical distance between themselves and Devin as possible.

Alex grew up unpopular and was hyperaware of the signs of unsympathetic strangers. Devin, who had signed his first autograph before she was born, didn't sense the danger. Not in a place with so many stimuli. When he'd likely focused his hyperactive senses on monitoring the approval rating of one man.

"Come with me." Alex tugged him urgently to the side, as far away from prying ears as she could.

"What's going on?" Devin frowned up at the VIP box and then stepped closer to her, his face drawing with concern. "Are people being mean to you?"

"What?" She blinked. Oh, right. For most of their brief acquaintance, that had been the case.

"Um, no. I'm okay." *In a twist of fate, you're the one people don't like right now.* How could she bring this up tactfully? "I was just thinking you might wanna back off a little out there on the court. Give the other players a chance."

"You're not serious." Devin ran a hand through his hair,

which had fallen, sweat damp, into his eyes. "I'm playing amazing. People can't take their eyes off me."

Alex had assumed that if things blew up in Devin's face today, it would be the wolf that ruined him. She hadn't stopped to consider that his greatest liabilities were human. All his finely honed skills—the charisma, the showmanship, the shamelessness—had been rendered dangerously potent by his years of relentless reliance on them to survive. Now, fueled by anxiety and supercharged by the full moon, they were poisoning him. And Devin couldn't even tell.

On the court, the Lakers' cheerleaders had the crowd clapping along to what looked like the grand finale of their halftime routine.

"Hey, listen." Devin caught Alex's elbow and leaned forward to whisper in her ear. "I might be showing off a little, but I have to make up for the fact that everyone here thinks I'm a dried-up joke."

Her chest ached with an almost unbearable tenderness for him in that moment. She knew how bad it felt not to be taken seriously, to have people dismiss the things you cared about and try, intentionally, to make you feel small. It was why she thought she could get through to him.

"Remember when you first told me you wanted to play in this game on the full moon?"

"You thought it was a terrible idea," Devin said, his brow creasing.

"I did." Alex took a deep breath. "But you asked me to trust you." She was going to have to be direct, to say the hard truth, knowing Devin wouldn't want to hear it, that he might hold it against her. "I know you can't see it, but all the spotlight chasing you're doing out there is not making you come across like some hot young hero. It's making you come across like a selfish jerk."

Devin reeled back like she'd struck him.

"What? No."

"Trust me." Alex took his hand. *Please.*

"You're wrong." Devin pulled away. His voice brooked no argument. "Brian Dempsey is eating this shit up. He came down here to give me a fist bump. He said I'm killin' it."

She shot her gaze sideways to where *The Arcane Files'* show-runner was chatting away to yet another reporter.

"Devin." Alex flexed her empty fingers. She'd come with him to LA, but she was still losing him before she was ready. There was nothing she could do to stop it. "Brian Dempsey is an asshole. He's not looking out for your best interests. He's never given a shit about you. I'll bet you twenty bucks he came down here to be closer to the press circle."

A whole flock of them stood together over there, unleashing a series of rapid clicks and pops of flashbulbs that made Alex see spots.

"You don't know him." Devin shook his head, stepping farther away, out of her reach.

"Back on the court in two minutes," his coach called out, no doubt worried about how far some of her players had wandered.

"I gotta go," Devin said. "Stick with Jade, okay? I'll be done soon."

He was right; he got thrown out of the game six minutes later.

"How was I supposed to know Justin Hartley had a bad knee?" Devin grumbled later, when they walked toward the exit after a tense series of team photographs.

"I think as a general rule you're expected to avoid trick shots in this kind of environment," Alex commented blandly. Her phone was burning a hole in her pocket, but she didn't take it out.

There was a zero percent chance Devin's antics weren't all over fan circles on the Internet right now. She didn't dare check what the group chat thought about all of this.

All Alex could do was hope that today taught Devin caution. That this disaster wasn't a premonition for later tonight.

26

THE TREPIDATION ALEX had felt about her friends finding out the truth hadn't been enough.

Before, they'd been playfully outraged. With photographic evidence of her holding Devin Ashwood's hand, they were sincerely, justifiably pissed.

Alex and Devin weren't even the focus of the image that must have gone out as part of some kind of press wire for the charity basketball game. But in the corner, in focus, there they were on her phone screen. Alex in profile, Devin turned more toward whoever had taken the shot. Their faces pressed close, trying not to be overheard. There was inherent intimacy to the distance between their mouths. What was the rule—sixteen inches for strangers, twelve for friends, and six for lovers? What did they say when you could count the space with the length of your finger?

Nothing good, as it turned out.

> **ELIZA:** what the fuck . . . this feels gross, Law.

CAM: Nothing about that body language says 'casual first time encounter'

ELIZA: WELP I guess we know now why she's been ignoring us

CAM: I never thought we'd fall in the intimacy hierarchy to Devin Ashwood

ELIZA: . . . this means she's been lying for a while, right?

CAM: I gotta put my phone down before I say something im gonna regret

Sitting on one of the white couches in Devin's living room while he took a shower, Alex stared down at her phone screen and tried to find words.

She was too old for this. For sneaking around, lying about a guy. She felt seventeen again. Only, when she'd been seventeen and had nothing, no one, least of all Devin Ashwood, Eliza and Cam were the ones who held her up, held her together.

In high school, it didn't matter that she got picked last in gym class, that she rode the bus all by herself. She'd always had friends at the tips of her fingers. Every horrifying embarrassment, every snub, Alex weathered because she knew somewhere out there in the world there were people who liked her. Now she'd gambled those same people for a fantasy that was slipping through her fingers.

> **ELIZA:** Did you tell him stuff we've said about him?

Alex's pulse slowed to mud, sludgy and dirty. *The Arcane Files* fandom was the foundation of their friendship, an experience they'd all shared, cultivated, come into as equals.

While they had since moved on to other fandoms, had extended their friendship beyond the boundaries of media properties, *TAF* had been their foundation, their touchstone.

And now it was rubble.

Alex had broken more than Cam's and Eliza's trust. She'd broken the bond that had brought them together.

She was here in Devin's Ashwood big cement house. She knew what it was like to kiss him, not just to imagine it. He'd held her. She'd made him laugh.

All of that was tarnished, tawdry, now too.

Her own naked motivations were no longer avoidable. Even as she'd told herself it could never happen, Alex had wanted what she and Devin had to become something real. She'd avoided her friends because she knew that if they found out, she'd have to choose: you couldn't be both fangirl and girlfriend.

She'd tried to avoid picking between who she was and who she wanted to be and came up empty-handed. Devin's behavior at the game showed her exactly where she stood—several rungs below Brian Dempsey and *TAF*. He still believed the showrunner had more to offer him than Alex did.

When her hero cut her down at that con all those years ago, she hadn't wanted to tell her friends. She knew how much it hurt to lose your idea of Devin Ashwood, of Colby. But she'd done it, revealed her humiliation even though it went against every safeguard she'd tried to build around herself since her mom left, and Cam and Eliza let him go willingly. For her.

Hating Devin Ashwood bonded them together more than loving him. The way he'd insulted Alex had been personal, while admiration for him was anonymous, ubiquitous.

Ever since she'd turned seventeen, Alex had built herself around a single truth: Devin called her unlovable; Cam and Eliza proved him wrong.

Devin found her crying into one of his overly firm throw pillows.

"What the fuck?" He knelt down in front of her, his eyes flashing silver. "Who did this? Who hurt you?"

"I did." Alex wiped at her eyes with the sleeve of her dress. She wished she could place some of the blame on his shoulders, but she'd known from the jump that caring for him would get her clobbered.

"What?" Devin's irises faded back to normal. He moved to sit beside her. "What do you mean? What happened?"

"My closest fandom friends found out I've been spending time with you. That I've been covering it up."

"And that's, what . . . embarrassing or something?" His frown deepened.

Alex couldn't explain how getting close to him in real life meant leaving Eliza and Cam behind.

She shook her head. "You wouldn't understand."

Devin flinched. "Why?" he bit out; the ego deflation he'd experienced at the game must have still been fresh in his mind. "Because I'm not some weirdo from the Internet?"

Her breath caught in her throat before a bitter laugh erupted, carved from the hollow space between Alex's ribs.

She got to her feet and stared down at him, this man she'd once wanted to save her. "I was so desperate to erase the version of you that hurt me that I let myself believe you'd changed."

Fool me twice.

It had taken—what?—a handful of weeks to convince herself Devin wasn't the selfish asshole she'd assumed. But the man she'd seen over the last twenty-four hours was still exactly as vapid, selfish, and carelessly cruel as she'd always feared.

At the first glimpse of Brian Dempsey and the weights and measures of the Hollywood machine, he'd stopped trusting her. Alex had let herself fall for yet another version of Devin Ashwood that wasn't real.

She had to get out of here.

"Alex, wait. Where are you going?" Devin scrambled to follow her as she collected her shoes and purse.

She didn't know. Out. Anywhere.

Reaching into her pocket, she came up with the purple flyer from the fellow fan at the stadium. Alex almost smiled. After all this time, the archive was still saving her ass. She ordered a Lyft, punching in the party address with trembling hands.

"What's going on?" Devin was at a total loss. "What did I do?"

Alex spun on her heel, her hands clenched into fists. "I lied to my closest friends about our relationship to protect you." *And you broke my heart anyway.*

"That's bullshit," Devin said under his breath.

Alex reeled. "Excuse me?"

"I'm sorry, but are you really gonna stand there and pretend this is the first time you've kept people at arm's length?" All of the frustration he'd carried on the car ride home from the stadium was back twofold. A shower couldn't wash it away. "You said it yourself at the cabin, the people you're closest to, they all get little pieces of you, but does anyone get the whole thing?"

"I . . ." Alex sputtered. She wasn't used to him like this, seri-

ous, almost . . . betrayed. How could he play the wounded party
here? When all she'd done since they met was try to help him?

Devin paced before his front door. She could see signs of the
impending full moon in his stride, the hulking movements almost a prowl.

She fought a sudden onslaught of guilt. She'd promised to
be here with him for this, the hardest part of his transformation.
The final test.

Devin ground to a halt and faced her. "I can't believe you're
chickening out right now."

Alex tried to gather the reins of her anger, but they were slipping. She hadn't expected him to know her this well, to care
enough about her leaving to fight her like this.

"I'm not . . ." That wasn't right. Was it?

"You do this to protect yourself." Devin stared her down, his
voice harsh and openly wounded. "Your mom took off when
you were a kid, and now you think if you don't give your whole
heart away again, no one can hurt you when they leave."

How dare he. That wasn't— She didn't—

"Think about it. Are you ever totally honest about what you
want or how you feel? Why are you pushing me away right
now? Why are you running?"

All this time she'd put Devin Ashwood under the micro-
scope, he'd been doing the same to her.

It was searing to be seen.

"You're mad at me." Devin's voice softened, so her surprise
must have shown on her face. "I get it. So stay here and yell at
me. I can take it. Just . . . don't leave."

Alex swallowed against a tight throat, helpless, caught.

"I can't." She stepped around him and reached for the
doorknob.

Every animal had a self-preservation instinct, even humans.

"You were right all those years ago," she said, not trusting herself to turn around and face him. "I probably am going to die alone." She'd fulfilled her own fate, followed his words like a premonition. "But guess what?"

Alex took her first step out into the balmy LA night, away from Devin Ashwood for the last time.

"So are you."

Full Shift, wiki article #707

Unlike Partial Shifts, which occur outside of the full moon, during a Full Shift, which can only occur when the moon is at 100 percent illumination, The One transforms into the body of a true wolf.

Mod Note: Because of budget constraints on the show, Colby was rarely shown in a full shift. Instead, this type of transformation was depicted using shadows until the final season, when the TW sprang for CGI, which was "poorly received" by the fanbase.

27

AS ALEX RODE away, Devin bent to pick up the crumpled purple paper she'd dropped on his front steps. The Prius that picked her up got smaller, slowly, as the driver hugged the spiral turns down the hills from his home.

MY BOSS IS OUT OF TOWN, LET'S PARTY, the flyer read, followed by an address in Silver Lake.

If Alex thought she was punishing him by running off to drink warm beer with strangers, she wasn't. He'd been to a thousand Eastside hipster house parties. You know what happened there? Small talk. *Good luck with that, sweetheart.*

He slammed his door on his way back inside.

Devin knew he'd fucked up at the game, okay? It had been like the shift; he could feel it happening, but he couldn't stop it. Alex's advice didn't land over the wolf's restlessness, the screaming panic in his bloodstream that stepping back into LA had brought on. He hadn't realized how bad this town made him feel until he spent a significant period away.

His footsteps echoed on the poured-concrete floors, too loud as he wandered aimlessly across his downstairs. The empty house held traces of Alex's scent—not the plastic, chemical compound of her new clothes but the pure, unadulterated notes that came straight from her skin.

Devin purposefully gave a wide berth to her sweatshirt hanging by the door.

The wolf wanted to bury his nose in it. Wanted to find Alex. Show her his neck.

Devin overruled his instincts.

Why should he run after her and apologize? She was the one abandoning him at his most vulnerable. When he needed her. The full moon would rise in a few hours, and sure, Devin could handle himself, but they'd arranged this whole thing so he wouldn't have to. Alex was supposed to be here, armed with emergency tranquilizers, her comforting scent surrounding him like a blanket, her sweet husky voice keeping him tethered.

Devin opened the fridge and let the blast of cool air hit him full in the face. He had no food in the house. He'd made a reservation for dinner for two at Crossroads on Melrose. It was supposed to be the best vegan food in the city.

He bet they wouldn't have any snacks she could eat at her shitty little house party.

The wolf whined, worried.

Alex is a grown woman. She can order herself a delivery salad if she gets hungry.

Devin pulled out a beer even though he hadn't been able to get drunk since his transformation. At least the bitter hops on his tongue matched his mood.

As he leaned against his kitchen island, the label came away under the pressure of his thumb.

Alex was supposed to be different. She wasn't supposed to leave him.

Just because he'd been selfish.

And pathetic.

And mean.

Fuck.

All these feelings he couldn't look at straight on swirled inside him.

He'd completely lost his head when she tried on new clothes—how would he react when she inevitably came home smelling like someone else? He was losing her, and he couldn't figure out how to stop it. What if she'd walked out that door not just for tonight but for good?

People left when Devin stopped paying them. His parents, his ex-wife, Jade, now her . . .

He didn't know what to do. How to make things right.

Alex loved *The Arcane Files.* At least if the show came back— if Devin was Colby again—he'd still mean something to her. She might insist she was only hate watching so she could tell him how bad it was. But whatever. He needed to matter to her in whatever way he could.

Try as he might to hide it, Devin had always been desperate.

He booked his first feature film at seven. A family vacation comedy with a veteran Oscar winner playing his father. The guy had made a career in Mafia flicks in the seventies, a frequent collaborator with Scorsese. He'd taken the easy-money role to combat mounting alimony payments. Though of course Devin hadn't understood that at the time.

He was funny with a big, belly-shaking laugh. Devin took to following him around after the cameras stopped rolling, calling him "Dad" even between takes. The guy had been okay about it at first, but then one day, after a series of shitty delays, Devin tried holding his hand, only to have it smacked away. *What's wrong with this kid? He doesn't know when to quit.*

The hit hadn't been hard, not enough to leave a mark, but yeah, Devin remembered the sting.

He thought he'd learned to live like this, constantly scared and unable to show it. But this whole werewolf thing made everything worse, more precarious. Because now, if he got too emotional—if he felt anything too strongly—he could lose control.

Seconds ticked by on the wooden Scandinavian clock his decorator had picked out. Every minute without Alex made him more anxious. It was like at some point, while Devin was obsessing over the moon, she had become his sun. Each step she took away from him pushed Devin further into darkness, into the cold.

How could he tell her he wanted her when he *needed* her like this? It wasn't fair. She couldn't save him indefinitely.

He needed to be able to control himself without her. To subdue the riot of his emotions all on his own.

Devin had spent an extraordinary amount of his life working out. He'd had a bunch of different trainers, but they all agreed on one thing: no pain, no gain. The second your body adjusted, you had to make it harder. Add more weight, more resistance. Cut time, increase the reps. The trials he'd done with Alex, honing his senses, finding his center, testing himself in increasingly stressful situations—it was the same. This was just the next step. His newest test.

Alex was a crutch. It had always been inevitable that one day, sooner or later, he'd be alone with the wolf when the moon came calling.

Devin went to the master bath to collect his phone from the pocket of his joggers. The thing had died on the way back from the stadium. He plugged it in at the kitchen island and then forced himself onto his too-stiff sofa, flicking on his grossly expensive TV.

The *Entertainment Tonight* logo flashed. Just as Devin

hovered his thumb over the button to pull up the on-demand guide, Brian Dempsey came onscreen.

Devin froze. He blinked at the caption. Then, when it didn't change, he got up until he stood two feet from the giant screen. Each letter of the announcement was as big as his palm.

LIVE: BRIAN DEMPSEY ANNOUNCES THE ARCANE
FILES MOVIE

"What the fuck?" Devin waited for the straight shot of pure elation to hit. *This is it.*

Despite what everyone had said, he'd done it; he got to be Colby again.

Except why did the role feel in this moment like a beloved jacket that he'd worn for many years, only to wake up one day and discover it no longer quite fit? Devin shook out his shoulders. That didn't make sense. He loved Colby and he loved *TAF.* Dempsey must have gone straight to the execs after today's game. Maybe something raw, something animal in Devin's play had sparked urgency for him to revisit Colby's story.

Devin turned up the volume on the TV, even though he didn't need to.

"We're so excited for this next chapter," Dempsey told the reporter, his red hair gleaming under the studio lights. "Gus Rochester blew us all away last year with his performance in *Shatter Me.* As soon as I saw that, I knew I needed to write for him again. We realized how much of his character's story we'd left on the table."

Fine. They wanted to show more of Gus? Let them. Contrary to popular belief, Devin didn't need the spotlight all the time.

The pretty reporter with the slightly orange spray tan held a finger to her ear, as if she was getting feedback in real time from the studio. "Is it true that the reboot was developed without a role for Devin Ashwood?"

Devin's ears started ringing.

"Yes, sadly." Brian Dempsey pouted, his forehead refusing to crease in the movement.

Bad Botox.

"We love Devin. He's great. But we just didn't see any more story for Colby. There's something a little sad about a forty-two-year-old werewolf."

Devin tasted copper, salt.

No. There'd been a mistake.

"He'll like you," the woman at the front desk said, the first time Devin went to Brian Dempsey's office to read for Colby.

"Why do you say that?" Devin was twenty-two and sleeping on his friend's couch between auditions, living off frozen Costco burritos. Too afraid to ask his parents for any of the money that he'd earned.

"You look like him," she said, and handed him a plastic security badge. "Only better."

That was almost twenty years ago. Devin had gotten old. Why would anyone want a self-insert with crow's-feet and bad knees?

A crash cut the air, followed by a streaming fizz. Devin looked down. He'd dropped his beer.

The broken bottle spun, leaking across his carpet, the neck shattered.

If Alex came back, she might step on a shard. He went to his knees.

His eyes blurred, burned, as he reached to collect the slivers of brown glass. As his hand made contact, he heard a series of clinks.

Claws.

Fuck. Fuck. Alex wasn't here. And Devin didn't know if he could hold back. Not now. Not this.

He needed the tranquilizers. He stumbled toward the guest room, but it hit him in the hall—Alex had taken her purse with her.

Devin tried to slow his breath, to find an anchor. He could stay conscious, in control, even through the shift. As he stumbled down the hall, the walls moved—no, not the walls. That was him, his vision again, going funny. Dizziness setting in. Was the bitterness on his tongue from the beer or the blood?

Need to call Alex.

He missed a step on the way into the kitchen and caught himself on the counter. Still plugged in, his phone lit up with a bombardment of messages, missed calls, emails.

> **ANTHONY:** Know you must be hurting, brother.

> **ERICA:** Don't do anything rash.

It was like someone had died.

And then it hit Devin. His career was over. It might as well be his life.

What else did he have?

If he was younger, his looks undiluted, his reputation unspoiled, he might've stood a chance at a comeback. But Devin was no longer some fresh, new thing waiting for a breakout vehicle. If he was honest with himself, his name had baggage in this town even before Venice. He'd come up in soaps, had a sloppy tabloid divorce. If he had more talent, perhaps these black marks could be overlooked, but Devin knew his ceiling as an artist. How many times had he been told by his parents that he skated by on his good looks?

He'd tried to control exactly what he revealed about himself
for so much of his career—of his life, really. And for what?

He wanted to be the perfect canvas for a character. Wanted
to be exactly what a director envisioned. Exactly the hero the
fans wished could step off the screen.

A new message came in as Devin stared at the screen. I'm so
sorry, from Jade.

A metallic crunch drowned out his jagged inhale. He'd accidentally crushed the phone in his fist.

Devin couldn't catch his breath. There was a weight on his
chest he couldn't shift, even when he tore off his shirt.

He'd seen something like this on TV once, a guy having a
panic attack—*oh. Oh.*

Blackness bled at the corners of his vision.

He'd trained for this. With Alex. But now he couldn't remember why he was supposed to fight it.

Darkness beckoned, an invitation. A reprieve.

*Alex reached for his hand earlier at the game, asking him to
trust her. Her palm had been so warm, the tender flesh soft, careful. And Devin had pulled back so he could keep showing off.*

He'd lost her.

He'd lost everything.

After a lifetime of seeking the approval of the anonymous
masses, he'd wound up completely alone.

Devin wouldn't know real love if it was standing right in
front of him.

After struggling for so long, surrender felt like release.

He might be worthless, but the wolf was strong, sure, unbro-
ken.

Devin opened his arms for oblivion and set his monster free.

28

CHIPTUNES SOUNDED LIKE a drunk person stepping on a child's light-up soundboard. Alex found, to her dismay, that not only did Viola and her friends make music by remixing video game sounds—club beats cut with blaring clangs and whooshes and beeps—but they insisted on playing this music for unsuspecting guests.

"This song is sick, right?" a white guy with dreads yelled from behind the makeshift turntable in the corner of the mid-century modern mansion.

Alex offered a weak thumbs-up as vibrations from the subwoofers blew back her hair.

She'd never gotten into video games. She lacked the hand-eye coordination. Also, they made you do battle too much when she just wanted to romance the fussy bisexual vampire.

And yes, she understood the hypocrisy of judging anyone for their niche media interests when she herself had once dedicated an entire eight-week period to cataloging the backstory of a tertiary character who appeared onscreen in *The Arcane Files* for a total of 234 seconds.

What could she say? Fandom was everything when you were in it and embarrassing as hell when you weren't.

Alex was too old for parties with kegs and no food. She made her way out to the back deck overlooking the swimming pool, hoping to escape both the music and the crowd. A cool breeze raised goose bumps on her bare arms as she leaned against the wooden railing. She wished she could text Cam and Eliza about this spectacle. If things were normal, she would have captured an audio clip inside and made them try to guess where she was. But Alex had lost that privilege.

The still water of the pool glittered in the falling darkness.

"Let me take him off your mind," Viola said, propping her elbows up beside Alex's. "Devin Ashwood, right?" The other woman had on a V-neck denim jumpsuit that showed off her long legs. The sun slowly sinking on the horizon cast a soft glow over her heart-shaped face.

"I saw you guys leave together after the game," she explained.

"Oh." A flush crept up the back of Alex's neck. "Yeah. He's a menace."

"I mean, I get it." Viola took a sip of her beer, leaving a ring of purple lipstick on the rim. "I used to have it so bad for Colby. That bomber jacket? Whoooo." She fanned herself. "It's funny, isn't it? A show ends and all the oxygen gets slowly sucked out of a fandom. Until one day you wake up and the fever dream is over. I was such a hard-core Nolby shipper, I'd get heart palpitations just thinking about them. But now?" Viola shrugged. "I mean, sure, I still got a twinge of fondness seeing Devin Ashwood at the game, but I'm not sick over it the way I would have been back in the dog days of 2018."

Alex wished she could say the same. Devin Ashwood had been the source of her constant suffering since she had braces, and she still couldn't quit him.

"Besides, I don't mean to be rude," Viola said slowly, cautiously, "but isn't he kind of a dick in real life?"

Cicadas sang in the early evening air almost loud enough to match the whir of the pool filter.

Alex didn't know how to answer. Yes, Devin Ashwood was a dick. Totally. Presented with the chance to dunk on him a month ago, especially armed with the kind of fodder she had now, Alex could have done some serious damage. She would have made this pretty woman laugh. And never thought twice about the real person behind the straw man she was tearing down.

"Ahhh," Viola said in the face of Alex's silence. "You like him anyway."

And there was the rub.

What could Alex possibly say? How could she explain to a stranger that it was worse than that. She didn't just like Devin Ashwood. She understood him.

As much as she wanted to pretend her affection for him was a weakness, a naivete left over from girlhood, she couldn't. Over the last month, she'd seen the good and the bad and the ugly of Devin Ashwood. The way he thought he had to be a flawless vessel for other people's fantasies, to make up for the fatal flaw of wanting to be loved.

The first time Alex fell for him, it was because of that performance. His face, his voice, his smile. Everything the wolf stole.

Alex had seen what was left when the supernatural carved to the core of Devin Ashwood and found he wasn't at all what she expected. Who knew that under all that self-serious bravado was someone playful and affectionate, wary but hopeful? Someone protective and stubborn. And tougher than anyone, especially Alex, ever gave him credit for.

His parents brought him here, to LA, *when he was seven*

years old and told him their livelihood and their love depended on his ability to get cast. Alex, of all people, should recognize regression. Was it such a surprise that he'd backslid from the second he decided to return to LA?

But she couldn't say any of that to this nice stranger.

"Unfortunately, I don't think I'll ever be normal about Devin Ashwood."

In the near dark, Alex couldn't tell whether that was a tragedy or simply fact.

The door slid open behind them and two guys walked out to share a joint, the glow of the cherry lighting their faces, one and then the other, as they passed it back and forth.

Alex's phone buzzed in her pocket.

"Sorry," she told Viola, her stomach swooping as she pulled it out. Alex was shaping up to be a real flop of a party guest.

The other woman waved her off. "I hope that's him and he's groveling. I'm gonna go grab another beer."

Music blared and then faded along with the opening and closing of the back door as she rejoined the party.

The notification was an email rather than a text—to her archive inbox—a Google Alert so long dormant that for a second Alex couldn't process the headline.

BRIAN DEMPSEY ANNOUNCES PLANS FOR <u>THE</u>
<u>ARCANE FILES</u> MOVIE

Mortifyingly, her fangirl heart soared. Alex found herself grinning into the night. It figured that Devin could act like a total clown for the last forty-eight hours and somehow miraculously still pull out the win.

God. She couldn't believe she was gonna devote more precious hours of her life to watching *The Arcane Files*, but it was inevitable. It was like when your ex posted vacation pics with their new partner. It didn't matter if you told yourself you weren't gonna look; sooner or later you caved.

Alex held the phone to her chest and closed her eyes for a minute, letting the nostalgia crash over her like a wave. *TAF* back on the air. When she was younger, when life was simpler, she would have dined out on this feeling—new content, new storylines, the return of her favorite characters, the return of this *fandom*—for a year. Maybe more.

If the last month had never happened, she would have stayed up all night, flipping between the group chat, Tumblr, Discord, and whatever last vestiges remained of Twitter. People were probably already posting predictions. She could almost guarantee someone had started new fic.

Knowing Dempsey, they'd play up the potential for *something* with Nathaniel in promos, then ship in another blond woman as Colby's latest love interest. But now, instead of rolling her eyes in frustration or silently fuming, Alex would watch Devin kiss someone else knowing exactly what it felt like. She imagined holding her breath, waiting to see if he cupped the back of their neck or kissed their jawline. She'd never enjoy *TAF* again purely as a (reluctant, long-suffering) fan. Not now that she knew what it was like to be Devin Ashwood's . . . someone.

He must be ecstatic. She could picture him getting the call in his kitchen: the wild spread of his grin, the inevitable fist pump. Everything he wanted, everything he'd worked for, what they'd all told him was an impossible pipe dream, finally, *finally* won.

Gladness spread like warmth in her chest. She wanted him to be happy, even if it meant he'd never belong to her.

She made herself actually read the article, expecting to see a projected filming schedule or release date, a timeline of how long she'd have to prepare herself.

Only . . .

> Dempsey shocked fans, revealing the recently
> green-lighted script does not include a role for
> the series' longtime star, Devin Ashwood.

A white-hot blinding rage burst from behind Alex's eyelids, making the text on the screen swim.

> . . . even costars caught off guard. "What do you
> mean Ashwood's not in it?" said Oscar winner Gus
> Rochester when called for comment. "We're
> talking about *The Arcane Files*, right?"

Alex let out a screech so terrible, it scared a nightingale out of one of the property's palm trees.

The couple to her side threw their still-smoking joint to the ground and scampered back inside.

Was this a fucking joke? Why would anyone continue *The Arcane Files* without Devin Ashwood? How could they, after everything he'd given them?

> Sources close to Dempsey hinted that the
> showrunner had concerns Ashwood's recent
> "lowbrow" antics in the press would upstage what
> he hopes will be a more "prestige" reboot of his
> debut franchise. "Brian doesn't want anyone
> thinking this is the Devin Ashwood show."

Of all the asinine, out-of-touch, self-important delusions. Objectively, Devin Ashwood—Colby—was *TAF*. The reason the fans who'd grown up watching supported the story long after the writers room jumped the shark. This was an overt slap in the face to Devin, but it was also a slap in the face to the fans. To the thousands of people so invested in Colby that they'd kept that ridiculous show on the air for so long.

Alex didn't give a shit if Gus Rochester had grown into his sideburns and learned how to do a British accent; he didn't love the show, or the audience, the way Devin did.

Brian Dempsey had always been a piece of garbage, but this was a whole other level of pettiness and self-importance.

That asshole had waved to them in the parking lot of the basketball game earlier, calling out, *Y'all have a great night.*

He must have known Devin looked up to him, that he trusted him implicitly. Even someone who hadn't followed the life of Devin Ashwood religiously could see that the show-runner had been a kind of mentor to him. Apparently, Alex thought with a sinking heart, just like Devin's parents, he'd only ever seen Devin as a product to be sold.

Devin Ashwood was selfish and shallow, but even as a were-wolf, he was more human than the people he trusted.

He'd be crushed when he saw this, and he was already vulnerable tonight because of the full moon.

Oh god.

The full moon.

And she'd left Devin alone.

FUCK.

With shaking hands, Alex tried to call him.

"Hey—"

"Thank—"

"—you've reached Devin. Leave a message. And if it's interesting enough, I'll return your call."

No, no, no. Alex looked around helplessly. What could she do? With less than a half hour before the moon rose, she was at this horrible party on the other side of town. It might be her first time in LA, but even she knew traffic on a Saturday night was unlikely to be kind.

Alex had no other choice.

She made a hasty apology to Viola and ordered another car. In the back seat of yet another Prius, she crossed everything that Devin could hold back the wolf until she got there.

If he lost himself tonight, Alex feared they'd never be able to bring him back.

29

IT DIDN'T MATTER how much Alex begged and bargained, her driver couldn't get past congestion on the freeway any quicker. She cursed every Prius in the seemingly endless line of head-lights ahead of them and tried Devin's phone again, and again to no avail. There was nothing she could do for him trapped in this four-wheeled prison. It would all come down to the hours of training as Devin fought to stay in control of his mind while the moon called forth the full shift.

Alex sat back against the vinyl seat of the car with a sinking stomach, trying and failing to remain optimistic. She'd seen Devin go to pieces over much less than losing his beloved franchise. Alex couldn't imagine the frantic man she'd seen at the basketball game deciding that a professional and personal betrayal like the one he'd suffered at the hands of Brian Dempsey was nothing more than a glancing blow.

Her phone vibrated on the seat beside her, and Alex's heart flew into her throat.

> **CAM:** We've decided to call parlay

Alex gasped, almost sick with fondness seeing her best friend's name on her screen.

ELIZA: Brian Dempsey green lighting a TAF movie without Colby is extenuating circumstances to your fandom probation

ELIZA: this has nothing to do with the fact that you've got some kind of in with Devin Ashwood and might have gossip from an inside source 👀

Desperately, Alex found herself smiling.

CAM: We've loved to loathe Devin Ashwood for the better part of our lives, but I've got to admit I feel bad. He made The Arcane Files worth watching and (indirectly) brought us together.

ELIZA: His various humiliating exploits have provided us with countless hours of joy.

CAM: he might be a slightly delusional prima donna but he's also our little meow meow.

> **CAM:** besides, if anyone can keep him in line, it's you, Law.

Alex couldn't help the tears that blurred her vision. She hadn't thought that she'd lost her friends forever—she wouldn't have let them go without more of a fight—but to have them on her side again, now, shored up her flagging courage.

> **ALEX:** I'm on my way to his house

It felt surreal to type, like she was the y/n self-insert in a Devin Ashwood/reader RPF.

> **ALEX:** I know I fucked up keeping secrets from you guys. I can't explain everything right now, but I swear I'm gonna find some way to make this up to you

> **CAM:** we trust you

> **ELIZA:** I expect to read the entire saga in fic form, as penance.

> **ELIZA:** #blackcat/goldenretriever #Enemies-to-lovers #Agegap 300K Rated E

By the time they finally pulled up to Devin's long, winding driveway, Alex had convinced herself that she could handle whatever awaited her at the top of the hill. That confidence wavered slightly when, about halfway up, the sound of a growl overtook the purr of the engine. The driver looked at her uneasily in the rearview mirror.

"That's, uh . . . my guard dog," Alex said, as confidently as possible considering the claw-shaped dents in the steel fence that wrapped around the property. "He's a Great Pyrenees."

At least she knew Devin was still in there. The security protocols designed to protect him from the rest of the world, utilized in reverse.

Her driver dropped her off and sped back down the hill, leaving tire marks outside the driveway.

Alex took a deep breath, steeling herself. She had handled Devin in a partial shift before, and the wolf had never shown violent tendencies toward her. That didn't stop her body from breaking out in goose bumps. She pulled her Taser from her purse, just in case.

Alex entered the code into the gate security system with sweaty hands. The metal groaned as it receded into the stone walls of the perimeter fence, shooting sparks as the warped shape grated against the rock.

Across the vast yard, Devin was nowhere to be found. There was, however, a wave of destruction that signaled a previous appearance. Grass torn out in clumps, ceramic pots overturned. This had to be at least ten thousand dollars' worth of gardening destroyed.

The back door, made of weatherproof glass, had been shattered by blunt force. Shards littered the deck like macabre confetti, along with a set of bloody paw prints that trailed back inside and then faded, as if the injured animal had healed in real time.

Alex tensed with worry but forced herself to stay calm. She made her way carefully through the foyer to find the living room in shambles, the TV on and blaring. She picked up the remote and turned it off, plunging the house into sudden silence. She realized the growling had stopped, departing with her Lyft.

On the kitchen counter she found the remains of Devin's pulverized cell phone. Alex took that as a fair indicator that someone had broken the news about the reboot. By all evidence, he'd taken rejection about as well as could be expected.

"Devin?" Alex called as she made her way down the big, open hallway. Her voice echoed off the stark white walls.

She found him in her guest room with her red sweatshirt between his teeth. Alex took an involuntary step back.

She'd known what to expect, had seen the paw prints moments ago; still, her body tightened with shock. *Oh, that's a real live animal.*

The wolf stared back at her, massive, with glowing silver eyes and a sandy-colored coat. The juxtaposition of the huge body curled up in the corner, his head resting on his giant front paws, stole her breath.

Alex had grown up around wolves. She knew the average adult male red wolf in Ocala could reach up to five and a half feet from nose tip to tail. Devin seemed about that size, maybe a little larger. It was hard to tell with him lying down. Thank god they weren't dealing with *Twilight*-sized giants or he'd definitely have destroyed more than the living room and garden.

"Hi," she said, inanely.

The wolf gave her a long look, then got up and turned, showing Alex his back as he once more curled around the sweatshirt. He seemed . . . grumpy. Sulky. His side-eye and huff somehow conveying the very human emotion of betrayal, the same one Devin had given her right before she walked out the door.

"Devin?" Alex said again, and the wolf's ears twitched.

She didn't know if that meant that he understood her or if

he was just responding to the sound of her voice. At least he wasn't in a defensive posture or showing any signs of aggression. She shoved the Taser back into her purse.

"If you can understand what I'm saying, blink twice," she said, taking a few steps closer and crouching down.

The wolf pivoted again so his big furry butt complete with plumy tail pointed right at her. Alex took that as a no. So far, there was a surprising amount of indignity in trying to communicate with a werewolf.

It was strange to see the signs of the partial shift in his fully shifted form. The familiar silver irises set in his lupine face, a long white muzzle, a black nose, and whiskers.

It was a struggle to make her brain process that this giant natural predator was in fact Devin Ashwood, or at least part of him. The most the audience ever saw of Colby in the full shift was a comical CGI rendering.

Alex had guessed that this would happen, but guessing and seeing it for herself were two very different things. A sliver of moonlight came through the open window, for a moment casting Devin's fur the same golden honey brown as his hair when he was human.

Upon closer inspection, the wolf was kind of filthy. Dirt covered his paws and legs, along with dark red dried blood. Alex didn't see any open wounds. The wolf apparently enjoyed accelerated healing.

"Don't think I missed your escape attempt," she told him.

The wolf tilted his head as if trying to listen to what she was saying.

"I guess the security system thwarted you, huh?"

She was surprised he'd come back here, to her room instead of his own. You'd think every other space in the house would be more familiar, more comforting.

She stared down at the sweatshirt he'd curled around.

Oh. Right. He liked her scent. A lot. His response to her LA makeover took on burgeoning context, his insults becoming, somehow, a poorly delivered compliment.

"Were you . . . uh . . . looking for me?" The idea made Alex's heart hurt. A fresh wave of guilt washed over her. She should have been here. They'd made all the preparations together, gone through all the training. She'd known he could be an asshole when she signed on to help him.

Since words didn't seem to be getting through to him in this form, Alex crouched down next to the big animal's body and tentatively reached out her palm.

The wolf allowed her to pet behind his ears, his soft fur moving like silk between her fingers.

He leaned into her hand. Apparently petting was an acceptable form of apology. His pointed ears relaxed, and he even turned to lick at the bare skin of her wrist.

"Oh, are we friends again?"

When Alex had imagined Devin during the Change, she'd certainly pictured more sinister scenarios than this. The wolf simply looked sad, weary. He sighed through his nose and once again lowered his big head to his paws. When Alex made to stand, to give him some space, he whined low in his throat.

"Don't worry," she said, folding herself into a seated position beside him, "I'll hang around until you're feeling more like yourself."

Was this what lay beneath the core of Devin Ashwood with every learned social response removed? Had he really withstood pain and resisted temptation all in a desperate bid to hide the fact that deep down he craved comfort and companionship?

Alex could handle that. He'd taken care of her, more than

once. Her insides twisted, remembering the tender way he'd held her when she was in pain. She could take care of him too.

First things first.

It took significant coaxing, including uncovering a jar of peanut butter from the pantry, to convince the wolf to climb into Devin's massive marble bathtub.

He didn't trust the rushing water coming out of the spigot and proceeded to both growl at and try to bite it in turns. That, more than anything so far, convinced Alex she was dealing with the wolf rather than Devin in the driver's seat. The latter never would have allowed himself to look this silly.

Alex stuck her own palm under the water while he watched to try to prove it was safe.

"See? It's nice." She'd deduced at this point that he couldn't understand what she was saying, but talking to him made her feel better. Plus, the sound of her voice seemed to soothe him.

The wolf gave her a brow-furrowed look that questioned her intelligence.

"You'll thank me once your human counterpart returns," Alex said as he sat, docile but clearly miserable, while she gently sprayed his feet clean with the detachable shower head. "This entire house is wall-to-wall white. You've already ruined several carpets."

The wolf let out a soft grunt that said she better appreciate the privilege he was bestowing, allowing her to bathe him.

It figured that Devin Ashwood would be spoiled in every form.

When the opportunity arose, the wolf took great joy in re-taliation, shaking his sopping-wet coat on the bath mat within inches of Alex's crouched body so that she got thoroughly spat-tered. It was remarkably disconcerting to see Devin's sly smile on the face of a predator.

After changing into clean and dry pajamas, Alex found the wolf curled up on the couch. She dropped down beside him and indulged his demands for ear scritches, which he conveyed by bumping his nose against her knee until she lifted her arm.

As both Alex's and the wolf's eyelids began to droop, she couldn't help but think how differently this night might have ended if Devin had never become a werewolf. In the least conventional way possible, he'd managed to avoid the fallout of the *TAF* news, the inevitable onslaught of phone calls and requests for comment. Of course the reprieve would only last as long as the full moon. Alex didn't have much hope the tranquility of tonight would carry over to morning, when Devin woke up forced to face a future without Colby.

30

ALEX AWOKE WITH immense relief to find Devin returned to his human form. Once more resplendent in full Hollywood Hunk™ status, he snored lightly on the opposite side of the couch in the same spot where the wolf had curled up over Alex's feet last night.

The long lines of his body were relaxed in slumber, the morning sun painting his bare skin golden. His hands had returned to normal, nothing of even the partial shift remaining in the fingers he had wrapped around a throw pillow.

Alex held herself perfectly still, not wanting to wake him just yet. When he rejoined the world of the domesticated, he'd have to process Brian Dempsey's betrayal. She would shield him from that just a little longer, if she could.

No doubt *The Arcane Files'* fandom, various entertainment press outlets, and the team of professionals paid to protect Devin Ashwood's image and interests were champing at the bit to get a comment out of him.

On a more selfish note, Alex indulged in these last intimate moments (not that she was full-on ogling—his curled position protected most of his modesty). She knew a series of awkward apologies awaited them when he awoke, along with the goodbye they'd both pretended wasn't imminent.

Alex would fly home tomorrow, and then what? They'd text? Call?

No. He'd get swallowed back into the machine of this town and forget about her. Hell, he'd almost done that in the last forty-eight hours. Alex didn't like it, but she couldn't blame him, really. It was the only life he'd ever known.

It was fine. They'd both go back to where they belonged. And in Tompkins, without debt hanging over her head, Alex would figure out how to open her heart. If she couldn't keep Devin, at least she could keep what he'd taught her.

Perhaps it was a bit of a lackluster ending to an outrageous month of adventure and poorly managed sexual tension, but Alex had always found that real life fell short of her fictional standards.

At least that's what she thought until the house's gate buzzer went off.

Devin jolted awake with a furious growl.

Alex barely had time to blink before he was charging, fully nude, into the foyer, flexing his fingers and baring blunt teeth.

Alex scrambled after him, her socked feet sliding across the polished marble floors.

"Devin, *don't.*"

At least he didn't seem to be going into a partial shift, the way he had when they'd been startled awake by her father. His body stayed in its human form while Devin stalked forward as if he hadn't even heard her protests.

He staggered as he walked, listing dangerously from one side to the other as if he were drunk or didn't know quite how to navigate his own legs. Near the doorway, he stumbled into a gilt end table and snapped his jaws at the offending object before righting himself.

The momentary delay was enough for the poor mailman to hightail it back into his vehicle and for Alex to throw herself in front of Devin, bodily holding him back from pursuit with two hands pressed against his heaving pecs and her back against the front door.

Devin froze, the growl cutting off as he frowned down at her hands, seemingly caught off guard by her inserting herself between him and the intruder.

"What the hell do you think you're doing?" she demanded.

Devin tilted his head, drawing his eyebrows together as he stared at her mouth in an eerily similar impression to the wolf trying to follow her babbling last night.

"Devin?" Alex's pulse began to flutter. Oh god. Saying his name had become particularly fraught over the last twelve hours. "You're, uh . . . at home, right? Behind the steering wheel?"

This couldn't be happening. He looked human. Eyes, claws, jaws—she scanned the pertinent features one by one and came up zero for three. There were no signs of a partial shift. But she got nothing back from Devin other than a warm huff of breath as he peered over her head to watch the delivery van drive away.

"Hey." She tried to catch his chin and regain his attention, only to have him snap, playfully, at her fingertips like she was teasing him, his green eyes sparkling as they returned to hers. He craned his neck to chase her fingers as she pulled them away, reeling back only to hit her head on the door with a crack.

"Ow." She cradled the back of her skull. Great, exactly what she needed while dealing with an MIA celebrity—a concussion.

Devin whimpered low in his throat, his face folding with distress as he leaned down to sniff at her scalp.

"I'm not bleeding," she said, sensing the question in his movements. "It's just a bump. But you know what would make me feel better? If you could say something."

Instead of words, the wolf herded her back toward the couch.

Alex sat down of her own volition when he began to pace, clearly agitated, again flexing his fingers like they weren't working right. If her best guess as to what was happening turned out to be correct, the wolf was probably even more rattled than she was that he'd somehow been left in charge of Devin's (naked) body.

Alex put her head between her knees and tried to breathe. She'd been prepared for the full shift, had known it was coming for a month. But this? Somehow losing Devin Ashwood after the full moon had set? This was so not canon.

Feral Colby was a microtrope exclusive to fanfic. To save him, Nathaniel often went on a dangerous quest or solved a sphinx riddle. On one memorable occasion he intentionally poisoned Colby with wolfsbane and then turned him into a vampire/werewolf hybrid as he lay on the cusp of death. Alex couldn't do any of those things. She was hopelessly, pathetically human.

Maybe the mental exchange would wear off naturally as they got further from the full moon, but they didn't exactly have time to wait. Here in LA, Devin was under constant observation, more so now that his antics at the game and the movie announcement had put his name once more in the press. The second his team showed up at his house looking for him, they were going to realize something was seriously wrong. Alex didn't want to get arrested as the unwell superfan trying to *Weekend at Bernie's* a TW network star.

For both their sakes, Devin needed to get back control of his body. Quickly.

Alex pulled out her phone and opened an Internet tab, but she didn't even know what to search at this point. For every other part of Devin's transformation, they'd had the show as a textbook. She'd been able to devise proxies and solutions based on that framework, but there was no blueprint for this in the scripts.

When he first came to Tompkins, he'd asked how to turn a werewolf back into a human. Alex told him then that you couldn't do it. It was irreversible. Now she needed to be wrong.

She couldn't even consult Devin the way she had when developing the trials. Talking to the wolf in this state had no greater effect than when he was on four legs and furry.

Even though it had always been a strange task, Alex had, naively, considered herself uniquely suited to guiding Devin through this werewolf transformation. No one knew *TAF* better than she did. Her experience at the vet gave her familiarity with dangerous animals. Plus, she had her dad's lifetime study of wolves in the wild to draw upon. But this? Alex was beginning to suspect this wasn't a werewolf problem but instead a Devin Ashwood problem.

At a complete loss, she texted the group chat.

> **ALEX:** So um Devin's not himself. I'm having trouble getting through to him

> **CAM:** oh man that same kind of thing happened with Michelle when they had layoffs at the firm last year. She was totally withdrawn.

"Withdrawn" was one word for it. If there was a way to avoid confronting the reality of the *Arcane Files* reboot happening without him, it made a certain kind of sense that Devin would seize it. And the wolf was always closer to the surface when he lost control of his emotions. Had it somehow become harder for him to take the reins back after the full moon?

> **CAM:** You need to gently remind him that he's more than a job.

> **ELIZA:** Even this one.

More than a job. More than a job. Okay. Alex could do that. She was here, in his home. This place must be full of personal memories that would remind Devin who he was.

She sprang to her feet, looking around the living room for signs of anything he cared about besides being an actor. The space was so sparsely decorated. Everything from the carpet to the walls to the furniture was white or glass and ruthlessly modern. The few pictures hanging on the walls featured stark black-and-white desert landscapes. If they meant something to Devin, Alex didn't know what it was.

She tried opening the cabinets in the TV console and found a slew of awards and plaques.

SOAP OPERA DIGEST—
BEST MALE NEWCOMER, 1996

TEEN CHOICE AWARDS—
BREAKOUT STAR, 2007

PEOPLE'S CHOICE AWARDS—
FAVORITE TV BROMANCE
(SHARED WITH ANTHONY MARIANO)

There were even awards Alex had never heard of:

THE SATURN
(BEST FANTASY ACTOR, 2013)

THE LEXXY
(BEST HAIR—MID-LENGTH, 2002)

There was something exquisitely sad about the fact that
Devin was proud enough of them to keep them polished but
didn't think they were worthy of being displayed out in the
open.

Acting, more than any other industry Alex could think of,
really trained its workforce to seek external validation. She wondered what it felt like for Devin to win something. How long the
sense of acceptance and accomplishment lasted before he
needed to seek it out again. A day? A week?

Speaking of, the room had gotten suspiciously quiet— *Oh
shit.* She spun in a circle. Her feral friend was nowhere to be
found. He must have wandered off while she had her back
turned. Fuck. She could not lose him. Especially when he wasn't
wearing pants.

Alex found Devin in the backyard, relieving himself against
a ceramic birdbath.

Well. At least he hadn't peed on the carpet.

"I'm trying to preserve your modesty," she told him ten minutes later, sweaty and red in the face after finally managing to

wrestle him into a pair of pants during an ordeal that was humiliating for both of them.

She was going to need a plan to keep the wolf on a leash until she could figure out how to bring Devin back. Luckily, Devin Ashwood, like many rich people in LA, had an impressive array of edibles in his nightstand.

Two hundred milligrams of indica and one Instacart delivery later, the wolf was slumped on the couch watching *Planet Earth* and eating a box of Cinnamon Toast Crunch by the handful. Crystals of brown sugar glistened in his beard. Estimating for a werewolf's advanced metabolism, Alex figured the drugs should buy her at least a few hours of triage time.

She was in the process of scouring the living room's copious built-ins when her phone rang with a number she didn't recognize.

It turned out to be Jade looking for Devin.

"Hey, I'm sorry to call you out of the blue. Though you should know your number is scary-easy to Google."

"Uh, thanks?"

"No one's seen or heard from Devin since the news about the movie broke," his former agent said, her voice threaded with tension, and then after a pause: "I'm really worried."

Everyone knew what *TAF* meant to Devin. What losing it would cost him.

He wasn't the only one who had been fighting for a reboot like this for years. Jade would have been in those meetings too. At least in the beginning.

"He's at home," Alex rushed to assure her and heard Jade exhale. "I'm here with him now."

Jade muttered something that sounded like "thank fuck" and then more clearly, "How's he holding up?"

"He's . . ." *Naked and high off his ass.* ". . . processing."

"Can I talk to him?"

Alex looked over to where Devin was gazing with heavy lids at the screen.

"I'm not sure he's up for conversation at the moment."

"Okay." Jade sighed. "I'll jump in with his team and do some triage, but tell him the longer he waits to make a statement, the more people will speculate. He can't hide forever."

"I will definitely pass along that message," Alex said, biting at her thumbnail.

"Can you also tell him . . ." The line went quiet for a moment. "Can you tell him I'm sorry that I forgot how to be his friend while I was busy being his agent?"

"I can, yeah." Alex just hoped the apology, which she knew would mean something to Devin, hadn't come too late.

After a quick thank-you, Jade signed off and Alex hung up the phone.

"I hope you know you're scaring people," she told the wolf, who was busy trying and failing to lick crumbs off the tip of his nose.

Alex thought she'd finally caught a break when she found a box of old VHS tapes and DVDs shoved into a cabinet under the TV. Nothing said childhood memories like home movies—never mind how in the hell she was gonna play them—but instead of things like *Devin's 10th Birthday*, the hand-printed labels read *Father of the Bride Audition, 02/89* and *Mickey Mouse Club Dance Routine, 11/93*.

Devin's parents had marked his adolescence by parts he'd never gotten cast in. And Devin had kept them.

Alex had read about him as a child actor with overly ambitious parents. He'd told her that even after their estrangement, he'd been taken aback by the way they seemed to love the lifestyle he'd afforded them more than they loved him. But neither

of those experiences prepared Alex for seeing the evidence of
their single-minded greed laid out before her. Her hands shook
as she folded the cardboard flaps, shoving the box back where
she'd found it and getting to her feet.

Devin's bedroom must hold more personal effects. Alex
knew he had help. He'd mentioned in passing a chef, a trainer,
cleaners, not to mention the myriad members of his manage-
ment team. If she had a continuous parade of people coming
and going in her space, perhaps she'd try to keep things more
Spartan too. Using a bag of Funyuns as bait, she managed to
lure the wolf into the primary suite.

In Devin's massive, immaculately organized closet, Alex ran
her fingers across the soft velvet of a purple suit she'd once
mercilessly mocked after he wore it on the red carpet during a
sweeps week promo. She hoped his expansive collection of expensive clothes and shoes might resurrect Devin's vanity.

She got her hopes up when he reached for a pair of Italian
leather loafers, but then he tried to bite them.

His vast array of hair- and skin-care products in the adjoining bathroom didn't tempt Devin either, though he did manage
to sneeze spectacularly into a tub of coconut-flavored body
butter.

The wolf didn't respond any better to the envelope of personal photos she found tucked into the back of the dresser. In
fact, he growled at an image of him and his ex-wife: a magnifi-
cent golden couple posing at the end of a dock, beaming on
their wedding day.

Nothing about Devin's life seemed to call to him.

Trying to appeal to his other senses, Alex poured Devin's
favorite whiskey and scrunched a bag of his favorite BBQ chips.
She even tried putting on "Love and Memories" by O.A.R. And
flashing him her bare boobs.

His lack of response to that last one stung.

Frustrated, Alex decided she had no choice but to try to use negative emotion to draw him out instead. If Devin ceded control to the wolf when he got upset, maybe somehow she could trigger the reverse response and make him so mad he clawed his way back to the surface.

"Chad Michael Murray is the most underrated cable TV star from the early 2000s," she declared.

The wolf blinked and then his gaze jumped over her shoulder to the window where, outside, a squirrel was climbing a neighboring tree.

Damnit.

This was a test: How well do you know Devin Ashwood? And Alex was failing.

She'd been all over this house, the wolf accompanying her like he was reluctant to let Alex out of his sight. He kept insisting on entering rooms before her, presumably to check for danger, but he wasn't particularly delicate about wielding Devin's body.

"Which one of us do you think is in charge right now?" Alex asked after he hip-checked her so he could rush first through the door to the small mudroom off the side of the house, the only remaining place they hadn't investigated.

The room was mostly empty except for a fancy spaceship-looking washer/dryer set and a cluster of Devin's suitcases from his trip to Florida. He'd probably brought them in here because someone else did both his unpacking and his laundry.

Alex eyed the luggage. Devin had been away from home for almost a month. It made sense that he'd have taken his most prized possessions with him, the stuff he couldn't live without. She knelt down in front of the first zipper bag with a rush of excitement.

As she folded back the top of the suitcase to get at the

contents, the wolf dropped to his knees beside her, his nostrils expanding on a deep inhale. Whatever was inside this suitcase, he seemed to recognize it.

Underneath a layer of clothes—a few faded denim button-downs, Devin's ludicrously soft white T-shirts, a pair of hunter-green cowboy boots for which she'd mocked him mercilessly—Alex's hand wrapped around something cold and metallic. She unearthed the horseshoe, holding it up so the light from the window winked off the gleaming steel. Someone, Devin, must have cleaned it, but Alex recognized the bend in the metal from a skittish Palomino horse.

Lou lost one of his shoes, Devin had said one day at the vet, soft and concerned. *Doesn't he need it?*

The wolf leaned over Alex, sniffing at the metal. His eyes went wide. He must be able to smell Lou. Another animal in his space likely raised territorial hackles. Alex handed over the shoe, not wanting to agitate the wolf. She expected him to take off and try to bury it somewhere. But instead, he simply clutched it, as if it were grounding, an anchor at sea.

Back in the suitcase, tucked further under the clothes, Alex found a Ziploc bag. Inside were a bunch of seemingly random items, but a flash of distinctive turquoise paper caught her eye. Alex had picked that color at the print shop because it was on clearance, too bright and beachy for most business customers. She unfolded the slightly bent pamphlet, tracing her thumb over the nineteen bullet points. The wolf poked his nose over again in a gesture that unmistakably meant *What do you have there? Is that for me?*

Alex forfeited the pamphlet. The wolf began to create a little collection for himself of items in his lap, looking down at them happily.

She carefully pulled out the paper clip next, crinkling the

Post-it folded into a square stuck through to become a make-shift badge. Devin's big, loopy handwriting spelled out *he/him* in a hasty imitation of Rowen's pronoun pin. He'd kept this. When he kept so little.

The wolf commandeered the pin too, his hands clumsy but careful as he added it to his pile.

If Alex hadn't pulled out the other items—keepsakes—she might have thought nothing of finding one of her father's text-books tucked into a front pocket. She smiled when the book naturally folded open to a receipt acting as a bookmark. Her father's messy, spiky handwriting sat in the margins, cramped—even when writing he was always in a hurry—calling out pieces of the writing he thought Devin would be particularly inter-ested in.

Devin had made connections in Tompkins that had nothing to do with Colby. The hometown that she'd always been half-ashamed of meant enough to him that he'd gone to the trouble of bringing pieces of it back to LA.

As Alex leafed through the pages of the textbook, she found other random trash folded inside, only . . . on closer examination that curl of yellow paper might have been the remains of his wristband from the beer garden at the fair. When she un-wrapped a tissue bundle tucked against the back cover, a burst of fragrance was released.

Alex's breath caught. Inside was the wildflower crown she'd made for Devin at the cabin in the woods as they lay together in the grass.

The small yellow and white flowers had curled and dried, leaving a fine residue of pollen against the paper.

The wolf was curious, trying to treat the delicate things with the same kind of care Alex did, cupping them in Devin's hands, his breath fluttering dried petals.

Here was evidence of his life outside of being an actor. Proof that Devin was thoughtful and surprisingly sentimental.

He'd wanted to be a part of something in Tompkins. He'd grown attached to an abandoned horse and a crumbling community center. He'd wanted to remember something of Rowen and Isaac and Alex herself.

Maybe he hadn't wanted her to come here with him to his home just because he needed her like a security blanket for the werewolf stuff. Maybe he was trying to hold on to her like he was holding on to these memories. Just a little bit longer.

The wolf brought a careful hand up to touch the tears tracking down Alex's face, frowning severely.

It felt like a privilege to know the parts of Devin that he'd worked all his life to conceal. To witness his messiness and the way he wanted. To get to see the strengths she never would have given him credit for from a distance: his generosity, his loyalty, his tenderness.

She felt protective looking at him. Possessive.

Alex had wasted a lot of time telling herself that she wasn't good enough for Devin Ashwood. That if he cared about her, it didn't matter. Because caring about her hadn't made her mother stay. Even the people who loved Alex didn't pick her.

She knew with unwavering certainty in that moment that she loved Devin Ashwood, really loved him. She also knew that if she said it right now, he wouldn't be able to understand her. She'd be saying it just for herself. Because it was true and she wanted to be brave.

When she was little, she had a VHS tape of *Beauty and the Beast*. Her dad kept a little two-in-one TV / VHS player in his office, and when she got sick he'd bring it into her bedroom. She watched the movie over and over, manually rewinding. When true love saved the prince, Alex had thought it was too neat, too easy, a cynical skeptic even at nine.

As an adult she appreciated how chaotic and complicated and scary true love could be.

Alex had people who loved her. But Devin was right; she'd done her best to keep them at arm's length. Attempting to prevent pain before it formed. But even though she could reach out right now and touch Devin's hand, his cheek, she'd lost him anyway. She couldn't imagine that letting him all the way into her heart could hurt more than this.

31

THE WOLF WASN'T supposed to be alone.

He and Devin were two pieces of the same soul. Split.

But the wolf was simpler. Instinct given form.

He didn't belong in this body. Hairless. Clumsy. Cold.

He wasn't made to lead for this long.

Humans had too many rules. Too many walls.

The wolf didn't blame Devin for wanting to hide. Fade. Make everything less.

Devin felt deeper. Different. Too much.

He thought in either form they were *AloneBadWrong*.

So sometimes he missed things that were good. Simple. Clear.

Alex *DarkBitterDelicate* was looking for him. Missing him.

Her scent soured with *FearSadnessPanic*.

She did not like this den.

The wolf didn't either.

It smelled *EmptyLonely*.

Alex searched the den for Devin. Tried to reach him with sounds. Scents.

But Devin was quiet. Dormant.

The way the wolf faded at the new moon.

The wolf did not know how to call him back. To the surface. To this body.

The tether was broken.

Alex did not accept that Devin had gone.

The wolf tried to trail her, to keep her safe, as she searched for him.

But then he ate something that made him *SleepySlow*.

When he woke, Alex had brought him things that smelled of her forest. *SunSoilFree*.

And her den. *SweetSafeWarm*.

Some of the things smelled of her pack.

The horse. *HayHair*. The elder. *KindWorry*. The cub. *Cheese-Mischief*.

Something inside the wolf reacted, pulling forward. Seeking.

Alex sat next to the wolf now. Making noises again.

Words. They were called words.

This body knew lots of things. When it was allowed to remember.

Her scent was shifting. Changing. Lifting. Lightening.

She felt . . . something the wolf did not recognize.

The wolf pressed his nose closer, breathing in, trying to place it. This new feeling.

Again he felt the pulling from within. Stronger now. Desperate.

The tether!

The wolf didn't know how to get out of the way. To make room in this body for Devin. But he could be still for a moment. He could breathe. Try.

The wolf filled his nose with Alex's new scent.

Until quietly, slowly, Devin stirred.

32

DEVIN CAME BACK to his body like red wine against a white tablecloth: a sudden, jarring splash. From the darkness, suddenly he found himself sitting on the stiff white couch in his living room as the sun set behind the wall of massive windows looking out over his backyard. The inside of his mouth was gritty with sugar as he ran his tongue across his teeth. He wore nothing but a thin pair of sweatpants, which appeared to be on backward for some reason.

Alex paced in front of his coffee table. She was talking to herself, her tone that of a pep talk well underway.

"This is silly," she said, shaking out her shoulders. "Just say it."

Her chest rose and fell with a long, deliberate breath.

If Devin thought her scent was appealing before, it was nothing compared to how she smelled now.

He could trace these notes in the middle of a hailstorm if he lost the use of his eyes and ears.

He could even, apparently, follow it back from the depths of his self-loathing.

Leaning forward, he inhaled, pulling the scent deeper into his lungs.

Alex didn't spare him a glance.

Devin knew the scent was tied to something Alex was feeling, but like the wolf, he couldn't quite place it. He had no frame of reference for this emotion.

"Even if this doesn't bring Devin back," Alex said to herself, "it's not like it'll be the most humiliating thing you've tried today."

Instead of the glaring emptiness of amnesia that usually followed a transformation, fuzzy memories of the last twenty-odd hours flooded Devin's mind like faded snapshots. He had the feeling it was the wolf showing him what he'd missed, opening the line of communication between them that usually went quiet after his other half took the wheel.

Devin's neck heated. Oh god.

He'd absolutely peed on a thirty-thousand-dollar Japanese maple in the backyard.

He was only wearing these pants because Alex was surprisingly strong, and the wolf had been too afraid of hurting her to fight back while she wrestled him into them.

He felt like he'd come back home after a long journey. For the first time in days, he had distance from his emotions. He saw himself a week ago in Tompkins: happier, lighter, easier. Learning how to care about things, about people other than himself. Then he saw himself as he'd been since returning to LA: the sharp, metallic fear; the anger; the ache. He'd forgotten all he knew about being kind to himself and—bile rose at the back of his throat—to Alex.

Devin had hurt her as she was trying to help him. He'd hurt her as he frantically tried to convince her to stay.

The wolf's behavior, fully feral, was less shameful than his had been by a mile.

But . . . Alex was here. He'd given her every reason to leave, and she'd come back. To take care of him after he'd done nothing to earn it.

Alex was still trying to save him. No, not trying. She had saved him. Her scent. This new feeling. Devin had been able to follow it back like a beacon.

"Alex," he said, hoarse from the wolf's abuse of his vocal cords. And it felt like a benediction. His first word, all over again. The effort, the importance of dragging the sound free.

She froze immediately, her gaze shooting to his face.

"Devin?" All the color drained from her cheeks. "You're back? You're you?"

"I'm so sorry." He got to his feet, taking a few steps toward her before halting. She might be afraid.

Alex threw herself into his arms. He caught her with a soft "oof" as she smacked against his bare chest. Having her this close, smelling the way she did, made him dizzy.

"I hate your guts," she said into his neck, the words muffled against his skin.

Well, that wasn't true. He knew exactly what that smelled like.

Alex poked a finger between his pecs in a gesture that she surely meant to be threatening, but the effect was dampened by the fact that her hand was shaking.

"Do you have any idea what I went through while you were gone?"

"Yes." Devin knew, and hated, the scent of her fear.

He caught Alex's hand in his. Her palm was sweaty. Touching her was bliss.

"I missed you too."

Alex huffed. But she didn't try to take her hand back.

"I thought you'd dissolved into the ether."

He wrapped one hand around her hip, letting his other cradle her jaw. "Not on your watch."

Alex's eyes were wide and dangerously glassy. "What the hell happened to you?"

Devin dropped his gaze to the ground and took a step back. He'd put her through the wringer.

"I don't want to say." He toed at the plush fibers of the rug under his feet. "It's embarrassing."

The way he'd behaved, yes, but even more than that, the way he'd given up.

Alex scowled.

"Do you see all of these feathers?" With her chin she drew attention to the snowfall of down littering the living room.

"Yes."

"They came from that pillow"—she pointed to a carcass of Italian cashmere—"which I watched you destroy *with your teeth* about an hour ago."

Okay, that was fair. Devin took a deep breath.

He'd been a product for as long as he could remember, his value fluctuating depending on how he looked, who he was seen with, whether or not audiences thought he could kiss and kill convincingly.

But here, right in front of him, was someone who, even after all he'd put her through, still wanted him around. He owed Alex an explanation. He owed her a lot more than that.

"So, you know how I like your scent?" Understatement of the century.

"I've come to recognize that general concept, yes," Alex said with a dismissive little wave.

It was probably for the best that she didn't think it was a big deal.

"Well, over time, I've gotten more and more used to being around you. I've built up some degree of tolerance." So that he didn't fly completely off the handle every time they were in the same room. "But the first time I caught your scent—undiluted by all those disgusting chemicals you work with—it hit me like an arrow through the chest."

Even now Devin could feel the impact, the urgency, of that moment in the forest.

"I had to follow it. To find you."

Alex's brow creased. "We're talking about that time you showed up at my dad's house randomly?"

Devin groaned. "For the last time, I did not know he was your dad."

"Yeah. Yeah." Alex smirked. "Get back on track."

Minx.

"Right. What I'm trying to say is something changed in your scent just now." Devin shook his head to clear it. "I don't know where I was—where I go exactly—when the wolf is in charge. It feels kind of like being in a dreamless sleep. Only this time I couldn't wake up. But then, out of nowhere, it was like you were calling me. Like I was summoned. Finding you, getting back to you, was . . . essential."

Devin knew it sounded impossible, silly even. He didn't know what he'd do if Alex laughed at him right now. But she didn't look at him like what he'd said was funny. If anything, she looked sheepish, her face going pink.

"And do you have any idea why my scent might change?" Her tone was careful.

It was a good question. Where previously Devin relied on Alex or *TAF* as the experts on his physiology, now his lived experience had gone beyond the bounds of the show bible. Devin himself was, alarmingly, the new de facto expert on a role for which he'd never been cast. He was the one who could, who must, define what it meant to be a werewolf from here on out.

"Your scent signature changes a bit whenever you're feeling something particularly strongly." Devin flipped through his sensory memories. He hadn't picked up on it at the time, but on reflection: "The adjustment is usually more subtle than this, but the same kind of thing happens when you're really pissed or you're really horn—"

"Got it," Alex said, cutting him off. "Thanks."

"But I actually don't recognize whatever you're feeling right now." Devin frowned. "Normally the emotions just kind of clock in my head. Like the wolf has got special receptors."

"Receptors," she repeated.

"I'm not a scientist, Alex." The word seemed accurate enough. "It's like—you know how birds can see more colors because they have more cones in their eyes?"

"Yes," she said slowly.

"What?" Devin shrugged. "Sometimes I watch nature documentaries to fall asleep."

Her mouth quirked to the side, Alex's trying-not-to-smile smile.

"So you can sense feelings, and whatever I happen to be feeling right now somehow acted as a strong enough sensory lure to pull you back from the dark abyss?"

"Yeah." That about summed it up.

Alex sat down heavily on the couch. "Oh my god."

Devin followed her, standing awkwardly at her shoulder.

"Are you good?" She looked a little green.

Alex shook her head.

"Okay, well, as stated, you're gonna have to spell out what's going on in your head for me because I can't tell if you're like super mad or having a nervous breakdown or just like a form of hangry I've never encountered."

"I'm in love with you," Alex said, looking up at him.

"What? *Now?*" Devin was appalled. He'd spent the last day and a half as an animal. "Didn't you watch me eat an entire raw steak this morning without using my hands?"

"Yes." Alex buried her face in her hands. "There's something seriously wrong with me."

Devin's heart tore at the words.

"Alex." He went to his knees in front of her. "I've fucked up so bad."

She lifted her head to look at him. "It has been an eventful week."

He almost laughed. "I know, but even before now."

Saying the words hurt, but Devin had been carrying them around in the pit of his stomach since the town fair.

"Growing up, my parents made me believe I was worthless unless I could make myself into what other people wanted." His voice came out as ground glass. "Even after they left me, I carried that belief around like a disease. And it's bad enough that I let it poison my whole life. But it's worse that I met you when you were young and impressionable and I passed that pain on."

Alex started to shake her head, but they both knew it was true even if it wasn't his fault.

"I don't know if I'll ever forgive myself for contributing to your idea that you aren't good enough." Devin cupped her jaw, his thumb caressing the crest of her cheek. "Because while it's true that you're one hundred percent a stone-cold weirdo, I am so fucking into it."

"*What?*" Alex said, half laugh, half croak.

"You're scary"—he kissed her brow—"and mean"—the

underside of her chin—"and obsessive"—the tip of her nose. "And I cannot get enough of you."

"You're so bad at this," she said fondly.

Ignoring the ache that had started in his knees, Devin tucked a lock of hair that had fallen from her messy bun behind her ear. "I don't know if it was the moon or fate or the universe that made me a werewolf, but, baby, you made me human."

Alex's breath caught.

Kick rocks, Brian Dempsey. Devin could write his own damn lines.

Sure, he was still getting the hang of being a once-in-a-generation supernatural creature. And yes, even though he was working on managing his other half, he'd probably always be anxious and odd and desperate for approval.

His acting career was almost certainly over.

The only long-term personal relationships he'd ever known had ended in estrangement and/or divorce.

And yet . . .

"I was thinking, if you'll have me," he said softly, moving to sit beside her, "maybe we could die alone together?"

Alex pressed her hand over her heart, looking slightly dazed. "Devin Ashwood wants to be my boyfriend?" She stared into the middle distance about a foot from his face.

"You know it's a little weird when you say my whole name like that, right?"

"This is real," Alex said flatly. "This is happening."

"Uh." Devin waved a palm in front of her face. "I can't actually tell if you're saying yes."

She whipped her head around to meet his gaze. "I don't want to move to LA. I know in a lot of ways it would probably be easier, but I belong in Tompkins."

"No, I know," Devin rushed to assure her. "I was thinking, I could go back with you. I'm gonna start a horse sanctuary for Lou and the other abandoned racehorses. I've got this whole plan. Don't worry about it."

He didn't need more proof than the charity game that being in this town, in a place with lists and constant cameras, where he was always trying to win someone over to succeed, was really fucking bad for him.

His parents had brought him to LA. It was Devin's decision alone to leave.

Alex raised a skeptical brow, but he would fill her in on the details later. At the moment he wanted her to understand the choice wasn't a sacrifice, not really.

"When I got the news about the *Arcane Files* movie, don't get me wrong, it sucked real bad. But there was about twenty seconds before I lost my shit when I was just . . . so relieved. I've been hauling this show, this character, around like a ball and chain for two decades, and only seeing Brian Dempsey's smug-ass face on *Entertainment Tonight* made me realize I've had the key this whole time."

Alex took both his hands back into hers. "Is this you having a midlife crisis?"

Devin tilted his head. It was a fair question. He'd spent so much of the last two decades defining himself by Colby, by the success (and failures) of the show. The wound of finding out it was over, not for everyone else but for him, still sat as a dull ache behind his ribs. There was something very cliché about an aging actor moving to Florida and dating someone a decade younger.

"That's what they call it when you wake up one day and you're scared and dissatisfied with your old life?"

"Basically." Alex chewed her lower lip.

"And so you make all these radical changes trying to figure

out how to be happy?" Devin reached up and used the pad of his thumb to gently dislodge her teeth.

He had plans for that mouth later.

Alex's pupils dilated as she nodded.

"Well then, yeah." He placed a kiss on her jawline, right behind her ear where the scent of her loving him was strongest. "I'm probably having one of those."

Thank god.

Alex traced the veins on top of his hand with her finger.

"Are you sure that you want to leave LA? I know Jade's not your agent anymore, but I think she genuinely likes you. I'm pretty sure she'd help you figure out a next step in this town if you wanted, as your friend, if nothing else."

Huh. Being friends with Jade might be nice. Devin could get the spinach-artichoke dip going again. But why was Alex trying to talk him out of this?

Oh. He should've realized.

"To be clear, I'm in love with you too." Even though Alex said it first, saying it back still felt like jumping off the edge of a cliff.

She snapped her head up. "You do?"

He nodded solemnly. "Devin Ashwood is in love with you."

Alex scowled. "You are not as cute as you think you are."

"I want to take you on dates," he clarified, ignoring that blatant slander. "And go grocery shopping together. I've got some really dirty ideas for sex positions that leverage my super strength."

He grinned at the bridge of a blush across her nose and cheeks.

"I wanna be there to see how you finally spend my money."

Alex's eyes were getting suspiciously watery again. Who knew behind all those tats and piercings she was such a big sap?

"I like taking care of you," he said gently.

As predicted, that snapped her from sentimental to mad in about two seconds flat.

"I don't need you to take care of—"

"Yeah, I know, Xena: Warrior Princess. Relax. It's not a need thing. I'm asking, Do you like it?"

Alex considered for a long moment.

"Yes," she admitted reluctantly.

Sometimes Alex missed things that were simple. Clear. Good.

"Then let's figure the rest out, okay? I don't know about you, but I think we make a pretty good team."

Thirteen seasons and Colby never got to be in love. Poor guy.

"I'd like that," Alex said, smiling at him with that gap he wanted to write poems about. "All of it."

"Yeah?" If Devin kept grinning like this, he was gonna sprain his jaw.

"Yeah."

Later, after he'd taken a human shower and brushed his human teeth, he followed his nose to find Alex. He caught her in the hall, her arms full of laundry. He'd have to get her to show him how to do that sometime.

"Hey," he said, doing Colby's signature smolder.

"Hi," Alex said, a little sheepish.

"What?" He dropped the smolder. "All of a sudden you're shy?"

"You're all wet," she said delicately.

Devin looked down. He'd wrapped a towel low around his waist, and he supposed his chest was kinda damp and glistening. He inhaled.

Oh.

As it turned out, the best scent in the world was Alex loving him *and* wanting him to fuck her.

"Well," he said, taking the laundry from her arms and walking toward the bedroom, "as you know, you just rescued me from a fate worse than death—"

Alex followed him. "Do we know that that's true?"

"—and as my hero—"

"Devin." A note of warning rang in her voice as she recognized some of the worst dialogue in *The Arcane Files'* long history.

"—you have won my favor."

Alex tipped her head back and groaned at the ceiling.

"And my flower." He dropped the laundry on a chair in the corner beside his bed as Alex came to stand beside him.

She opened her mouth against the pulse point on his neck to apply soft suction. "Who says I want your flower?"

"Doesn't matter." Devin's knees threatened to buckle. "It's yours."

Vibrations from her soft laugh sent goose bumps trailing from his throat to his navel.

Alex guided him over to the foot of the bed and then shoved softly at his shoulders until his ass met the comforter. She knelt with her thighs bracketing his, and scraped her teeth across the tendons of his throat.

"Do it," Devin said when he clocked the question behind the first hint of pressure from her jaw, the soft flick of her tongue against the thin skin.

Giving Alex permission to bite him felt almost as good as when she did it.

Devin grunted at the first flash of discomfort as her teeth pressed down.

"Harder."

She indulged him.

Oh fuck. Oh fuck. Oh fuck.

He was shaking by the time she moved her mouth back to his, adrenaline spiking so hard he tasted copper.

Alex traced the marked skin with her fingertips as she kissed him, slow and filthy.

"Does it hurt?"

"Yes." He sucked on her tongue, wishing he could drown in the taste of her.

In the dim room there was only the sound of her breath growing more ragged with each press of his lips, her heartbeat racing in his ears. Devin wanted to taste every part of her, leaving traces of himself across her skin.

Having her this close was almost too good, too much. He never thought he could be this happy.

Devin ghosted his own fingers over the imprint left by her teeth and groaned.

So this is what it feels like to belong to someone.

EPILOGUE

A FEW MONTHS LATER . . .

ALEX APPRECIATED DEVIN'S offer to come over and help her unpack in her new apartment, but she also desperately wished she could have figured out a non-suspicious way to decline. She kept putting her body in front of a specific set of boxes tucked into the corner of her new bedroom. Her choreography grew more and more obvious as the amount of cardboard in the room dwindled.

After spending the last month working with a small group of carefully screened, NDA-gagged professionals—a doctor, a therapist, a psychiatrist, and his former physical trainer—Devin's comfort and aptitude using his enhanced speed and senses made him wildly efficient. Especially when he applied himself.

After much deliberation, they decided revealing his transformation to a select few, with the most expensive legal muzzle money could buy, wasn't ultimately that risky. If someone wanted to gamble their life savings by going to the press, well, most people wouldn't believe the truth anyway. The worst they could say was Devin Ashwood was once again pretending to be a werewolf, and at this point that was small potatoes, public humiliation–wise.

"You're supposed to use the little wrench they include with

the packaging," Alex said when he started putting the screws in her IKEA bed frame by swiveling a single clawed fingertip.

"Oh, is that what that is?" Devin gazed up at her from where he sat on the carpet. "I thought it was just a misplaced piece of someone else's order."

Alex shook her head solemnly, turning back to the half-hung curtains before letting herself smile.

This apartment, a fourth-floor corner in a new building within walking distance of the community center, wasn't forever. But for now it was perfect, as Alex was working as deputy director, helping oversee planning for the TCC's next act.

She'd even convinced Devin to volunteer with the kids' summer stage production. All the preteens treated him like a golden god. It was good for him, Alex privately thought, not to have to go totally cold turkey on that kind of attention.

The pay for her new role wasn't great, but with the money from Devin buoying her bank account, Alex could have quit working at the vet even with her new rent. But when it came time to put in her notice, she swerved at the last second and asked about going part-time instead. She would have missed Dr. Wronski and Seth and the animals. Even Snowball. Plus, she figured having continued access to animal healthcare wasn't a bad thing, considering her werewolf boyfriend.

Falling in love with Devin Ashwood didn't magically fix all her problems.

She still worried about her dad being on his own. Though as the result of a conversation she hadn't been invited to, Devin began shadowing him at work a few days a week, an informal apprenticeship. Apparently they both had things to teach each other about wolves. Her dad also offered to help her turn the now-empty loft into a dedicated art studio, so they'd both still have plenty of excuses to check up on each other.

Unfolding sheets and hanging picture frames in her new home felt like a ritual. Like with each personal touch she laid down an intention to take up space.

Pete Calabasas and the country club contingent reacted as one might expect to Devin Ashwood moving in full-time. He and his friends took to double-parking their massive trucks in front of the community center's new wheelchair-accessible entrance, a pretty pathetic protest. Alex called the cops a few times, trying to get them towed, but of course they all had friends and family on the force who let them off with smirking warnings.

Had to cancel senior chair yoga, she texted Devin the third time it happened. Half the participants use either walkers or wheelchairs and we couldn't get them all inside.

He hadn't seen the text until late, when he and her dad got back from monitoring the red wolves' new habitat, but the next day Pete Calabasas pushed open both doors of the community center like an old-timey sheriff and slapped a hand down on the reception desk in front of her.

"A fucking wolf scratched up the entire left side of my truck last night."

Alex turned her laugh into a noise of faux concern at the last minute.

"Sounds like you need a body shop."

While she didn't explicitly condone vandalism, in this case, she made an exception.

"It's not just me." Pete's face turned puce. "All my buddies have similar damage on their vehicles, even though we weren't parked anywhere near each other."

"Maybe Carla Venetti down on Bleeker will cut you a two-for-one deal?"

Pete loomed over her. "I know you had something to do with it."

"You think I have the power to control wild animals?" Alex pitched her voice with incredulity.

"Yes," he said, belligerent and also visibly afraid.

"Don't be silly." At her nod, Jameson, the burly security guard Devin had insisted on hiring, escorted him out.

Once the bed was assembled, Alex managed to divert Devin's attention away from the compromising boxes, distinguished only by the black X she'd drawn in the left corner, by asking him to unpack linens in the guest room.

He narrowed his eyes at her in a way that said he knew she was being fishy.

"I want to make sure I have enough towels for when the group chat comes to visit next week."

Instead of leaving her bedroom, Devin walked toward her. Toward the boxes.

"You're never gonna learn, are you."

"What do you mean?" Alex heated under the force of his gaze.

He just shook his head.

Over the last few weeks she'd collected all kinds of mundane details about him. How he liked his eggs (soft-boiled—gross). If he'd ever had a pet (yes, for a few short days, a goldfish named Gilda that a PA had let him take home after they starred in a cereal commercial together; he'd cried when she died). What he'd been thinking when he got his heinously ugly bicep tattoo. ("That it would look badass. Which it DOES.")

Still, Alex had a feeling she'd have a crush on him until the day she died.

"The sooner we open them, the sooner you can get over whatever's making you so embarrassed."

"Do we have to open them?" she pleaded.

Devin didn't dignify that with a response.

"Fine." Alex stepped aside. "But I want you to know not all of it is mine. I'm holding on to some stuff for a friend."

He had the first box open before she'd finished her sentence.

Because there was no justice in the world, the first thing he picked out was the poster.

"Wait." She tried to dive for it, but Devin easily caught her with one arm and slashed through the rubber band, keeping the picture rolled with a claw on his left hand.

It felt like slow motion as the paper unfurled upside down to reveal his younger self, wearing a crop top, leaning against a barn with his bare arms crossed and a truly explicit pout on his face.

Devin stared at the image for a tense ten seconds.

"Holy fuck."

Alex debated going limp, playing dead.

"Were you kissing this thing? I can still smell the remnants of bubblegum lip gloss."

Apparently, it didn't matter that she'd drawn devil horns and poked out his eyes with a Sharpie. Devin's ego was positively vibrating.

"I meant to throw that out."

"Did you?" He rubbed his thumb across her flaming cheek, looking for all the world like he'd like a poster of her. "Then I'm keeping it. You got any more in there?"

"No," Alex said, lying.

She nudged the box away with her knee and kissed him.

GQ EXCLUSIVE—
15 MINUTES WITH DEVIN ASHWOOD

*More than twenty years after the TV show first premiered,
the* Arcane Files *film launched this week at South by
Southwest—without its former star.*

By Eden Fienberg

Shortly after it was announced that his claim to fame
would head to the silver screen without him, TV's most
famous werewolf quietly purchased two hundred acres of
farmland in northern Florida with plans to turn the
property into a sanctuary for retired racehorses. Today,
One-Trick Pony has thirteen occupied stables and
counting. We caught up with Devin Ashwood to talk
happy endings.

EF: What made you decide to forgo the spotlight after
over thirty years in front of the camera in Hollywood?

DA: *laughs* I'm sure you can see the obvious parallels
between a racehorse and a child actor. I need the fresh air
and tranquility as much as the horses. We're all working
on getting over our baggage. On starting again. I recently
brought on some goats and a few donkeys. They're good
companions for skittish horses. We're all on a journey
together. I've got everyone in therapy. It turns out a
bunch of us have low-key internalized disordered eating.

EF: Oh. Well, I must say all the animals look very happy in retirement. They seem to enjoy visitors.

DA: Racehorses work very hard and give so much of themselves to make people happy. I'm glad that people want to come and celebrate them later in their lives. A few days a week, we allow visitors to stop by and take photos, that kind of thing, and those ticket sales help support our costs and programming. We're lucky that we attract a lot of tourists and horse enthusiasts who flock to the area for the nearby racetrack. Our horses know they're special, and while we try to give them many other types of care, they do seem to flourish in the face of adoration.

EF: There's no way to talk around this. When Brian Dempsey announced the *Arcane Files* film would go forward without you, hundreds of thousands of fans signed a petition in protest. What would you say to those people who are disappointed that Colby Southerland won't return for another chapter?

DA: First of all, I'd say I really appreciate the support and enthusiasm that folks have shown for this character for going on two decades. It was one of the great honors of my life to portray someone who meant so much to so many. The love for Colby is not something I take for granted. I don't like to think about where I'd be right now without this fandom. That said, Colby's been through the wringer, and we all know how much the writers love tying him to a cross. I think it's okay that we let him sit this one out.

EF: Since we won't get to find out onscreen, what would you say Colby's up to now, as the actor who portrayed him?

DA: I think he and Nathaniel are off somewhere in a remote cabin, living off the land. Or maybe they're running a small-town coffee shop or a bookstore. I can't take credit for those theories. They're just my favorite of the fandom's fix-it tropes.

EF: I'm sorry, are you saying that you believe Colby is canonically queer? Because to my knowledge you've never addressed the huge lobby for that ship online.

DA: Oh yeah. Why do you think he looked so sad for all those seasons? Poor guy's been waiting twenty-odd years for that vampire to ream him against a wall.

EF: Um. I don't know if we can print that. Brian Dempsey has always fervently denied queer fan theories about that pairing.

DA: Well, I no longer work for him, so he can deny my theories too.

Acknowledgments

I am really lucky to have formed relationships with so many people who enable me to be weird, in art and in life. This book is a direct result of their guidance, encouragement, collaboration, and gentle herding.

Thank you first to my publishing team for your professionalism and compassion while I tried to finish a book during one of the most change-filled years of my life.

My editor, Kristine Swartz, helped guide the development of this project to be as sexy and coherent as possible—two equally noble goals. Thank you for all the work you've put into this book, Kristine. I hope you're proud of the end result.

Jessica Watterson, thank you for tirelessly cheerleading for this idea, for fielding many anxious phone calls, and for always supporting my growth as an author.

To Mary Baker, Kristin Cipolla, Yazmine Hassan, Jessica Mangicaro, and the extended Berkley team—I know so much more work goes into bringing books to readers than authors ever see. I am endlessly grateful for your resourcefulness, collaboration, and compensation for my lack of attention to detail.

My cover artist, Roxie Vizcarra, and the Berkley design team. Thank you for making a cover that perfectly captures the specific unhinged vibes of this story.

Romance readers and reviewers. Thank you for your early excitement for *Fan Service* and for championing our genre. A major theme of this book is how an audience uplifts and extends canon through their passion and creativity. I am constantly in awe of you.

Sarah Younger. Thank you for seeing potential in me and my work and for helping me navigate publishing with authority, insight, and a sense of humor.

Melanie Arndt. Thank you for reading early and swiftly. You saved some of my favorite lines. All typos and continuity errors should fear you.

Sonia Hartl and Jess Swinco—my alpha readers. I seriously can't believe you managed to not only get through such early versions of this book but also somehow find nice things to say about it at that stage. I couldn't have trusted anyone better.

Leigh Marr and Laura Piper Lee. Thank you for letting me join your writing retreats this year. So many critical pieces of this story came together at your side, with your encouragement.

Olivia Dade, Rachel Lynn Solomon, Alexis De Girolami, and Martha Waters—my "US writers living abroad" support system. Thank you for your tremendous friendship and support in all areas of my life, across time zones and great bodies of water.

Christina Hobbs, Lauren Billings, Susan Lee, Julie Soto, and Ali Hazelwood—my very own fangirl group chat. You bring so much joy into my life and make the bitter moments sweeter.

To my sensitivity readers, Leigh Kramer and Mary Roach. Thank you always for helping make my work more inclusive and honest.

Big thanks to Alexa Martin, Denise Williams, Alicia Thompson, Jen Comfort, Rachel Runya Katz, Jo Segura, Regina Black, Ava Wilder, and Lana Ferguson for being the best coworkers.

Quinn, Marisa, Emily, Ilona, Dave, Ryan, and Frank. Some of the funniest, sharpest, truest moments of friendship in this book were inspired by you. I am so glad every day that none of you work in publishing.

Sarah and Hannah. Thank you for answering so many strange questions about veterinarian work for my research. Hopefully neither of you ends up on any government lists because of those texts.

Jen. Thank you for being a wonderful teacher and for always asking questions that would never in a million years occur to me.

Ruby Barrett. Sometimes I'm in charge and sometimes you're in charge, but either way I always feel safe holding your hand. This book would have had a lot less horse stuff in it if not for you.

My family. It has been a gift to be closer to you this year, to share more moments of this precious life with you. Thank you for all your support and love.

Micah. I usually try to make these romantic, but I've left the acknowledgments to the very last minute and my brain is mush at the moment. I love being your partner and building a life with you. I really appreciate how you do almost all of the wet chores.

Keep reading for a preview of

DO YOUR WORST

by Rosie Danan

AVAILABLE NOW!

WHILE OTHER WOMEN inherited a knack for singing or swearing from their grandmothers, Riley Rhodes received a faded leather journal, a few adolescent summers of field training, and the guarantee that she'd die alone.

Okay, fine, maybe that last thing was a slight exaggeration. But a unique talent for vanquishing the occult, passed down from one generation to the next like heirloom china, certainly didn't make dating any easier. Her matrilineal line's track record for lasting love was . . . bleak, to say the least.

Curse breaking—the Rhodes family talent—was a mysterious and often misunderstood practice, especially in the modern age. Lack of demand wasn't the problem. If anything, the world was more cursed than ever. But as the presence of an angry mob in any good folktale will tell you, people fear what they don't understand.

To be fair, Gran had warned Riley about the inherent hazards of curse breaking out of the gate. There was, of course, the whole physical danger aspect that came part and parcel with facing off against the supernatural. Riley had experienced everything from singed fingertips to the occasional accidental poisoning in the name of her calling.

As for the personal pitfalls? Well, those hurt in a different way.

She'd grown up practicing chants at recess and trying to trade homemade tonics for Twinkies at lunch. Was it any wonder that, through middle school, her only friend had been a kindly art teacher in her late fifties? It wasn't until tenth grade when her tits came in that guys decided "freaky curse girl" was suddenly code for "performs pagan sex rituals." Riley had been almost popular for a week—until that rumor withered on the vine.

It was like Gran always said: *No one appreciates a curse breaker until they're cursed.*

Since she couldn't be adored for her talents, Riley figured she could at least get paid. So at thirty-one years old, she'd vowed to be the first to turn the family hobby into a legitimate business.

Still, no one would call her practical. She'd flown thousands of miles to a tiny village in the Scottish Highlands to risk life and limb facing down an ancient and unknowable power—but hey, at least she'd gotten fifty percent up front.

Hours after landing, strung out on jet lag and new-job nerves, Riley decided the village's single pub was as good a place as any to start her investigation into the infamous curse on Arden Castle.

The Hare's Heart had a decent crowd for a Sunday night, considering the total population of the village didn't break two hundred. Dark wood-paneled walls and a low ceiling covered in crimson wallpaper gave the already small space an extra intimate feel. More like an elderly family member's living room than the slick, open-concept spots filled with almost as many screens as people that Riley knew all too well back home.

Hopefully after this job put her services on the map she could stop picking up bartending shifts in Fishtown during lean months. For now, her business was still finding its feet. The meager income she managed to bring in from curse breaking remained firmly in the "side hustle" category—though it was still more than anyone else in her family had ever made from their highly specialized skills. Riley had always thought it was kind of funny, in a morbid way, that a family of curse breakers could help everyone but themselves.

Whether out of fear or a sense of self-preservation, Gran had never charged for her practice. In fact, she'd kept curse breaking a secret her whole life, serving only her tiny rural mountain community. As a consequence, she'd never had two nickels to rub together. She and Riley's mom had weathered a few rough winters without heat, going to bed on lean nights—if not hungry, then certainly not full.

Riley had never faulted her mom for ditching Appalachia and the family mantle in favor of getting her nursing degree in scenic South Jersey. It was only because she'd never been good at anything practical that Riley found herself here in the High-lands, hoping this contract changed more than the number in her bank account.

If word got out that Riley had taken down the notorious curse on Arden Castle, she could go from serving small-time personal clients to big corporate or even government jobs. (She had it on good authority they'd been looking for someone to remove the curse on Area 51 since the seventies.)

Perching herself on a faded leather stool at the mahogany bar that divided the pub into two sections, Riley had an excellent vantage point to observe the locals. Up front in the dining room, patrons ranging in age from two to eighty occupied various farm tables brimming with frothing pints and steaming plates.

Her stomach growled as the scent of melting butter and roasted meat wafted across the room. After ordering a drink, she'd ask for a menu. As much as Riley didn't mind charging into battle against mystical mysteries, she was terrified of plane food, so she hadn't eaten much in the last sixteen hours.

Next to her, a middle-aged man with face-paint-streaked cheeks bellied up to the bar to speak to the hot older woman pulling pints.

"Eilean, come and sit with us." He thumbed at the more casual area in the back of the pub.

Over her shoulder, Riley followed his direction to a cluster of rowdier guests on the edge of their seats in a haphazard cluster of well-loved armchairs. They all had their necks bent at uncomfortable angles to watch a small, shitty-looking TV hanging from the wall.

"We need you. The game's tied and you're good luck."

The bartender—Eilean—waved him off. "Even if that were true, I wouldn't waste it on you lot and that piss-poor excuse for a rugby club."

She smiled at Riley when he turned tail back to his buddies, but her eyes held the kind of guarded interest reserved for interlopers at a place that served almost exclusively regulars. "Can I get you something?"

Without hesitating, Riley ordered an aged local scotch on the rocks, hoping the quick, simple order would convey that she came in peace.

While she waited, the face-painted man and several of his buddies took turns heckling the sports teams onscreen, their impassioned shouts cutting above the dining room's steady din of conversation.

Riley smiled to herself at the colorful insults delivered in their thick Scottish brogues. A similar disorderly air erupted in her mother's living room every time neighbors and friends gathered to get their hearts broken by the Eagles. Even though she'd never traveled abroad before, suddenly Riley felt a little more at home.

"You've got good taste in scotch." Eilean placed the highball glass of amber liquid in front of her. "For an American," she said, warm, teasing.

Apparently, in a village this small, even a few words in her accent stood out. Riley raised her glass in acknowledgment before taking a sip.

She savored the sharp, smoky flavor of the smooth liquor, a subtle hint of spice lingering on her lips after she swallowed. Good whiskey tasted like indulging in bad decisions—that same satisfying burn. This job might kill her, but so close to Islay, at least she could enjoy single malt without paying shipping markup or import tax.

"I'd ask what brings you all the way out here," the silver-haired bartender said, "but there's really only one reason strangers come to Torridon." Almost imperceptibly, her gaze strayed to a couple tucked in at a corner table wearing a pair of what looked like homemade novelty T-shirts reading *Curse Chasers*.

Riley winced. Reminders that her real life was someone else's sideshow circus could make a girl feel cheap, if she let them.

Accustomed to using people's drink order as a bellwether for their character, out of habit, her eyes fell to check what they were drinking. Riley groaned.

"Not mojitos." Far and away the most tedious cocktail to

prepare. She revised her previous analysis of their threat level. To make matters worse, their table held the remnants of several rounds.

"All that muddling." She rubbed phantom pain from her wrist.

Eilean barked out a laugh. "You've spent some time behind a bar, then?"

"More than I'd care to admit."

They shared a commiserating sigh.

"Do you get a lot of gawkers?"

"Not enough," Eilean pursed her lips. "The Loch Ness monster is obviously a big draw for bringing supernatural enthusiasts to the Highlands, but unfortunately for us, the curse on Arden Castle scares off more tourists than it brings in." She grabbed a rag to wipe down the bar where a bit of beer had splashed. "The latest landlords have promised to make a big investment in turning the castle into a vacation destination that will 'revitalize the whole village,' but we've heard that promise enough that we try not to get our hopes up anymore."

"Maybe these guys will surprise you." Riley pulled a card out of her wallet and extended it to Eilean. No one really used business cards anymore. Even though she'd gotten them on sale, they'd been an irresponsible purchase. But they added an air of legitimacy that her unconventional offering still required.

"At the very least, they hired me." Based on what Riley could tell from their website, her new employer, Cornerstone Investments, was a land developer based in London. The latest in a long list of investors both public and private who had inked their name on Arden's deed, they were a relatively young company with eager, if green, staff.

"A curse breaker?" Eilean arched a finely crafted eyebrow. "No wonder that weedy project manager looked right pleased with himself last time he came in here."

Considering how frazzled and desperate he'd been when they spoke on the phone a week ago, Riley took that as a vote of confidence in her abilities.

"Still." As Eilean handed back the card, her voice took on a new note of gravity. "Arden Castle is no place for the faint of heart."

Riley's ears perked up at the first hint of a lead.

"You believe in the curse, then?" Not always a guarantee, even among locals.

"Oh, aye"—Eilean laughed humorlessly—"and anyone who thinks I've had a choice in the matter hasn't been here long. I've seen enough people broken by that curse over the course of my lifetime to know that the land doesn't want to be owned and the curse ensures it won't."

When a guest at the other end of the bar held up two fingers, the bartender nodded and began pulling a pair of fresh pints while simultaneously finishing her warning. "I hope you know what you're getting yourself into."

"I'm a professional," Riley assured her firmly as she slipped the card back into the pocket of her jeans. Part of the gig was projecting confidence in the face of the unknown. Gumption, as Gran called it, was an essential trait for curse breakers. "But the more I can learn about the curse, and quickly," she said with a meaningful head tilt, "the better my odds."

The little time she'd had to research in the short period between receiving the assignment and arriving in Scotland had left her with more questions than answers. Arden Castle didn't attract the same obsessive analysis and "eyewitness account" forum fodder as other Highland supernatural stories. A cursory Internet search hadn't turned up many hits.

Maybe it was like Eilean said, that the close proximity of Loch Ness, or even the standing stones at Clava Cairns, simply drew interest. Or maybe it was because castles, cursed or not, were a dime a dozen in the UK. Whatever the reason, Riley knew she would have to tap into the firsthand experiences and folklore of locals like Eilean—people who had grown up in the castle's backyard—to get this job done.

"Very well." Eilean's mouth pulled to the side. "I suppose it's better you hear it from me than the sensationalized tales of these hooligans." She raised her chin toward the armchair crowd from earlier.

Riley eagerly pulled out a pocket notebook and pen from her purse. "Start at the beginning, please."

It was curse breaking 101: pin down the origin.

In their most basic form, curses were uncontrollable energy. And power stabilized when you completed a circuit back to the source. Riley's first task was always uncovering specific details: who, when, why, and how.

"Now, I'm not a historian, mind you." Eilean popped open a jar of olives and began to spear them in pairs while she spoke. "But based on what I've always heard, the curse started roughly three hundred years ago."

Riley leaned forward. An origin date somewhere in the eighteenth century was a broad window, but it gave her something to start with in terms of timeline.

"A land war had broken out in Torridon between the Campbells, the clan who held the castle at the time, and the Graphms, who controlled the region to the east." Eilean kept one eye on her customers as she spoke and patiently spelled out the Gaelic version of "Graphm" when Riley jotted down the names.

"The fighting was so bitter and so deadly that it nearly wiped out both clans."

Already the set pieces were starting to make sense. Gran had taught Riley that curses came from people, born out of their most extreme emotions—suffering, longing, desperation—feelings so raw, so heavy, that they poured out and drew consequences from the universe.

A blood feud made the perfect catalyst. All that burning hatred, the sheer magnitude of anguish from so many lost loved ones.

"The tale goes that when both clans' numbers had dwindled so far that it looked like the castle might soon belong to no one," Eilean said, her low, lilting voice weaving the story like a tapestry, "one desperate soul went into the mountains, seeking the fae that lived beyond the yew trees, determined to make a terrible deal."

Ah, the infamous Highland fae. Riley loved a good fairy tale, especially when they were real.

"But which side did the person come from?" By the sounds of it, a member from either clan would have enough they stood to win or lose.

"The name is lost to legend, I'm afraid." Eilean frowned. "Whoever it was, they made a bad bargain, because the last lines of both clans fell, and the castle lay dormant for years before a lieutenant from the Twenty-First Light Dragoons purchased the place in 1789."

The bartender paused to hold up the bottle of scotch from before.

With a smile, Riley tapped the bar next to the glass, accepting the offer of a refill.

"Whatever that sorry soul was promised by the fae remains unfulfilled"—Eilean delivered a generous pour—"and the curse persists as a consequence, driving any- and everyone away from that castle."

Riley bit the inside of her cheek while the bartender went to help another customer. She knew there were tons of regional

ROSIE DANAN

nuances to curses, but even though popular lore cast the fae as tricksters and mischief-makers eager to make deals with desperate humans, Gran's journal didn't say anything specifically about their influence.

Whatever Riley was up against here, she had her work cut out for her.

A bell chimed over the front door of the pub, pulling her attention from the first stirrings of a mental pep talk.

Holy shit. Her breath caught in her throat at the sight of the man who entered.

Everything from the harsh line of his jaw to the broad stretch of his shoulders pulled tight with a specific kind of tension that seemed . . . tortured. Even though that didn't make sense. The expression on his face was perfectly neutral; he wasn't limping or dripping blood.

As he walked in and moved toward the bar, Riley had the sudden visceral memory of a painting she'd seen once. She was far from a fine art lover, but back when she was in the sixth grade, her whole class had gone to the Philadelphia Museum of Art on a field trip.

Riley had found the whole day unforgivably boring—none of the work moved her. But then she'd come to this one massive canvas, and it was like her feet sprouted roots into the marble floor.

All these years later, she still remembered how the artist had captured an angel suspended midfall. She'd felt the momentum of that still image within her own body. The way anguish strained his face and form until his plunge became like ballet, like poetry.

She felt it again—the painting feeling—now, looking at this stranger. Heat licked up her spine, as swift and sudden as wildfire.

Looking back, that painting had probably been some kind of sexual awakening. For even though the man at the bar was fully dressed, coat and all, the angel had been naked, his modesty preserved in profile.

Riley had found herself fascinated by his body, the high contrast of strength and vulnerability. Sharp ribs and taut thighs versus how tender the pink soles of his feet had looked. How those massive indigo wings had folded as he fell.

Looking at this real-life man who reminded her of an artist's rendering, Riley realized something new about the painting.

It wasn't the despair in the pose that had drawn her in. It was the defiance.

It was that even in the act of falling, the angel had flung up one arm, fingers curling, reaching for the only home he'd ever known, refusing to go quietly, while the other arm remained tucked to his breast, protecting his heart.

The man with his dark head bowed over the bar looked similarly braced for impact. For the fight that inevitably awaited a fallen angel on land.

What did it say about Riley that his weary resilience called to her? Probably something twisted.

Since she was someone trying to make curse breaking into a career, it wasn't a great secret that Riley wanted to save people, but she feared the parts of herself that wanted to be saved in return.

"Who is that?" She hadn't meant to speak the words out loud, but Eilean heard and answered anyway.

"Oh. *Him.* He's been causing quite the fuss ever since he came to town."

Wait, that guy lived here? Forget the curse; *he* should be Torridon's new claim to fame.

Though if the unimpressed look on Eilean's face was

anything to go by, she was seemingly immune to this guy's whole thing.

Riley leaned forward, lowering her voice. "What do you know about him?"

"He's English." Eilean moved to restock some napkins. "Like the land developers who hired you, though blessedly he doesn't work for them. He comes here most nights, so he probably can't cook. And he's an archaeologist hired to—"

"An archaeologist." Riley's ears perked up. "Oh, that's perfect. I just watched a movie about archaeology on the plane!"

Eilean's slate brows came together. ". . . So?"

"So that can be my in!" Riley didn't remember all the details of the film—she'd nodded off a bit in the middle—but it had been based on a true story. The main character was ripped directly from the pages of a best-selling memoir after some major film studio purchased the guy's life rights.

"Wait." Eilean stopped working. "You're not going to hit on him, are you?"

"I mean, yeah," Riley said, "but, like, respectfully."

She didn't make a habit of picking up people in bars, but she certainly didn't have a problem striking up a conversation with someone she found attractive. And this guy was hot like burning—even dressed in the repressive layers of a Ralph Lauren ad, with a button-up under his sweater and a tweed blazer over top.

"I don't think that's such a good idea." Eilean began to shake her head. "The assignment you took—"

"Oh, don't worry." Riley could already tell that Eilean saw everyone under this roof as her responsibility. "I'm not on the clock until tomorrow morning."

She didn't mix business and pleasure at home, but that was mostly because she didn't want to pollute her potential client pool with former flames. Since her first trip to Scotland was likely to be her last, that didn't seem like an issue here.

"Do I have anything—" She bared her teeth at Eilean.

"No," Eilean said after a quick glance, and then, crossing her arms, "I suppose, in your line of work, you know your way around trouble."

"Huh?" Riley had gotten distracted looking at the guy again. Before tonight, she hadn't even known they made cheekbones that sharp.

"Never mind." Eilean ushered her forward. "Good luck to you, curse breaker."

Photo by Sylvie Rosokoff

ROSIE DANAN writes steamy, bighearted books about the trials and triumphs of modern love. Her work has been optioned for film as well as translated into nine different languages and counting. When not writing, she enjoys jogging slowly to fast music, petting other people's dogs, and competing against herself in rounds of *Chopped* using the miscellaneous ingredients occupying her fridge.

VISIT ROSIE DANAN ONLINE

RosieDanan.com

🅾 RosieDanan

Ready to find
your next great read?

Let us help.

Visit prh.com/nextread

Penguin
Random
House